Xsardis

To Kathy,
God bless,

Sessu
Mm

Xsardis

Xsardis

Book Three of the
Xsardis Chronicles

By

Jessie Mae Hodsdon

Adventure with a purpose

Xsardis   4

Text Copyright by Jessica Mae Hodsdon

All rights reserved. No part of this book may be reproduced or transmitted in any form or by any means, electronic or mechanical, including photocopying, recording, or by any information storage and retrieval system, without written permission from the publisher. For information contact Rebirth Publishing by mailing PO Box 1006, Bangor, Maine, 04402; or by emailing rebirthpublishing@issym.com.

ISBN 978-0-9843386-2-7

Cover Art by Ande Binan

Published by Rebirth Publishing, Inc.

Printed in the United States

Visit www.issym.com

Bible quotes taken from the New International Version, 1984.

Acknowledgements:

Well, we made it to book three, friends. Thanks for following my journey and the journey of Xsardis! Rebirth's team and I could not have done this without you. It's hard to believe the Xsardis Chronicles have concluded, but I look forward to the new worlds I will share with you.

To my ever-supportive parents: you pulled late nights and early mornings; you made me coffee and moved cars; you counseled and encouraged; you supported in more ways than I can describe. Thank you!

Dearest Kate, I owe much of this book to our 'kitchen counter discussions'. As always, you were a strong support in a busy time.

To my mentor, Kelly, and to your entire family: thanks for being there in the rough spots and in the happy times. I'm so glad you guys are in my life!

To my editors—Julie, Chuck and Judy: you guys rock. Thanks for all your willingness, determination and hard work.

And to my sweet Jesus: words cannot begin to pen all that You have done for me. You remain my rock, my joy and my purpose. Praise Your Name!

Xsardis

For our service men and women, especially my friends recently or soon to be deployed:

Zach, Adam, Victoria, and Seth

Xsardis

Introduction

The fine-featured young woman shrouded herself in the curtain of the stone doorway, peering at the ailing uncle she loved so much. His ashen face momentarily renewed with some of the old rosy color as he fingered her delicately written scroll. It was for him she had labored such long hours, desperate for his approval of her second historical manuscript and for him to have the joy of reading it before he passed.

Sounds of the busy life already brimming in the castle filled her ears as the sun cast its rays on her uncle. Her sharp red satin dress displayed her prominence in the kingdom. At that moment she should have been by the king's side, counseling him, but no one could strip her from the bedside of the man who had raised her.

"Reesthma," the long-bearded old man called with a warmth that masked his failing body.

She moved into the small room, her feet barely touching the ground, and knelt by his side. "What is it, Joppa?" she spoke softly.

Placing a rough hand around hers, he commissioned her, "Soon I will not be history's keeper any longer. That will fall to you."

"No one could ever replace you, Joppa," she returned sweetly.

"That is what they said of Issym."

An understanding smile graced her lips as she recognized the tone of storytelling.

"Every great man has his origin. So does every villain. Often, the two are connected."

The old man slipped easily into his story, "Issym had devoted himself to defending the innocent. His training, even at his young age, exceeded many of his older counterparts. His natural combat reflexes and hunting skills had persuaded any warriors he met to teach him everything they knew. As he exerted himself as the land's protector, Issym was burdened that he could not save all. He had abandoned the comforts of home and normality and lived a life

Xsardis

10

of sacrifice, but he still could not defend the entire land. While he battled to save the life of a village on one side of the continent, on the other side a caravan would be decimated. The millstone of shouldering a country had caused his skin to toughen and his eyes to bag long before their time.

"On a rainy night Issym scanned the forest around him for a cave in which to pass the storm. He had saved a girl's life that day, but he could sense the trouble far away that he had not been able to avert. His eyes finally landed on a large cavern and he ran up the muddy hill towards it. After shaking out his long hair, the warrior began his exploration of the tunnel. Instantly he was confronted by a young dragon.

"Most men would have drawn their swords or run, but Issym, with the fearlessness for which he was already being noted, approached the creature with his hands outstretched. The dragon snorted, smoke coming from its nostrils as it began to circle Issym. Though it was small and inexperienced, the leviathan could have slain him with his sharp talons and large teeth. But regarding Issym carefully, he allowed the man to touch his snout.

"Issym tamed the dragon and christened him Santana. He soon realized that he was more than an animal, but an intelligent creature. Determined now to protect and train Santana, he taught him to speak. As soon as the dragon was large enough, Issym flew with him to battle. He would drop from his back and send Santana from sight in order to protect him. Issym's wisdom warned that if the leviathan was known by the people of the land they might call for his death or try to use him for their own purposes. Santana had already exhibited his love of freedom and his dislike for the masses. Issym gave him as much liberty as he dared and kept the truth a secret from all but a precious few.

"His mind was focused on how much more quickly he could travel on the back of a dragon—how many people would never have to die. But Santana had plots of his own.

"The dragon was a jealous beast and he grew envious of Issym's now-widespread fame. Deciding that infamy was better than seclusion, the dragon subtly turned on his master and friend. At first, his acts were small—stealing cows and burning empty buildings. This was too little to quench his insatiable thirst for recognition.

"Santana abandoned Issym, conquered a mountain, and began to loot treasures and stockpile food. He drew to his side the cutthroats Issym was devoted to stopping and took the name Smolden, ridding himself of all memory of his old 'master.'

"Brokenhearted at the loss of his ally to the grip of evil, Issym struggled to stop Santana with a fury he had never before felt, but it was too late. The dragon was beyond his control. For years the two feuded in epic battles. Issym struggled only to contain Santana, holding out that there was some small goodness still left in his friend. The few times the dragon spared his life falsely confirmed Issym's beliefs.

"After the warrior left for Asandra's land, Smolden began to destroy Shobal's kingdom, bitter at the lost rivalry. Years later, in desperation, King Shobal learned of Issym's strange connection with Smolden and sent for his help. Asandra pushed Issym to go and he went.

Xsardis

11

"Issym and Santana neither slept nor ate for two days as they dueled in Kembar Plains. Words passed between them that Issym dared not even breathe to Asandra. With help, Issym banished Santana to the underground. The leviathan watched his rival go, calling one last taunt, 'I will destroy your family.'

"Santana's words burned in Issym's heart though they were not fulfilled for many years. Asandra was a majestic queen, but so often the greatest among us are the most damaged. Asandra grew ill—by Smolden's hand, most said. Streaks of grey finally claimed Issym's hair as he sat at his wife's deathbed.

"'You, my love, are a mighty warrior. I know you are weary now, but you must continue to defend this world until God raises some else up,' she spoke, placing her weathered hand on his face.

"The warrior king had faced all and conquered all, but this new enemy he could not destroy: grief. Asandra crumbled before his eyes.

"Issym left the land not long after that, taking his place at Shobal's side to guard against another attack from Smolden. For years after the king's death, Issym led the land. His feud with the dragon only grew. One day he took a commission of his strongest men into the underground. They never returned.

"People questioned how anyone could defend them as Issym had. For a long time there was no use for such a warrior. A century later, when the need arose, so rose a hero.

"Out of nowhere she would appear and into nowhere she would disappear. Leaping off of walls and wielding every imaginable weapon with a proficiency unmatched, this warrior of legend could single-handedly rout bands of criminals. Throughout the centuries she has continued to arise, gaining only the name 'The Legend.'"

"The same woman…" Reesthma whispered, her eyes recalling a memory.

"The reports say that it was the same," Joppa replied, heartened by the interest he could still capture in his niece.

"Well perhaps my book can shed a little light on that," she returned.

He unraveled the scroll and began to read:

Xsardis

Chapter 1

One strike of his sword after another, the youthful warrior barreled through his enemies. Fat or short; tall or thin; average or strong—it did not matter. With only one swing they fell to his superior skill and focused rage.

He moved toward the wagons. The army began to part for him—no one wanted to get in the way of his slashing blade. They were puzzled by the strange respect for life exhibited by this boy-hero. He was trying only to wound them.

He jumped into the first wagon in the open field and closed the curtain behind him. The warrior had only a few seconds before the soldiers' superiors forced them to follow. A nine-year-old girl looked up at him, wiping off the dirt and tears with her bound hands. "Come with me," he instructed, after loosing her wrists. She followed him to the front of the wagon without debate. His eyes flashed with the courage of battle, but the mark of tenderness could still be found in them.

Taking the reins of the horses, the warrior forced them to move to the right of the other wagons and to go up the road. There were only a few horses with the army, so only a few could follow. Maybe they would get out of this alive. He heard the thudding of boots as someone jumped in the back and he felt the way the wagon rocked as another soldier clung to the sides. "Take the reins," he said, and shoved them to the girl.

She protested, but attempted to take control of their wild chariot.

Standing, he gripped the wooden post that held the fabric of the wagon and swung towards the side. The force of his feet knocked the soldier off the wagon. The youthful warrior was instantly back by the girl and his sword lanced into the remaining soldier's shoulder as he was reaching for her. He fell back.

The horses were going off the road. The warrior took the reins, correcting their course. He then looked around him, getting ready for the next attack. The enemy's horses were pounding towards them. Too many. "Come here," he snapped with frustration. The girl obeyed. "You're going to have to

Xsardis   14

jump when I say."

Her eyes flashed, but she said nothing. They were coming toward a corner. They would jump as they moved out of sight. "Now!" he called, and gave her a push so that she would not lose her nerve. He was less than a second behind her.

The impact caused his shoulder to burn as a stabbing pain wrapped around the bone, but he propelled himself to his feet, pulling the child deeper into the woods. He heard the crunching behind him and pushed the girl down headfirst into the bushes so that her curious nature would not get her killed. "Don't move!" he hissed, turning to face whoever was after them.

With a shout of surprise he parried one blow from the dwarf before him, then swung his sword toward his enemy's head... He stopped short. The dwarf knocked him back with his strong foot and could have given a killing blow, but he too stopped. The youth looked familiar. His hair was longer, he had some stubble on his face, his eyes held more heaviness, his frame was stronger; but even so... "Seth!" The dwarf offered a hand up.

"Lotex," he accepted the stubby hand, then motioned that the girl could rise. She clung to Seth's side.

For a moment, the dwarf stood staring at the two. Then he broke out of his own thoughts, "We should go; they'll be coming after us."

"What are you doing so far from the dwarf outpost?" Seth sought to process information as they moved swiftly.

"The king and queen summoned me," he replied, not sounding pleased. "And as I was hurrying along the road, I saw a youth battling an army of fifty by himself." He used his ax to cut branches out of his way. "I was going to help him until I saw him take a captive. Who's the girl?"

Seth shrugged, "I was on my way to you, when I heard her screaming." He turned to her, "Who *are* you?"

"Laneena, from the village of Palla. Sasha's cutthroats stole everything we had!"

"So you went after them?" Lotex chuckled.

"I was not going to let them get away!" She turned to Seth, feeling utterly belittled in front of such a great man. "Are you really Seth, hero of Asandra?"

His eyes glazed over. Hero... Some hero he was. He had let his best friends die in a world that wasn't even theirs. He shook his unkempt hair and brought his focus back to the present. "Next time, Laneena, stay home and leave Sasha's men to me. Where is your village?"

"Over the hill," she answered.

"Good," Lotex moved faster and looked to Seth, "because when the king and queen sent for me, it sounded urgent."

"If you left the dwarf outpost, they must have been very convincing." For some unfathomable reason, the dwarves were anxious to get back to their barren island of Noric. They desired as little contact with Asandra as possible. They were focused on their mission. Nothing else.

"Their messenger looked grave," Lotex affirmed.

Seth had to admit that he was glad for the dwarf's company. To be sure, their first few weeks together had been agony as Lotex had put him to

Xsardis   15

work in the mines of the island, but they had been a proving ground. Seth had established himself through hard labor and diligence. What was so surprising was that Lotex had won Seth's friendship. Once Seth had suspected him of trying to kill him; now Lotex was an invaluable ally both in and out of a fight. And it had been Lotex who had convinced the other dwarves to return to Asandra for battle.

They walked into Laneena's village as the sun set. They were instantly surrounded and practically carried into the tavern for a celebration. Seth kept an eye on the door—looking for his opportunity to leave. Although he loathed the attention, it was more than that. The people did not have the supplies to be wasting on such a banquet.

Food was short throughout Asandra. Sasha's men had taken much of what had been grown; the sprites had burned the rest. Even the manna, which grew on its own by water, was in short supply. The winter had been hard. The many blizzards had been unexpected even by the fierce standards of Asandra's climate. *What caused such storms?* Seth's imagination wondered.

Finally the townspeople retired, giving Seth and Lotex rooms in the inn. Without collaboration, each one lay on his bed, listening for the sounds of the town to die down. As soon as it was quiet enough, they slipped back onto the road. Seth was used to traveling in the darkness. To him night and morning were the same thing; hunger and fullness; sleep and wakefulness. Life had lost its senses. Lotex's heavy footfalls beside him were about as rhythmic as life got.

The wounds might still have felt fresh, but five months had passed since Rachel, Max and Prince Evan had died in Maremoth—a day that had been dubbed 'The Day The Whispers Became Trumpets' by hundreds of villagers throughout Asandra. It was an odd name, but it had stuck, then had shortened simply to 'The Day'.

That day had changed everything on Asandra. Their deaths had made them martyrs, and that had a powerful effect on a people who had forgotten what it was liked to be truly loved and sacrificed for. Love had been a forgotten concept on Asandra. Everyone had grown used to looking out for themselves. Rachel, Evan and Max had kept pushing to help the people even when they did not want that help. It was a special kind of love and it had made an impact. With much weeping, the people mourned their deaths. A change of heart swept through Asandra following 'The Day.'

Scores of prisoners had escaped Maremoth on that day and had returned home to tell of Sasha's cruelty. No longer able to hide from the truth that the shifter was a malevolent usurper, many of the people of Asandra turned away from Sasha, resisting her at every turn. The citizens took the blame for the three's death, believing that if they had only listened when Evan and Rachel had come to them for help, they might have survived. Rachel, as Asandra's imaginer, had a special place in their hearts. Prince Evan's death had swung favor back to his parents. They had sacrificed a child. Much damage was repaired simply by that fact and that King Remar had been imprisoned in Maremoth for years himself hiding under the name Nicholas.

But, surprisingly, it was Max who had caused the largest stir. Seth often caught himself laughing at the irony. The once-troublemaker, with no

Xsardis

16

connection to the world, was most mourned. It was, however, exactly for that reason that people commemorated him. He had had no reason to even come to Asandra, but he had given his life. All the people who had truly belonged and had been unwilling to help burned with shame.

A preacher named Zachary had fanned the sparks created by the three's deaths into flame. When Seth had first learned of Zachary, who had apparently allowed himself to be kidnapped to help Rachel and Evan, he had begun searching for him. He had gleaned that after his capture, Zachary had been forced through town after town as Sasha's guards continuously collected more prisoners. He eventually was imprisoned in Maremoth weeks before 'The Day The Whispers Became Trumpets.' He had escaped with many of the others. With a new boldness, he began to preach.

Zachary's message drove home the sacrificial love of the three and then he revealed the sacrificial love of Christ. He preached hard that all must love each other and God in the same way if Asandra were to see change. His words stirred the hearts of all Asandra. "Jesus replied: "'Love the Lord your God with all your heart and with all your soul and with all your mind." This is the first and greatest commandment. And the second is like it: "Love your neighbor as yourself,'" he would quote from Mathew 22:37-39.

Lotex purposefully brought Seth back from his distant thoughts. "If you were coming to see me, you were going the wrong way,"

Seth managed to jump right back into reality, a skill that showed his experience in the blur of existences. "Not the wrong way, just the long way."

"Right," snorted the dwarf, coming to a crossroads and arbitrarily picking a direction.

"Don't go that way," Seth whispered, his tense posture alerting Lotex of some unseen danger.

The dwarf stopped his confident gait and listened, gripping his axe for comfort. "What is it?"

"Vaylynne has a camp up there."

"Ah, ah-ha, ah-ha-hah," Lotex bellowed. "The so-called freedom fighter? That's what has you so worried?"

"Are you trying to get us killed?" Seth pulled him down the right-most way.

"Her army is practically depleted..." the dwarf was laughing too hard to resist Seth's pull.

"But her principles have captured the people's attention," he whispered sharply in the moonlight. "And you should not underestimate her skills as a warrior and a leader."

"Seth, everyone knows that we have not seen a fighter and a leader like you since Issym himself, or The Legend, if she's even real. And you're afraid of some rebellious teenage girl?"

The youth's eyes smoldered. "I know better than anyone what a teenager can do."

"Yes, but you always remind me that it is what God does through you. She is godless."

Seth made out a figure in the woods. Lotex followed his gaze and smiled as he readied himself for a battle. "No fighting her today," Seth ordered

Xsardis   17

and began to run.

"For a warrior," Lotex panted as he struggled to keep up with the agile Seth, "you do not have much of a heart for battle."

"I have seen enough death and sorrow for several lifetimes," he answered.

But the fact was, as Lotex well-knew, that while Seth fought like a wild tiger, his marks were aimed with precision to keep his opponent from getting back up for a few hours, but never aimed to kill. It was risky—especially to the people fighting with Seth. Lotex had pushed and pushed in an attempt to explain it, but there was little ground he could keep in an argument with the boy. And, after all, he had Issym's example. That great warrior had done the same thing. Or so Joppa the historian's many lectures had led him to believe.

They slowed, realizing that no one was following behind them. There was one topic on which Lotex had a chance of besting Seth. "Then why don't you go back to Earth? Max and Rachel's families deserve to know what heroes they were. You deserve a normal life."

"Normal?" Seth choked. "Without them? I couldn't live knowing that they had given their lives for something I had quit on. And besides that, God still wants me here."

Lotex grunted. Seth sounded a little more rehearsed than sure. The dwarf could not blame him. Battle was not easy on anyone. Seth had a skill that he could never have naturally possessed, but he called on the imagination that had woven Xsardis by God's power and used the skill he had granted to Issym in his games. It was necessary to summon mental blocks in order to survive in the middle of so much death; Issym had had plenty of those. Even half a year ago Seth had held some youthful innocence. Now he carried the weight of a true warrior.

The sun had not yet risen when the dwarf and the teenager came to the incomplete fortress of Saphree. In the short time that the king and queen's army had occupied it, they had made enough improvements on the dwelling that had once been Sasha's to use it as the base of their future empire. Early in the war, Sasha had demolished their palace. After escaping Maremoth, the king and queen were forced to look for a new home. They took Sasha's Saphree for their own.

The gate was quickly opened, despite the earliness of the hour, and the guards stood at attention as their hero and the well-respected dwarf walked past them and into the castle. Entering the dimly lit stone entryway, Lotex was quickly shown into a room to rest until the king and queen woke, but Seth was ambushed by Princess Katarina.

As her rebellious nature had been washed away, so washed away her boyish attire. She was now fitted into a regal, crème colored nightgown—even that was a dress. It fit the authority she carried in her step as they walked together through the rooms of the palace, her blue cloak flowing behind her. They spoke in soft tones after her initial sharp rebuke, "You are trying to get yourself killed, aren't you? Do you think a man who has captured the devotion of a people can be easily replaced?" She sounded so like her mother.

Seth had declined to be the captain of the king's army. He preferred to

Xsardis   18

work alone. Nevertheless, he was still the spirit of the battle. He represented the three heroes and the many others that had died to bring the land peace. His deeds had already become part of the lore of the Asandra. Seth was half man, half legend. But he preferred it that way. He could live in the shadows unbothered, but in a position to do good.

They moved into a room that was still being constructed, sitting in their usual high-backed chairs with the wind blowing in from the open wall in front of them. Staring into the wooded land, Seth attempted once more to explain himself. He was tired of the constant rebukes from everyone who knew him as more than a warrior. "You know that we do not have time to stop and feel. Grief and fear have been put aside like all the other feelings."

"Perhaps you do not have the time to grieve," her voice trembled with emotion, "but I do. I rarely leave these walls."

Katarina could not stop blaming herself for Max, Evan and Rachel's deaths. It was she who had led Max unwittingly to Maremoth. If she had not, Seth and the others might not have attacked the fortress when they did and the three might still be alive. Her mother would be dead and none of the prisoners would have escaped, but it was her deception that had killed three people. Her repentance to God had been real and the transformation, she knew, had been profound, but the darkness of her past still filled her with grief.

Seth could have told her that they only had to hold on until the army of Issym came. He could have told her that this would all soon be over. But they had both become disillusioned, so instead he assured her, "Your brother would have been proud. You have done much good."

The princess chuckled, "I thought he was an idiot for continuing to fight for Asandra. I asked him a hundred times to run with me to Issym. To keep us safe, my mother would have given us what was left of our inheritance, but Evan would never leave and I could never go without him. I was furious with him for being determined to stay. Now I realize how incredible that was."

When Seth said nothing, Katarina glanced at her friend. His eyes were focused on some unreal object in the distance. "You should sleep."

"Your parents were in a hurry to have me back. We'll probably get summoned in an hour or so. There isn't much point."

"I don't mean now, stupid. You should try sleeping at night, like normal people." She tried to tame her unruly side when around others, but with Seth it did not seem to matter.

He rolled his eyes. "There isn't time," he insisted, leaning forward in his chair and speaking in the deep tones that he had grown into. "Every day I am out there, I save lives. And you want me to stop and take a nap?"

"I don't want to lose you too," Katarina whispered. There were days it felt almost normal to live with the grief she carried, but other days, pressing on seemed unbearable. She had spent a lifetime ignoring her emotions as much as possible. Now...

Seth softened. "I don't intend to die and leave the work unfinished."

She re-masked her concern. "What do you know about this meeting?"

A look of surprise filled his face. "Lotex didn't tell me anything, but *you* don't know?"

Katarina shook her curly head. "No."

Xsardis

19

Frustration burned through her eyes. To her parents, she was still a child, but she keenly felt the adulthood that is brought about by tragedy.

The corners of his mouth turned up in an understanding smile. Whatever changes had occurred in her, she was still good old Katarina. He gestured to the sun as he rose. "Your parents will soon be calling us together. I should change."

"You don't want to appear before them dusty and scraped?" She pushed herself to her feet.

"I don't want to have them breathing down my throat like someone else I know…"

Seth felt like he was stepping into someone else's room as he entered his own. His bedroom on Earth had born witness to what he thought had been a busy life. This dwelling's pristine order showed that he was so busy he was never there.

Pouring water from a jug into a basin, Seth bent over and felt the cool of it take his mind back to another cold day—the day he and Max had woken up in the middle of a forest on Issym. Max's snarky comments had been so annoying then. Now the memories made him laugh.

He splashed water on his face and was gripped by another vision. "Then no matter what we encounter, don't run." The force of Galen's words and Rachel's deathly pale faced flashed through his mind. He shivered.

"Get a grip!" he snapped at himself as the all-too-familiar nausea threatened to engulf him. Once more he splashed the water on his face and rubbed at some of the grime. This time he saw Rachel and Max, tired but happy, mingling with hundreds of various creatures after the battle against Smolden had been won. They were so much fun when they were happy. They had jigged into the early hours of the morning.

Roughly wiping at his face with a towel, Seth locked the memories in a safer part of his mind. He left his brown pants and green shirt in a basket for washing and donned a blue tunic, black pants and fresh boots. Strapping his sword around him and straightening his shoulders, Seth began to feel in control again. He had gone from looking like a child of the forest to a prince in only a few moments. It would keep Queen Juliet from saying he was letting himself go. For that he was grateful. Katarina's less-than-gentle knock startled his short nerves, but he opened the door for her with a calm face. "They're ready for us. Finally," she said.

Now she wore a patterned dress, the same blue cloak, and earrings that fell almost to her shoulders, evident since her hair was swept into a bun. "What?" she asked, catching his funny look.

He laughed at the smallness and stupidity of what he had been thinking.

"What?" she asked again, the twinkle in her eye showing her amusement.

"I thought… that you guys didn't wear earrings. I never saw you with them before."

"It's not like they're really practical for battle," she retorted. "But I'm trying to live up to the expectations my people have for their future ruler. And that is not exactly a boyish princess."

Xsardis

20

"*You*," he emphasized, "are going to be a great ruler. That will have nothing to do with your earrings."

As they approached the thick wooden door, they both stopped, unwilling to enter. Katarina was mustering her social skills—they never came easily this early in the morning. Seth hated meetings. As the conversation went around and around, people were dying—people he could have been helping. At least he could usually catch a nap. Nobody noticed as long as his eyes stayed open.

Lotex's heavy footfalls sounded behind the two. He shoved one bulging arm in between them and pushed the door open, grunting at them to move in. A wave of heat washed across the teens, carrying with it the smell of stuffiness. The council room was small, with no windows and a thick door. It had a table and several chairs with their backs leaning against the walls. It was built to contain the sounds of their voices so that decisions could be made in safety.

Jeffery and Sphen, known as The Brothers, were already in the room. They were tall men in their late twenties, who had several years ago had an undiscovered talent for battle strategies and commanding men's hearts. This talent had been buried by years of mischief ranging from staying out late to burning down a part of the forest. They had been imprisoned for that when Sasha came to the town, demanding recruits to take to Maremoth. Their town offered them up to appease the shifter.

Jeff, the taller and more broad-shouldered brother, and Sphen, the wiry and elder brother, then found their skills. They did not give the least amount of resistance until Sasha was gone. They then broke from their chains and, as they fought with their guards, released the other prisoners. They led their band of forty to King Remar whose battle commander had recently turned traitor. The Brothers somehow rallied men's courage, and Remar put their various, somewhat strange, and somewhat illegal—if that concept still existed on Asandra—talents to good use.

Queen Juliet had her own uses for them. After Remar's capture, she swore them to a secret oath to protect her children. She used this promise to get them to leave her side when they received news that Sasha had discovered her hiding place. Jeff and Sphen spent the next two months tracking the prince and princess, coming near them several times until they themselves were captured by Vaylynne, leader of the independence movement. She tried to persuade them to join her cause until they escaped—Sphen gaining the scar that now ran from the top of his forehead to his nose. By then, they had lost all trace of the prince and the princess and did not find them again until they reached Saphree.

The Brothers sat at the council table, arguing. Jeffery boomed, while Sphen offered quippy comments when his brother paused for breath. They could agree about nothing outside of battle; but in it, they acted as one man.

The king and queen sat beside each other. Queen Juliet looked preoccupied, but despite the white that now took a lock of her hair, she was quite beautiful. King Remar was old—his hair half fallen out and the rest of it gray. His body was still twisted and malnourished from the years in Sasha's fortress. His air was heavy, but he broke from his staring at the table to grip Seth's hand and say, "So you did make it back to us. Good, good." The

Xsardis 21

distraction of his mind did nothing to lessen the sincerity with which he treated every member of his kingdom.

Seth took his seat. Unfortunately for him it was by the queen, who constantly chastised him for his recklessness. "You leave when darkness falls one night and come back a week later before the sun has risen. You tell no one where you are going or when you will return. And you take no one with you. We never know if you're dead or alive." She spoke in her usual gentle tones, which somehow hit harder than a shout would have. Juliet reminded him of his own mother. The soft eyes, the long hair, the perceptive nature...

Seth squirmed. His fresh clothes had not saved him after all. He was rescued by the entrance of the last member of the council—Joppa, history's keeper. Still reading a scroll, he took his seat. The king called for attention.

The Brothers ceased their verbal battle, but maintained it in spirit, their postures turned away from each other. Joppa took the scroll from his face, putting it on the table, but keeping his eyes focused on it. Seth and Katarina's attentions were on the door as if it was a valid exit from the meeting. Only Lotex and the queen paid any real attention to King Remar as he solemnly said, "Sasha is not our only true enemy anymore." He paused, letting his words sink in and bring the attention of the others. "A day ago, Vaylynne attacked one of our cities' leaders on the road. He and his wife are dead."

"Who?" Seth demanded.

"Harvey."

Katarina's face instantly washed out. Harvey and his wife Elizabeth were her friends. Not only had they risked their safety to rescue her and Max from a blizzard, but as soon as the king and queen took over Saphree, they had led their city back to God and into the service of the royal family. Elizabeth's kitchen was one of her only comforts.

"One of my men returned to me with the news," Sphen affirmed. "He saw Vaylynne himself."

"No," Seth was firm. "Vaylynne hates you," he stared into the eyes of the king and queen, "but she wouldn't murder them."

"Are you calling my man a liar?" Sphen and Jeffery both looked towards him.

"No. But I know better than anyone how convincing Sasha can be. She could have formed herself to look like Vaylynne."

"Why would she do this?" Katarina asked, breathless.

"To get us fighting amongst ourselves. To get our attention off her," Seth finished.

"Vaylynne is not one of us!" Jeff pounded his fist on the table.

Without realizing it, Sphen rubbed his temple where the scar ran. It was a nervous twitch he had developed.

"But think about it," Seth pushed.

Katarina had been thinking about it, for months. "This is what I don't understand. If Sasha is as powerful as we know her to be and as intelligent, then she must know Issym's army is coming and realize that she has to act before they get here. Why does she do almost nothing? It doesn't make sense."

Seth nodded. This bothered him too. Day and night he attempted to understand.

Xsardis

22

King Remar spoke decisively and returned the conversation to the matter at hand. "I have already made my decision. We will battle Vaylynne. She has been saying that she wanted a war. It is time we gave her one. That's why I summoned Lotex here. Jeff and Sphen's men are already far too spread out. I would like the dwarfs to lead the attack."

"You can't be serious!" Seth felt the world swirl. Why did the king even call him here? He must have known how opposed he would be to the plan. More deaths!

Sphen spoke distantly, "I have no lost love for Vaylynne, but I think Seth might be right. She would not murder good people like Harvey and Elizabeth. And such a battle would stretch us far too thin."

"I won't let people get murdered," Katarina's voice trembled. "These aren't just casualties of war or some kind of statistic; they are people! What we decide results in death or life. But we can't assume Vaylynne's guilt either."

Jeff declared, "We must not let her grow any stronger. Already she is too powerful."

Seth stood and drew all their eyes and attention, even Joppa's. The historian leaned back and waited expectantly. As the king had made his decision, so Seth had made his. "I'm going to find Vaylynne and convince her to come and make a treaty of peace with us."

"Seth," the queen's tender voice made him feel like a four-year-old, "why do you think she would listen to you?"

"Vaylynne let me go once—I think she respects me. I can talk her into this."

"If you are wrong, you won't get out of there in one piece." Sphen met the eyes of his fellow man with a deep respect and an even deeper warning.

Seth turned to the king and spoke firmly, "We will lose hundreds in a battle with Vaylynne. If there is a peaceable solution, I intend to find it. With all due respect, Sir, you'll have to arrest me to keep me here."

Katarina put a hand on his arm and looked up at him with her deep green eyes. "Don't do this. Don't commit suicide like this. She won't spare you. I know she's probably innocent of this, though I want nothing more than to convict her for all the trouble she's caused, but it doesn't mean you have to risk your life to stop a war. She's always wanted one!"

Remar told him, "My daughter is right. This *is* suicide and I won't allow it."

Now Joppa spoke for the first time: "Let him go."

All eyes turned to him in surprise.

"I think he's right to try. Our history shows that often one man's sacrifice leads to the salvation of many."

Remar looked back to Seth and, after several moments, gave a heavy nod. Seth walked quickly to his room, packed his small bag and slung it over his shoulder. Katarina caught him in the door and pushed him back in. "Kat, don't…"

"No Seth. Hear me out!"

"I can't slow down," he pressed his thoughts out. Why did she always insist he *feel*?

"You *won't* slow down!" she yelled. "Are you determined to be a

Xsardis

23

martyr like them?"

"I must do this! We don't have to lose those lives."

"You say you don't feel, but you don't make any logical decisions either. Stop being brain-dead and think!" she chastised.

"I have no time. I have to keep going." He tried to move past her. They fought fairly frequently, but this was different. She was digging inside him and it stung.

"Until when? Until Sasha's dead?" the words tore out of her angrily.

"Until Asandra is whole."

"Why?" she shouted, turning towards the door in frustration and clenching her fists.

Seth waited until she was looking at him again. "Because I'm not strong enough to take the time to grieve! If I stop to feel like a human again, I'm done. And I can't be done. Xsardis needs me. God has a plan for me still. Or else I'd be dead with them. I'm sorry that's not good enough for you, Kat, but it's all I have."

"Then let me come with you."

"What?" The words shocked him.

"You heard me. I am like Vaylynne. I never wanted to do things the long, drawn-out, right way. I took shortcuts and sacrificed things and messed up all of Xsardis."

"Katarina…"

She put up her hand to stop him, "And Vaylynne is the same way. I can reason with her."

"Your parents would never risk the heir of the throne…"

She nodded and was silent. When Katarina spoke again the flame was gone from her eyes, "Be careful. She's not going to spare you."

He stepped back. "How do you know?"

"Because if I was Vaylynne, I wouldn't."

Xsardis

Chapter 2

In every home on Asandra a name was mentioned... it was not that of a fallen hero, or of Seth, or of King Remar, or of Sasha. It was that of a simple preacher: Zachary.

Rumors abounded... that he had helped Rachel and Prince Evan and that he had allowed himself to be captured by Sasha to give them time to get away. For months after that, no one knew what had happened to him. In truth he had been kept as a prisoner and forced to make the slow journey to Maremoth as Sasha's troops collected other prisoners. He arrived a few weeks before 'The Day' and escaped with the others.

Those prisoners returned to their old homes and told of Sasha's injustice and abuse. No longer able to hide behind the belief that Sasha offered 'jobs' or 'servant' positions, it was now completely clear that the towns had sold their own kinsmen into slavery for the self-serving reward of Sasha ignoring them. The terrible thought seared Asandra with grief.

Instead of returning home, Zachary had begun preaching, starting with the village closest to Maremoth. He boldly declared that God was King over all the universe, that the people had to repent, that they had to begin to change their ways. He challenged them to reject the vileness or the comfort of evil and to stand for right. He told them that the only way they could hope to accomplish this was to trust Christ for their salvation. He said nothing of battle or of politics, but as his words stirred people to begin to take their faith in God seriously, they no longer could live under Sasha's lies. They broke her shackles and began to fight.

And Zachary kept preaching, from town to town to town, until everyone knew his name in the east and the west, the north and the south...

Xsardis

26

After years of diligent recruiting and training, freedom-fighter Vaylynne had small contingents of her army stationed across Asandra. She made a point of never telling anyone where she was going, which forced her camp leaders to constantly stay prepared for an inspection. Despite her youth, she was intimidating to all who met her, and the consequences for failing an inspection were too high to risk.

Perpetual readiness was doable, for most, but not for Caleb—the fifteen-year-old who sat on watch staring out at the blank woods. He had left home to do something great. Most of history's leaders did not sit on watch, but Vaylynne wanted everyone equal. So Caleb sat on the tree branch, soaking wet from the rain, when he could have been inside finding a way to make his troops respect him.

Caleb was young, but so were all the others sitting in his cave. By now, everyone who was still working for Vaylynne was as young. She had lost most of her camp leaders after 'The Day The Whispers Became Trumpets'. People went home, either to find their released families or because they realized Queen Juliet held real power again. Mention of that day still threw Vaylynne into a dangerous mood. She had had to promote unskilled officers to leadership, but no one was as unskilled as Caleb. So far, he could not fight; he could not plan; he could not earn people's loyalties; the poor kid couldn't even eat without spilling his food everywhere.

Why did she pick me? Caleb wondered. At first he thought she had seen something deep inside him, but after his last lecture for a failed inspection, he knew differently. He had tried to be intimidating and commanding, but he had failed—as he would always fail. Caleb was only five foot three and very thin, with a squeaky voice. So he tried to be a friend to his troops; that didn't work either. Caleb knew that he needed one chance—one moment to make his troops and Vaylynne respect him. One day and everything could change. He feared that day would never come.

As his chance for respect walked towards him through the rain, he had no idea what was about to happen. It was another young person, probably searching out the legendary Vaylynne. This one was tall, well-built. He was succeeding at looking cool with a scruffily beard and green clothing that blended in with the thick forest. He walked with his head down and his arms together to preserve warmth in the chilling rain. Caleb could not see much of him, but his sword poked out of the edge of his cloak. That was good. He came already equipped. Weapons were in low supply, just like people.

The 'leader' scanned the area to make sure there was no one else with this new recruit. Then he jumped down and stood right in his path, his feet sinking in the mud and his body lurching forward. He stood up with a face-full of mud. "Who are you?" he had meant to sound menacing, but after getting a better look at the guy with the soldier's gait, Caleb found he could only speak with a broken voice.

"I could ask you the same question," the man answered, walking by. How did his feet glide over the mud?

Caleb wished he had the stranger's deep voice or his manner—either one would have gotten him at least some acknowledgment. "What's your business here?" he demanded, as he ran awkwardly through the mud to keep up

Xsardis

27

with the man, and used his sleeve to clear his face.

The stranger found some patience and stopped, Caleb finally getting in his way. The man replied, "One question at a time. My name is Seth."

Caleb found that the little courage he had possessed had slipped away, "Not... not the..."

"Yes," he rolled his eyes. "Now answer my question. Who are you?"

"My name..." *Why can't I talk?* "is..." he cleared his throat and wiped off more of the mud from his face, "Caleb. I am the leader of this camp of Vaylynne. And it is my duty to take you back."

Seth drew his sword, making the air sing. Caleb struggled several moments to get his out. "You don't want to do this," the warrior warned.

"I... have to." Caleb knew he was going to die; die a miserable whelp covered in mud. His troops would probably have a celebration, if they even bothered to look for his body. At least his humiliation would be over and at least he would be felled by an incredible warrior. Maybe he would be remembered kindly by his family. Maybe word would get to his parents that he was a hero.

Their swords clashed together and Caleb almost dropped his with the weight of it. He closed his eyes to accept his fate. A few moments later, Caleb was still alive, amazing as it seemed. He popped open his eyes and saw Seth, waiting, observing, boring into his soul...

Caleb shouted and charged Seth. Minutes later, when he was still alive, Caleb began to wonder if he had some unseen prowess after all. He doubled his attack, though fatigue and cold were setting in. And then, Seth was on the ground, his sword somewhere else. *How?* "S...tand up. Slow...ly."

Seth obeyed in one swift movement—even the way he got up was cool. His eyes kept staring into Caleb. "Drop all... your weapons."

Seth complied, setting his sword gingerly upon the wet land and letting two small blades fall beside it. "Now walk up to that cave." *I'm not stuttering. I'm not!* Caleb's mind screamed.

He moved Seth to the cave, the tip of his sword in the warrior's back. They entered the large body of his hideaway. Thirty youths—some barely tall enough to handle a short sword and none old enough to have a shadow of a beard—filled the space as they ate, talked and practiced. The clatter brought back Caleb's nerves as he called for attention. No one paid him any attention. He tried again. No one looked in their direction.

"Attention!" Seth's powerful voice cut through the group and they instantly gave him their focus.

Offering a strange look, Caleb addressed his troops, "I have captured the legendary fighter, Seth."

The room roared with laughter, but a few were staring at Seth—he *looked* like a warrior. He fit the description of Seth, too. "I am Seth," he said quietly, but everyone heard him. The teen had a voice that people listened to.

Why don't I? Caleb could not understand.

The troops looked toward Caleb with more respect and suddenly they all cheered. He pushed Seth forward to be bound and put in another room, where there would be no chance of escape. He walked by his troops, receiving pats on the back from them all. Someone actually brought him water to wash himself, and a change of clothes. As he sat down to a hearty meal, he triumphed, *I am finally great!*

       Katarina swung her bag over her horse's saddle and glanced around the courtyard for Jeff. She had insisted that the group going to Harvey and Elizabeth's funeral be small; it would attract less attention from Sasha and Vaylynne. Her mother had insisted that she take her bodyguard. Katarina had swallowed the rebuttals that sat at the edge of her tongue.

       It wasn't that she minded Jeff coming. In fact, it brought a sense of safety that she had not been anticipating. But Jeff and Sphen were in charge of the army. With Seth gone, both needed to be fighting for Asandra, not defending one princess. When her father had threatened to send a whole troop to protect her—believing that Vaylynne would be searching for royal blood—Kat had quickly accepted Jeff's presence, along with those of another fighter and a girl that had almost become her lady-in-waiting. She refused to think of her as a servant, but only as a guest accompanying them. The princess could not say friend. She had no more trust to offer and no more of her heart to give away.

       Noticing the agile presence of Reesthma, Katarina adjusted the straps of the saddle, doing anything to look busy. Kat had been avoiding Joppa, and his niece Reesthma too. It was Joppa's fault that Seth was gone. It would be Joppa's fault if Seth died. Joppa cared only for his scrolls! And because of that he did not even notice the princess's fury. Reesthma, however, noticed and cared.

       The fifteen-year-old girl looked and acted nothing like her uncle. He rarely spoke to a living person; she could not stop talking. He was white, average height and slightly pudgy. Though he had been taken by Sasha's army, Malcon had placed Joppa in holding in his own dwelling, with orders to feed and clothe him as well as any of the guards themselves. So he had suffered, but not as much as he might have.

       In the last five months Reesthma had transformed. She had gained four inches, so she now stood a little taller than her uncle. Reesthma was thin, with dark skin and dark hair that she had in a long ponytail at all times. This left her dominate feature to be her brown eyes and long, dark eyelashes. Her childish form had left and been replaced with great beauty. The curves of her face were perfect. She was prettier than anyone else in the palace, Katarina included. Not that that was one of the reasons Kat was miffed at her…

       Reesthma walked around the horse and ran her fingers down its nose. The princess knew she could not ignore her any longer. "Hey, Ree."

       "Katarina, I know my uncle…" her voice had lost any nerves or high pitch.

       Katarina cut her off, "Seth's choice. He would have gone even if my father had said no." In only a few seconds she had finally come to believe that.

Reesthma smiled. "I brought you something."

"What is it?" the princess hid the sigh that threatened to creep into her voice.

"It is the last scroll that Joppa read to me before Sasha took him." Reesthma had the large volume in her hands. "I think you'll like it."

"History?" History had been school; never choice.

"You should really read it. You'll understand why Joppa did what he did."

"Ree, I'm leaving. I'm going to a *funeral*. I don't have time to read a book."

Reesthma slid it across the saddle, "Please."

Kat was saved from answering as Jeff's hulking frame moved towards them. She already knew that his slow gate meant that they were not leaving that night. His words only confirmed it. "Your father orders that we leave tomorrow morning at first light. He does not want us to travel in the dark."

Katarina groaned. "It's safer at night. We won't be seen."

Jeffery shrugged. "Depends on how you look at it. And I follow my king's orders. He would not even have let us come if not for the protection of your illuminescent."

Zara, her deep red color unusually shiny, surfaced from Kat's saddlebag. "Or my insistence on your behalf," Zara added, quickly flying back into the palace to find Hector, the blue illuminescent who was once Evan's. The two were an inseparable pair except during the times the princess needed her for anything. Then the red illuminescent was completely devoted, bound by some strange tradition more than by a true connection between the two.

"I guess you'll have time to read the book," Reesthma smirked.

Kat sighed. Jeff studied her weary features. It was probably good that they were leaving in the morning, despite his own reservations. She looked exhausted. "Rest. We leave early. I shall stable your horse," he spoke.

She nodded and handed him the reigns.

A year ago, Jeffery would have worried that she would sneak out and go by herself to the funeral. Now he knew her to complain about the edicts she disliked, but to obey them with a sense of duty few possessed. She was such a different person.

Remar sat in his bed, his eyes reading a letter but his mind absorbing nothing. The slight smell of smoke filled his nostrils as his wife blew out the few candles in their room. Sitting beside him, she pried the letter from his hands.

"I shouldn't have let him go," the king sighed.

Xsardis

30

"You know he would have gone anyway," Juliet answered.

"The army from Issym needs to arrive. It will not be long before Sasha attacks."

"Remar," Juliet put her hand on his, "you don't have to put up that front with me. You know she isn't waiting."

"But I can't figure out why," he sighed again. "What could possibly make her hesitate? No stones to harm her; we are not yet strong. Once Issym gets here she'll be easily defeated. There is no reason to delay. Unless..."

Juliet snapped to a new attention, "Unless what?"

"Unless Issym's boats are never going to make it."

"She couldn't have defeated them!" his wife gasped.

"They may have died of disease; may not have brought enough food; may have fallen to the sound sprites; or may have been taken by that legendary whirlpool. Truly, we don't know much about Sasha's power. Or theirs..."

"You really do think she killed them while they were still vulnerable on the seas... before our two armies could unite." It was starting to make sense. "How could you not have told me your suspicions?"

"You carried Asandra while I was in prison. I did not want to worry you unduly."

"I pray you're wrong."

"So do I."

Chapter 3

Vaylynne knew that she would have to replace Caleb. He had already failed so many inspections. But her reasons for putting him in charge were still valid. Sure she had lost all truly competent leaders, but there were others left with at least a skill with the sword. Caleb's strength was not in his fighting or leadership but in his passion. He longed to make Asandra better. He would not hesitate to give his life to do so. All the others were mindless warriors or kids looking for an escape from reality. Caleb cared.

Don't go soft, Vaylynne... Tahath's recent words drifted into her mind. She had replayed them again and again as she replayed all his counsel. The times when she could seek his insight were now precious and limited. She longed for the days when it had been just her and him leading a small contingent of idealistic and determined teens.

Tahath was now her second-in-command, and had always been her friend. At one time he had been opposed to her movement. Close to her since childhood, he had not hesitated to tell her what he thought of her new ideals. Their constant debates had finally won him over. He respected Vaylynne on a level that most people could not begin to mirror. She was only a figurehead to them. Sometimes she was so human and wrong to Tahath that it made her boil.

On the long nights where prospects seemed dark and hope slim, it was Tahath who kept her firm. And it was that firmness that would send Caleb away if he had not improved.

Walking through the trees, she saw that the lookouts were in prime places. None of them were asleep. Upon entering the body of the cave, she found that all of the troops were working. Some were training. Others were cooking. Still others were moving supplies around or sharpening weapons.

Caleb ran towards her. "Vaylynne, I have a gift for you."

"There is no use for such flattery on the battlefield. Show me your food supplies."

"No. Vaylynne you need to..."

"No?"

Xsardis

32

Who knew that one word could sound so terrifying?

Caleb quickly explained, "What I mean is that I fought Seth and captured him."

She shook her head. Caleb might have been idealistic but he was clearly too young to lead. "Why would you joke?"

"I wouldn't joke with you, Vaylynne," he promised.

"You would lie to me?" the warrior practically whispered.

Caleb was alerted from her posture that she was about to do something drastic. A moment later, his body slammed into the cave wall. She pinned him to it with one hand, her pretty face distorted with anger, her other hand bringing a dagger ever closer to his chest. "Wait!" he cried. "Go to the back room and look for yourself."

Vaylynne moved swiftly away, the dagger still in her hand. His eyes told truth… or insanity. She grasped a torch from the wall and entered the room. It almost fell from her palm. Hands and feet bound, Seth was leaning against the wall with an all-too-calm look marking his face.

"*You*," she was indignant. She had let him go once and he got caught again? Didn't he know what would have to happen now?

He nodded. "Vaylynne."

He was not the Seth she remembered. His arms were stronger; his eyes were darker; he had grown a beard; he had a different way of holding himself—it spoke of a change similar to her own so long ago. "Why did you let yourself get captured?"

Caleb slipped away from the door, where he had been standing in order to, for once, hear praise for his good work. *Let himself? He* let *himself get captured?*

Seth leaned his head against the wall, too calm for her preference. "I wanted to talk to you."

"There were better ways!" she chastised in a low voice, stepping toward him. "You know that I cannot let you go again."

"I don't know why you let me go the first time."

His placid nature caused Vaylynne's irritation to rise. "Do you think this is a game? I wish you no harm, but you are my enemy!"

Having Seth as a captive would do much for her movement, but she wanted him free now more than ever. There was something so similar in his weary eyes. Hadn't he known that she had let him pass through the night with his dwarf friend? Even that was too generous! "Give me the weapons you have hiding in your boots," she commanded. There was nothing she could do now. He had allowed himself to be captured after all. "This had better astound me."

He handed them to her, then settled back against the wall. "The attack against Harvey and Elizabeth…"

"I didn't touch them. You have my word. Sasha must want us fighting."

"*I* know that, but my king and queen don't. They're readying for war against you."

She smiled, to let him think she was more prepared than she was. But the smile was a hideous scowl underneath. This was not good news. She needed more time. Sasha's ploy had worked very effectively. Her army would

Xsardis

33

wither. Vaylynne shrugged. "It was going to happen."

"Our forces are prepared for a battle against your small army. You *will* lose. Your people will die. My people will die. And no one will respect Remar and Juliet after they demolish freedom fighters. You were some of the only people who had been willing to stand up for the villagers while Sasha was in power." He paused, then added, "I know you don't want this loss of life."

"You assume much after one meeting with me," Vaylynne glared.

"Talk peace with the king and queen," Seth persisted.

"I will not settle. What is there to talk about?"

"It can do no harm," he insisted.

Vaylynne sniffed. "It can do a *lot* of harm. It will make my people think that I have lost my resolve, but you know that. That's your plan. Do you think I'm stupid? I didn't get here by making idiotic decisions."

"Come on, Vaylynne. Would I put my life in your hands for something that trivial? We don't need to have war!" his voice bellowed. "Hasn't there been enough death? Come and talk."

"We've had fifteen years of war that wouldn't have happened if we had an independent government. I will save lives in the long run." She kept going before he could offer a rebuttal. "Is that all you came for?"

"Yes."

"Rot then, Seth," she spat, "until I decide what to do with you."

Hours later Seth twisted in his itchy bonds. They were not that tight. He could have gotten out of them. But it was not time. He had always known Vaylynne would not listen, not unless she thought she could gain something from the meeting. Now she simply needed to realize that she had in her possession the greatest bargaining chip she could have wanted. With him as a prisoner of war, she would believe that much could be gained in a meeting with Remar and Juliet. Or so he hoped. It was what he had bet his freedom on. His life he had bet on her valuing him too greatly to kill.

He lay down on the hard floor. He had long ago decided to stop comparing everything with the comforts that used to be his on Earth, so it was not that unbearable. But there was something about the cold and damp floor that took him back to memories he hated reliving.

Seth fell into a fitful sleep.

Rachel lay on the couch, an arm draped across her eyes to block out the light of the day. They had been at an all-nighter with her church and they were both tired, but Seth was content merely to stare at her peaceful face. She rolled over and her eyes flicked open for a few moments, gazing back at him. Then with a smile she drifted back into a restful sleep.

Max was sleeping underneath a pile of leaves. Seth was surprised that his friend could sleep in such an uncomfortable position. Where were they? Hadn't they been in a living room watching a movie? It seemed odd that he had fallen asleep just as the film's hero was attacked by the leading lady.

Rachel's sword clattered against Seth's as they dueled. He became distracted for only a moment and she locked her leg behind his to trip him. He grabbed her waist and they tumbled to the ground, laughing.

Seth could see the happiness that marked Max as Seth passed him the ball and he made the shot that won the basketball game. He fell to the ground,

Xsardis

34

panting.

Rachel's face was pale, her breathing shallow. Seth heard Galen's voice saying that she would not make it through the night. It was over.

It was over. The dragon would reach him before he reached the cliff. But suddenly he roared and turned, showing that Max was gripping onto the beast's tail. When he had finally been dislodged, Seth was ready. Jumping onto Smolden's snout, he shoved the gem sword through Issym's enemy's eye.

A woman was holding a dagger to Rachel's heart. Seth felt the panic surge. It could not be happening. Not after everything they had already made it through. The woman turned her attention to Seth. He watched as Rachel dove for a bow and arrow, shooting Sasha. They ran to each other and he felt her arms wrapped around him.

Rachel wept on the breathless body of Prince Evan. He saw the illuminescent. Evan would live.

The young woman would live. Thanks to him. But now he was surrounded by scores of the enemy. He spun his sword for affect and fought his way out. Every blow he inflicted on the enemy, he felt. Every step cost. All he saw were attackers.

They were surrounded by attackers. Prince Evan, Max and Rachel were up in the tower. Fire consumed them. Sasha snickered. The bile came out of his throat. They were gone—dead. No!

Seth bolted upright as he heard someone hollering in terror. It was him. He stopped himself, panting and sweating. He could not escape the grief. It cut off his air supply.

A form brought a torch into his dark cavern. It was Caleb. He approached with timidity but it took great boldness to enter a room with a screaming warrior. "Are you okay?" he whispered sharply.

The capturer who cared if he was okay… Xsardis *was* messed up. "Go away." Seth lay back down, setting his head on the hard stone floor.

"Are you hurt?" Caleb persisted.

Seth sighed and let out the anguish with it, "No."

Caleb sat down across from him. He did not have a weapon. Vaylynne's orders. She warned that Seth would disarm anyone who came in with a blade and use it to escape.

"What do you want?" Seth questioned with irritation, his eyes still closed.

"How did..." he took a breath and forced himself to go on, "you become who you are—that great fighter everybody knows about?" Caleb inquired softly. It didn't matter that Seth was on the opposite side of the war. No one cared about that. Everybody hailed Seth as a hero. Caleb was no exception. Seth had risked everything to do the right thing. It was rumored that he had even killed a dragon!

The warrior opened one eye and lifted his head long enough to say, "You captured me, remember?"

"I heard you and V…Vaylynne talking. I know you let me win. How did you learn to fight like you do?"

"Believe me kid, you don't want to learn my secret," Seth spoke with finality.

"I know you're supposed to be my enemy, but I'm trying to do a good thing here and I can't lead my troops. They don't respect me and why would they? Can't you teach me?" his voice rose to a high pitch.

Groaning that Caleb was still there, Seth sat up and leaned against the wall. This time his motions were not swift or cool; with his feet and hands bound, they were laborious. "Teach my enemy? No."

Caleb took it as a good sign that Seth was sitting up and continued, "Where you always... a hero?"

"Once I was very much like you—afraid, trying to do the right thing in the wrong way, a poor leader, and a useless fighter."

Caleb winced, knowing the words were true. "So what changed?"

"I had to make a choice. To do what was really right—knowing what it could take from me—or to run for the rest of my life. I choose to do what was right."

"So you gambled."

Seth weighed the words. "I accepted the risks."

"And you won."

Seth shook his head, his gaze becoming distant. "I lost. But Xsardis is winning."

The words swirled about in Caleb's mind. Didn't Seth know how to give a straight answer? "How did you learn to be fearless?" he demanded, forcing the question to be clear before he could change his mind. Maybe he did not want to learn Seth's secrets, but he needed something to change or he would lead his troops to their deaths in battle, if they would even follow him.

An all-new heaviness settled on Seth as he thought about whether or not he would answer. He finally declared, "I lost what I loved most."

"That's what you were dreaming about, isn't it?"

Seth had been right. Caleb did not want to learn to be fearless.

Katarina was awake at three in the morning. Nightmare after nightmare about Evan, about how she had betrayed Max, about how she had screamed at Rachel and, now, how Seth had died at Vaylynne's hand. Harvey and Elizabeth's faces danced through her subconscious. After that she had finally given up trying to sleep. It would only be a few hours until she left for the funeral anyway.

In the stillness and dark of her room she let herself shake with the sobs she could not control. Death was a terrible thing. No wonder Seth had risked his life to stop more of it. War destroyed not only the bodies of humans, but their spirits. It had destroyed hers.

For so long after her father's capture she had believed that there was no happy ending, no way out for her, her family, or her country. So she had done whatever it took to ease the pain of her soul, but it had only made things

Xsardis

36

worse. Each selfish decision destroyed those around her, until only one person remained by her side—Max. He had challenged her constantly. She had been so furious with him for saying that she was not a Christian, for daring her to do better. Max had shown her the depth of pursuit of the love of Christ. As she suffered in Maremoth, Katarina had finally learned that while surrender stung, it brought healing. She had given herself fully to Christ.

The princess understood that now she was new—God's creation. But the wounds she had inflicted in her life before Christ were numerous and the guilt threatened to choke her. "Oh God," she trembled, not for the first time. But this time, she truly longed for help that she knew she could not give herself.

And suddenly the princess felt a peace surge through her. She was reassured of the love of God, the forgiveness. *Therefore, if anyone is in Christ, he is a new creation; the old has gone, the new has come!* 2nd Corinthians 5:17 rushed to her. She had studied the Scriptures after settling in at Saphree. And the more she studied, the more steadily it came to her when she needed it most.

But how can I go on without them? This was supposed to be Evan's position. I'll never be able to lead these people. If Seth is dead...

Katarina knew her parents were barely hanging onto the kingdom. It was Seth's and her presence that had won the people back. And the look she could sometimes discern on her father's face showed with a grave reality that his life would not last more than a few years.

The tears were gone but the numbing pain remained.

But he said to me, "My grace is sufficient for you, for my power is made perfect in weakness." Now it was 2nd Corinthians 12:9 that was almost spoken in her room. The verse had a profound effect.

Katarina rose, lit a candle and washed her face. She spoke softly, but defiantly to the room. "God's strength. No longer my own. Now I am His. That's all that matters. The rest is up to Him and He won't fail."

The realization, the strength from those words sent Katarina's grief to the place it would always be. Present, but not overpowering.

Now awake, she could not fall back into sleep. Her eyes landed on Reesthma's scroll of history. "No. I'm not reading that," she whispered to herself, but already her hand was reaching towards it. "No." She pulled it back.

After several long moments in the oppressive stillness, she gave in. Her bare feet skimmed the cold stone floor as she obtained the scroll. The orange flame of her candle cast its homey glow on the parchment. Katarina crawled under the covers, for a chill had overtaken her.

Thunder rippled across the frozen lake.
Water sheeted from the blackened sky,
banging on the windows and roof of the costly house.
Bolt after bolt of lightning struck, brightening up the world for less
than a second
and then leaving it in greater darkness than before.

So Joppa did know how to write interestingly, but it was an odd place to start a story.

Xsardis

Tension reigned in the house's living room.
Another bolt of lightning flashed,
and the thunder that followed was so loud
the teen could barely hear the four-year-olds' high pitched screams.
The twin girls buried their faces in her shoulder and lap.
The sitter liked rain, and even enjoyed thunder,
but not when she was the sole semi-grown-up in a big, empty house.
Her imagination ran away with her
—wasn't this the same scenario every horror movie that she refused
to watch started with?

Movie? Katarina was utterly confused. This was not what she had been expecting.

She shook her head.
Her charges were sobbing.
She needed to act like an adult.
"Mary, Elise, do you know where lightning comes from?" she began.
The identical faces looked up at her.
"No, Rachel," they declared in unison.

"Rachel," Katarina breathed. This was the story of Rachel and Seth in Issym. She had heard things from Max's perspective, but Seth had not wanted to talk about it. It *would* be an interesting read.

Xsardis

Chapter 4

Caleb recognized that Seth did not want to talk with him again, but he also knew that Vaylynne would not leave the hero of Xsardis in the camp for long. If he was ever going to get real training, he would have to act now. As the feel of destiny, and the determination to do right, had pulled him from home, so now it pushed him beyond his usual boundaries of timidity.

The rest of the camp was asleep, except for those on watch outside the cave. He walked into Seth's room, lighting the torch only after he was in. "Good eve...ening," Caleb tried to look strong, but only ended up looking like a chimpanzee to the warrior.

Seth was staring at him. Caleb groped for words, "I've come for a lesson."

"I told you I wouldn't help my enemy."

"The way I figure..." it took Caleb a lot of effort to swallow, "you don't want people to die or else… you wouldn't do what you're doing. You saw how clumsy I was and if you don't help me, I will die in battle."

"You would be a fool to go into battle," Seth's harsh words were meant as a life-saving warning.

"I... believe in my cause."

"And what is your cause?" Seth was entirely frustrated with Vaylynne and her troops. Everyone else had rejected Sasha and was supporting Remar and Juliet. Vaylynne was what was keeping the country from completely uniting! He might have understood if her troops had been hopelessly devoted to the cause, but it seemed that they were only run-aways, united by another stray. The reason for their war didn't matter to them. Or maybe they simply longed for freedom from laws…

"We fight for independence. We want to be free," Caleb answered.

"Free from what?" he pressed.

Caleb repeated what he had heard Vaylynne say, "The wars wouldn't have happened if we were free."

"That, I can guarantee you, is not true. *I* know Sasha better than that."

Xsardis   40

And Seth did know plenty about Sasha. She was the master of deception, a creature who took pleasure in ravaging not only people's health, but also their dreams. The sinister look in her face still filled his mind.

The first time the shifter had tried to kill him, Seth had just returned from defeating Smolden. He found Sasha about to kill Rachel and captured their enemy's attention. Rachel had shot the vile woman. It should have been done at that. But Sasha lived on.

On 'The Day,' Sasha had morphed into a giant fire sprite and sent flames from her hands, consuming the people he loved most. Her laughing sneer after she had crushed his future still rung in his ears. He could feel the wave of heat that had remained a minute later when he reached the tower and saw that Evan, Rachel and Max were gone.

"You actually met Sasha! And survived?" Caleb's wide eyes and awed words brought Seth back from his memory, but the warrior said nothing.

When Seth did not answer, Caleb slunk to the ground and offered with shrunken shoulders, "Vaylynne says we're doing something important."

Seth pried his thoughts from his own memories and studied Caleb, suddenly aware that the kid was seeking more than training. He was searching for answers. He wished he could ignore that violently clear voice of the Holy Spirit telling him to talk with Caleb, but he could not. "Look, I know what it is to want to be important…" he began.

With bitter regret Seth remembered how he had forgotten Rachel and imagination, and truthfully everyone that was not popular, in a desperate attempt to rise to the top. When he had first come to Issym, he had cast Rachel aside in order to please Max. A divine change had taken him then, but all the years before that? They were gone and he was never going to get them back. Seth could not go back in time and follow through on their childhood promises that they would e-mail every day. And he couldn't make it up to her now either. She was gone. With trembling passion, he emphasized, "But you *need* to know the costs of war."

"I grew up in war," Caleb returned.

"You grew up in a coup. War, actual battle, is even more wretched. Asandra must avoid it all costs. That's why the king and queen want to meet with Vaylynne."

It took the young boy a few minutes to find his voice again, "I don't want to die, Sir."

Seth sighed. He really should not train the enemy, but Caleb's ignorance and folly would get him killed. Seth could have no more deaths on his conscience. "Did you bring me a sword?"

Caleb excitedly stood up and threw one to him. Seth cut his bonds and gratefully rose, massaging his torn wrists. It felt good to move again. "The first thing you have to do is this: stop stuttering and stop apologizing." His own voice reminded him of the one Elimilech the fairy had used to instruct him in wielding the gem sword—the only weapon that could stop Smolden.

Seth went on, "In war you have to act like you know what you're doing and you're capable—even if you are not. Make your opponent afraid of you and you've won half the battle."

In what seemed a different reality, his basketball coach had once given the team a similar, less intense, speech. It was funny how common-place memories were accentuated by his grief and distance from home. Seth could not go back for years—until this was finished. And that was if he went home at all. How could he face Rachel and Max's parents? How could he face his own? How could he explain anything?

"Stand straighter," Seth instructed, pointing with his blade. "Now put your sword in your hilt."

Caleb glanced at him. Was Seth going to hit him over the head and escape? But he had begged for this training and he had to be willing to risk that. He sheathed his blade.

"Draw it out in one fluid motion," Seth commanded.

It took Caleb several tries but he finally got the gist of it. He was such a short person to deal with such a large weapon.

"Everything is fluid. When you move your sword, your whole body needs to be connected. You tighten your stomach, your thighs; you lean forward."

Caleb found the coordination difficult. "Is this really necessary?" he asked.

"A good base will improve your whole skill," Seth replied. His air had turned fully-adult as the instruction poured out.

"How old are you?" Caleb wondered aloud. Seth talked like he was fifty.

Seth tapped Caleb's sword with his own. The kid lost balance almost completely. "Caleb, focus."

Katarina could not tear her eyes away from the scroll even when she heard the knock on her door. "Come in," she said absentmindedly.

Reesthma entered and hopped up on the bed beside her. "You look like my uncle."

"How did he get all this information?" Kat looked up with wonder.

Smoothing out her long hair and her colorful dress, Reesthma replied factually, "A boat came to us with some scrolls. It was an exploring vessel, sent by someone called Universe Girl. The captain and crew told their side of things. My Uncle Joppa also talked with Edmund the shape shifter."

"It is incredible."

"Jeff sent me to wake you." Reesthma was always one of the first people awake. Her duties in the palace included helping with the meals. "It's almost time to leave."

Katarina knew she had to get moving, but in the story Seth, Rachel and Flibbert were battling a group of bandits who had attacked them and had wounded a frog woman. She had to know how it turned out.

"When you're done with that scroll," the stunning girl spoke with a timidity that reminded Kat of the younger Reesthma, "would you look at another? I wrote it about... their time on Asandra. I meant it for Joppa—he learns better by reading. He says he thinks it should go in the tree, but I want to know whether it has really earned that or if he is just flattering me."

Katarina froze. To walk back into those memories... "Okay, Ree. Okay."

With that the princess rose and quickly dressed in brown pants, a green shirt and a leather vest. It was much closer to her dressing style of old, but on riding days she allowed herself to wear what was practical, not what was proper. She descended the stairs five minutes later to find the three others already on their horses and waiting. With a heavy heart, she jumped onto her own steed, and they began their long journey to the funeral.

It was one thing to have an enemy. It was an entirely different thing to have an enemy who was your brother.

Sasha knew it was more than Edmund's 'brilliant' plan that had him walking around her fortress. He was the only person she had ever loved... other than herself, of course. Love was a great risk—one she tried to avoid at all costs. One made mistakes for love. And love meant trust—a trust she was extending to Edmund even though he had already proved to be full of deceit.

She should have killed him for his treachery on Issym, but since only the stones could kill him, she did not have to worry about that, yet. Still, something should have been done to the one who had ruined everything on Issym.

Issym's army was on its way. It was common knowledge. She was wasting time on Edmund's plan, but what choice did she have? Hidden from the whole world, she was breaking apart. She had to have eternal youth—only that could save her. With a desperation that now often swept over her emotions, she was reminded of how she craved the artifact that she could feel out in the abyss.

It was that artifact that Sasha was hoping Seth would remember when her delay aroused his curiosity. That tool birthed by imagination would prevent her from aging and give her power over the cursed stones of the frogs. Edmund, having an understanding of Seth's mind because of the time the two had spent together, had assured his sister that Seth did not yet remember the artifact but that he would if he was pressured to. As Sasha's armies offered few attacks—despite the urgency of the war—Seth would begin to wonder why and search his memories.

Once Seth believed she was going after this powerful weapon, he would risk everything to get it first. Edmund could follow him and steal it from the boy then. It might just work. Sasha held onto hope that it would. Maybe there was a better plan, but the cursed pain in her side would not let her think it through.

Xsardis

43

Part of Sasha doubted that Seth could figure out her scheme. Maybe only Rachel had the memories?

Rachel... she half-smiled. She remembered the look of agony on Seth's face when he saw her die. That was reason enough to keep going. The 'heroes of Issym' would never be the heroes of Asandra. If only Rachel's death had not made her a martyr, Sasha could have enjoyed the taste of sweet revenge. Revenge on a girl who did not even deserve death. Living misery always made far better punishment.

Smolden's fixation with Seth's destruction had been foolish, but Rachel was an enemy worth destroying. The girl had dared to impose restrictions on a shifter's power! It was those restrictions that were destroying Sasha's insides more as each day went by. And Rachel had not even remembered it. She had imagined Asandra a bountiful land and kept the shifters locked on Issym. She had cursed them with her imagination that if any tried to become too powerful too quickly, they should be devoured by their own lust for power. Ill? She was a shifter. Shifters did not get sick!

To spite the one person who had ever controlled her destiny, Sasha had broken both of Rachel's rules. She had claimed Asandra as her own and had quickly amassed power. As soon as Sasha had the artifact, then her victory over limitations would be complete. Her victory over all of Xsardis would follow shortly thereafter.

"You sent for me," Edmund bowed stiffly.

Sasha had not even noticed him, but her eyes fell on her brother with pleasure, as she looked down from her high throne. She liked seeing him subservient. Her half-smile was replaced with true happiness. "I did. What news?"

"None, Sasha. I told you I would keep you informed." He stayed bowed but his eyes taunted her.

The cocky attitude opened the anger in Sasha. "I don't think your plan was as smart as you thought it was," she challenged.

Edmund did not want to be serious; he wanted to tell his sister to try a different dress. Her clothes got more and more exotic every day, probably an outward symbol of her deteriorating mental health. Oh, sure, she believed no one else knew about her 'problems' but Edmund was not only a fellow shifter, he was her brother. He could see right through her transparent eyes. Before answering, he shoved his thoughts beneath the surface, where she might once have seen them. "We need only wait."

"Wait!" she exclaimed, then glided down the steps with a grace and speed he thought she had forgotten. She might have been growing weaker, but she was still perhaps the most powerful figure on Xsardis. "Wait until Issym comes? I gave you a second chance! You realize that if this does not work, you will die a long and painful death."

But Edmund no longer quivered at her threats. Perhaps he had learned that the more elaborate the words, the less she truly meant them.

Sasha recognized that he knew far too much. She needed to send him away. Yet, there was some small comfort in having him around. Someone who so completely understood her, who had been betrayed by shifters and men, who loathed Seth, who shared her goals...

Xsardis

44

The empress hated the weakness her brother made her feel. Before she had made alliances with Smolden, the two siblings had been a powerful pair. It was not easy to seize control of a group of beings as powerful as the shifters, but she and Edmund had done it! He was so strong; they had been so close as children… Edmund was significantly weaker, she reminded herself. And as long as she could keep him believing that, he would stay weaker.

"If you are too impatient, I'll just…" he turned to leave.

"Wait!" she called after him again. "Edmund," she began, pulling him to where she could look at him in the light streaming from the window. "There are reasons for the things I have done. For why I left you without completing your training. For why I pushed you. For why I now give you a second chance."

"I don't care," Edmund answered, but he was interested. Something about her look was off—even for her recent illness. She was white as a sheet, trembling, her eyes were drooping. She was struggling to maintain form.

"I know you won't fail me if I tell you all."

Edmund nodded.

"Father died young, very young. Do you remember?"

"Barely."

"He tried to attain different shapes far too quickly. It made him sick. I watched him shrivel. He asked me to look out for you. But I was a foolish teenager with his blood running through me. I succeeded where he failed. I have mastered all shapes. But I could not defeat the sickness that came with age and skill. I have used up my one life and now need another. I left you so that you would not achieve what I had achieved. I left you to find a way out for me."

The secret to excellent lying is to tell half-truths, Sasha knew. Half of what she had said was really the heart-wrenching parts of their childhood. She was hoping it would distract him from the other half which was pure fiction. It didn't.

"You don't believe me?" she questioned, still holding onto him. It had been a long time since he had seen her this way.

A sudden thought propelled through Edmund's mind, causing intense pain as it arrived. If Sasha really was melting from the inside out, maybe Kate was too. No matter how he tried to forget Kate, she remained the love of his life. He would do anything to protect her. Edmund asked a simple question, "Would your sickness happen to anyone as talented?"

"Yes! It is the curse of power."

Edmund nodded and knew what he had to do.

They stood side by side for a few moments, each thinking their own precious thoughts. In a single second Sasha hardened. She had revealed great weakness to Edmund and that in itself showed the extent of her weakness. He could cause much trouble for her if he stayed in Maremoth. "You are leaving," she barked suddenly.

The change in her was clear. She was controlling, vindictive, and mean again—the sister he knew. "And where exactly am I going?" he inquired.

"To Saphree. You earned Seth's trust; use it."

"But Sasha, you're risking everything!" Edmund protested. "You must give this more time."

"Silence!" she command. "This will be *my* world. I make the decisions. Now you are leaving... alive or dead; it's your choice."

Edmund stared at her for a long while, but finally made another bow and walked away. Kate could be dying at that moment and Sasha was risking the only scheme that could save her for the sake of her pride! He would need to alter his strategy a little.

As he walked out of Maremoth, Edmund chose to stay in human form. Saphree was a long way to walk; but that was good. He had no intention of hurrying.

Vaylynne was walking to another cave to do an inspection there. She would return to Caleb's forces after. *That should give Seth enough time to get away,* she calculated. No one would believe that Seth had 'escaped' on her watch; but it wouldn't take Seth much time to break out of the cave without her presence. If only he would realize that!

She felt her insides churn within her at the thought of Seth. He was making her job more difficult than it needed to be. He was the reason Juliet and Remar were gaining power. He was her enemy and he was quite the prestigious prisoner to have. She should have hated him and killed him on the spot. But there was something about Seth that was so honorable. She saw why people followed him. And now that he had lost Rachel, there was something even more alluring about his character. They were similar now. She simply couldn't add to the pain he carried with him every day—she knew that pain far too well. Maybe now he understood. Maybe now they could join forces.

Tahath would have counseled her to cut her emotions from the situation. And he would have been right.

Vaylynne walked into the cave before the sun had risen—none of the scouts were in their positions. Odd. The cave seemed unusually quiet. She lit a torch and walked through the hallways, expecting something to jump out of the darkness around every turn. She rounded a corner into the open area that should have been occupied by her fighters. Empty. No signs of battle or struggle. The whole group had deserted.

She had lost a whole cave full of her fighters! Vaylynne kicked a nearby stone in her frustration; its rolling sounds echoed throughout the cavern. How long before others followed them?

The timing could not have been worse. They were right on the verge of war. She had to turn the tide back in her direction. It was now or never.

A cold steel hardened in Vaylynne as she came to terms with what she would have to do. Seth's life and struggles now meant nothing. She would have to sacrifice him to save Xsardis. Juliet would never let Seth die; he would be the biggest bargaining chip Xsardis had ever known. If Remar wouldn't

Xsardis

negotiate, Vaylynne understood that she would have to be willing to let Seth die. She steadied her breathing, cementing her resolve, channeling Tahath's support. She would do what she had to.

Chapter 5

Caleb was getting a little better. He could keep his feet, at least. It had only been two days, so Seth was not expecting much.

As Seth brought his sword down hard against Caleb's, it dawned on Seth that he had underestimated Vaylynne. She wanted him to escape. That's why she had left, but he could not ruin his own plans like that. He was going to stay where he was until she returned in a fury and played right into his hands.

Caleb's sword almost nicked Seth's arm. He was not following his own advice to focus. When he went on the offense, Caleb was not even competent enough to successfully switch to defense. The youth stooped to pick up his fallen sword, just in time to defend a blow by Seth. "You're still too afraid!" their blades were locked.

"You're scary!" the kid protested, trying to stand up against Seth's superior weight.

"If your troops see fear, they won't follow you. If your enemy sees fear, he won't run. If..."

"Did you know them well?" Caleb cut him off with his piercingly quiet question. He explained, "The people who died 'The Day The Whispers Became Trumpets'? I have to know."

"You *have* to?" Seth pulled back. The change in pressure sent Caleb down. "Why do you have to?"

In an instant the boy was back up, attempting in vain to fight with Seth. Again they locked blades, this time Caleb bearing down on Seth before getting thrown against the wall. Caleb charged, missing Seth completely. "Who are you? Why are you here? Who were they? Please. There are so many rumors, I don't know the truth!"

"Please—another word you should never use in battle," Seth corrected him. He pushed the kid to the ground, his sword above Caleb's throat—he was in a dangerous mood. "I'm not telling you a bedtime story."

"Years from now, they'll be legends. The whole word will talk of them and they will inspire a new generation of heroes. They wanted to inspire

Xsardis

48

people. They could inspire me!" Caleb persisted, crawling backwards until he reached the wall and could move no more.

Seth pressed the cold steel against Caleb's neck, then pulled back, taking a seat on the floor and drinking some water from his canteen. He wiped the sweat off his brow and answered, "I didn't know Prince Evan very well, but I knew Rachel and Max. There were no two people closer to me. They helped me save Issym and they were family on Earth."

"If they are dead, why do you stay here?"

Why did everyone ask him that? "I could not leave their work unfinished." Seth handed his blade to Caleb. "The lesson is over for today."

Caleb didn't take the weapon. "Why did it destroy you so much? Everybody dies!"

"In battle you don't merely fight alongside people. You learn to trust them with the very fiber of your being. There is a closeness between comrades that you know will never fail you. You risk all for them and they risk all for you. You anticipate their movements; they anticipate yours.

"Rachel and Max were comrades in battle, in politics, in adventures and in the everyday. We saved each others' lives again and again. They trusted me and I led them into a deathtrap. They can't be replaced like a soldier who abandons you. Someday you may lead men into battle, Caleb, and only then can you know the pain I feel."

"Why did you all risk everything for Xsardis? I don't get it. I want a better future, but you guys never lived here!"

"Love is a powerful thing. It motivates you in ways you'll never know until you experience it. My love for God, for Xsardis, for all life… I could do no less than what I've done. I was destined to help Xsardis. It's like James 4:17 says, 'Anyone, then, who knows the good he ought to do and doesn't do it, sins.' I knew I had to help Issym. I couldn't wait to help Asandra. Now I have to finish what we all started together."

"But…" Caleb was going to keep pushing, but a heavy step fell behind him.

"Well, I get to replace you after all," Vaylynne stepped into the room, her dark mood almost suffocating.

Caleb was immediately at attention, "You're back."

"I directly ordered you never to give him a weapon."

"But he's..." the stutter was back.

"You're one of the few who actually has a family; go home to them."

"Vaylynne..."

"Vay," Seth said. "He was using a bizarre interrogation tactic. It was working, until you showed up."

"How nice for you both." She pointed to the door. "Get out. I'll decide what to do with *you* later."

Caleb was quickly out of the room.

"You stealing my people's loyalties?" she glared at him and took the blade.

Seth shrugged. "You left me here."

She tossed a rope at him, "Tie yourself up. You missed your opportunity for escape."

"Where are we going?" he asked as he complied. He could tell by the way she carried herself that she had determined her next steps. She would not allow him to escape now. That chance had come and gone.

"I'm going to that meeting with your precious king and queen. But you're going to be my bargaining chip."

"What will you do if they don't meet your demands?" he questioned, although he already knew the answer.

She stared into his eyes to let him know how serious she was. "I will kill you."

Galen remembered wondering how Issym and Asandra could possibly have fallen in love on the journey from the one continent to the other. It was not much time, after all. After seeing Andrea the first time, he knew—it must have been love at first sight. Even if it was not, he now realized, you got to know people a lot better on a long voyage than anywhere else. If their affection could last through the close quarters of a voyage, then the love must have been true.

The constant waves and clouds were all that there was to distract the sailors—how he wished there was something, anything else. Everyone's nerves were low. They had been sailing for months, moving away from their families, not knowing what they were getting themselves into. They had been gone so long, through storms, some food shortages, attacks from sound sprites... The crew was beginning to wonder if they would ever arrive. It was the illuminescents that had solved their most basic problems, but they never acted until the crew was in desperation.

Flibbert hopped into the room, not knocking—the frog never knocked. "What are we going to do with Philip once we land?"

"Are we even close to landing?" Galen was lying on his bed, trying to beat the nausea that had been constant since day one. It was not just from the waves. There were so many worries. Was Issym alright? Were the shape shifters who had formed themselves into boats still alive? And now Philip? He had to admit that this was the least of his concerns.

"Galen, don't you even care?" Flibbert criticized.

The king sat up. "Yes, yes... we will watch him closely. He does not want to fight so we don't have to worry about him fighting against us."

"But he could murder us in our sleep!"

"You are far too worried."

"And you are not worried enough."

It was the most civil conversation they had had in weeks. If Galen was upset, Flibbert was ten times as much. "What's your problem?" Galen questioned him. "You didn't even leave a family behind!"

"Do you think I like being alone?" he tried to jump out the door, but

Xsardis

Galen stopped him, swiftly sitting up and stopping the door with his foot.

"Get back here." Three-fourths of the time they fought, but the other one-fourth, Flibbert was a truer friend than any other. In total, they acted like brothers. "What's going on?"

"You don't know her, but I do."

"Who?" the high king massaged his temples.

"Ethelwyn," he squatted with his long legs.

"This is about Universe Girl? Still?"

Flibbert leaned what resembled his chin into his fingers, sounding more like a youth than Galen had ever heard him sound like before. "She wouldn't have stayed behind unless there was something wrong—I mean really wrong. And I don't know whether it's about her or about me or about Issym or about Asandra or about Xsardis. I know that she was trying to tell me and I didn't understand."

"*I* don't understand."

"Galen, the only reason she would act the way she was acting is if someone was dying. Dying!"

Whatever the frog was driving at it was important. "Well, what do you want to do?"

"I want to talk to her but I can't so I..." he stopped. "I'm worried. Maybe she was just trying to warn us. Whatever the case, we need to be careful."

Katarina and her companions arrived at Clidrion an hour after darkness fell. In the light from the large bonfire, faces she recognized surrounded her. They showed confusion, sorrow, fear. But the most chilling were the faces that showed understanding. Nobody should have to be that comfortable with death.

She dropped from her horse almost before it had stopped, shedding the skin of a perfect princess and carrying herself as a member of this community. In that moment she felt she was. She welcomed the hugs of the few women that had been part of Elizabeth's inner circle, offering whatever comforting words she could find.

The town had held back the ceremony, waiting for her arrival. As Jeff watched her mingle with a truly open heart, he realized that she had no idea how much good she was doing these people. They loved her. They trusted her. Each kind word she spoke, they would remember long after she had forgotten.

The list of names read before the bonfire was seventeen long. Each death read off by Thaddeus, the new governor of the town, was accompanied by the person's loved ones throwing some memento into the blaze. Katarina felt the heavy weight bear down on her shoulders. They had been told only of Harvey and Elizabeth, but the whole caravan had been destroyed. Grief hung

Xsardis
51

like a fume that would forever taint the air; she knew it all too well.

When the entire list had been read, Thaddeus offered a prayer and the people dispersed to their homes. It was not disrespect, Kat knew, that had kept the funeral so short. It was custom for people to honor the dead in their own way in their own homes. *Evan will never have a burial...* the thought was impossible to stop or banish as it washed over her.

Katarina stayed in her spot, offering reassuring looks and words to any who passed by her. Jeff and the others stood unmoved at the edge of the fire; they would not stir until their princess did.

Finally Thaddeus' wife drew her toward her own home, where a few of the key leaders in the town had gathered without prearrangement. Thaddeus caught Katarina's elbow as she entered. He was a tall man, bearing the scruff of a few days without shaving. His thick hair swept over his ears, but ended above the neck. His clothes were those of a pauper, but whose weren't in those days? "We hardly expected you to come, Katarina." He used her name without hesitation. Kat reserved the term 'princess' only for those she disliked or did not know. "The roads are dangerous. I am surprised your father permitted his only surviving child to come."

She was at least five inches shorter than him and looked up as a cool wind from the still open door swept the wisps of her hair back. "*Are* the roads dangerous?" her soft question accompanied by her perceptive green eyes held a piercing tone in the eerie mood after the late-night funeral.

His eyes flashed and they instantly understood each other. "I know not."

"Then you do not believe it was Vaylynne who attacked the caravan?" she spoke quickly now. Though the others were drawn away by the fire and Thaddeus' wife's offer of drinks, their distraction would only last so long. They had only a moment of privacy left.

"What do *you* believe?" he returned, pulling her to the side of the room for a few more seconds as Jeff and the others entered and closed the door.

"You and I both know that Vaylynne might have killed Harvey, but all the others? Those are the people she is fighting *for*! It couldn't be her, could it?" Kat's brain wanted to refuse to believe that it was not Vaylynne. She wanted to know that whomever had killed her friends could be brought to justice. Sasha might never be...

He opened his palm and led her to the group sitting around the fireplace, some in wooden chairs, most on the ground. The large open room held a few beds on the far end, containing children who were sitting up and refusing to sleep. Kat took the seat of a man who moved for her, accepting the offer of a gentleman. Her eyes looked for Jeff and saw him immovable by the door, observing everything and saying nothing.

An older man across from Katarina met her attention as the group fell suddenly silent, "We understand that King Remar believes that Vaylynne is responsible for this?"

The princess confirmed it wordlessly. The old man looked to Thaddeus and at his nod continued, "Forgive us simple peasants, but we do not believe it is so."

"Go on." She suddenly felt the restraints of her position like a weight

Xsardis   52

on her tongue or a seal on her lips. As a representative of King Remar, she could not simply say what she thought. Every word she spoke carried consequences. But these people were her friends. How could she keep silent on such a night as this?

"As you said in the door," Thaddeus responded, "Vaylynne would not harm the villagers of this town simply to make a statement. And if it was a statement, why has she not taken credit for it?"

His wife glanced at him sharply, but his calm demeanor told what she needed to know. Katarina observed it, saddened that the people felt a need for the precautions they were taking. They had ensured that the princess would take their side before they had been bold enough to speak their fears. But one could never be too careful in these times. Treason was a dangerous word, and it sounded very similar to 'disagree'.

"Give me a moment." Katarina stepped into the cool of night and stared up at the moon. Zara's red form swept past her eyes and disappeared. It should not have been hard for her to walk back in and tell them that she agreed, that she would go to her father and stop the war with Vaylynne, but it was.

King Remar had been through much. He had to reassert his power, and sometimes that meant using an iron fist. He pushed those who disagreed with him away. Katarina wanted to obey his words, to be in his inner circle, to follow her king and her father to the ends of Xsardis. Her heart churned at the thought that she would make a selfish decision this night to agree with Clidrion instead of her father. She had changed. She had tried to be obedient. She had tried to become the leader that Evan would have been.

But Remar was wrong. There was no way this was Vaylynne's attack. It was so clear. Seth had seen that. He had risked himself to prove it. And her father had just cast Seth out—let her friend put his neck before Vaylynne to disprove something Remar never should have believed. Had the king's time in Maremoth blinded him?

Katarina already knew what would happen if she returned to Saphree and spoke to her father about her concerns. He would say the risks were too great, that war would come sooner or later, that his decision was made. And Seth would die. As soon as the king declared all-out war Vaylynne would kill the warrior who held Asandra's heart… if she already hadn't.

The princess had to speak. She couldn't. If she took a stand against the king, others would start to. The unity that Asandra had begun to see would disintegrate. *She* might be cast off. Katarina was so tired of being the enemy of both sides.

Unity or truth? "Oh Evan," she whispered, "I wish you were here." He would have known exactly what to do and done it without hesitation. And however she had complained, he would have stood his ground.

The door behind her opened and shut just as quickly. Jeff moved to her left and said nothing. She turned to look at him. "Do you agree with them?" He was not the usual person she would have turned to for counsel but it seemed appropriate under the circumstances. Jeff knew all the people involved and understood the consequences of each action.

"They argue with great wisdom," he replied. She turned back to the open road. Moments passed before Jeff spoke again, "I know what runs through your mind. Only you can make the decision of what to do. But know this: you have come to this village for months to give them a voice in Saphree. They now ask you to use that voice."

"But..." she turned and protested.

The solemn shaking of his head silenced her. "When your mother asked us to flee the underground as Sasha came to attack, I was faced with a similar one. Which commitment did I honor? That to my country or to its princess? These decisions are never easy and they are not simple to live with. But, Katarina, you are not simple. You were created exceptionally strong."

"Strong?" she chuckled, raising an eyebrow.

He put a rough hand on her shoulder, "Yes, Katarina, You are one of the strongest people I know. You carry on when others would falter. You learn when others would rather forget. You forge your future when a future seems impossible."

The man of few words had spoken many, but they now dried up inside him and he walked inside the building with only one more comment. "Say nothing to them tonight. You have the ride home tomorrow to consider this, for there is much to consider."

Stewart paced Maremoth, unhappily embroiled in his own thoughts. His plan had been simple but excellent. Earn Sasha's trust. As Sasha grew in power, so would he. But now...

Sasha had become inconsolable after the battle in Maremoth. She should have been happy because, after all, Rachel and the prince were dead. But no! Her increasingly disturbed nature had even brought her brother back from exile. What was she thinking? Now she was wasting their army! Something had to be done. Stewart was losing all his power.

He had to remind his empress that Edmund was a traitor. Only then would things turn around. She had wasted so much time hoping that Seth would pursue the talisman that offered her eternal youth. She could afford to wait no longer. Issym's cursed army might arrive any day.

Stewart had sacrificed everything to be Sasha's right hand. He devoted himself; did not allow himself to rest. He commanded her army well. He took care of the things she would not bother with. And Sasha did not even notice!

He poured himself a drink from the flask on his table and downed it. "I work hard enough. I should be a very important person," he whispered. He poured himself another drink and finished it off. "I'm smart enough. I'd be a good ruler. Juliet couldn't see it. Sasha can't see it. No one can see it." He finished a third drink. "Why do I even bother?"

He stared at the bottle, deciding. He swallowed a fourth drink. His throat burned. "But someday the whole world will know what kind of ruler I

Xsardis

54

will be!" Stewart staggered toward his fireplace, running a hand through his slick hair. He emptied the bottle into a fifth glass, drank it, then threw the cup into the fire. "And then they will regret ever having opposed me!"

Chapter 6

Vaylynne pushed Seth at a brisk pace, knowing that any day now King Remar would realize that Seth was not going to make it back to Saphree and would declare war. She had to hide Seth somewhere from which even he could not escape and make it to the fortress before the king's patience wore out.

"Do you think your people will meet my demands, or will they let you die?" she queried.

"I don't know," he answered. Seth hoped that Vaylynne and the king and queen would come to a compromise, but there was no telling. He had known the risk that they might not when he had allowed himself to become Vaylynne's bargaining chip. He felt a twinge of guilt, manipulating his own people, but there seemed little choice.

They were in an open plain with nothing but grass and a few stray boulders for as far as the eye could see. The sweet scent of summer filled their noses.

Seth glanced back at her and said, "Most of your men don't know why they're fighting, but you must have a reason. What is it?"

Resting her hand on the hilt of her blade, she replied, "I grew up on a farm, with uncles and aunts and cousins and grandparents that I don't think we were even related to, and a troupe of siblings, and, of course, my parents. Those were happy days."

Her voice darkened, "I watched them all die—every one of them. Some to Sasha's men in battle. Some to disease from poverty because of the taxes leveled by your Remar. Eventually all that was left was my uncle and I and his two beautiful daughters. The lawless burned our home to the ground. I tried to rescue the baby, but she was dead before I even got her out of the house. My family was gone and I was alone and I realized the problem. Remar was wrong. Sasha was evil. It left the average unprotected. Only if we were governed by the average would things change.

"I've spent the last several years learning how to fight and making a stand. I don't ever want to watch those I love die around me again." She

Xsardis

56

paused. "And you? Why do you fight even now that those you cared about are gone?"

"They gave up their lives in this fight..."

Vaylynne cut him off, "A hopeless fight for a hopeless king! All these deaths are on his head."

Jaw clenched, knuckles white, eyes dilated, Seth turned. "You make their deaths sound like they'll never matter. Did you ever think that this is *your* fault? If you had not taken half our army in your independence movement, maybe Rachel and Max and Evan would be alive right now!"

That sent her reeling, "You have no idea what you are talking about. You came from a whole different world. Why did you have to mess *mine* up? You should have kept them home—safe."

"You're saying it's my fault their dead now?"

She was too upset now to hold back. "You were their leader."

Seth turned from her. And instant later, he spun back, barreling her off her feet. His hands were free. His eyes were wide with anger.

"How?" she breathed, knocking him off her with a powerful kick.

Seth stood, covered in grass, and rolled his hands into fists. She drew her sword. "I'm not letting you escape."

Escape was not on his mind. Making her calloused words hurt her as they had hurt him was.

"Ah!" he yelled as he charged her. Her blade nicked his arm.

When she brought her sword over her head, his forearm stopped her arms. He struck her stomach. In the wake of pain's distraction, he gripped her wrist, twisting until it almost snapped. Vaylynne cried out and dropped her sword.

Vaylynne thought he might kill her there, but footsteps were coming toward the sound of their fight. She glanced up at Seth. His eyes were searching for the source of the sound. She snatched her sword.

The first of the men jogging toward them came into view on the horizon. "They with you?" she asked.

"No." He forced himself to trust her. "Which way to safety?"

Despite the bad news she had to offer, she spoke without hesitation. "Its miles before there is anywhere to hide, in all but one direction."

"Through them," he surmised.

More and more men were coming into view. How many, he could not be sure. But there were well over a dozen already.

"What's the plan?" she asked.

Seth did not answer. He simply charged the enemy. Without waiting for her, without a weapon, with certain death staring him in the face, he ran toward them. He dodged the blow of the closest human and punched him in the jaw. He fell down and did not get up. Stooping for his enemy's sword, Seth drove his way farther into the group. Vaylynne went after him—stabbing blindly, often hitting a target.

Pushing herself to run, Vaylynne moved through the heat of the day toward Seth. By the time she reached his side, they were in the middle of the pack of attackers. Few wore armor—Sasha had little of it left. The two of them were surrounded. She put her back to his and nudged her left foot until it made

Xsardis

57

contact with his where she could sense if he cut a way out. In sync, they battled the enemy that far outnumbered them.

Thrusting and blocking, Vaylynne protected his back as he protected hers. In minutes, her clothing was more tattered than whole as she barely escaped blows meant to kill her.

"Now!" Seth shouted and lurched through a small opening he had found in the army.

The few of their enemy who realized that the pair was no longer in the center were unable to keep the others from caving in on them.

Vaylynne and Seth sprinted together to the forest's edge, lashing out at anything that got in their way. He paused behind a knoll. Only then did he let himself draw in the deep breaths that his shaking body so needed. His hand was white with the grip on his weapon.

The sounds of the enemy started to get closer. "We need to move," Vaylynne had not even finished the words before Seth was on his feet and running deeper into the woods. The loud sounds of a pounding waterfall were growing. Seth and Vaylynne moved toward it; their feet often slipping from fatigue. How long had they battled?

Seth came to the edge of the cliff and looked down. The blinding sun shone brightly on seven waterfalls cascading down into their own pools. Each waterfall was one of the colors of the rainbow. Each basin touched the peninsula of lush grass. "Rachel," he mouthed. It fit her whimsical side.

The sounds of the falls drowned out the enemies' footfalls, so that they could not determine how far ahead of their pursuers they were. Vaylynne tied a rope from her bag to a rock and began to descend the cliff.

Seth glanced at her. "This is your shelter?"

There was no option but to follow. Once, he might have climbed like this for fun. Now he raced for his very life and his muscles pulled at the strain. His boots thudded as he hit the ground.

"Peace for now?" Vaylynne made certain as she leaned in to be heard over the deafening sounds of the falls.

He gave his consent with a simple blink.

The two were completely surrounded by the folds of the cliffs. "The army," Vaylynne explained, "will have to come down one at a time."

"And what if they shoot us?"

"Sasha's archers aren't that good a shot. I didn't see very many bows."

Seth rolled his eyes, unsatisfied. He gathered driftwood, built a fire, and sat down. Vaylynne kept her eyes trained on the cliffs, though after a few minutes she knew that Sasha's men were not going to follow. "They're going to wait for us to come up."

"Yeah; I know," he answered shortly. Vaylynne had worn out any respect he had possessed. His eyes stared into the flames as darkness fell.

Vaylynne accepted her error, "I shouldn't have said that, Seth."

"No. You shouldn't have."

"If you could have escaped even after I came back for you, why didn't you?" she pondered, putting things together. "You *wanted* to get captured! You knew that I would only talk peace if I had an important prisoner to bargain with."

He threw a long piece of grass into the fire and it sparked blue. "So what?"

"You were right when you said that I don't want to lose all those lives. Join me in freeing this people."

"No."

"Why? Because you feel like you have some debt to Rachel?"

"No! Because I know what's right and what's not. You're the one who's blinded!"

"You—a foreigner—know? Hah!" She stood in frustration and began a series of exercises that would maintain her balance. She felt his eyes on her. "What?"

"We just escaped from near death, almost killed each other, scaled a wall, are in the middle of waterfalls, will soon have to face an army again… and you're exercising?"

"Never give up a routine that makes you stronger, especially in a time of battle."

He let her work for a little while before speaking again, "You know things that I, the foreigner, don't know." She peeped open her eyes to look at him. "Like why Sasha is waiting to attack us."

She stopped. "Oh. You won't like it."

"Try me."

"Edmund is working with her."

Seth felt his mouth go suddenly dry. He and the shape shifter had, at least in Seth's mind, become friends during their time on the island of Noric. Edmund had assisted Seth in convincing the dwarves to fight Sasha. But when Seth had given them a chance to back out of the war, Edmund had punched him and disappeared. "Are you sure?"

Vaylynne nodded.

Edmund had refused to accept Christ. He'd tried to stay in the middle. He'd failed because it wasn't possible.

"I'm surprised Sasha would let him," Seth murmured.

"He apparently offered something she couldn't refuse."

"What?"

"I thought you would know. I don't, but it has me pretty scared."

The clear morning sun met Katarina as she stood after a night of fitful sleep. Normally she hated short trips. She would rather have escaped Saphree for weeks than for a single day. But at that moment she was ready to begin their journey back to the palace.

Her thoughts wandered over her history and Seth's. She had finished Joppa's scroll on the way to Clidrion. It afforded her the time on the return trip simply to process what she had learned. The sheeting rain that had assaulted them in the early afternoon worsened her already unhappy mood.

"I must tell you," Jeff had said almost an hour ago, "that I agree with the people of Clidrion, after hearing them speak. I will tell the king my position, but you must decide yours."

The princess was torn between her longing to please her father and her need to stand for what she believed. The town was right. Vaylynne was not responsible for the deaths. And they knew that if a war started with Vaylynne so many more, maybe of their own people, would be lost. Katarina could not remain silent.

Seth and Rachel might have kept quiet and out of the way when they had first been brought to Issym. Joppa's scroll showed that they had wanted to. They had tried to flee, to keep away from taking sides, but they had known when the time came to stand. Rachel and Seth had given everything to make that stand. And when she and Evan had brought them to Asandra, they had made that stand again—despite Katarina's less-than-grateful attitude.

With silent displeasure, the princess knew that her time to stand had come. Her father would give Seth maybe a week to return with Vaylynne. If he did not, war would be declared. Seth would be slaughtered as the first prisoner of war and many more would follow. Before that happened, she would have to speak.

The fairies and the mushnicks had been paired together for centuries. The mushnicks were a peaceful and jolly people, who, most admitted, kept the fairies from being too serious. And for centuries the fairies had tried to keep the mushnicks out of battle, not wanting their way of life to be disrupted.

Only the fairies realized that the clumsy mushnicks were quite noble. They self-sacrificingly gave gifts, offered comfort, immortalized the kind in song. They were wise in their own way. But none of that made them noble; they were noble because they never thought of themselves, never. With a crazy love for everyone around them, they would make sure that the whole of the fairies had all they needed or could want before any mushnick would eat or rest.

Because of this, when a contingent of the mushnicks had begged to come on the voyage to Asandra, Elimilech—the fairy captain—had been unable to refuse them. Now he wished he had. They were nearing Asandra and despite months of training, the mushnicks were still incapable as warriors. Their short, pillow-like bodies lacked the quickness needed for battle; their jovial personalities had trouble even clashing swords with each other in preparation; and their bright colors would attract too much attention. Some, to be sure, did know how to handle a sword. After all, they had routed Sasha with Rachel and some others' help. But even these... Elimilech sighed.

The broad-shouldered fairy did not fit his green wings—they were

Xsardis 60

dainty, and there was nothing dainty about Elimilech's forceful spirit. Many soldiers used broadswords, but even those were too small for the bulking man. He had had a special one made. Although not an elegant blade, it was strong. His traditional white tunic was cut at the shoulder to leave room for his muscular arms. Months without shaving had allowed a trim red beard to grow, making him, except for the wings, look more like a lumberjack than a fairy.

Elimilech flew towards Galen, who was at the helm, steering one of the three ships from Issym. The fairy saw the king's eyes hesitate on the helpless mushnicks. "We can't let them fight," Galen broached the subject first, putting his focus on the fairy for a second.

"I had come to the same conclusion," Elimilech answered heavily. Their hearts would break.

"We should give them some other purpose." Galen was already a politician. *We* effectively meant *you.*

"I've been thinking about that too. Mushnicks grow and gather almost all of our food on Issym. War-torn Asandra most likely has all it can do to find food for itself. We should not burden them any more than we need to. With your permission, I will put the mushnicks in charge of finding our food."

"An admirable task for an admirable people," Galen agreed, his eyes locked on the waves. They rose and fell like the nausea in his stomach.

Elimilech began to leave but turned back, "Sir."

Galen braced himself. *Sir* always meant trouble. "What is it?"

"I've been thinking about what the sprites said... that prophecy about Rachel. And how she was going to burn."

"They were trying to weaken our moral. Nothing else." Galen's mind returned to the day at sea when three sound sprites with their melodious voices had almost destroyed the vessels.

"I don't think Flibbert believes that."

"Neither do I," Galen whispered under his breath as the fairy flew away.

Chapter 7

"Leave Vaylynne and Seth! Sasha's orders!" Edmund demanded, getting right in the face of the leader of one of Sasha's companies and commanding his attention. If there was anything he had learned from his sister, it was how to get someone's attention. The shifter had grown a few extra inches, but it was his tone that was the most intimidating.

"You're her half-witted, treacherous brother; why should we listen to you?" the man mouthed off, testing Edmund's cocky exterior.

"You remember Sasha's threats for long and painful deaths?" he replied in his creepy voice. This was vitally important for both his plan and his sister's. He could not fail. Seth had to be allowed to escape. "I've seen her carry them out for less disobedience than what you are showing me now. If you capture Seth her whole plan will be ruined! You know I'm back in her good graces. Do you think it was easy surviving outside them? You want to give it a shot?"

Edmund got in the face of the second-in-command and then proceeded through the men. "Do you want that? Do you? How about you?"

The leader was losing control of his soldiers. "Fine!" he caved. The shifter returned to his side and he asked, "You are sure?"

"If you don't believe me, pursue them and find out," Edmund offered.

"No, no. No."

When the army had turned around, Edmund flew down to the basin of Dye Falls. Morphing into a small human as Vaylynne stared at the cliff face and Seth slept, he spoke quietly into the youth's ears. He would make Seth remember the artifact while he slept.

Xsardis

62

Vaylynne was hovering by the fire, keeping watch over the cliffs. She had to do something with Seth. He was too powerful an enemy, far too committed to his cause. And she needed him if she was going to prevent war with Remar.

Vaylynne knew what she had to do. She could subdue him now with one of the herbal remedies her uncle had taught her. So why was she holding back?

Thinking it could only be a lack of courage, Vaylynne forced herself to ready the mixture. It did not take much to cause unconsciousness. She could drop it into his mouth while he slept. He would not wake up for several days which she could use to get him to a secure cave—but she could not carry him and had no horse. How was she ever going to get him over the waterfalls?

Vaylynne not able to capture a guy who's sleeping next to waterfalls that are so loud he cannot hear a thing you do. It was almost as if Tahath was talking to her. *You just don't want to.*

Seth went from a dead sleep to being on his feet. She spun around to face him. Was he going to add 'mind reader' to his list of talents? He was hurriedly strapping his sword to his belt, getting ready to leave. Sweat poured from him. His pupils were wide. "What on Xsardis is wrong with you?" she questioned as she rose quickly, hiding the concoction.

"I know what Sasha's doing," he told her. Now he was slipping daggers he had retrieved from the battle into his boots and belt. "Why was I so…" he muttered, and Vaylynne could only pick up some of his words. "It was… Fool!" He spoke more clearly: "If only I had known all of this was going to be real!"

"Tell me what's going on, right now!" she ordered, a sudden fear seizing her.

He spoke to the fire instead of to her, "As a kid imagining all of this, I thought that the stones of the frogs were too easy a way to defeat the shifters…"

Too easy? she wondered.

"So I pretended," he continued, finally looking at her, "that there was something… something that would make them impervious to those stones and grant them eternal youth. She doesn't need to be fighting us, because that is all she needs."

He was done talking. He walked to the cliff and started climbing.

She followed. This concerned more than Remar and Seth. If what he was saying was true, the whole world was in terrible danger—a danger greater than any they had yet faced. "Where is it?"

"I don't know," he replied without pausing. Seth did not care if there was an ambush waiting for him at the top of the cliff. He had to get back to Saphree and warn the others.

She followed him up. Once they were on the top, she pulled at his arm and demanded, "All of Xsardis is on the line and you don't know!"

"I can't remember!" he returned gruffly.

"How can you not remember?"

He ripped free, "I just don't! And there isn't time!"

Seth was moving quickly. She kept pace with him. All thoughts of subduing him were gone. Inside Seth's mind might be the only way to stop Xsardis' greatest danger. "Tell me there is some way around this," her voice trembled.

He shook his head in the pale light of the moon.

"How can there not be? What kind of imagination do you have?"

"I got distracted imagining Smolden," Seth answered. "And Rachel... never liked shape shifters."

"You got distracted!" she screamed at him.

"I didn't know it was real!" he returned with force. Now he broke into a jog.

"Where are you going?" she demanded.

"To Saphree."

"Saphree is two days away. I know these woods. Judging from your reaction to the Dye Falls, I'm betting you don't. You need a guide."

"Leave me alone, Vaylynne."

She gripped his arm again and stopped him. "Look, forget our history. This is my world too. That makes this my fight."

He nodded.

"Land ho!" voices called from the crow's nests of the boats.

Every eye turned towards the distant land mass. "Asandra," Galen muttered. He called out orders, which Flibbert and Elimilech oversaw. With armor and weapons ready, the crew made for the small harbor that Philip pointed out.

Finally, land.

Longboats dropped from the ship, bearing the many soldiers and what supplies were left. Fairies and airsprites flew from the vessels.

"Get every piece of stone armor off the boats!" Flibbert shouted.

"Move!" Elimilech bellowed, though the troops did not need his charge. They were desperate to set their feet on solid ground again.

When Bridget and Brooks had first come from Asandra with the news of Sasha's aggression, Issym had known that they had no time to waste in building boats. Three shape shifters had agreed to form themselves into those shapes, but not without great self-risk. The shifters believed that if you stayed in one shape too long you would never come out of it—in an inanimate form, death.

Galen and Flibbert were in the last long boat to disembark. The king wore chain armor, while Flibbert donned his traditional frog stones. Most of the army wore the light frog armor. Only a few used heavier mail or plate armor.

"Get these people away from the boats," Galen directed. "I'll join you as soon as the shifters are free of their boat forms."

"This continent is at war and you are our king," Flibbert pointed out.

Xsardis

"Someone should stay with you."

Galen grasped his shoulder, "Already these shifters have been in this shape too long. I must see that they live. Don't waste any more time. Go!"

It took an excruciating amount of time for that many people to get onto the land and move away from the vessels that had born them across the ocean. Silence set in long before the shifters were able to change. Galen was so grateful for that quiet! It was like long ago when his only companions had been the birds and the trees and the wind. Pulling a flute from his belt, he began to play a merry tune. By the third song, his thoughts grew dark. Would the shifters ever return to their normal shape, or would they be the first casualties of this war?

He heard the ships begin to break apart. As the masts fell, the boats snapped in two. Though he was on land and safe, Galen cringed at the mighty sound of destruction. The vessels sunk into the ocean. And then there was silence.

Water shot into the sky. Three forms propelled from it on magnificent wings. Changing from airsprites, to animals, to objects, the shifters tested their 'muscles.' After several long moments they landed before Galen, in human form. Pale—but alive.

The second Katarina's feet alighted inside Saphree, she knew something was wrong. She glanced at Jeff. His stance showed the same awareness. They tossed their reigns to their companions and jogged inside, still looking tousled and muddy from the pouring rain through which they had ridden. Heedless of the dirt they left behind them, they made their way past countless people to the council chambers, only to find them empty.

Katarina's loud sneeze showed the cold that would grip her if she did not change into something warmer. "I'll find your father," Jeff said. "Hurry to change. We may need your skills of persuasion in a few minutes." He did not wait to see if she listened, but went off to seek the disaster they both felt so clearly.

Knowing his motivations, the princess moved quickly back to her room. She exchanged her riding clothes for one of her finer dresses and her warmest cloak before washing away the grime and sweeping her hair back into a controlled bun. In only a few minutes' time, she swung open her door and ran full-force into her mother. "Oh Katarina!" Juliet exclaimed, pushing her back into her room and closing the door.

"What's going on?" the princess demanded.

"Your father grows impatient," the queen exclaimed, her eyes wide with knowledge.

"It's been two days. He can't be that impatient."

"A scout reported seeing Seth and Vaylynne surrounded by fifty

Xsardis

65

armed men—presumably Vaylynne's. She had Seth tied up. It's clear that Seth's reasoning with her has failed. The council met an hour ago and decided to declare war in the morning."

"This is ridiculous!" Katarina's brain was working too quickly for her to process. "We can't do that." She saw in the queen's eyes that she would or could do nothing to change her husband's decision. Kat brushed past her and ran to her father's room.

The princess stopped outside the door, offering a prayer and cooling her voice. A rushed explanation would destroy her cause. She knocked and heard her father's low voice say, "Come in."

Katarina entered, summoning her authority. She passed Jeff as he exited, receiving a reassuring glance. Katarina stopped before her father.

"You're back," he smiled.

"I have to talk to you."

"Go ahead," he said with open eyes. Her voice faltered. She did not want to disappoint him. "What is it?" Remar asked. "You look so troubled."

"When I got to Clidrion, I was surprised. We had heard only that Harvey and Elizabeth died." She spoke somberly and slowly. "But fifteen others were killed."

"It is terrible," he replied, though he had already learned the news from Jeff.

"That act does not fit with what we know of Vaylynne. She would not harm innocents. The people of the town wondered the same thing. No one really believes it was her."

The king sighed, "The decision has already been made. Please do not try to…"

"Dad, let me finish. The people of Clidrion are scared of more death and more war. It's not what Harvey and Elizabeth would have wanted. None of us want that. And then there's Seth…"

"He threw his life away," the growl entered his voice. Remar hated believing that, but he did. As far as he was concerned, Seth had died the second he left Saphree.

"No, he didn't! He risked his life because you would not listen to reason."

The king's face flushed with displeasure. "He's been waiting for a mission where he can die since 'The Day.'"

She pushed herself to keep going. "No, you're wrong."

"You know him so much better?"

"Yeah, I do," she fought against the frustration that wanted to consume her. Was her father even listening? "And not just because he's my friend. I read the scroll of Joppa's that told about his time on Issym. Seth wasn't trying to kill himself.

"Once," she continued, "Seth was no warrior; he was a normal kid. He was asked to fight a dragon and he was terrified. But he did it, because it was the right thing to do. He came to Asandra because it was the right thing to do. He gave up Rachel and Max because it was the right thing to do," her voice choked but she pressed on. "And he went to Vaylynne because it was the right thing to do. Seth has been called by God to stand up when others won't or

Xsardis 66

can't."

"This doesn't change anything," Remar returned.

"It changes everything! Seth gave you his service—he had no reason to. He risked his life to stop needless deaths. And you aren't even letting him have a *chance* at finishing his mission. Why did you let him go if you were simply going to consider him dead? There is no way he could be back by now."

"Katarina, stop. You need to learn to listen."

"Me?" she shook incredulously. Strands of her hair slipped from the bun.

"Seth has failed his mission already."

"An extra day won't hurt you at all, but it can save a man's life—a man who has given everything for us. Don't do this for me, or for Seth. Do it because it is right."

"No," he barked.

"You say you've changed," her voice was full of emotion. "The people have given you a second chance. But you haven't changed at all."

"That is absolutely out of line! You need to grow up, right now."

Her ears burned as she recalled the memories of which he was thinking. Her foolish childhood battles. "I'm not asking you if I can climb a tree!" she sputtered. "I'm asking you to spare a life."

"How many times do I have to say no?"

Katarina remained silent for a few moments. "You think I'm opposing you, don't you? I'm trying to save you!" Her eyes watered with her sorrow for him. "These people loved Seth and what he represented. *He* unified them. Without him, you are going to fall. I'm trying to prevent that."

King Remar looked away.

Her heart threatened to burst from her chest. "I can't sit by and support you while you make this grave mistake." She whispered her next words, not believing them herself: "I'll have to leave."

Chapter 8

Katarina fingered the weathered bag that had once had a permanent resting place over her shoulder. Those were the days when adventures still thrilled her; when she and Evan could get out of any plight; when being a princess required little and being a refugee meant you followed few rules. Now adventure seemed only to lead to death; Evan was gone; she longed to do what was right, but she would never be a princess again.

Her disagreement with her father ran too deeply to be overcome. When she left Saphree, she would be abdicating her throne. Katarina could not stand beside him, encouraging people to follow him.

Once again having exchanged her fine dress for a set of riding clothes, Kat stood unable to move in her room. Her hair was firmly tucked up and out of the way. What jewelry she felt was truly hers and not the kingdom's was safely hidden on her person. She swung the bag around her shoulder and strapped her sword to her waist. Her trusty bow and quiver of arrows waited only for her to reach out for them.

The agony of having to oppose her father was unlike any other she had felt. The Bible said to honor your father and mother. Since she had become a Christian, she had tried. But to stay in Saphree went beyond submission. She would be asked to do what was wrong.

The sounds of the castle had grown but as yet Katarina had not heard anything that either confirmed or denied her suspicion that she had failed to convince her father. Waiting until the morning to leave had defied her nature. She would rather have slipped away, but this was not a thing to do in secret. Katarina would not run away from her home. She was making an adult decision and she would bear the consequences as an adult should.

But as her hand hovered over the doorknob, she wished she had gone secretly. Jeff would try to honor his promise and come with her. And Zara would feel obligated as well. She would not take them away from Saphree, but she had no idea how to stop them.

Unable to control her exhausted nerves any longer, Katarina thrust

Xsardis   68

open the door and stepped out into the hallway of the place that had begun to feel like home, but would be home no more. When Jeff saw her, he hurried to her side. "We had a thorough council meeting this morning," he announced in deep tones. "I counseled on your behalf and, because of you, the king kept an open mind."

"He didn't sign the edict," she breathed, barely able to hope.

"No; he did not." Jeff glanced at her bag, "I think you should speak with him."

Hurried footsteps ascended the stairs and their owner bowed before Katarina, words stumbling out of his mouth, "There's an army at the gate."

The princess turned to Jeff, "Get my parents quickly." She spoke to the messenger, "Inform Sphen. Hurry!"

The king and queen were only seconds behind. Remar instantly took control, "Get every able-bodied man armed."

Jeff ran at full speed, hollering orders as he went, "Archers to the battlements! Arm yourselves!"

Remar turned to Juliet, "Take Katarina and get her somewhere safe."

"Like that will work," Juliet answered. Her daughter already had battle in her eyes.

Remar sighed and turned to Kat, "Take your mother and hide."

"Like that will work." Katarina had received her obstinacy from her mom.

The three hurried down the stairs, met by a guard whose eyes showed bewilderment. "A delegation is coming this way. Should we open the gates?"

Remar nodded. "And close it behind them. Bring them to us."

It seemed like hours as Katarina's nerves flipped inside her. They weren't strong enough for battle yet. Was it Vaylynne's forces? Sasha's? She hoped against hope that it was the people of Issym, but part of her doubted that they were even coming. They had been so long.

The doors to the castle opened and in stepped a man wearing fine clothing, with a crown on his head. There was a radiance about him that was inexplicable. With him was a man-sized frog and a strong man with wings coming out of his back. This explained the bewilderment on the guards' faces. Katarina felt her own awe at the sight of them. Seth had described talking frogs before, but this one looked so… real.

The man with the crown spoke: "I am Galen, High King of Issym."

Juliet sighed gratefully. They might have doubted the story, but the fairy and the frog were enough to convince them.

"I am King Remar; this is my wife, Juliet."

A rush of excitement took hold of Katarina. These were the people of the story; courageous men who would give all for her people.

"This is Flibbert, the frog, and Elimilech, fairy of the green," Galen introduced.

"Fairy, frog and king of Issym, welcome," Remar greeted and called to a soldier, "Let that army in."

"I am Princess Katarina," the girl spoke softly, but Flibbert recognized the wildness in her green eyes. "I am a close friend of Seth's."

Flibbert bowed to her, flipping his top hat off his head. "It is a

Xsardis

pleasure, Lady."

"Do you need food or drink?" Juliet offered.

"Better to discuss the war at hand first," Galen replied. "We heard you were in some trouble."

"And we have heard rumors that you can stop shifters," Katarina returned.

"That we can," Flibbert beamed, puffing out his chest to show off the armor of the frogs—the armor that could save Asandra.

Two more figures walked through the front door. "Seth!" Katarina shouted, more relieved than she could say.

The three turned and instantly Seth was absorbed by them. Such happy sounds of greeting.

"Perhaps we could continue our conversation in our council room," Remar broke in.

Asandra's royals went ahead. Seth and Vaylynne moved slowly onward with the three from Issym. "Where's Rachel?" Flibbert tried to ask the question lightly but the prophecy had terrified him.

Seth's blank stare told them what they needed to know. It was only then that Galen realized how old Seth looked, how worn. Vaylynne kept walking, but the others did not have the heart.

The sickening grief rolled through Galen, but part of him held onto hope that Seth would open his mouth with a story about her being sick or kidnapped—not dead.

"Max, Rachel and Asandra's Prince Evan fell to Sasha in battle. Their deaths bought us time enough to wait for your arrival," Seth explained. His mouth was so dry. "They just stood there while she came after them..."

Flibbert keened and dropped into a crouched position. Galen sunk to the ground with the news, his forehead in his rough palms. Elimilech remained still, silent until he discerned the important parts of the story. Only then did he slip away to manage things until Galen was back on his feet.

Seth sat down with Galen and Flibbert and told them everything. No one bothered them as the three sat for almost an hour in the middle of a hallway.

Seth met Galen's eyes, not hiding the horrible pain that he had born for the last six months with as much silence as he could. Galen suffered all the more when he saw the anguish his young friend carried. It would change his life forever.

"Flibbert," he began, "you don't know how much Rachel loved you. She would constantly tell stories about you and with a sigh wonder if she would ever see you again. She would brag about how noble you were; how courageous; how you had inspired her to fight Smolden."

"I don't typically like people—especially humans," Flibbert admitted. "But I loved her like the sister I never had."

The youth looked at Galen, "You were more than a mentor and protector to both of us—you were our friend. She felt safe with you."

Rachel and Max's deaths were so unexpected. They may have had the prophecy of trouble-making sound sprites, but... it was Rachel and Max. They were essential to the fight. They were legends. They were children. They couldn't die like that.

Now Flibbert stood. His muscles tightened, his eyes narrowed. He was transforming from mourner to warrior. "Where are you going?" Galen questioned, alerted to the frog's aggressive intentions.

"Rachel is not about to give the ultimate sacrifice in vain!" Flibbert shouted.

Galen and Seth rose. The king declared, "You can't go after Sasha."

"Rachel was my sister. I will avenge her death." Flibbert gripped his cane.

"She was mine too. We will stop Sasha. And I'll need you alive to do it."

"Come talk with the king and queen," Seth recommended. There were no more words to be said, no more emotions to feel. There was a task that needed to be done; two armies that needed to be encouraged; and a shape shifter that needed to be stopped.

"The best way to honor Rachel is stop Sasha—not to die trying."

"Vaylynne," Kat scowled as she recognized the girl who entered the council room, "have you come to talk about a treaty of peace?"

"We don't have time to fight each other right now," Vaylynne replied, sitting down and addressing the king, determined to ignore the princess. "Seth knows why Sasha waits to attack you." She explained his theory briefly.

"You're right, then; we don't have time to be enemies," Remar responded. "But I don't want you in my fortress."

"I intend you no harm." Vaylynne opened her hands wide as if to show her innocence.

"Like those words make you any safer," Katarina scoffed.

"Look," Vaylynne leaned forward, "if you want Xsardis to survive, you are going to have to trust me. And no," she answered Remar before he could ask the question, "I didn't kill Harvey and Elizabeth or anyone else from Clidrion."

Kat glared at her, "We still don't need your help."

Vaylynne had the presumption to come into their fortress. Not even to bargain peace but to ask for her army to be allowed to continue to grow while she had full access to the royal family and the fortress!

Once the princess had respected Vaylynne. She had been her hero—a truly free creature—and Evan had been her idiot brother, living under rules he didn't have to follow. Now the roles were so reversed... She wanted the rebel gone. And she wanted her brother back.

Vaylynne was not about to get kicked out. "You don't know how much you need me," she said confidently. "There are three powerhouses on Asandra. The one that stays in the middle often hears things the others don't.

As you communicate with me, so does Sasha. I know her business and you need what I know. The two of us against Sasha will be stronger than one against Sasha."

"You admit that you have contact with the shifter and you want our trust?" Remar questioned.

"Perhaps we would be a better team," Juliet spoke calmingly, "if we established a more permanent alliance?"

"I want complete independence. That I know you will not give."

Remar glanced to the door. He had ordered some trusted soldiers to keep The Brothers out of the room for as long as possible. If they saw Vaylynne, there was no telling what they would do.

The army of Issym entered the gates of Saphree. Bridget felt her body stop moving, repulsed as if by a magnet. The high stone walls, the cruel architecture, the guards at the entrance. Her world started to spin. She was completely disoriented. Where was she? She was burning up.

Focus! She forced herself to breathe.

"It is a lot like Maremoth, isn't it?" Brooks' voice filled her ears. "We don't have to go in. We got the army this far."

"We should have stayed on Issym," she lamented. Fifteen years of her life spent in Sasha's prison. Brooks had just been another guard until he helped her escape. Together they had fled and warned Issym about Sasha.

"Maybe," he responded carefully. "But we're here now and you tell me that everything has a purpose."

"You're right." She stared into the fortress. "And this place is different."

"Of course," Brooks knew there was a note of skepticism in his voice. It really did look like Maremoth.

Bridget did not believe herself either. So much of Saphree bore witness to the shifter who had commissioned it. She could still feel the terror she had struggled with each day, wondering if it would be her last.

"We don't have to go in there," Brooks repeated.

"What are we going to do? Sleep outside?" she laughed. "I can't live in fear."

Brooks watched as Bridget was encompassed by friendly mushnicks. They loved her; as everyone loved her. The colorful heads came up to her waist and they all reached for her hands, drawing her toward the castle with chattering voices. A smile lighted on her face, thanks to them, and she allowed them to pull her in. Brooks didn't know whether it was by complete accident that they took this moment to surround her, or if they had some natural instinct when people needed their jolly natures, but whichever way, he was grateful.

Bridget belonged with such good people. He didn't. She was a woman of virtue, a woman who carried beautiful scars. He would always be the former servant of Sasha—distrusted.

His own feet would not allow him to enter the fortress walls. He would only tie the armies down as they supervised him. He needed to find his own place in the world and that wasn't going to happen here.

Knowing what he had to do, Brooks set out to seek a new identity and to bury his old life. He simply hoped Bridget would be okay.

Deception had been a powerful tool. How had Sasha allowed herself to lose it?

Stewart knew that they were in a dangerous position. For some reason, unknown even to him, she was waiting to attack Remar's forces at Saphree. That might have been manageable, but all of Asandra groaned for freedom now. The prisoners' escape from Maremoth on 'The Day' had cause irreversible damage and untold danger. Asandra now realized how terrible Sasha was. A decade of lies washed away in a day! It would have been better to kill every prisoner inside than to allow them to return to their villages with true tales. That's what Stewart would have done. But no one listened to him…

Though he was a tall and handsome man who had always drawn the eyes of those around him, Sasha had never fully appreciated his potential. That lumberjack Zachary with his tall frame, blond hair, and bland face had somehow managed to capture people's attention. Stewart knew that he was behind much of Asandra's recent conversion and changes. His words or, more likely, the Word that he preached held more effect than the memory of the three's deaths and more even than Seth's leadership did.

If Stewart was ever going to take control of Asandra, things would have to change, dramatically. Sasha had to fight again! Her frazzled state allowed him to exert his control right underneath her nose, but to usurp her power was not enough.

At least the traitor Edmund was gone.

Standing in the center of Maremoth, where scores of slaves had once moved about, Stewart could barely tolerate the silence. The few slaves still left in Maremoth served Sasha's growing desires in the castle. His eyes scanned the fortress walls, discerning the guards and their lack of attention. He would have scared them into watchfulness, but a fire sprite landed before him.

"Golesha," he addressed her. She had pushed three sprite leaders from their places and had ruled the others for months now.

"Where is Sasha?" Golesha barely noticed Stewart as she whipped back her red hair. He was second-in-command; and in her mind, he might as well have been a common soldier. Her inflated self-view left her speaking with no one but the powerful. Someday she would serve *him*!

"Tell me your news," he commanded. This sprite would not have

Xsardis

73

come to Maremoth herself unless the news was of great weight. He wanted to hear it first. "Sasha does not wish to be disturbed unless it is important."

Golesha would have remained silent but that her news would win her the awe of this human. "Issym's army has arrived."

Stewart lost his composure. Sasha had waited too long. Together the two hurried to her throne room. Golesha flew past him as he raced up the stairs. She had already told Sasha the news when Stewart arrived. The shifter's face was a painful arc, but she said nothing. Golesha flew lower, having expected some reaction. Stewart forced the sprite from the room and shut the doors. "What are your orders, Empress?" he bowed before her.

Sasha looked down at him. "Prepare the army, but do not move them until you hear from me."

"Empress?"

"Issym will spread its troops over the land to try to prevent me from having free reign of the country. You will wait until they thin themselves out and then pick them off, group by group."

Stewart nodded. He would enjoy that.

Xsardis

Chapter 9

It did not take long for Flibbert and The Brothers to realize how similar they were. The frog loved his job. While Galen talked politics with Asandra's king and queen, Flibbert got to exchange battle stories and strategies with Jeffery and Sphen. The Brothers were wise to include Flibbert in their planning, not just for his immense battle-knowledge, but also for his own sake. His grief could still cause him to be reckless.

"The stones can only affect so much area. We'll have to spread our armor out," Flibbert explained, setting the armor of the frogs onto the table before them. They had taken over the kitchen so that the kings could have the council room. The frog hoped Galen and Remar could come to an arrangement. He did not relish the thought that they could have come all the way from Issym to turn back. Flibbert doubted that would be the outcome. With Seth already fighting by the king's side and the threat of Sasha more dangerous now than ever, Galen would be no fool. He would do what had to be done and that meant entering the war.

Jeff heaved the chainmail armor Asandra employed onto the table beside Flibbert's. "We're short on armor. We have some mail, but many of our soldiers use leather."

Sphen added the leather armor to the table and Flibbert inspected the designs. "Good, good," he squatted to get a better look in the dim light.

Spreading out the map of Asandra, Sphen spoke, "Once Sasha knows that you're here, she'll move rapidly in her last attempts. We need to send our troops out quickly."

With that the three set to work with the map, stationing men as best they could.

"No, not there. They are better defended here," Jeff smacked his finger down at a spot on the map.

Sphen actually laughed. "Yes, but they do the town absolutely no good there."

As if Flibbert had been the missing third of triplets, he pointed to

Xsardis

another place. The Brothers looked at each other and nodded.

Flibbert watched as Galen swept past the kitchen with Remar and Juliet. The frog knew what the look on his face meant. "Well boys, looks like you have yourselves a partner in this war."

The frog moved out into the hallway, waiting for a moment to speak with his friend out of the hearing of the others. They caught a few minutes of quiet in the shadows of a hallway.

"We're going to fight," Galen confirmed. He wanted to say something else; to address the grief they both carried like a fatal wound; but he found no words of comfort. "Do our people know?" It was all he could ask.

Finding a voice, Flibbert replied, "No." He forced himself to continue: "Galen, you know what Rachel—even Max—did for our country. Our people here, including those who never met them, loved them. We need to mourn them in our own way."

"Rachel once told me," Galen began, realizing how painful every memory had become, "that on Earth they have days to commemorate fallen heroes. Let us do the same for her and Max. Every year we will celebrate them; the first of those celebrations will be tomorrow."

"Though for our people," the frog moaned, "tomorrow will be much more like a funeral."

A loud clatter filled their ears as some object was overturned. Flibbert ran back to the room with Sphen and Jeff. Jeff was blocking the way out, hunching his shoulders into a defensive stance. Sphen had knocked over a chair. The pitcher of water was across the room. "She can't stay here!" he was shouting.

At the feel of Flibbert's slimy fingers, Jeff moved aside enough for him to enter. "Vaylynne captured us, tried to force us to help her," he explained.

Sphen leaned forward as he stormed before the far window and pointed to the scar on his face. "And she gave me this as a souvenir. She is a deceiver and an enemy. There is no way I'm letting her hole up in our fortress."

"Seth seems to think we need her help," Flibbert risked saying.

"Then let me talk to Seth," Sphen practically shouted. He held a high regard for the boy, but on this, he would not be dissuaded.

"Our king wants her here, for now," Jeff point out. "And there is no debating that."

"Then I'm leaving!"

"We'll keep you separate," Flibbert held up a hand in front of his face. "And it will only be for a few days—or else I'll help you deal with it."

Sphen growled, but nodded his assent.

Caleb let out a holler, tore leaves from the trees, kicked a rock...

"Ow!"

Did he really need a sore foot on top of all his other problems? Vaylynne had always told them that the day would come when they would question their task, so they needed to be ready. He had thought he was. But now! Now he was doubting. Word had come that an entire cave had quit, on top of all the others that had left. There were no adults left—only the children freedom fighters. And Vaylynne would gladly have sent him away if she could have.

The question was not: was it safe to continue? The question was: why continue?

So many had left. Why? Because Asandra had hope again. And Caleb and the freedom fighters were fighting against that hope. Seth had trained him—his enemy—in order to save his life. King Remar valued life. Vaylynne took lives to get her way. How was that right?

There was hope again. King Remar was reasonable. Why was he fighting it?

Because he had committed himself to this task. Until when? Until he was the only one left? Even his own cave members were leaving, and he could not stop them. Seth's presence had changed things. Despite his despair, he had showed mercy, compassion, courage, love, kindness... Seth was the enemy, so Vaylynne had said. But he had not acted like the enemy.

You're one of the few who actually has a family; go home to them. Vaylynne's words rang in his head. He did have a family. A family he loved. He had done this for them, to liberate them. *Or did I?* But now his town seemed to support the king. Was he fighting against his own loved ones?

And then there was the fact that one of these days he would be asked to take a life. He finally knew he never could. Life was far too precious. Seth's grief showed that.

So what was left for him? How could he simply leave his cave? How could he ever go home? He still longed to make a difference.

Who was Caleb, really? Vaylynne had told them to put aside the individual—to learn to think and act as one. He had followed her orders to the letter. Who was *he*?

Caleb stared up at his cave, his home for so long, the place where he had been a leader, part of a new family. He wanted his own family. But how could they ever take him back?

With solemnity, he left the cave. He did not know where he was going, but anywhere had to be better than where he was.

Vaylynne stayed in her room at Saphree. She was not welcome here. She was the enemy and she was treated like one. That made the room seem restrictive. It made her twitchy. This was not the place she wanted to be.

Things were coming to a head. Issym's army was here; Saphree knew

Xsardis

about Sasha's plans; the shifter had a big head start. And her freedom fighters were not even in the race!

Sitting motionless on the bed of her small room, she rethought her actions. She had captured Seth and then let him go back to Saphree. Was she growing weak? No. Even Tahath would have recognized that she had no other choice but to help Seth destroy the mysterious artifact.

"Come in!" Vaylynne answered the knock on the door with a snap of frustration.

Seth shut the door behind him. She stared into the face she could not read as he asked, "Do you know what Sasha's after?"

"Not specifically," she told him, sitting down in her window.

"Then I don't get it. Why are you here?"

"Seth, I'm here to help." She tried to seem convincing, but her sweet words only made him certain he was being deceived somehow.

"Help who?" he moved towards her with a threat in his eyes. "I brought you in here. I trusted you. So I'm responsible for your actions. What are you up to?"

"I would rather die than have Remar on the throne, that's true enough; but I would rather have everyone I love murdered than see Sasha there!"

His gaze pierced hers. Finally, he spoke, "Okay. But keep your distance from Sphen."

"At least Jeffery stands up for me," she smirked, having heard of the conflict. Dividing The Brothers...

Seth turned back, "Jeff would destroy you with much less regret than his brother, but he's biding his time—waiting for the right opportunity."

"Until I've outlived my usefulness," she suggested. "I won't let that happen, then. You do know you need me, right, Seth?"

"Unfortunately."

There were hours until dawn when Katarina set her bare feet on the stones of Saphree and slipped from her room. She had not slept, but had been captivated as she looked out her window over the courtyard that was now filled with strange creatures. For months they had simply been praying that God would keep them alive until Issym's army arrived, and now it had. It was the first time she had felt this joyful since before 'The Day.'

She stepped outside the castle and allowed the grass to fill her toes. Tents and creatures filled her view, but they had kept part of the land clear for sword practice. The air was cool; the moon full; the noises plenty. Night had not brought rest to anyone; there had been too much to do.

The lean figure of Seth moved toward the door behind her and stopped when he saw her. "You're up late," he commented.

"How could I sleep?" she pondered, spreading her hands out over the

Xsardis

79

magnitude of what she saw. Their low tones were inaudible to others in the din of life that had finally filled Saphree.

He stepped out of the castle, taking it all in. He had spent hours mingling, answering questions, setting up tents, catching up on Issym's history. There was something about being surrounded by his old friends and creatures of his own imagination that had revived him.

"Finally," Katarina breathed. "They're here."

He paused so long she thought he was not going to speak. "It feels different than I had expected."

She turned to face him, "What do you mean?"

"I kept telling myself to hang on because I could hand over the reins as soon as they arrived. Instead I'm still leading. And I'm not ready to stop."

"Does it surprise you that they look to you for leadership?"

"Yeah," he chuckled. "You guys saw the older, more experienced Seth. Not the selfish, useless fool who arrived on Issym with no intention of following, let alone leading."

"But you're not that kid anymore." She shook her head. The moon glinted off her eyes. "Galen and Flibbert recognize that. You were *meant* to lead."

"You're not bad at it yourself," he commented.

The princess caught his look. "You heard?"

"You stood up to a king. It spreads around…" He paused. "Were you really going to leave?"

She sighed and rubbed her arms, suddenly cold. "I was close." Katarina changed the subject, "Issym wants to…" she paused, "have a ceremony for Max and Rachel. I didn't know Rachel very well, but Max saved my life in many ways. I want to go."

"He would have wanted you there."

They went their separate ways in the night. Tomorrow would be the death of a long struggle and the birth of a new one. Only now, they had hope.

Xsardis

Chapter 10

The last six months had been a grief and battle-filled blur. The fresh strength of Flibbert, Elimilech, Galen and the army from Issym had brought life back not merely to the fortress but to Seth. Even so, as Seth finished dressing for the ceremony that night, he could feel the heavy weight of grief. *Why can't I let you go?* he wondered. Galen had said it would take time. Seth knew he was right. At least the burden of telling Issym that they were dead had been removed. And maybe that night's memorial could offer some finality to the situation.

Shaved and dressed in Asandra's finest, Seth offered his arm to Katarina and moved toward the crowded courtyard where so many waited.

A glance at the princess showed her strong exterior. Whatever openness she offered in the quiet early-morning hours had been replaced by her firm poise. She had braided her auburn hair, but left a few wisps loose. Her cream dress was pristine; her long earrings had been crafted by Reesthma; her brown boots were freshly cleaned. Especially strange was the slender silver crown that glimmered on her brow.

Together they walked out of the palace and through hundreds of Issym's creatures. Kat drew closer to him as she was overwhelmed by the compact space filled with immeasurably strange creatures. They could see a clearing far ahead of them, with two coffins prominently displayed. They pushed forward as Seth was clasped on the back by many who knew him.

At the edge of the onlookers, Katarina stopped. Seth went forward to stand with Galen, Flibbert and Elimilech. They spoke a few words to each other. Seth protested. Flibbert nodded vehemently. Elimilech put a hand on Seth's shoulder, bent down, and whispered something into his ear. Finally Seth nodded. Clearly, they had persuaded him to speak.

In the flickering of torchlight, each breath Kat took hurt. Around her people relived memories, their voices rising and falling like a funeral dirge. Her gaze could not resist resting on the empty coffins. "Oh Max, I'm sorry," she whispered, keeping her posture straight and her breathing steady despite the

Xsardis

82

pain. "Evan... it should have been me, not you."

And suddenly the crowd fell silent, as solemnness descended on them like the rain, first hitting a few, then hitting everyone else. They looked to Seth and he met their gaze. "Good friends," he began. His tone held that of a heavy conversation with old friends, not that of a speech to throngs of strangers. "Knowing that we will fight together again gives me a courage that I have not felt in a long time."

Eulogies are a terrible idea, Seth thought before pressing on with his words. "You know Rachel and Max. They are heroes to you not because they came from a far-a-way land or imagined your world, but because you saw how they lived.

"Who, in the face of grief, does not question God? I did. I challenged God because Rachel and Max had trusted Him and I felt like He let them, and me, down.

"But I have come to realize that God did not fail us. His plans are beyond our comprehension, but they are made for our good. Rachel and Max are in a better place, away from war and tragedies. They gave their lives to save this world. The best way to honor them is to finish what they started."

In his pause for breath, no other sound could be heard. Despite the large crowd, there was no movement, no quiet whispers, only listening. He spoke again, "Legends will hail them as heroes, but we have the opportunity to hail them as friends.

"We have all lost people in battle other than Rachel and Max. Remember your loved ones today. Remember their sacrifices, as I will remember Max and Rachel's." Seth stopped, distracted by a sound he could not identify. "Don't just grieve them; be inspired by them."

The sound grew until he was sure that there was a banging noise coming from inside the coffins. Seth's face was ashen.

"What a sick joke!" Flibbert croaked, drawing his sword and leaping towards the casket on the left.

Galen's usual think-first, fight-later nature was replaced by one that drew his sword and moved to the other coffin. Elimilech took one side of the lid and he took the other, lifting it and casting it aside. Galen's face showed no emotion—not surprise, nor shock, nor anger, nor happiness. Flibbert pulled the lid off the other. He slipped, then jumped back to his feet. "What on Issym?"

Seth's eyes were torn between the two coffins. Nothing had surfaced yet from the left, but to his right two young men were climbing over each other in an attempt to get out. The unmistakable figure of Max leapt free.

"What kind of shape shifting trick is this?" Seth demanded, finding the trusted shifter Kate pressing towards the front of the crowd. Her face showed disbelief. She purposefully met his eyes and shook her head. This was no trick.

Glancing at Max and a form that he guessed was Evan's, he turned back to the other coffin. Brown hair fell over Flibbert's shoulders as he hugged a girl still seated in the casket. Seth's heart beat loudly in his head as he stumbled toward them and pushed the frog aside. "Rachel..." he whispered. The eyes... the nose... her presence... the fairy dust necklace. "Is it really you?" he asked, standing a few inches back, unable to step any closer.

"How?" she breathed, her eyes wide and wet in the moonlight.
"Tell me something only you would know."
"When you found out you were going to move, you and I stockpiled food in my playhouse so that you could hide out there," she began.
"But your dad caught me the second I ran away from home..." Seth finished.
"It is you..."
Seth grasped the phantom before she could slip away. Their foreheads were in each other's shoulders. Neither had the courage to say more for fear this vision would disappear. He closed his eyes and held her. For the first time since 'The Day' he felt truly strong, invincible.
A hand on her neck, he pushed her back enough that he could look into her eyes. "I'm so glad you're alive."
In the deafening roar of the army behind him, her smile filled up her face, and somehow he knew that this was no trick or dream. Rachel, Max and Evan were back. He helped her from the coffin and she ran to hug Galen and to take in the whole of Issym's army.
Evan had an arm around Katarina. Seth moved forward and grasped Max. He was as real.
Elimilech thrust the teens inside the palace as the crowd threatened to trample them. In the chaos, Seth slipped his hand into Rachel's and held on. She was not going to disappear again.

Hours before on Earth:
The teenage girl yelped with surprise at the figure before her, then her face turned cold. "What are you doing here?" she demanded.
"Hello to you too," he answered, having expected her 'welcome.'
"You shouldn't be here," she pushed the freckled teen towards the window and ladder he had climbed up. "My parents gave strict orders not to let you in, Max."
He almost fought with her. Rachel, hero of Issym, was scared of her parents finding out she was talking to a friend. Max stopped himself and instead bent down beside her, kneeling in the soft blue carpet where she was sorting through a cardboard box, and won her attention. "Rachel, they are not dead."
"Didn't you see all Xsardis burn, Max?" she broke out. Why did he have to keep tearing at old wounds? How could he have such a calm voice? "*I was supposed to be the decoy. I promised to let Sasha come after me to save the queen and Seth and Asandra—but I failed. Now I'm alive and they're dead. Not only them, but all of Xsardis!*"
Max rolled his eyes. How had the girl turned so irrational? "I saw it," he persisted. "You think I could get those images out of my head so easily? We

Xsardis 84

were on the tower. I was trying to save your life—if you remember—and the world burned. An explosion erupted from Sasha and she was taunting us, 'If I can't have Asandra, no one will.' But it looked more like computer graphics than reality."

"Computers on Asandra? Come on! *Attempt*," she emphasized, "to put it behind you. I'm trying to pull a life back together. You should too."

"You think you are the only one who is hurting? Get a grip, Rachel! Why would we have survived that?"

"I've told you this a thousand times." She unzipped her red sweater and cast it aside. Cold wind blew in from the open windows, but her anger and the pain of the memories were causing her to burn up. "Ruby used her powers to protect me. Sasha couldn't affect me. When there was no world left, I was transported to Earth."

"And me and Evan?"

"You were touching me. It must have passed on to you."

"But if Ruby died, then you would have died too. Think, Rachel. I know I'm not that bright, but it doesn't make sense!"

She stared at him as if to continue their discussion, but her face grew devoid of emotion. "Go home, Max."

"What home? They think we're crazy. No one believes us."

"You think I don't know that? I spent a lifetime earning respect, securing trust, building a life that now can never be. My church, my parents, the people I babysit for—they do not think I am insane, they think I'm a liar. And Seth's gone. Xsardis is gone. Everyone we know is gone. And I can barely survive knowing that. Every time you come back here asking me to believe, you make it worse. And I can't disobey my parents, again. They don't want you here."

"Do you remember how Seth's parents looked when we tried to explain?" he did not stop for a moment. He hated causing her the pain, but he somehow he *knew* that they were alive.

Rachel swallowed. "I remember." That had been the most painful of all.

"They cast me out, Rachel. They think that I am part of the reason their son is dead."

"And we are," Rachel shook her head. She rubbed at a tear that had fallen from her eye. "Can't you understand? I have to forget!"

Rachel violently set her filing box with the others. When she turned away, Max caught them from teetering. He understood her reaction. Like she had to forget in order to survive, he had to believe in order to survive.

He spoke more gently, "I refuse to believe that God brought us to Xsardis and let us fail to the implosion of an entire world. They're alive," he insisted. "What we saw was a show—I'm sure of it."

"Even if they were alive..." she softened with a sigh. Max was not the problem, but he perpetually brought the problem with him. "What would you have me do?"

He stood, glad for the new reaction. "Imagine again. Maybe it will work."

Rachel leaned against the wall and supported her head with her

Xsardis

85

fingers. "I haven't pretended since I found out that it was all becoming real."

"Try," Max implored.

Her voice choked, "No; I want to forget."

"Just a few years ago your imagination was so brilliant a whole world was formed. You can do this. Say something like," he forced his brain to push through the block, "in the attic where two teenagers mourned a lost world, a... forgotten orb—one of Universe Girl's—was found in the walls. They used it to go back to that lost world and appeared as it mourned them."

"Go home, Max," she decided, and started packing boxes again.

"If they are alive and you are abandoning them..."

"Go home!" The bite in her words bore finality.

Max looked at her sorrowfully. If she was right, the grief would destroy him too. But she just couldn't be. He shook his head. Maybe in a few months, or years, she would be willing to listen. Until then, he had to stop hopping on buses every month and trying to convince her. Maybe they *were* all dead. Katarina and Seth... No. He shut his mind to the possibility.

Max suddenly felt a cold suspicion jump through him. It took hold of his very mind. "Fine. After all, why remember Seth when you can move on to Evan?"

She sent him a fierce glare. "I'm not moving on!" she returned. Then more meekly, "I don't know that I ever can."

"Oh, lots of girls crushed on Seth," Max continued, having struck a chord. "You're no different."

"It wasn't some crush!" Rachel picked up a few items and threw them into another file box. "It was the most real, most profound thing I have ever felt. It was almost beyond belief. Seth and I weren't a casual couple. We fought wars together; we shared a bond. I can't move to Evan just like that," she snapped her fingers. "I wouldn't even want to. But if you think that, you clearly don't know me. Now I would like you to leave."

Max knew that he had crossed a line, so he gave up. As soon as he had descended the ladder, Rachel's shoulders shook with sobs. She so desperately wanted to believe that Max could be right, that Seth and the others might be alive. But it was a foolish hope. Holding onto it would make it harder to adapt to life on Earth again. As it was, she had a lot of re-planning and repairing to do. She really could not blame her parents for not believing her, but it was still almost unbearable.

"Why God?" she whispered. "Why would You allow all of Xsardis to be destroyed? Why not only me? It was supposed to have been me!"

Shaking her head, Rachel pulled open the wall cubby with all the force of her pent-up frustration. She swept away the trash that cluttered the floor. Her hand felt the cold of a hole in the wooden panels. "No..." she breathed. With the last bit of faith she had, Rachel reached into the crevice and felt the object wrapped in cloth. Her hand tingled wildly. She knew what it was.

Barely able to get the covering off with her shaking hands, she saw the orb. "Max, wait!"

The once-prince Evan winced as he shoved his shoulder into the door to get it open. He didn't bother with a key. The lock was beyond repair. He sighed as he saw the apartment that was almost worse than the hiding-places he had kept on Asandra. The dwelling was heated by the pizza shop below, but the cold from his walk home had caused his chest to ache and stab with pain.

Gingerly, he removed his coat. He slumped over to the mirror in his small bathroom and pulled up his tee-shirt, revealing the medallion-sized bright red scar that marked his chest near his shoulder and throbbed uncontrollably. It was probably never going to heal. It would always be a reminder of what he had failed to protect.

The wound had almost killed him. Sasha had thrown her poisoned dagger at Rachel, but he had taken the blow. For a long time she had struggled to save him. Rachel and Seth had figured out a way just in time. He put a hand on the injury he never spoke of. The illuminescent had mostly healed him, but Sasha's dagger had been meant to destroy.

Gripping the edges of the sink with arms muscular from hard labor, Evan weathered the pain of the wound and of his failure to protect his homeland. "Why did you spare me, God?" he wondered aloud. He would rather have died with his people than gone on living. He had to believe there was a reason he was still alive. That was why he worked so hard. School, a job, taking care of Rachel when she would let him. The culture of Earth was so different! He spent most of his time trying to figure out what was going on.

After putting a cold towel on the wound, Evan flopped onto his bed and lay there unmoving. "Katarina..." he whispered the name. They had been an inseparable duo—even when they had not wanted to be.

When a knock came to his door he did not bother to move. If whoever it was wanted to get in, they could let themselves in.

His night shift at work had turned into a double. He usually did not mind. He wanted as much work as he could get. He was determined to make something of himself on Earth, no matter how long it took.

But last night had been filled with lifting and pulling boxes. His shoulder wound was close to reopening. And Sasha had never been meant the injury to close. Without the power of illuminescents, if it opened, he would probably die. That would be ironic. To survive the explosion of his entire world only to be killed by a wound that should have been healed.

The knock did not repeat itself, but the door opened. Evan sat up with a groan, hand still holding the towel in place. He saw the form of Rachel reflecting from the window. Quickly he dropped the towel, pulled on his shirt, hid the pain, and walked out to meet her.

"Hey," she spoke softly, an unusual gleam in her eyes.

"Hey," he returned, surprised at her happiness.

She turned as Max entered the little apartment. "Evan," Max nodded.

Xsardis

87

"Max…" The prince raised a brow. He was aware that Max and Rachel had not been getting along. Evan's eyes flipped between the two. He recognized the strange energy in the room. "What's going on?"

Max took a seat on the ratty couch, salvaged from a street corner. Rachel closed the door and pulled out the milky orb. "Do you know what this?" she asked, her voice trembling with awe.

Evan shook his head. "Should I?"

"It's one of Universe Girl's orbs that I was telling you about—a special one, a lost one. If Max and I are right it can take us back to Xsardis."

"But doesn't that take all the orbs?" Evan pondered slowly, resting against the wall as the wound kept hurting.

"Not this one… Max imagined it today."

Evan's face dropped. His pulse beat fast. He finally understood what they were hinting at. "But if Xsardis was destroyed you shouldn't have been able to imagine anything… right?"

"That's our theory," Max smiled.

His excitement fell as his optimism was smothered by logic. "No... We can't trust that. Maybe you imagined this before."

Rachel shook her head. "I don't think so."

"If Xsardis is gone and we try to go back there," Evan spoke slowly, "we'll die." His face changed and once again he carried the authority of a prince. "I'll go first and make sure things are safe."

"No way," Max protested.

"I am Asandra's prince. It is my duty." He added, "And my privilege."

"And I'm Xsardis' imaginer," Rachel pointed out. "We could all argue about who is going, but I'm not staying behind and I don't think you two are either."

"Rachel…" Evan started.

She caught his eyes and whispered with a hope long forgotten, "I believe, for the first time in months, that they may still be alive. I won't wait. I have to go back there."

Evan rubbed his temples, "I want to believe too. But if Xsardis is still there, why has Seth not come looking for us?"

Max cleared his throat. After a moment, he spoke sheepishly, "There's something I didn't mention. I think when I was imagining the orb, I might have—accidentally—designed it to only work once and then disappear."

Rolling her eyes, Rachel questioned, "Why would you do that?"

"Oh, seriously!" Max responded. "Your imaginations had all kinds of strange ticks. At least I actually know what mine are!"

Evan ignored the bickering and tried to protect the others once more. "If I get through I can send an illuminescent back for you."

"I'm not staying behind." Rachel was determined.

"Are we going to go dressed like this?" Max was not getting stuck on Earth either.

"Let's just go!" Rachel answered and began to tap away at the surface of the orb. She looked at her companions. "Either we die or we find our lives again."

Xsardis

With that they disappeared.

Chapter 11

Present time:
The king and queen were quickly downstairs, hugging their firstborn. But there were only a few moments of pleasantries before the important things had to be dealt with and they moved into the council room. They had outgrown the confined space, between Asandra and Issym's officials, and now the return of the three who had been believed dead for six months. Several people stood behind the chairs, mashed against the walls.

"What did you see?" Seth questioned Rachel as they sat side by side.

"Xsardis exploded," she replied. "We thought all of you were dead."

"Sasha must have created some kind of two-sided illusion, because we saw you three burned alive."

The newly-arrived three were informed about the state of Asandra as concisely as possible. Then they were released to be together once more.

There were plenty of people whom they needed to see, but it could all wait until after they had had time to absorb that this was real. After changing into era-appropriate clothing, they moved to the kitchen and ate with the first real appetite they had had since Sasha's illusion.

Somehow Seth ended up against the wall, Rachel leaning beside him. Max was cross-legged on the floor. Evan and Katarina were sitting on the kitchen's chairs. Noises filled their ears, but caused not the smallest distraction for the core they had become.

They exchanged stories quickly, but they learned most by the obvious changes. Seth carried himself stronger and bore the air of a competent leader. Katarina was dressed like a proper princess and held a certain grace that had been lacking before. Max kept smiling and telling jokes. Evan possessed a new confidence and the same quietness. Rachel was almost too joyful. Seth knew that things had not been well on Earth.

"But here's what I don't get," Max said as things grew serious again. There was enough happiness to last for years, but the truth was that they were still in a war. "If Issym's army only now has showed up, why has Sasha not

Xsardis

totally annihilated you guys?"

Seth sighed. Only Max would ask the question like that. "There is an…" he searched for an explanation, "artifact or something that Sasha is pursuing. If she finds it, she will be invincible—to injury, to death, even to the stones. We'll have no chance then."

Rachel suddenly saw an island in her mind's eye. Her vision narrowed in, but she lost it. "It will give her eternal youth, too."

"You guys have got to be kidding," Max protested. "What were you thinking imagining this?"

Seth and Rachel interrupted their conversation to send a glare Max's way. "Rachel, what do you remember?" Seth questioned. "I barely know anything about it. It's taken me six months to figure out what she is planning."

Six months, Katarina mused. She glanced at Evan to be sure he was real. She did not need to look at Max. His loud mouth assured her that he was, in fact, back in her life.

"I think," Rachel mused, as her mind wandered back into her imaginations, "that it's on Noric."

"That would make sense," a new voice spoke. Vaylynne had entered the room. "After Issym, Sasha went to Noric."

"What is she doing here?" Rachel instantly became tense.

"She is, temporarily, not our enemy," Katarina replied unhappily.

"Temporarily," Vaylynne emphasized.

"If we put Rachel and Seth's imagination with some history, maybe we can figure this out. I'll go get Reesthma." Katarina did not trust Vaylynne. She either needed to escape from the girl's presence or claw her eyes out. She hurried out of the room.

Evan stood and asked Rachel, "What is *it* exactly?"

Rachel searched for the memory again, but saw nothing more than before. "It's like a dream that I can almost remember, but I can't push through. Maybe with more time," she shrugged. "But I doubt it."

"If we both have memory of it," Seth theorized, "then we must have imagined it together. Which means it made its way from Issym."

"There was a riddle." Reesthma stepped into the kitchen with Kat. Ree had changed. Tall, she walked with grace and her voice had matured. Rachel welcomed her hug. Stepping back, the girl explained, "It is rumored that there was a scroll, passed down by a powerful shape shifter family. It tells the riddle. If Sasha has the scroll and can decipher the truth…"

No one wanted to hear the end of that sentence. "Then someone has to go to Noric," Max cut in.

"I agree," Evan added. "Issym's army can keep Sasha at bay here while we make sure she can't find this… whatever it is."

"We just got back and we're going to leave again?" Max queried, but adventure was already in his eyes.

"You don't have a choice," Vaylynne pointed out. "Now that Issym is here Sasha will search with a violence and speed that you can't begin to anticipate. If we don't act now, it will be too late."

"But if it's a trap," Evan pondered. "If Sasha wants to follow us to it?"

Xsardis

91

The group weighed the words. "It is a possibility," Seth admitted.

"It's too great a risk not to find it," Rachel decided. "We have to go."

"What will our parents have to say about this?" Evan questioned his sister.

"Our father will hate the idea," Katarina answered him. "But he's used to Seth running off."

"And Galen will trust us," Seth finished, offering an amused glare at Kat's teasing.

"When will you leave?" Reesthma inquired.

"When will *we* leave?" Seth corrected.

"We?" Her face instantly glowed.

"Yes, we. We'll need your help—all that knowledge. And hopefully, tomorrow."

As Reesthma moved with joy to pack a bag, Rachel got Seth's attention, "You think that's wise?" Reesthma had grown, but she was still young.

"How much older were we when we came to Issym?" Seth countered.

"Between the different worlds and the time shifts, I don't even know how old I am now!"

Max yawned, knowing that he was going to sleep well tonight. He started with the others for his bed, but held back. Katarina was standing in the hallway. The moonlight shone in through the open window and lit her face with an ethereal glow.

"Can't sleep?" he asked softly, stepping beside her.

"Never could when I was excited," she replied. "I can't believe you're alive."

"Or you." She kept her face turned from him. "What's wrong?" He shuffled even closer.

"Max," her voice trembled with an unusual guilt, "I thought, all these months, that it was my fault you were dead." Her green eyes locked on him. "I led you to that death trap. If it wasn't for that, the attack on Maremoth might never have had to happen. And you and Rachel and Evan would have been alive. I kept thinking about how you didn't walk away even after I had deceived you and falsely led you towards Maremoth."

"Even then, you couldn't go through with it," Max pointed out. "But you're a new person, right?"

"I certainly am."

Max spoke after a moment's hesitation, "Despite all our bickering, I missed you. Rachel wanted to forget about you guys. I couldn't give up the memories. If I had believed that you—all—were dead, I couldn't have gone on. But I don't think I ever really expected to see you again."

"I am so glad you are home."

"Home," he laughed. Never had Xsardis felt like home before. But now it felt so right.

"Bridget," a voice more hearty than she remembered it being filled her ears.

Bridget turned to see King Remar and with a smile greeted him by the name he had used in prison, "Nicholas!"

"I thought Sasha had killed you, despite the rumors that you got away."

His face was more joyful to see her than she could have expected. He was a king, after all, and she had never been more than a prisoner. "She would have, had not the guard Brooks helped me escape," Bridget answered.

Remar put an arm around her and steered her to the kitchen. "Come, let us eat and be happy. My child has returned to me!"

"It is wonderful," Bridget smiled at him. Nicholas was still thin, but there was a strength and a hope returning to him that he had not possessed in Maremoth.

Selecting an apple, she took a seat by the window and looked out over Saphree. "This is a wonderful stronghold."

"But rather like Maremoth," the king replied. "Is that what troubles you?"

She turned her eyes from the window to meet his, "I did not realize I looked troubled." When he said nothing, she allowed herself to answer honestly, "In part, it is these walls. And in part, it is that I have many thoughts running through my mind. For the last fifteen years—almost sixteen now—I have been a slave or aboard a vessel. Now the choice for my future is mine and I have no idea how to make it."

Remar took a long sip from his drink, then set it down. Bridget had been a counselor to him in Maremoth; he would be the same to her now. "What do you want to do?"

Taking a breath, Bridget thought carefully. "I still want to follow wherever God leads. I can't imagine myself in battle or here in Saphree. But I cannot leave this war unfinished."

The noises of the cooks and early-risers in the castle were already filling their ears, but they could not distract Remar from the importance of his young friend's words. He took her hand, "Bridget, listen to me. No one else could have done what you did for the prisoners in Maremoth. You have fought this war since the day you entered the prison.

"But things are changing. You are not only entitled to, but you need to take a few days or weeks or months to discover what God wants you to do next. I know you are strong, but you still need to heal. Making a decision now would not be wise. Neither would staying here. Does your village still live?"

Bridget shook her head, "It was burned long ago."

"If my kingdom was secure, I would send you anywhere you wanted to go and establish you in any life. But since I cannot do that, allow me to set

Xsardis   93

you free of feeling like you must help Asandra by staying here. I commission you to go."

Bridget took the first bite of her apple to afford herself a few seconds to think about what he had said. Finally, she nodded. "I'll need to find Brooks and tell him that I am leaving."

"The guard who helped you?" Remar thought for a moment. "I was told by King Galen that he had left. He never even set foot in Saphree."

"He's gone?" Bridget's eyes widened. "Why would he leave without saying anything?"

"Perhaps he believed that a former servant of Sasha would be distrusted here. If so, he was wrong. Anyone who aided you would be welcomed in my fortress."

Despite the news, Bridget could not help but offer a small smile. The kindness the king was showing her was beyond any she had ever hoped to receive.

"Where would he head?" King Remar finished his drink and leaned back in his chair. "Home?"

"I don't think so," Bridget returned. She had learned much about Brooks on the voyage back to Asandra. He feared he would not be accepted or that he would not fit at the farm he had abandoned. She guessed he was running, not to something but from something. That was dangerous these days.

"He has no allies; nowhere to go." The last time he had been in that position, Brooks had turned to Sasha. What would he do now when the road grew turbulent?

"I have to go after him."

Xsardis

Chapter 12

"You are underestimating the danger," King Remar challenged Seth. "Think about it. If Sasha had the scroll, she would have already found this... artifact. She's using you."

"You could be leading Sasha right to the artifact," Juliet added, her eyes pleading with Seth to listen to her wisdom.

He met her gaze and assured her, "We will destroy it before she has the opportunity to use it. This is our only course of action."

Remar pointed out, "It doesn't make it the right one."

Stepping beside Seth, Evan said, "I agree that there are dangers, but I also agree with Seth that we have to take those risks."

The queen recognized there would be no dissuading the two young men, "If you are going, are you sure you should be taking Vaylynne?"

"She's a good fighter; she knows things we don't. I want her along." Seth added, "As long as she's helping us, her army won't be fighting us."

The prince nodded to Seth that he could leave. He would carry the conversation with his parents from here.

As Seth exited their chamber, he was met by the bushy eyes of Joppa. At first Seth could not discern what was different about the aging man, until he realized: Joppa was not holding a scroll. This would not be good.

"Walk with me?" the historian half-invited, half-directed.

Seth fell into step beside him, fully aware that this conversation would be about his taking Reesthma to Noric. He broached the subject before her guardian could. "About Reesthma... I really believe we need her, but I won't go against your wishes. Do you want us to leave her behind?"

Joppa shook his head no. They were near a set of stairs leading directly to the kitchen, and the aromatic smells wafted through the air. "I would keep her here, but she deserves the same opportunity to help her world that the rest of us have had."

"Then what is it?"

Xsardis   96

"I want to tell you a story."

Seth glanced at Joppa. Was he serious? They were leaving the fortress in a few hours and he wanted to waste his time with a story? The sincerity in the historian's eyes convinced Seth to stop and listen as they stood beside a window sill in the crowded corridors.

"Listen carefully, Seth. It is not what you think. Do you remember Jarek?"

"Asandra's body guard," Seth confirmed. "Issym's ally."

"Jarek's descendants became as renowned for their battle skill as he was. It was not long before they had formed the Sululie, a warrior tribe. Throughout the generations—to this very day—they have served honest kings and queens loyally.

"While our own Juliet's father still ruled, there was a Sululie named Rodika. She was not only an impressive warrior, but she was most beautiful among women."

His eyes stared at the wall now as his thoughts took him over. "She was sinewy and tall, with fair skin and a captivating smile that made you long to listen to her wisdom. For too long that smile had lain dormant, as she devoted herself to protecting Asandra. Then she met a farmer.

"You know where the story goes from here. They fell in love. Rodika buried her sword and married him. It was not long before they had a child."

"Reesthma," Seth surmised.

"Reesthma," Joppa acknowledged. "When Sasha started to gain power, she knew the Sululie were a threat. She hunted them down and killed all of them that she could find. When Sasha came for Rodika and Reesthma, she found only the farmer. He died that day.

"Rodika understood what was happening. Though she had never trained her daughter in the ways of the Sululie, Reesthma was still in great danger. Desperate for her safety, she brought the child to her husband's brother."

"You?"

"Me," Joppa nodded. "Rodika picked back up her sword and sacrificed herself not long after." There was a weight to his words. Joppa had loved Rodika like a true sister. He still grieved for her and for his brother. Taking a breath, he went further: "Before she left, she begged me never to train Reesthma in the ways of the Sululie. Rodika knew how grave the life of a warrior could be. As you now know."

Seth's distant blink affirmed Joppa's words.

The old man continued, "I have honored that promise despite the war that has claimed Asandra. Reesthma has the blood of a warrior in her. Look at how she moves; how she perceives; how she thinks. Open her to battle and she will become a Sululie. I will have failed her mother's last wishes."

Pausing before he answered, Seth knew what he had to say, "Joppa, we are going to find an artifact that Sasha is seeking. I cannot promise to protect anyone who comes on this journey from battle. It may be that if you send her with me that she either fights or dies. Would Rodika want her to perish?

"Sasha will be pursuing us. The others have accepted the risks. You

Xsardis

97

and Reesthma must as well."

"I only ask that you try to shelter her from the battles you will face." Seth nodded. "I will."

Having satisfied—to an extent—both Joppa and Remar, Seth hoped he might be able to pack and then return to his companions. But with so many passionate people in one place, nothing was ever simple.

Lotex marched toward Seth, cheeks red with fury. "What do you think you're doing?" he called, still a long way off but moving his stout legs with great speed. "You should not have planned this without talking to me! It's *my* island."

"*Your* island?" Seth had learned to laugh off Lotex's stronger feelings.

"I've searched every inch of that place and there is nothing there," the dwarf affirmed.

"Then why are you so angry?" Seth crooked his head. "You found *nothing*?"

"Nothing."

"Then it shouldn't be a problem for me to go and see for myself."

"We need you here."

"You have Issym's army. You don't need me."

Lotex barked in frustration, "I don't want you on my island."

Seth stared at him. "Tex, what are you keeping from me?"

"Get off my back, Seth! And trust me."

"You're not acting like I should get off your back. What do you know?"

"Please, Seth. Listen."

Startled by the world *please*, Seth knew that Lotex was consumed by something, but he would never say what. Part of him longed to bend to Lotex's leadership, but he had to be the leader now. "I'm sorry," Seth replied and walked away.

Entering the armory, he took a new pair of bracers from the stacks. A small grunt of frustration escaped Seth's lips as he tried to tie one on. Rachel moved into the room and took his arm. "That's a nasty gash," she whispered in the stillness. She rubbed her finger across the large scar on his forearm before tying a knot in the bracer. "That could have killed you."

"It tried," he answered. "Hector, Evan's illuminescent, saved me."

Rachel tied on the other bracer. As she moved her hands away, he caught and held them for a moment. "I'm grateful to God beyond words that you're back."

Seth released her hands as she mused, "The way people talk about you—it's like you're Issym himself. I don't understand how you stayed here, thinking we were gone. I wouldn't have had the heart to continue fighting."

"Honestly, I thought about never going home. To make a life without you two. To abandon this work that we started together. To have to tell your parents that you were dead..." His face dropped as he suddenly understood what had been bothering her. "Did you tell my parents?"

Rachel nodded. "They didn't take it well. No one did. We only tried to explain to a few people, but they believed we were lying. It would have been

Xsardis

98

better if they had called us crazy."

Though Rachel might have said more, a feminine voice filled their ears, "You were looking into shape shifter lore and you didn't ask me?"

Turning, she saw Kate. Rachel smiled. There was something wonderful about this defiant shape shifter who had shaken off the long bonds of wickedness and power and led her people back to God.

"Good to see you alive, Rachel," she spoke, sweeping back her brown hair.

"You changed your hair color."

"Some things about my old life are best forgotten. It's odd but every time I looked at my hair I remembered who I had been." *Edmund liked blondes,* she thought.

Kate was dressed simply but still looked radiant. She was comfortable with a weapon easily within reach. All of Xsardis had become twitchy.

"Have you heard of this scroll?" Seth asked, setting his arms on a barrel.

"It was in my family's possession."

From her timid demeanor it was clear that this was something Kate did not talk about, or even think about. It took her several seconds to find her voice again. It was almost dreamlike, "It was passed into my hands by my aging grandfather. In a hundred years I had never once met him. He had spent his life in pursuit of what you now seek.

"Sick, he had come home to die and begged me not to follow in his steps as he had his own grandfather's. I held that scroll close to me for days that turned into weeks that turned into months. I had neither the courage to get rid of it nor to pursue it.

"All the time, Edmund begged me to go after the artifact and get enough power to rid us of his sister. I was so tempted. I knew things were wrong amongst the shifters. I thought if I had the power the artifact could give me, I could change things. The longer I held onto it the more tempted I became.

"I was only saved by some small but even more powerful Voice that called to me. God promised to save me and to use me, but not through the artifact. Perhaps it was vision, or just a certainty, but I knew that if I possessed the artifact, I would become as evil as Sasha.

"I sat in front of the fire, Edmund's hand in mine beseeching me to keep it, and I threw the scroll—and our love—into its flames."

Kate blinked away the memories and her voice grew solid, "That's when I began to take some shifters away from the camp and everything changed."

"So the scroll is gone?" Rachel questioned. She did not know how to address the secrets the shifter had shared.

"I believe so, but I cannot be sure. Edmund might have saved it when I walked away."

Seth queried, "If he had, wouldn't he have searched for the artifact?"

Shaking her head, Kate responded, "He wouldn't have risked his position as second-in-command to Sasha to run after a fairytale. But when you two fought before the battle at Maremoth, he might have given Sasha the scroll to spite us."

Seth nodded. "You're right. He might have."

Silence filled the space as Seth and Kate's thoughts wandered over Edmund and their sorrow at his refusal to follow God and what it would cost. In the past years, they had been his closest friends. Even now, Kate and Seth held out hope that some small goodness was left to be awakened in the shifter.

Rachel broke their reverie. "Did you burn the scroll before you had read it?"

"I'll admit," Kate began, "that I glanced at it, but I've blocked what I read out of my memory. Most think that the scroll was merely a taunt by one of my family's enemies—a cruel trick to make us squander our lives. Otherwise, how could my grandfather and his grandfather and his grandfather have searched and never have found the artifact?"

"Do you believe it exists?" Seth would trust her opinion.

Though she shrugged, Kate's opinion was clear.

Rachel might have asked her to come with them to Noric, but given Kate's reaction to the memories of the scroll, she would not tempt Kate to go near the artifact. With the smell of leather armor overwhelming them, Rachel and Seth thanked Kate and walked out of the armory. She called after them, "Remember well the Word—capital 'W.'"

"What?" Seth stopped.

"That's the only thing I remember. I don't know why the scroll would be referring to the Bible, but it was."

"Thank you, Kate," Rachel answered over her shoulder, walking and bumping into a hopping Flibbert. Galen walked at a steady speed and was only a few paces behind. Flibbert's eyes were wide, clearly disagreeing with Galen on something. "I'm going with you," the frog declared.

"They need you here," Seth reasoned.

Galen nodded to Seth. "I *do* need him here."

"These teens have a pension for disaster," Flibbert argued.

"You do too," the words slipped out under Galen's breath.

Seth slung his bag over his shoulder. "We'll be fine, Flibbert."

"Yeah, right!" He took Rachel's hand and gave a bow, "Let me come, fair lady."

"Your flattery is not as persuasive as it once was," Rachel replied with a broad smile.

Galen shook his head, "Already the group is too large for the secrecy their mission requires. Please, friend, stay. They are fully capable."

"I appreciate your confidence," Seth gripped Galen's hand. "Take care of Asandra for us."

"You're babying that shoulder," Katarina pointed out as Evan sat

Xsardis   100

down on her bed. "You okay?"

"It's nothing," he brushed off her question.

The two siblings were staring out the window at the many creatures of Issym, bewildered both by their appearances and the long-forgotten feeling of victory. "This is good, Evan," she whispered, setting her fingers down on his good shoulder.

Her brother squeezed her hand. For so long it had seemed like their lives would end in the darkness and obscurity of the underground. But now they truly had a chance of freeing Asandra from Sasha, and of surviving. "This trip will make Sasha hunt us," he spoke openly with her. "Father admits that someone must destroy the artifact, but he believes we should stay behind."

Katarina took a seat beside him. "Maybe you *should* stay." When he began to protest, she forced her voice over his, "Evan, you're the heir to this throne."

"What kind of a future king would I be if I hid in Saphree while you accepted this task? Yes, it is dangerous, but the future of our world depends on it. I can't stay here."

She smiled. "You're still the same old Evan."

"You're not the same Katarina," he replied. "You're different."

"Better or worse?"

"Matured-- a leader-- at peace." He let his words sink in, then said, "Dad's not what I remember either."

Katarina walked back to her door and shut it before she answered. "He is different. Sometimes his decisions make me boil, but he is trying to do right by Asandra. I think he has changed for the better."

"Our mother glows when she mentions you. She says you're quite the princess."

"I had tough footsteps to follow." Kat stopped as she realized what he was working toward. "You want me to stay."

The prince explained quickly, "That way, if I die, Asandra still has an heir. Mom says that you have been a driving force behind our father's acceptance by the people. I know he is good, but there is so much debate surrounding him. And look at him. He's old. He needs someone to fight beside him—someone willing to stand up to him, someone that the people can trust."

"How does word about our conflict spread so quickly?" she broke in with frustration, standing up and pacing through the room. Calming herself just a little, she went on, "Our mom can do what I would do."

"You know she'll support him, no matter what."

"And I would follow his commands until he asked me to do wrong!" her voice implored him to understand. "Evan, I can't stay here. Then I become the coward you don't want to be." She gestured out the window. "Issym is here. No one will turn against our father now. King Galen can stand up to him, if need be, but I don't think the need will arise."

"I trust your opinion of our father."

Sighing, she kneeled beside him, "Evan, I know that when he was in prison, you took on the responsibilities and concern for Asandra that a king should possess. I've had the last five months to learn about him and you haven't. It must be hard to trust Asandra to someone you barely know and he has made his mistakes in the past. But our father is a good king. You can trust him."

He nodded. "I'm always stronger when you're fighting beside me, Sis. If you don't think you should stay, then I want you to come."

"Rachel is back?" Sasha gripped her throne so tightly her hand went white. Her troops thought she had killed the teen. When this word spread she would lose all respect. And Rachel was back!

There were two men before her. She turned to the other, "What do you have to tell me?"

"Good news."

Sasha morphed two of herself and two of her thrones. The one on the right was angry. The one on the left was calm. "What good news?" asked her friendly-self, while her unfriendly-self demanded, "You said there was other bad news. Speak!"

The lucky man answered, "Seth, Rachel and some others are heading to Noric on some secret mission."

That made Sasha smile. "Have we heard from Edmund?"

"He's following, Empress. But there is one thing: Vaylynne is with them."

She dismissed his words with a wave of her hand, "That means nothing. You shall be rewarded for this news. Bring me Stewart."

Meanwhile the unlucky man was telling the other Sasha, "We have begun to see strange creatures bearing strange armor throughout the land."

"Issym? Already! Get out!"

Stewart walked quickly to her side as she ordered him, "Offer a reward for every piece of stone armor that Issym brought with it. A very rich reward. Stop at nothing to destroy it. Crush their army."

He bowed, "With pleasure."

Xsardis

Chapter 13

The sun beat upon them as they rode along the path, listening to the birds chirping, the squirrels chasing each other, and the conversation that passed easily between them. A soldier had come with them in order to bring the horses back to Saphree once they reached the waterside. He said little. The joy of day was keeping the dark understanding of the importance of their mission from stifling them. That Sasha might really possess such a powerful artifact was too horrible to consider.

The group was making good time. They came to a sudden stop as a big purple feathered bird blocked their path. "Firil!" it squawked.

Rachel smiled. She descended her horse and leaned into him—the warmth feeling like a blanket, the soft feathers like a pillow. "You're smaller, Firil." She knew that birds like Firil grew smaller throughout their lives, but it still astounded her.

Evan laughed, "I'm not riding that again."

"Where have you been?" Rachel asked the creature in soothing tones. He was squawking loudly and had wrapped his long neck around her.

"We haven't seen him since Maremoth," Seth told her.

"How did you find me?" she whispered.

"They have incredible hearing," Reesthma explained. "As soon as he heard your voice, I'm not surprised he came to find you."

Tethering her horse to Seth's, Rachel struggled onto Firil's shifting back and felt the wobbling three legs pick up speed.

After Max had grown bored of watching the bird's funny movements and Rachel had slowed Firil to a steady trot beside Reesthma in the back of the group, Max asked Seth, "So what's the plan? Are we just going to swim across the ocean to get to Noric?"

"Vaylynne has a nearby camp. I'm sure she has boats we can use." Seth spoke without looking at her.

The warrior stared unhappily at him, but nodded to Max, "I do."

A wicked laughter echoed around them, disorienting everyone. At

Xsardis 104

first, Max thought he was imagining it—imagining all of it. He closed his eyes, expecting to wake up disoriented in his bed with the TV on too loud, knowing that his friends were still dead. He forced himself to open his eyes and recognized how real the mocking echo was, how real all of Xsardis was. There was a strange mix of gladness and fearfulness in him. The laughter was getting closer. They were clearly in danger.

Seth urged the group to push forward, but the sound was scaring even the horses. Reesthma's fell behind. Rachel stopped Firil to stay back with the girl. Seth tried to turn his horse, but on the narrow path with the others in his way it took too long. He watched as Reesthma and Rachel were encircled by fire sprites whose vicious frames racked with chortles.

"You escaped us once," one said.

"And our leader was transformed," said another.

"So now you die!" finished a third.

As laughter poured from their mouths, fire came out of each of their hands—lighting the trees and bushes surrounding the girls. Rachel and Reesthma were closed in.

Firil thrashed about. Flung from his back, Rachel grabbed his face and pulled him to the ground. With fearful eyes, he obeyed and stayed still. She turned her attention to Reesthma. The girl's eyes were wide, but she was calm. It was only then that Rachel felt her own panic. Maybe Seth could rescue them, but from the thickness of the flames it seemed doubtful. The grim reality of the war still waging on Asandra finally settled on her again; and with it, an understanding of the vital necessity of stopping Sasha. The passion to set Xsardis free rushed through her veins anew. Too late.

Her lungs were already blocking up, asthma making the thin air almost useless. The fire sprites' snickers dissipated. They were leaving them here to die. She and Reesthma lay against Firil, mouths covered with their cloaks, waiting for the inevitable. *Seth will find a way,* Rachel believed.

The blaze consumed the forest before Evan's eyes, growing steadily and enclosing around his friends. To his left Katarina's eyes flashed as she searched for a plan. To his right, Max's hand on Seth's arm held him back from charging through the flames after Rachel and Reesthma.

The flutter of small wings filled Evan's ears as he slowly turned to face the sprites that had caused this inferno. But it was not fire sprites that he saw. The small creatures' light blue robes and eyes were unlike those of any sprite he had yet seen. Though he had never even heard of them before, the prince knew that they were water sprites. "Help us," he pleaded, trusting a peace in their eyes.

"There are people inside?" a sprite girl flew forward, joined by a boy her age.

Evan nodded. Rapidly, the two led the others as they flew towards the fire and pushed water from the air with their hands. As the pressure increased and began to beat back the flames, smoke rolled into the sky. The second it was safe, Seth dodged into the steamy air calling for them, "Rachel! Reesthma!"

"Here!" came Reesthma's reply.

"Firil! Firil!" the bird squawked, guiding Seth with his boisterous sounds.

Seth reached out and felt Reesthma's hand in his. "Come on," he tried to pull her up.

"Rachel first!" the girl determined and helped Seth find the unconscious Rachel in the haze.

The air was damp and hot. Seth coughed, then held his breath. He bent down and gently lifted Rachel into his arms. Her head fell against his shoulder; her lungs heaved with effort.

Beside him, Evan's voice spoke to Reesthma. The prince helped her drag an unwilling Firil into clear air. As Seth distanced himself from the fog, he felt Rachel's breaths come more easily. When she awoke, she stood up on wobbly legs, using his arms for support. Seth took in his own breaths of fresh air gratefully.

Max and Katarina were facing the sprites, already questioning them. Both their blades were drawn, but at their sides. Evan caught his sister's glance in their direction and her intense relief to see them all unharmed.

"Who are you?" Max inquired.

"We have not seen your kind before. How do we know you are not some shifting trick?" Kat questioned, using a gentle but piercing tone.

"Why would we have helped you if we were a trick?" inquired the sprite girl.

"We have lived secluded by the sea," the male sprite answered, taking her hand in his own. "Strange occurrences have led us to believe it is now time to return to your country. We have no knowledge of a 'shifting trick.'"

"What kind of occurrences?" Reesthma was instantly interested, alert despite her oxygen-deprived system.

Katarina looked for Vaylynne. She and their adult companion had gone to find the horses that had scattered in fear of the fire. Kat did not like the fighter being out of sight.

"Sound sprites told us terrible things," the girl replied. "Boats have come over the water again. Fish have been in short supply as if other food has been depleted. We just know that something is different."

"We are at war," Evan confirmed.

Rachel's eyes settled on the two. "I know you."

"We have never been here before," the male sprite reaffirmed. "You could not know us."

"You're Lilly and Lucas."

"How do you know that?" Lilly investigated.

"The story you told Mary and Elise the night you came to Issym?" Katarina remembered from the scroll.

With awe, the two sprites inquired, "How do we best serve you, Imaginer?"

Rachel looked to Evan. He told them, "Go to Saphree, our fortress. The kings will find a place for you."

With the satisfying knowledge that he would no longer have to watch Asandra be overrun by the enemy, Stewart led his hand-selected men out of Saphree. They rode for Syvillis, a little town that would be lightly patrolled. It was a good place to start the battle. He, alone, would get the reward for the stone armor that would be destroyed. He, alone, would earn the glory of this battle.

Glory was particularly important to his cause. If he was going to wrench the kingdom away from Sasha, he would first need to wrench away the army's loyalty.

Finally there was no Edmund to steal his honor and no Juliet to refuse his plans. He was in total command and he was about to bring a havoc that Asandra had not known in far too long. Death, destruction and gloating. What could be better?

Syvillis would be the beginning. He would go on to re-conquer all the cities Sasha had allowed to grow fat and lazy in the last few months as she had squandered precious time on her brother's plan.

"The scouts say there are a large number of strange creatures guarding Syvillis," a man—his temporary aid—said as he rode his horse next to Stewart's.

"Strange creatures?" Stewart laughed. Nothing could hinder his optimistic mood.

"Frogs and beasts…" the aid explained.

"Lore of men too scared for battle. They will be punished upon our victory, after we demolish this puny village."

Flibbert grumpily rode patrol around the town of Syvillis, a horn on his neck in the unlikely case he saw an army coming their way. He usually liked being in the action, but today there were other places he longed to be. The first was obvious, with Seth and Rachel.

If Galen would not allow him to go with them, then the king could have at least kept him by his side. But while The Brothers and King Remar and Galen planned for war, Flibbert was patrolling some small town that no one would have bothered to attack. Even Elimilech had stayed behind to help with the planning.

It was in the midst of these distracted thoughts that he saw them—an army of thirty coming straight for him. The warnings had been right. Sasha was sending out her forces. She would target the smaller towns, where she could be assured of victory and crush the heart of Asandra.

Help was minutes away. The frog blew the horn with one hand as he drew his weapon with the other. He rode back only to a line of trees, longing to keep the battle from the unfortified town itself.

Slashing mercilessly, Flibbert fought to stay alive until the others could arrive at his side. As the first of his fellows reached him, his horse fell and he leapt from its back. He jumped from place to place, defending the troops of both Issym and Asandra. Despite the superior numbers of the enemy, the tide of battle stayed even. Sasha's forces were too shocked by the appearances of the frogs and minotaurs to wage battle as they should have. Finally, Flibbert's skilled warriors began to win out.

It was then that Elimilech and a few other fairies arrived and drove a final wedge of terror into Stewart's army. They were easily routed. Flibbert caught the leader's eye across the battlefield. If the two met again, one of them would fall.

"Did you need some help?" Elimilech's gripping voice brought his attention back.

"As always, a pleasure to serve with you," Flibbert answered. He could not take offense. The fairy had just saved them all. "Surely there was some reason you came."

"Galen sent me to relieve you. He wanted both of us to glean an understanding of Asandra's land and people. You've had your chance; now it's my turn. He wants you back with him, now." He paused to allow Flibbert's smirk, as the frog realized he had not been cast off by the king. Then Elimilech continued, "Seems like you'll have much to report to him."

"You could come with me, Drainan," a man in his early-twenties spoke quietly as they stood at the entrance to one of Vaylynne's many caves. They were barely protected from the sheeting rain that made their breath visible.

"Are you sure you won't regret disbanding?" Drainan asked, arms crossed in front of him and back leaning against the slick wall. Despite a wild beard and clothes in need of washing, he was more alert than ever. "You won't get a chance like this again."

"No, I don't think I'll regret it," the man beside him chuckled. "You've seen my fiancée. And you know she won't have a rebel for a husband. I've given Vaylynne all the time I have. There's no point to this anymore."

"When are you going to tell your troops, Cain?" Drainan questioned the rebel-leader who had become his friend, despite the circumstances of their meeting.

When Drainan had still been traveling with Rachel and Prince Evan and a preacher, Vaylynne had used her knowledge of him to track them. She had knocked Drainan out and dragged him to this cave in time to save him from Sasha's attack. As leader of the cave's forces, Cain had been his prison guard, under strict orders from Vaylynne not to let him escape. "Who knows what stupid thing he'll do next?" she had scoffed.

Over time, Cain—by far the eldest of Vaylynne's remaining troops—

and Drainan had grown to have a mutual respect. Drainan had ceased being a prisoner in Cain's mind and become part of the cave. Even if he did not fight or follow Vaylynne's orders, Drainan did his share in training the others. Vaylynne had come frequently to converse with her cousin, and eventually, had freed him to leave.

It had taken a long time for him to gain that freedom. Drainan had been more angry than he could express for what Vaylynne had done. If it hadn't been for Zachary the preacher's willingness to sacrifice himself, which had allowed Rachel and Evan the time to escape, all three would have been taken to Maremoth—not just Zach. All because of Vaylynne!

Drainan had not known if he could ever forgive her, but time and the bond of family had healed their wounds. Only then did Vaylynne release him, though he had stayed with Cain to this point.

"I'll tell them soon," Cain promised. Then he implored, "Come with me to my village. When Vaylynne brought you in kicking and fighting I thought you'd be no end of trouble. But you've proven to be a valuable friend."

"Thank you for the offer, Cain, but I can't. Vaylynne cut short my help to Rachel and Prince Evan. Now that they've made their miraculous return, I must offer my sword and finish what I started."

Cain shook his head, but accepted his fellow's words. "I'd best tell my own men that I'm leaving. I bet most of them will follow." He offered his hand, "It has been my honor."

Drainan shook it, pulled his hood over his head and walked into the rain.

Ahead of Bridget was a figure, ambling forward and muttering to himself. She fought the urge to go off the road when she saw people. She remembered all too well the stories of many a prisoner in Maremoth who had been traveling when they had been ambushed.

The man stopped in midsentence when he saw her, but no rush of color or embarrassment came to his cheeks despite his rambling. He tipped his hat to her as they came close, then stopped. "Good day, Lady," he spoke cheerfully.

Bridget discerned from his still-furrowed brow that he had been in a serious train of thought. "What is on your mind, Sir?" she questioned. She innately found herself trusting the blue eyes and the youthful face as she gazed at him. He was lanky and simply dressed. He carried no weapon.

"I must have seemed a bit crazy," he laughed heartily. "Forgive me. I'm a pastor and was in the midst of sorting out my new sermon when I saw you before me."

"Don't let me bother you," she answered kindly and started to move on. Bridget stopped herself. "You haven't seen a man on the road, by chance?"

Xsardis

109

He faced her again, removed his hat and scratched his blond head. "I've traveled from Maremoth and back several times in the last few months. I've seen many travelers."

The word sent her blood cold. "Why Maremoth?" she whispered, without even realizing it.

"I escaped from there with the other prisoners." He knew the look on her face. "You as well?"

She nodded, her mouth dry.

He introduced himself, "I'm Zachary. I wasn't there very long, but long enough." When she said nothing, he further inquired, "And you?"

"Bridget," she replied, absentmindedly. "Fifteen years I lived there."

Zachary's observant nature and experience pastoring led him to understand exactly what she needed. "Perhaps you will have lunch with me?"

Dropping to take a seat on a large boulder by the side of the road, he pulled out resources from his bag. Bridget took a seat beside him, the road muddy from the earlier rain. As they ate, Zachary revived her with tales of helping Rachel and Evan before being captured.

"Now then, who was it that you were looking for?" he asked, brushing the crumbs from his lap.

"A man named Brooks," she answered.

"The guard from Maremoth?" Zachary was shocked. He had met the man a few days ago on the road, but he never would have imagined that someone as frightened of Maremoth as Bridget could have any alliances with a former guard.

"You saw him?"

"He was heading north and was planning on stopping for a while in Ganetiv. He said he had some friends there. You can probably catch him if you hurry."

Xsardis

Chapter 14

It had taken Seth and the others well into the night to finally reach the water's edge. They had been forced to keep riding in order to make up the time the fire sprites had cost them.

Katarina stared forward as her brother built a fire for them. The guard from Saphree was already curled up for some sleep. He would leave early in the morning to head back to the fortress. Seth had gone with Vaylynne to find the boats at her camp. Reesthma, snuggled on a chatty Firil, was conversing softly with Rachel.

Evan took a seat beside his sister with a sigh and dusted off his hands. "Why are we trusting Vaylynne?" he questioned.

"We aren't," Kat answered. Her thoughts had been in exactly the same place. "Seth is using her, thinking she'll do more good than harm. When the risks grow too high, he'll deal with it."

"You sound pretty confident," Evan responded unhappily. "What do you think, Max?"

Max rolled his eyes before turning to them. The last thing he wanted to do was get in the middle of this fight. He had been disagreeing with Seth's calls since they were kids-- on how to fight in video games, which plays to call in basketball, which songs to sing at their concerts, and how to wage war on Xsardis. He chose to follow his friend because Seth would make the hard calls, and, usually, they were right. "I haven't been around. How should I know whether or not we can trust Vaylynne?" he replied. "But I think she's outnumbered five to one. There's not a whole lot she could do."

"I still don't like it," the prince murmured. "We've not only shown Vaylynne Saphree, but we're letting her get to know *our* strengths and weaknesses. Something we say casually could change the tide of battle. After we get those boats, we should leave her behind. She's too great a risk."

Evan fell silent as Seth and Vaylynne returned. Neither was blind to the awkward stillness that filled the air. Vaylynne chose to lean back against a tree, her hand on her weapon and her eyes scanning the trees. Seth stirred the

Xsardis

fire before taking a place by Rachel. Discerning from her that whatever conversation he missed he was better off not knowing at all, he said, "I saw the Dye Falls."

It took Rachel only a moment before she remembered imagining them. "Really?" A touch of envy crept into the word.

"They were stunning." He accepted the canteen she offered him and savored the drink. Asandra's waters tasted better than anything he could get on Earth.

"When this is all over, you'll have to promise to take me to see them."

Seth nodded.

"Did you ever wonder," Rachel began, "why some of the names of our friends here sound so different but some sound so similar? You have names like Elimilech and then some like Kate…"

"I figure, sometimes we got creative with naming people, and other times we didn't. As our imaginations grew, our name choices probably got cooler," he responded. "But what I'm curious about is how they have the Bible—the same exact, letter for letter, Bible that we have. New International Version from 1984."

"I never thought about that…" Rachel returned. She glanced at Reesthma to ask her, but the girl was already asleep. Morning would come in a few hours. Rachel should have followed her example, but the adrenaline in her system would not allow her to miss a second of her time on Xsardis. Not for the first time, she set her eyes on Seth to assure herself that he was there.

Seth was not ready for sleep either. He asked her, "How does it feel to be back in a run-for-your-life, never-know-what's-around-the-bend adventure?"

Taking a deep breath of the crisp night air, she replied, "Actually pretty good."

"Not the answer I was expecting after today."

"It didn't feel real to me. I keep expecting to wake up and find myself stuck on Earth."

He lowered his voice, "Of all the emotions to be feeling when that fire was wrapping around you and Reesthma, there was only one: disbelief. I couldn't fathom that God would bring you back to me only to take you away that quickly."

Rachel sighed heavily. "I'm glad He didn't. But," she paused, then made herself continue, "you and I both need to understand that if we get to Noric and Sasha's there, we are going be fighting for our lives every day. We might not all make it back this time." She cast her eyes over their little group.

"You're right," Seth leaned his head back against the tree. "You know me, Rachel; I like to control every little thing. But I can't keep any of you safe. I have to give you over to God and accept the consequences. He's certainly proved that He can protect you better than I can."

"So you turn into mushrooms when you become adults?" Kate tried to discern from Abigail, the leader of the sprites, as they stood in the gateway to Saphree.

"The first time we earth sprites get scared, we become mushrooms to hide," Abigail explained. "It's a natural instinct. Unfortunately, we've forgotten how to turn back. The longest anyone has held out against becoming a mushroom was a few months."

The sprite wore a green dress over her thin, tan form. Membrane-like wings fluttered behind her as she stayed at Kate's eye-level. Abigail did not represent an intimidating creature, yet all of Asandra seemed to fear the sprites. "And you're still in your child form?" Kate queried.

"For now, but not for long. I can feel the change coming."

"You're transformation into mushrooms cannot be that different from our shifting. Maybe I could help you rediscover your abilities."

Abigail's weary face lit up for the first time since Kate had seen her and what little was left of the peaceful child inside her was evident. The shifter recognized that it was not only physical combat that had aged her, but the struggle to win her people's acceptance among the armies of Saphree. That was a battle Kate knew all too well. Her own shifters were widely distrusted.

Suddenly turning to face the forest, Abigail flew well above Kate. The shifter followed her gaze, but saw nothing. "What is it?"

"Sprites," Abigail informed. "I think..."

"You think?"

"I can hear their wings, but they don't sound right."

The sprite's attempt at an answer left her companion only more confused. Kate drew her sword and commanded a nearby guard to alert the kings of the sprites' coming. The seconds ticked by slowly until the many sprite forms came into view through the forest. Dozens hovered before Kate and Abigail.

"Water sprites?" Abigail guessed from their appearances.

"And you are of earth?" a girl flew forward, her hand interlocked in her husband's.

A grand air came over Abi as she set her feet on the ground beloved by all earth sprites. She spoke with authority, "Abigail, head of the sprites supporting King Remar. Name your purpose."

"I am Lilly. This is Lucas. We were sent here at the request of Prince Evan and the imaginer Rachel."

"Where did you meet them?" King Remar questioned, stepping in front of Kate. Galen, Flibbert, and The Brothers were steps behind.

Lucas looked down, then met the king's eyes, "There was a fire, caused by other sprites. We saved Rachel and Reesthma's lives."

Galen made his voice heard, "No one was hurt then?"

Xsardis   114

"No," Lucas confirmed.

"Galen, I should go after them. Look at what happened in a day!" Flibbert was adamant.

Drawing the frog towards the castle, Galen again talked him down from his determination to follow Seth and Rachel.

Glancing at the guards still standing with swords drawn, Lucas offered, "We are sorry for what other sprites have done, but we are not your enemy."

"We have not been to the mainland in a very long time," Lilly went on. "We sensed a change in the waters and returned. Prince Evan told us that you are at war. We want to help."

"If you haven't helped us in this long, why should we trust you now?" the voice came from a fire sprite drawn in by the commotion.

"We did save your prince's companion's," Lucas pointed out, the irritation in his voice clear. "This is not a welcome reception and we have done nothing to deserve this. Please, drop your guard!"

Lilly put her free hand on his shoulder to stop the flow of emphatic words. "Forgive my husband," she addressed King Remar. "We have not been exposed to war and we do not understand the aggression you seem to show your allies."

King Remar looked to Abigail for direction. At her nod, he ordered his soldiers to stand down. "Welcome to Saphree. Thank you for saving our people. Abigail and Kate, our new friends are in your care." He moved off with Jeff and Sphen.

After Issym's arrival, it had seemed wise to leave Abigail over the sprites, but to assign her to report to an adult from another race. Seeing the similarities between the plights of the two races, Galen had wisely chosen Kate. The shifter's nature had soon set Abi at ease with her new superior.

Studying the thick group of sprites dressed in blue and grey, Abigail pondered where they would be best assigned. Though all their hair was curly, some possessed a glossy green, others a silver and still others a blue so light it was almost indiscernible. They hovered above the ground, as if loath to touch it. Many wore bangles of sea glass or jewels.

A whispered conversation with Kate led Abigail to bring the sprites to a place to rest. She would then converse more with Lilly and Lucas about the water sprites' abilities.

Kate was held back by the urgent appearance of Nevel—a shifter who preferred a handsome human form and whose passion for God had quickly promoted him to be a leader among the shifters. "What is it?" she asked, turning to give him all her attention.

"A fight is brewing," he reported. "Many of the fairies don't want to fight beside us shifters. They say we aren't trustworthy."

"They've been saying that for as long as I've been alive."

"They threw it in our faces. You know that some of us can be quick to anger. I barely stopped a brawl. Think how that would make us look. It would only confirm their fears."

"Oh..." Kate sighed, wiping a hand against her forehead. The sun seemed suddenly blazing. "If it was only the fairies that were so bigoted," she lamented. "But they're just the ones bold enough to admit their prejudice."

Could the world not see that shifters had a unique perspective born from long life experience with Sasha? Could they not comprehend that without the power of the shifters the war would have been lost already? Couldn't they see that they were pushing for a confrontation? This bias would cause her fellow shifters to one day turn against Xsardis. She could not put out Issym's biased fires forever if they were determined to keep lighting them.

"I'll speak with Elimilech," she informed him. "Go make sure our shifters are calming down."

Nevel nodded and walked away. Kate was more grateful than she could say for his constant attention to the many things she simply did not have the time to perceive or handle. Nevel had longed for freedom from Sasha even before she had. Now that he had it, he was determined to protect it. Sometimes she thought he would make a better leader of the shifters.

Shaking herself from her thoughts, Kate marched into the castle to have a lengthy conversation with the battle commander of the fairies. Elimilech approached her in the open hallway with as much firm intent as she carried. "Do you know what's going on?" he demanded.

"Do you?" she retorted. To reason with the fairy in his current mood she would need to show her strength. Kate got in his face and elevated her voice, "Your fairies taunted us, proclaiming that we aren't trustworthy enough to fight alongside them. They were asking for a battle!"

"Your shifters have itched for conflict," Elimilech countered.

"How long do you think anyone can stand being rejected and insulted?" Kate pressed. She softened herself, "If we do not heal these wounds, more will follow."

"Is that a threat?" the broad-shouldered fairy raised himself to an even taller position—if that was possible.

She persisted, "It is a statement of fact. We add immeasurable power to your army and we offer a comprehension of how to fight Sasha. Yet you refuse to heed even *my* counsel and you treat us like secondary citizens. You are inviting trouble."

He brushed past her with a last remark, "We're ready for it."

News of Stewart's failure at Syvillis reached Sasha's ears only hours after his defeat. She shook her head in her frustration. Edmund had made her wait too long! Had it been deliberate sabotage or was he simply an idiot?

The shifter knew that she had only herself to blame. She had allowed herself to be led astray by her love of her brother. Yet his plan had had merit. She needed that artifact. It was more than the intense craving that had been there since birth for powers beyond measure. Only the artifact could undo the damage she already carried inside her.

With her whole being she longed to go after Edmund and make sure he did not fail, but she knew that Asandra needed her here. Already Issym's forces had spread out and limited her powers. The recent demolition of Stewart's small army confirmed that it would take her overseeing to keep any power she still had on Asandra.

But Sasha had not taken her position by simple luck. She was the mistress of planning. When one plot when awry, she had another to take its place. When Smolden's failure had cost her Issym, she still had Asandra. Edmund and Stewart's ineptitude did not mean her destruction, but it did mean that she would need to ask the help of dangerous allies. She hated to awaken a sleeping giant, but the risks were worth it. Once she had the artifact, she could banish them once more to their home in the heavens.

Sasha rose from her chair with a deadly determination and went to summon an elite killing force. She was loathe to ask for help, but these creatures were her only chance.

Stewart led his defeated men through the forest toward Saphree. He knew how devastating the effects of his failure at Syvillis were.

But what chance had he had? Those wild frogs and beasts that had fought with a courage unrestrained were powerful and strange creatures. How was he supposed to lead his men against an enemy that arose every superstition amongst them?

In order to gain back his empress' and his soldiers' confidence, he would need to do something bold. Stewart planned to wait outside the fortress of Saphree and capture a key prisoner. To be this close to the stronghold of his enemy with only a dozen men was insanity—or greatness.

He saw a single wagon come out of the fortress. "Ready yourselves," he commanded his troops. They slid into positions on either side of the forest road far enough from the fortress that help would take time to arrive.

The wagon wound its way toward them as the hot sun beat down upon them. "Now!" Stewart shouted and jumped out before it. His men surrounded all sides. Two of Saphree's soldiers launched themselves at his troops. They were soon unconscious. One man emerged from inside. He wore no sword, but neither was he dressed in royal garb. Stewart recognized a look in his eyes that betrayed that his heart was not devoted to Saphree. "Who are you?" he demanded.

"Philip."

"And what ties do you have with Juliet and Remar?"

Philip stood and hopped off the wagon. "None."

Stewart smiled.

Chapter 15

It was not easy for Edmund to follow Seth and his tight-knit group as they made their way to Noric. They were armed with the stones of the frogs, which caused a deep fear to seep into the shifter. Every instinct in Edmund told him to get away from the accursed restrictors, but instead he was following them—keeping just far enough behind that the stones could not hinder his abilities. Still, he had to be close enough to feel them in order for him to follow the heroes no matter where they went. That closeness caused the terror that now slowed his movements.

Or was it something else? He sensed an animal below him. He was in a shark's form, and nothing should scare him, but this presence did.

Then Edmund saw it. The creature was big enough to swallow him without chewing. Each of its broad shoulders was larger than its head. In between them was a protruding sharpened fin. The monster propelled itself through the water with its huge, bumped arms and clawed hands. Its lower half was a smooth, three-pronged tail. Edmund was glad he could not see its front.

At first glance, the shifter had not even been able to distinguish it from the shadow of a sunken mass. The creature of the sea swam past without showing the least interest in the shifter-shark. Its steady movements showed a purpose, as if it was called by some unknown master.

Seth's quest might soon be over. This monster was swimming towards him.

Seth kept his strokes even as he paddled the boat in which Vaylynne and Reesthma sat. They had been taking turns for hours and it seemed like they would never reach Noric, but they could not be far.

Xsardis

118

To his left, Rachel slept while Evan rowed. To his right, Katarina chastised Max on rowing wrong. With a guilty smile he said, "You do it, then," handed her the paddles, and curled up for some sleep.

Firil had stayed behind on Asandra, apparently petrified of the open sea. His sorrowful eyes had pleaded with Rachel to stay, but in the end he had simply stood with his clawed feet in the water, moaning after her, "Firil! Firil!"

Taking with him a few stones, Seth had left behind his armor, as had the others. Their mission was about speed; forget safety. Armor would only hinder them. As long as they destroyed the artifact, nothing else mattered. He was actually beginning to believe that as he thought over the faces he had saved in the last five months.

It was nice to be safe on the seas for a few hours. *I never should have thought that,* Seth realized. He saw a creature fluttering in the heavy mist nearby. Maybe more than one creature. "Vay," Seth whispered.

Her eyes were already boring into the mist, "I see."

Seth pulled his dagger from his boot, leaving the bulky sword in its resting place. A screech erupted from the mist as three creatures flew at them, then doubled back. They made no attempt to make the noise beautiful. Instead, their song instilled fear in each of the teenagers' hearts. Rachel began to shake with a nightmare before Evan woke her up.

"What do you want?" the prince called to the creatures. One flew above each boat. They were ugly old hags. One had silver hair, the second gray and the third white.

They stared at Rachel, "We told your friends you would die. If they would only have listened, they might have understood the truth."

"You're sound sprites," Rachel summarized both from the story that Flibbert and Galen had told and from her own imagination. These creatures knew no boundaries. Rachel looked to Seth, "We should go."

But out-paddling sound sprites was not an option and fleeing would only make them angry, so the three boats stayed where they were. The gray-haired one asked, "Did you meet a minotaur named Joeyza?"

Her companions' snicker forced her to be silent. The silver-haired one said, "We have a prophecy for you."

"That was so helpful to our friends before…" Seth replied, recalling Galen's tale.

"What he means is we don't want your help." Max just wanted out of there. These were the mean girls at school—the reason he had allied himself with Seth and the popular group. He had always wanted to stay out of their grasp. Only these mean girls might actually kill them.

The silver-haired one spoke again, this time her voice eerily distant. "Do you still dream of the dragon's claws, Seth? You will face them again."

Seth did not know that he shuddered.

The white-haired sprite waited a few moments before saying her own prophecy, "Rachel, you will fight a person you honor and cherish—a friend—to accomplish your quest. She will lay down her life if she must to stop you."

"Go away, just go away," Rachel's sorrowful voice begged.

"But that is not all. Tell them," the silver-haired one prodded the ever-silent gray-haired sprite.

Xsardis   119

The gray-haired sprite looked sheepish, but gave in, "Not all of you will walk the path a second time."

"Of course, this only matters if you survive the next few minutes," the silver-haired one added before she and her white-haired sister let out a low moan, sending anguish into the hearts of the companions. With chortles they flew back into their mist. The gray-haired sprite tried to find some words, but in the end, she returned to the mist with her kin.

"*If you survive the next few minutes?*" Katarina repeated, breaking herself from the daze the strange sounds had affected upon her.

The water rippled beneath them. A sharp, pale-gray fin, half the size of their boat in width and the size of their boat in length rose to the top of the water. "Rachel," Seth's voice was strained, "did you ever imagine a sea monster?"

Max's face went pale, but he said nothing. Rachel shook her head, "I can't remember."

Their boats rose out of the water as the back of a long, bumped gray body picked them up—the fin sliding between two of their boats. They sank again and Reesthma could not keep in a scream, "The pitara!"

"The what?" Seth's mind craved facts as it always did when danger surrounded him and others. Somehow in a single second he could sort those facts, weigh the many options and outcomes, and make a solid decision. But now he did not have the facts with which to plan and choose.

"The reason no sailors go between Asandra and Issym," Reesthma attempted to answer his question. "It can swallow a whole boat! The sprite's moan brought it here."

"They must really want us dead," Evan groaned.

Rachel turned to Seth, her cadence was controlled but fast as she worked out the problem, "If the sprite's moan attracted it, then some kind of sound must repel it." Already, she could see the ripples of the creature circling back for them.

"If a moan of pain brought it," Max launched his idea off of Rachel's, "then perhaps a shout of joy will send it away."

"I don't feel very joyful!" Reesthma cried as their boats rose again— they were sitting on its powerful shoulders, unable to see the front of its body or head. Was the creature more than a beast? Or was it simply a predator?

The boats descended with a splash, almost tipping over. Katarina refused to fall into the open water with such a monster. She forced her sword out of its sheath, fighting against the close-quarters to do so. If the pitara came back, she was going to stab it.

Like that's going to do anything but make it angry... Max lamented. Seeing in his friends' faces that no one else would lead the sounds of joy, he began himself to laugh. With no other option available, Rachel and Katarina joined him. Reesthma was far too dumbfounded. Vaylynne and Evan stared on. Seth laughed only when he realized that the pitara had not yet resurfaced.

For minutes they kept up a stream of constant nervous laughter. It was only when they had paddled their way out of the mist and they saw the outline of the island of Noric that they gave up their 'joyous' sounds.

Seth felt the cool of the water revive him as he jumped from his boat to pull it to shore. Vaylynne, unable to remain sitting any longer, helped him drag it onto the sandy beach. She stared back out at the water. "Never in my whole life have I heard of something so ridiculous as a sea monster that is scared of happy sounds…" Her eyes narrowed on Seth, "You don't really think that's what drove it away."

He shrugged, strapping his sword back around his waist and keeping his eyes on the sea. "I don't know, but it seemed to work."

"That thing was out for blood. No wonder boats stopped passing between Issym and Asandra," Vaylynne stepped back several feet as she spoke.

"This isn't right," Seth gasped, turning to face the island. He was confronted by lush grass and trees. It was a thriving forest.

"What's wrong?" Evan inquired, snapping back to his feet on the sandy beach.

"The last time I was on Noric it was bare."

"It was winter," Max pointed out.

"No, I mean really bare. No grass, no trees, nothing. We're in the wrong place."

"This *is* Noric," Vaylynne confirmed. "I know we went the right way."

"Maybe we got lost in the mist…" Kat pondered.

"It had *no* trees before?" Max asked skeptically.

Seth's face told Max how certain he was. "There was only one tree. Lotex said they liked to keep one around. The others they had cut for wood."

"Sounds pretty stupid," Max countered.

"Yeah; it did." He glanced at them all. "You believe me?"

Moving inland as her wet boots attracted sand, Reesthma observed the landscape and looked back at the water. "I've seen a lot of maps at Joppa's tree. As far as I can tell, we really are on Noric." She glimpsed at Seth, "But that doesn't mean you're wrong. Maybe something has happened to this place. I'd love to find out what."

"That's not all you'd love to find out more about," Max spoke with an almost indignant awe. "You're excited you got to see the pitara, aren't you? You want to write about it!"

Reesthma nodded. "I was scared at first, but then I realized what an opportunity it was. Only a few sailors have ever survived an attack from the pitara. Joppa and I have never gotten a good report on him. Honestly, I thought he was a myth."

"I wish he had been," Katarina muttered, then rubbed her arms. "I never want to see that thing again."

"There's no more time for this idle chatter," Vaylynne said gruffly. "There's only one way to find out if we're in the right place. Let's move."

"We attack tonight!" Stewart gleamed to his men. His now-replenished, if still small, army had been heartened by the spy he had found. Still, they doubted him; but soon he would have set that right. "I have been assured by my spy that none of these foul creatures protect Ganetiv. We will demolish it before they get the chance."

After careful consideration, Stewart had allowed Philip to go back into Saphree to glean more information. Though he understood that he did not truly hold Philip's loyalties, the spy had little information to offer from the outside. As long as Stewart kept paying him, Philip would stay faithful. And no matter what he was offered, he would tell nothing to Saphree about his disloyalty. Philip was bitter against his king and some frog named Flibbert. He would not tell them anything—even if they bribed him.

Philip would be a spy that could only be trusted so far, but if Stewart was to ever take power, then he needed this man's help. Stewart would have to set Issym, Asandra, Maremoth and even Vaylynne's troops against each other. In the wake of the destruction caused, he would rise as the benevolent dictator he had been destined to become.

Sasha had been a fool for lying to the world, especially her own troops. Her claim to have killed Rachel had earned her little but hatred; the fact that the girl was still alive had secured the contempt of her troops. Stewart would be ready to present that fact to the army and earn their loyalties for himself. When the time came…

Loyalty? It was a myth. Princess Katarina had betrayed family and friends. Edmund had turned against both his sister and his girlfriend. Sasha had lied one too many times. Maremoth's former prisoners had been turned in by their own towns. The entire concept of loyalty was a lie that would be eroded under his reign. He would look only to himself. As for his subjects, he needed only discover their true masters and exploit them.

Philip was the beginning of Stewart's plan, but he was not the end. Sasha had captured Asandra by utilizing its bitterness. Stewart was going to corrupt the new-found alliances and capitalize on Asandra's distrust. Sons would rat out fathers when he was finished. He could hardly wait.

Sasha hated being humble, but there was no other way to approach her killing force. Long ago she had learned of them. Long ago she had asked for their help. Long ago they had refused her. But as her power had risen, their willingness had come. They told her to call on them only in her dire need. That need had arisen.

Such a powerful group of creatures, she knew, was best left untouched. She had little choice, however, if she was to maintain her control of Asandra.

Her body rose to the clouds easily. She was so thin these days. *Never*

Xsardis   122

mind that. Stay focused, she reminded herself.

When the shifter landed on the clouds she was in tightly-fitted black clothing, an inky black cloak around her to shield her from the wind. These were not the enchanted clouds of Issym. This was the arena of the dark clouds—a place from which no one ever came back.

As soon as Sasha had entered, the clouds seemed to encircle and engulf her. The orange sky above her was lost. She was trapped in a prison of gray and black. Only a few clouds were blue.

Energy in the form of light filled several of the clouds, shining through with their power. The dark clouds rippled with thunder. She was being shown how powerless she was. Unfortunately for the dark sprites whom she sought, their display had a reverse effect. The challenge to her authority made her stand up straighter. She became more defiant. *I am Sasha! None is more powerful than I!* her own thoughts stirred her. With a mighty bellow she called to the airsprites, "Come if you will and meet your master!"

The thunder yelled even louder. Bolts of lightning flashed. The clouds became a blackness of no light—Sasha was for all purposes blind. They shifted underneath her feet, making her feel as if she was on the rolling sea. "Hah!" she called. "Give up your fancy show and meet me!" her voice became scratchy and deep. She felt the surge of power run through her.

An opening in the clouds allowed a little orange light to glow upon a figure emerging from the mist. The airsprite wore a fitted black leather vest and a longer black skirt, which seemed on the top to be fabric but to be mist by the time it reached the bottom. Her skirted feet appeared to be absorbed into the clouds. "What do you want?" her voice had a possessed tone, but in Sasha's mood, nothing turned her nerves.

"It is time for you to serve me, to give the help you promised," Sasha informed the sprite.

Two more openings allowed two more figures to move toward her. Their controlled movements showed intense power and grace. She turned her body in a slow circle as she spoke with them. "Will you deny me this?"

"We deny you nothing!" retorted one with hair almost indistinguishably dark. Her irises were of the same black color.

"We have promised you nothing!" added another, as several more emerged from the clouds. The darkness was slow in filling around her again. Sasha memorized their locations in case she had to fight her way out. The concept of that fight awakened her even more.

"The time for victory is at hand," Sasha promised. "Join me now!"

"And what would we gain from this?" asked the first one, still in her haunting tones.

"You are supreme warriors. But what honor do you have? The world has forgotten you! Fight and prove your skills," Sasha responded.

Three more came through the clouds. "We need to prove nothing," answered a newcomer.

"Your own kind has forgotten that you exist," Sasha challenged. "They are here now and know nothing of you. They have lived in peace and respect among their people on Issym. What have you accomplished?"

The dark airsprites grew angry and began to gnash their teeth and

Xsardis

shriek at Sasha. But they all became still as one giant orb of light emerged from the clouds and developed into a pure white haired female. Her solid white eyes set her above the others just as much as her posture and slow wording, "We will fight."

Xsardis

Chapter 16

As they passed the decrepit old tree that Seth had once been forced to climb, he had to accept that they were really on Noric. It was too strange to be comprehensible, but they were on an island that not too long ago had been completely barren. If that was possible, then certainly the sprites' prediction that he would face the dragon again could be true as well. The thought made him twitchy. He looked over his shoulder so often that even Vaylynne saw that something was wrong with him.

Smolden was a relentless adversary in his dreams. When you imagine a monster and then meet it in reality, it will haunt you forever. The youth had gone over and over it in his mind. He should not have won in the fight against Smolden. Even with the superior skills he had learned since then, Seth understood that he could not keep himself or his friends safe from such a beast. It had been a stroke of luck, or divine blessing. It had had little to do with him. And to a warrior who had learned to control everything, the inability to stop an impending danger was almost too much to bear. The prophecy that one of them was going to die, or more specifically, "not walk the path a second time"—was it going to be his fault?

Max pulled Rachel back to a safe whispering distance, "Seth's being..."

"Weird?" she finished. It was more than a couple of looks over his shoulder. He was cringing, ducking like something was going to drop out of the sky.

Max nodded, "We need our leader right now. I want to help him. Am I talking to him or are you?"

"I will," she replied. With that she called a halt and asked Seth to help her fill their canteens from a stream that he was sure was nearby. As soon as they were out of earshot, Rachel spoke, "I know Smolden was hard on you."

Seth sighed. "You remember when you yelled at me on Issym?" She colored, but he kept on going. "You told me that I was not only being a complete jerk, but was putting a whole lot of people's lives on the line because

Xsardis

126

I was not willing to explore my imagination."

"You were miffed at me at the time."

"But you were right, and I knew it. So I tried to remember, mostly. But when it came to Smolden, it was like my mind would seize up. I would start thinking about him and the hours of creativity I poured into him and I would get lost.

"The first time I really saw him, I actually thought about letting him go. *I* imagined him and yet he turned out so terrible."

"Didn't you imagine him as terrible?" she questioned, kneeling in the soft bed beside a stream.

"No," Seth shook his head. "I imagined him first as Santana, friend of Issym. And I gave him strength unmatchable. His betrayal suffocated Issym— me. He could never kill him and I never wanted to. I had to kill a friend. The more time I spend here, the more I remember Issym like I was him. I realize what I did and I don't know that I could do it again."

"Seth, that day you did the right thing and you've been doing the right thing since. Whatever obstacles we face, I know you'll keep doing the right thing."

"Did I stop him?" he pressed. "Or did I close a blind eye to Smolden's supposed death? The sprites say he'll be back. What if he found a way to heal himself? What if he has been behind this war the whole time? And what if I could have finished him just by thinking?"

Rachel could hardly believe what she was hearing. "We can live on our lives on what-ifs, but it doesn't change anything. You faced Smolden. You defeated him in all but one way. He lives on in your mind to torment you."

"What did Issym—what did I—do wrong? What happened to Santana?"

"The sprites said what they knew would hurt you the most," she snapped to get his attention. "Like they told Galen and Flibbert that I would die. I did burn, but I did not die! They've spread the same lies to us. Do you think I want to press forward and fight someone I respect? I don't, Seth."

He looked to her, "Should we have imagined this place?"

"This place is wonderful... believe me."

The bitterness in her words was what forced Seth back to reality. "Why did you say it like that?"

Rachel instantly realized that the tables were turning. No longer would she be interrogating him; now it would be the other way around. "Nothing..."

"Something. What?"

"Before Issym you were focused on popularity, right? You would do anything to get it."

"Sadly, yes."

"Well I spent my life building trust," she chose each word carefully as they stood and began to walk back. "I was the golden child of my church. The parents of the kids I babysat adored me. *My* parents adored me. It left me unpopular with the other teens. I was simply a goody-two-shoes, an outcast. But I had trust; I had respect; the doors were open to me with good grades and scores of references. That's all I focused on.

Xsardis
127

"When I got back to Earth without you, we had been gone for six months. At first everyone was so happy to see me alive. Then I told my parents what had happened."

"They thought you were crazy," he inferred.

"No. They thought I was lying, which was much, much worse. In an instant, I lost the respect and trust that I had spent a lifetime earning. The police couldn't understand how I could say you were dead but not know how. The church people wouldn't talk to me. It was my fault."

"No, it…"

She broke through, "Seth, if I had told my parents the truth when we had first come back from Issym then this wouldn't have happened. I had Ruby to prove it then. I should have spoken. The only reason I didn't is because I wanted a secret—something that defied everyone's view of my predictability, even if only I knew about it."

Seth was aware there was more to the story than that. "The night we left for Asandra you wanted to tell them and I wouldn't let you. I should have; and I'm sorry."

Arriving back to the others at that moment, they dropped the conversation entirely. A look at both of their faces and Max guessed that Rachel had done little to fix Seth's distraction, but as they began their march again he could note a difference in his friend's posture. Seth's alertness was back.

It was a little before dark when they arrived at the dwarf mines. Hiding in the trees, Seth scouted to make sure everything seemed in place. Six stocky dwarfs guarded the entrance.

Glancing at the scowling faces, Reesthma inquired, "Do we have to go in there?"

"Lotex knew something he wasn't telling me," Seth replied. "My guess is that someone in there has the same information. If it's about the artifact, we need to know it."

"Do you know any of the guards?" Katarina asked.

"Just one…" Seth groaned. With that he began a fast-paced walk toward them, leaving the others to wait. "Beatrice," he said to the only woman in the group of guards.

She brandished her ax. "What do you want?"

"There were never guards before," Seth remarked.

"You should know why we have to have them. You made us enemies of Sasha."

He shrugged. That was true.

When he said nothing, she guessed at the reason for his appearance, asking, "Is my brother dead?"

"No; Lotex is fine."

"Then what is it that you want?"

"Information."

"You're distracting me from my work. I don't have time right now."

Seth knew he would get nowhere with this sister, who was every bit as stubborn as Lotex. "Then may I go in?"

She stared at him. "*You,* I know. You're friends hiding in the bushes, I don't. They stay."

Xsardis   128

He nodded and entered the tunnel, keeping a brisk pace. There was only one other dwarf he could count on to give him an accurate report, but the interview would not be pleasant.

Coming to the small door, he knocked on it. A thin dwarf man appeared in the frame, his voice a high pitch, "Seth! I do hope you have not come back for more hospitality. I already put you up once. Though it was my pleasure to serve you and I would gladly do it again."

"Blowen," Seth interrupted, knowing that the dwarf would go on forever contradicting himself. "Where did all the trees come from?"

"Hmm? Oh yes. We cut most of them down for the winter. The others fade. When its spring again, they grow back."

"I don't understand," Seth responded. "They *fade* and then they grow back in a few months?"

Nodding, Blowen asked, "Why does that surprise you? Though I could understand if…"

Seth cut him off, "Blowen, I need your help."

"Come in then. Wipe your feet first."

Ducking to enter, Seth was confronted by the hearty smells of the soup cooling at Blowen's small table. "I would be happy to offer you food even if it would tax my meager supplies."

"It's alright. I just have some questions for you."

"Go on." Blowen sat down, spread a napkin on his lap, and began to eat.

"My friends and I have come because we think there is some kind of artifact here on Noric. Sasha the shifter is going to come looking for it. Or she may already be here. We have to find it first."

Blowen nodded, then shook his head. "I don't know anything about that."

Seth sat down in disappointment on the dwarf's bed, despite Blowen's many protests. He sifted through the various pieces of information. Sasha was looking for eternal youth—a youth this island seemed to possess as it constantly returned to fruitfulness. "The tree you never cut down… is that important?"

"Important?" Blowen snorted. "It's only death if you harm it. Seems unreasonable, but they must have a reason."

"Where would its roots be?"

"I don't know!"

Seth stood in frustration and left the room, determined to make Beatrice answer his questions. After Blowen had made his bed, he called to Seth, "But there is one tunnel we never explore. It was here before we dwarves settled Noric. We like our own mines so we've ignored it ever since."

The warrior paused. "Where is it?"

Having received directions, Seth returned to his fellows. They journeyed as dusk settled upon the land. "It's almost night," Max pointed out. "And yesterday was a very long day. Are we going to sleep anytime soon?"

"We could just press on through the night, but we're going to have to sleep eventually," Rachel thought.

"Let's get into the mines, find out what we're dealing with, and then catch some rest," Seth decided.

"We should gather some of this fruit," Evan declared, looking at a forest full of edible things. "Our own supplies won't last forever."

They picked the fruit and finished their brief journey, lighting their torches once they were inside the mine. As soon as the teens had entered, they were faced with a choice. Five different rocky pathways stood before them. "Splitting up," Vaylynne figured.

"No. Follow hard the Word," Prince Evan answered.

"Wide and narrow," Reesthma muttered.

"We take the narrow path," Katarina walked into it. It certainly was narrow. They would have to walk one at a time and sideways from time to time. The cave jutted out at parts so that even Katarina could barely squeeze through. It was going to be a long walk.

When Seth moved to follow her, Vaylynne put a hand on his arm and whispered sharply, "You cannot be serious. We have to explore all the options. Sasha will be!"

"Follow hard the Word," he whispered back. "This seems clear to me."

"What if the Bible is not what it meant? And even if it was, what if this narrow thing is not the part we are supposed to be following?"

"Vaylynne, it's okay. This is Bible basics."

"Bible basics. You're risking Xsardis on Bible basics?" her voice trembled with rage.

She sounded like Edmund. "You're welcome to go down another path," Seth offered.

"Are you two coming?" Rachel was stopped in the entryway of the tunnel.

Seth waited for Vaylynne to answer. "Yes."

As Edmund followed the teens into the mine, he focused his mind on the stones. He had to know which tunnel they had taken. Of course, it just had to be the most narrow. He groaned as he shifted down to a smaller size. The stones really shouldn't have affected him at that distance, but they made shifting uncomfortable.

The sea monster had not ended the lives of Seth and his companions. Odd. It had seemed so determined. He had been sure that it would eat his once-friends. His mind accidentally thought, *Maybe God protected them.* Edmund spewed vehemently, "Luck protected them. God had nothing to do with it."

After his outburst he was more silent than ever. No need to risk being overheard.

It had been two days since the teens had left Saphree, and they were making remarkable time. It would not be long before his far-too-trusting but very impatient sister came to Noric.

Edmund's plan was far from certain. With a wholly-consuming passion that he assured himself was completely different from Sasha's, Edmund knew he had to find the artifact. Not for him and certainly not for his sister. He would never let Sasha have it. She would become far too powerful and not even he wanted to see her on the throne of Xsardis forever. But Kate... she would be a just ruler.

All too clearly he remembered the months after the scroll that told of the artifact had been brought to her. They had produced a change in her. Her brow had been ever furrowed; her usual smile had disappeared; she had been tormented. The day she had burned it, Kate had looked so relieved. In simple tones she had explained to him that if she kept it she would be destroyed, either by her failed pursuit or by the realization of absolute power. She would have been corrupted.

Now that was Edmund's goal. A corrupted Kate was still better than a Sasha; and a corrupted Kate would take him back. Together they would rule, ensuring the balance between good and evil.

He still regretted not pulling that scroll from the flames, but even the concern that it still existed had been enough to bring Rachel and Seth to Noric. Now, if he was to steal the artifact from under both Sasha's and Seth's noses, he would need a partner. Vaylynne would be perfect.

Edmund did not have to worry about approaching her. With her battle-heightened awareness, she would sense the presence of a stranger and come looking. And then they would form an alliance strong enough to weather the changing tides of Xsardis.

"We took minor losses," Flibbert boasted to Galen as he entered the temporary council chambers for Issym. "They outnumbered us, but we fought them back."

"Good, good," Galen answered distractedly. "I just don't understand it. Why wait five months, then attack once your enemy has reinforcements?"

"The desperate move of a crazy shifter," Flibbert scoffed, taking a chair.

"Perhaps..." the high king's eyes drifted out the window.

"What can be bothering you? We just had our first of many great victories. We should be rejoicing." The frog placed his top hat regally on his head and propped the familiar steel cane on his lap.

"I never rejoice in death, Flibbert," Galen replied. His eyes landed on the warrior's hat and he chuckled, taking a seat. "Why do you love that hat and cane so much?"

"Surely you know this." When the king shook his head, Flibbert

leaned forward and explained, "It's a symbol of being an airsprite guardian."
"And the cane?"
"You wouldn't understand…"
"Try me."
Flibbert conceded. "I hide my bit of a limp, but it's there—left over from some battle I can barely remember."
"There's another reason," Galen perceived.
The frog nodded. "It is a promise to my people that I will fight until I am crippled, and then I will keep on fighting."
"What a strange fellow you are," he said with a grin.
The man and the frog fell to their own thoughts. Flibbert considered strategy still to be discussed with The Brothers. Galen pondered his short reign. Would the legacy he left Issym be the slaughter of its young men in this war? He shivered.
"What's wrong?" Flibbert questioned.
"Can't you sense that brittle cold feeling?"
"It's nothing more than the draft coming through the window," the frog answered so quickly it sounded like he meant it. But Flibbert *could* feel it, and had been feeling it for some time.
Galen walked to the window and looked up. The orange of the sky flitted through the dark clouds. "It seems as if the sky has grown black and the air grown stale. As if a cold enemy is rising from a long sleep," he fell into a whisper.
"Galen," Flibbert moved towards him, aware of his king's keen perception. "What do you think it is?"
"The reason we have to hold on and hope that Seth and Rachel win this battle for us. We may have had one victory, but I fear we will have many losses."
He turned to Flibbert suddenly, "I'm sending you back out. Encourage the troops. Keep them on the ready. Tell them of the danger we sense. And when battle comes looking for us, find out all you can about this new enemy."

Bridget hurried her step. The empty night roads made her want to stop and make some safe camp, but she was so near Ganetiv. If Brooks was still there, as the preacher had said, her search would be over. How she would lament her fatigue if she missed him by one morning!
The village of Ganetiv had neither gate nor stronghold. It was a cluster of homes. As she entered, it reminded her of her old village.
Her footsteps made no sounds against the grassy floor as she moved through the town. Bridget was heading toward the sounds of conversation and occasional laughter—the center of the village—where Brooks would be. She

Xsardis

132

spared a moment to look up at the brilliant stars and be grateful for the light they afforded as she stepped over sticks and stones. Still, there was an eerie stillness that warned her to be cautious.

Moving close behind one house, she finally caught sight of Brooks, barely a few feet away from her. She was sure it was him; he always scrunched his shoulders when he was thinking. Smiling, Bridget slowly reached out her hand to touch his arm.

In an instant a rough hand gripped her mouth and an arm slid across her waist, pulling her behind the house and to her knees in one swift movement. She struggled and attempted a scream, but his hold was unyielding.

She heard the rush of bodies slamming together as someone tackled Brooks. The whistling of arrows filled the night. Cries went out, a bell was rung, movement filled the town. It was chaos now. She heard sword swing against sword and hollers of life and death. In her shock, Bridget gave up the struggle with her captor. He had pulled her away just in time. "Let's get out of here while we still can," he cautioned sharply, as he released her and stood to his feet.

As soon as she had risen to her own, he grabbed her hand and was pulling her into the woods. He carefully judged the distance between each house as he stayed out of sight of the town's adversaries. His grip gave Bridget no choice but to follow. They moved hastily, but not altogether quietly. The trees blocked out the starry light and she tumbled to the ground, only to be pulled back up again.

Finally safe in the deep cover of the forest, they rested. The moon persuaded the trees to let through a little light. In it Bridget could make out the man's face. He had a beard and wore dark clothing. The reflection of the moon caught his eyes. The blade he held in his hand was a crude weapon, made for killing, not for elegance. She stayed silent, ready to run the moment his eyes trailed away from her. She could not be sure whether he was friend or foe, but she doubted he was the former.

The sounds echoed from the town, finally ending as the attacking forces road off on loud hoofs. "I'm going on," his voice was surprisingly deep. "You can come until we get to the next town. Or not."

"Who are you?"

"I'm the man who saved your life," he answered, then began to walk.

Bridget followed to learn more. "But how did you know about the attack?"

"I felt them. I saw them. But it was too late to warn anyone but you."

"We have to go back to the town and help them!"

"It's too late for that." He stopped and observed her, "You're not from Ganetiv. But you know someone there?"

"One person."

"Probably long gone by now. Either they killed him or they took him captive. Sasha's men don't know another alternative. You have to think about your survival now. Coming or not?"

Bridget could tell that if she went with this stranger he would keep her safe. In the darkness of what they had barely escaped, she longed for that security. Surely he could mean her no harm. But there was something more

Xsardis

133

important to consider. The survivors from the village would need help. "I'm going back."

The stranger paused a long time watching her go. With a groan he followed.

"What are you doing?" she inquired. Why was he coming? Her suspicions arose again.

"I'm going to help," he replied.

"Why?"

"For the same reason I helped you, which you still need to thank me for, by the way."

Bridget sighed and walked faster. "Maybe you should look out for yourself."

If only to irritate her, the stranger pressed on by her side. The whole town—what was left of it—had gathered in a circle on the outskirts. Children clung to their relatives. There was not a tear in the crowd; just alarm and disbelief. "Why now?" questioned one man bitterly.

"That's Remar for you!" shouted an older woman.

"He didn't do this. Sasha did," spoke a young man passionately.

"Who was taken?" Bridget asked, stepping into their gathering.

"Only a few," spoke the youth again. "When they found a visitor, they didn't want anyone else."

"But they burned my home!" yelled a new voice. The stranger glanced back to the village. A house at a distance was already destroyed amidst the orange flames. It was far enough not to be a risk to the other dwellings, so Ganetiv had given up trying to put out the fire.

"What was the visitor's name?" she breathed.

"Brooks," he replied, confirming the dread in her heart. "One man was shouting something about how guards shouldn't run away and how he was going to make an example of him to the rest of Maremoth."

"That was your friend?" the stranger asked Bridget. She nodded, then turned suddenly away from the group. They did not need her help, but Brooks did.

"Don't," he called, his long strides catching up with her.

"Don't what?" she questioned.

"Go after him. You don't know what you're getting yourself into."

"You don't know anything about me," she turned on him. "And I don't know anything about you. So why don't you leave me alone? Thank you for the rescue; now go away."

"At least let me tell you who I am," he kept on, not bothered in the least. He began walking again when she did. "I'm Drainan, cousin to Vaylynne and, more notably, someone who served with Rachel and Prince Evan—for however short a time. And you?"

"Bridget," she replied, surprised at his credentials. "Prisoner of Maremoth for fifteen years. I know how terrible the place is."

"And you really think you can get your friend out?"

"If I don't, Stewart will kill him."

"Why is this so important to you?"

"He helped me escape."

Xsardis 134

"Well alright then," he decided.

"Alright what?"

"I'm coming with you."

"No..." Bridget stumbled. "That's not a good idea." She went on with honesty, "I don't trust you."

"That's harsh, but it's okay," he shrugged. "I trust myself."

She rolled her eyes. "I don't need your help."

"I can tell by your stance that you can't hold a weapon, so yes, you do."

"Oh, the guards were anxious to teach me swordplay," she retorted with sarcasm. "I can figure out a rescue."

A set of running footsteps cut their argument short. A youth joined them, panting for air. "Are you really Vaylynne's cousin?"

"Yeah, why?" Drainan asked, staring at him.

"I'm Caleb. I used to be one of her cave leaders."

"Used to be?"

"I'm not much of a leader, but I'm determined. Brooks and I were friends. I want to help."

"We're going to Maremoth," Drainan cautioned.

"Good," he was surprised to hear himself saying—Seth's cocky influence. "Then I can prove myself."

Bridget got in Drainan's visual path, "Hey! No way. He's too young to come to Maremoth. I don't even want you along."

"He was a cave leader for Vaylynne. He'll be fine."

"He's a boy! I won't put him at risk."

"I'm putting myself at risk," Caleb re-put. He almost said 'please' but remembered Seth's words. "Let me come. You could use my help. After all, I trained under Seth."

Concession was inevitable, but Bridget fought back. "You can join us for the journey, but that's all."

"Of course," Drainan replied.

"Most definitely," Caleb added.

Drainan winked at Caleb and Caleb winked right back.

Chapter 17

Beatrice had boarded a boat and set off for Asandra, cursing Lotex as she went. As soon as she had landed, she had marched herself to the dwarf stronghold, grabbed her brother by the ear and dragged him into another room. The occupants scattered quickly. "Lotex, how could you?" she questioned.

"Don't you dare treat me like that!" he shouted, cheeks red with fury.

"When you're this stupid I'll do whatever I have to! How could you?"

"How could I what?" he asked gruffly, shoving her back and rubbing his hairy ear.

"You knew Seth was coming to Noric and what he was looking for. But you didn't stop him. Do you care more for the boy than for our gem?"

"You know I'd do anything to protect the gem."

"Would you?"

Lotex opened his mouth to explain but Beatrice kept on, "Prove it. I let Seth go on to give you the opportunity to do what you know what needs to be done. Either do it, or I'll do it for you."

The dwarf sighed heavily and nodded.

Evan led the group deep into the tunnels, his sword arm drooping with the steady weight of the blade and the pressure it sent through his aching shoulder. They stayed constantly alert for battle. Sasha could be anywhere, if they were even in the correct tunnels. One phrase from a riddle could be taken out of context so easily. *Where is Sasha?* They seemed to be missing something.

Behind him Katarina exclaimed with delight, "Max, what is this

Xsardis   136

stuff?"

"Kool-Aid," he acted like it was not that cool, but his smile revealed that he was glad to please Evan's sister.

"And it comes from that little pouch?"

Max nodded, "You had the last of it. I found that in my jeans pocket."

"Didn't bring your iPod this time?" Evan rolled his eyes. The wonders of Earth might be something new to Katarina, but they had long ago lost their shine to him.

"Sad, I know," Max's smile was mischievous as he took out his headphones.

"You brought it?"

Putting the headphones away, Max took a sip out of his own canteen, the water flavored with the first half of the Kool-Aid pouch. His sword was in its sheath. In the middle of the pack on these narrow tunnels, the youth felt no need to have the weapon out.

Vaylynne did not agree with him. Despite her position behind him, her blade was in her hand and her eyes were scouting. A scowl was on her face.

"What is wrong with you?" he asked with his usual brashness.

"This is serious, Max," was all she replied.

"Oh no…" Evan muttered as he rounded a corner.

Rachel pushed her way to his side. "Dead end."

Vaylynne could not see the sheer wall of which they spoke, but she barked, "We should have spread out. Now we've lost all this time!"

Seth moved past the others to stand nearest the high wall blocking their path. As he set a hand on it, Rachel shivered with deja vu. The look he bore was of the playful, imaginative little boy she had once known. He leaned himself against the wall.

Deciding to utilize this opportunity for rest, Katarina dropped to the ground and massaged her weary calf muscles. Rachel and Seth sat on opposite walls near the dead end, legs stretched out beside each other. "What are you thinking?" she tried to peek inside the creativity she noted in him.

"I'm not sure yet."

Reesthma distributed the fruit from her pack, knowing it would not last long jostled about in her bag. "Maybe we missed something," she said.

"There were no turns to miss," Vaylynne assured her. "We just came the wrong way."

The rebel leader studied Reesthma's nimble movements as she maneuvered about the small space. She had a balance none of Vaylynne's troops possessed. And though there was much of a child left in Reesthma, she had a perceptive mind. She would have made a great fighter under different circumstances.

Handing fruit to Seth and Rachel, Reesthma bent before them. "Seth, I heard you talked with Joppa. What did he say?"

"He made me promise to keep you safe."

Reesthma nodded, but her own intelligence was too great to believe that was all. "He told you something about my past, didn't he?" Seth made no movement but she knew it was true. "Do you know, Rachel?"

"I don't, Ree; but digging around in your past before its time…"

Xsardis 137

The girl cut her off, "Do you know how long I've read through history book after history book but have never known my own?"

"Someday Joppa will tell you; that's the way you should hear it," Seth answered, determined to keep the historian's confidence.

In silence, Reesthma returned to her seat by Vaylynne. Suddenly, Seth jumped to his feet and commanded, "Max! Give me your iPod."

"What?" the teenager protested.

"Give it to me," Seth ordered.

Max pulled the technology from his pocket and dropped it in Seth's hands, skeptically. Seth scanned through the music selection until he found a punk-rock song that started with a beautiful violin intro. Pulling the headphones out and dropping them to the ground, he turned the volume up all the way.

"Hey!" Max complained. "Careful."

Consumed by the imagination stirring within him, Seth pressed the iPod close to the stone wall before him. Rachel stood, unsure of what Seth was doing. Suddenly the ground trembled as the stone wall before them began to rise. The teens were all thrown against the walls or to the ground. When the trembling stopped the barrier was gone.

"How did you do that?" Rachel inquired of Seth.

"What just happened?" Vaylynne demanded.

"I'd read in the scrolls rumors that some dwarf had developed a way to use music as a sort of a key, but I didn't think it was real!" Reesthma exclaimed. She had kept her feet, but she rubbed her arm where she had fallen against the wall.

"Should we hurry?" Katarina asked, not at all in wonder of the imagination or the history. "Is it going to close on us again?"

"Not soon, but we should keep on," Seth responded.

The group pressed on. Max rewound his headphones carefully and sent a glare Seth's way at the use of his iPod. Seth spoke to Rachel after his thoughts had time settle. "I think I've been here before."

"With Lotex?"

"No…" he shook his head. "As Issym."

Rachel stared at him. "Do you remember what story?"

"I only know that whatever he buried here broke his heart. I feel this sickly mourning every step we take—like when I watched you guys die."

Not knowing how to answer him, Rachel fell silent. Hours passed as the group continued onwards, not wasting any time. Seth lost the air of imagination as he took on the familiar stance of a warrior.

Max was dragging his weary feet, waiting for someone to decide to stop. He had not expected Vaylynne to call the halt as they came to a larger section of the cave. "Do you *feel* that?" she looked to Seth.

He nodded, as if already aware, "Yes."

Vaylynne stared through the rest of the group as if they were not there. "I don't know what it is, but its staying just far enough behind us," she commented dryly.

Max was wary of Vaylynne's intent, but if she was right that something was following them it needed to be checked out. He was already picking up from her heavy nature that this girl did not have the kind of childhood that had offered laughter or relaxation or even safety. She had been pushed and pushed until whatever true freedom she had possessed had been driven from her. But her eagerness did not mean she was wrong.

"I don't intend to let it catch up with us on its own terms," Seth decided. He made to double back.

"No, Seth, let me go," Vaylynne blocked his path. "I'm dispensable. After your show with the music, it's clear you're not."

He weighed her motivations, then nodded. Vaylynne moved back into the tunnel, soon out of sight.

She wandered, taking her time and allowing herself to lock onto the presence. Quieting her breathing, she knew she was getting close. Vaylynne could see clear down the tunnel, but could distinguish no figure. Where was this phantom?

Edmund materialized before her. She recognized his appearance, having met him once before. Then he had worked with Seth and she against him; now things were reversed. "Speak quickly, shifter, before I strike you dead," she spoke confidently, but the sudden appearance of such a powerful creature was alarming even to her.

"You can't touch me," he replied coolly. He was pale, almost dark, and it had nothing to do with the cavern's lighting. "You've wandered too far from the stones."

"Is this a trap, then, or do you have something to say?"

"Where is she?" Seth was ready to go after Vaylynne. His pacing showed that.

Max answered from his slouched, almost asleep position. "Give it some more time."

Rachel and Reesthma were discussing history. Reesthma related other myths like the music key that might be true.

"If she goes too far back and the enemy is a shifter, she'll be powerless. She doesn't have any stones!" Seth spoke to the air more than to any one person. "Why didn't we give them to her?"

"Because we can't trust her with them," Prince Evan responded. "If she finds a weakness in the stones… or if she turns on some of our shifters…"

"There is no weakness in the armor," Seth returned, annoyed.

"You're so sure because you imagined it, but you also imagined the artifact that might give Sasha Xsardis for eternity!"

Seth put up a hand of deflection. "Don't."

Katarina smacked her brother's knee to get his attention. "Leave him alone."

"You his protector now?"

"Don't turn on me."

Xsardis   139

"Come on guys; cool down," Max spoke through closed eyes. He was trying to use this extra break time to catch up on a little sleep. The stress level wasn't helping.

Rachel moved to stand beside Seth and captured his attention with her train of thought, "Something doesn't make sense. Even with the barrier, following a tunnel shouldn't have taken hundreds of years like it took the other shifters *with* the scroll. Do you think we're in the wrong place?"

"I don't know," Seth answered, leaning against the cold stone wall. He jerked his body away from it. "It's wet."

What he wouldn't have given for a real drink of water! But they had not yet come upon any kind of stream in the tunnels and their supply was both dwindling and precious.

"I know it's on Noric. I remember that much," Rachel started to organize what few facts they had.

"I agree. After all, Lotex was hiding something," Seth added.

"So you recall being here as Issym?"

"Sometimes I feel like I know exactly where I am and what's coming around the bend. Other times it's like I've never been here."

The longer they spoke, the more the two turned to face each other. With animated gestures, Rachel continued, "We know that the island seems to have eternal youth."

"That trees grow back when they're cut down."

"That a rocky shore turns into a sandy one in months."

They were running their streams of thoughts together, pressing toward some ultimate conclusion that seemed far off, but reachable.

"What's to say other unusual things don't grow as well?" Seth pressed on.

"But rocks can't grow…" Max voiced. They ignored him.

"These aren't mine walls," Seth spoke clearly. "Look at them! They are sheer rock, almost hinting at a blue color."

"Valean rocks!" Rachel triumphed.

"What are Valean rocks?" Katarina broke her silence to ask.

They turned to her to answer, but Reesthma beat them to it. "They're found in the ocean. They look like rock, but they're more like plants. They grow and change as long as they have water. It can take many years before any noticeable growth occurs."

"They've been seen to change their shape entirely in a matter of seconds, right?" Rachel thought.

"But that only happens once in their lives," Reesthma replied. "And only a few Valean rocks have ever been found. None since the time of Issym."

Seth's eyes flashed. "We're walking caverns I believe Issym was responsible for."

"I don't understand," Katarina admitted.

"We imagined them to strive to grow into columns, or buildings, when they were placed together. They almost had architecture in mind for their growth," Seth tried to answer.

"So you're saying that these mines are made of Valean rocks?" Evan inquired.

Xsardis

140

"Yes," Rachel nodded.

"But they grow so slowly," Reesthma doubted. "And they only change once."

"But what if every time Noric returns to its youth, the Valean rocks can shift again?" Rachel suggested.

"These tunnels could be constantly changing. No one could find their way to the artifact," Seth finished.

"So if we keep searching," Evan gleaned, "we might not be able to find our way back. And who's to say we can even get to the artifact? Maybe the entire room where it was placed is cut off."

"Do we have to worry that right now Vaylynne is separated from us by a changing tunnel?" Max queried.

"We would have felt it if the caves had changed," Katarina knew. "But Evan's right about our journey."

"Not all the tunnels are Valean," Seth guessed. "Otherwise I couldn't have followed a path."

"There are probably just enough Valean tunnels to get us lost," Evan hoped he was wrong.

"So are you suggesting that we turn back?" Reesthma asked the prince.

Evan responded, "We can't do that."

"Yes, we can," Max replied. "If we can't find this artifact, there's no way Sasha will. Isn't it better if we leave well enough alone?"

"I agree with Max," Kat admitted. "While we're here, what's happening on Asandra? We always knew that Sasha might be wanting us to go after the artifact. This seems to confirm that theory."

Vaylynne's sudden return startled them. She had overheard enough of the conversation to know what was going on. "We can't give up," she voiced her own opinion. "Asandra has two armies—three if you count mine—defending it, but it has commissioned us to make sure that Sasha can't find the artifact. We have to keep going."

The length of her absence required Seth to stare into her eyes to make sure he knew who he saw. It would have been easy for a shifter to have replaced her, but the eyes were the one thing not even Sasha could mask. "What did you find?"

"A few rodents. Nothing more. I wanted to be sure so I went back a ways. I knew Max could use the break," she joked.

Seth kept staring, his eyes loudly warning her that it would be a mistake to lie to him. "Is that the truth?"

"It is," she lied. "Now tell me you guys aren't giving up."

Seth could feel the group's eyes as they looked to him to make the final decision. If they continued, they could get lost forever. If they did not, Sasha might gain access to the artifact. With a prayer, he answered, "We press on."

Chapter 18

Rachel saw Evan handing out the last of the fruits for breakfast. She also saw him hand his to Reesthma. "Why did you give her another?" Rachel whispered, dropping down beside Evan, their position slightly separated from the group.

"She seemed weary. Nothing like fruit to keep you from getting sick." Evan waited a moment, but drew her focus back, "Rachel, I know you don't want to hear this, but it is too dangerous to let Vaylynne stay with us. We all recognize that she's hiding something. Maybe yesterday's disappearance was occasion for a meeting with a partner or an army she has tracking us. I can't sit by and watch the danger grow."

"Look," she began, "I understand your point. I want to protect our friends and our mission as much as you do. But think about it. Katarina admits she's out of practice with her sword. Reesthma is to be kept out of battle. I'm an archer. I can barely use my skill down here. Max has some Xsardis training and what a Renaissance Faire nut could teach. When Sasha attacks, Seth can't stand alone. Vaylynne's blade offers him a capable ally."

"Only if she is our ally." He took a breath, "Can't I fight?"

Rachel leaned forward. "You're nursing your shoulder wound. How long do you think you can stand in battle?"

Knowing she was right did nothing to change his opinion.

"There's more bothering you than that," she perceived.

Though he was not sure if he should answer, Evan spoke, "I left here a prince. I came back a commoner."

"That's not true."

"Seth leads; Katarina leads; people follow. All I represent to the world is my father's mistakes."

"Evan…"

"Even you look to Seth. As prince of Asandra I could order us to leave Vaylynne behind, but would people follow? I don't think so. I don't know where my place is anymore."

Xsardis

142

"If you're so bitter, why don't you just challenge me to an old fashioned duel and be done with it?" Seth scoffed as he stood above them.

Rachel stood up and snapped, "You're not helping."

"If he has a problem with me, he can say it to my face. This behind-the-back spread of discord will get us all killed."

"Fine," Evan decided, rising. "You want to know what I think of you? I don't really like you."

"I don't really like you either," Seth shot back.

"You just hate that Rachel might take my side—opposite from you."

Seth formed a fist and let it go. "I'm not afraid of her opinions. I appreciate them; that's why we're close."

Rachel closed her eyes and wished she wasn't hearing what she was hearing. "Stop it. There will be time for teenage melodrama later. Not now. Now we need to focus on stopping Sasha. Duke it out later. Anything but the mission is a distraction we cannot afford."

"Rachel is right. We have bigger problems here than your egos," Vaylynne added. "Our rationed water won't hold out much longer. Every minute we move forward is a minute we'll have to retrace if we run out of supplies."

"There has to be water," Reesthma joined them. "Valean rocks need water to grow."

Kat agreed, "We've got to believe that. And we've got to keep going."

"We'll head back only if we absolutely have to," Seth determined.

"For once I agree," Evan voiced.

"Then let's move." Vaylynne strode forward; despite the limited sleep, long hours of walking, and the strange environment, she showed not the least signs of fatigue.

They were barely into their walk when they were forced to make a choice to go right or left. "Have a Bible answer for this too?" Vaylynne jibed.

"I think we go left," Seth answered, searching his memory.

"You sure?" Kat asked.

"As sure as I can be."

Throughout the morning Seth was forced to make several similar decisions. With each passing choice he grew in confidence as the memories came back to him.

The afternoon brought sounds of water. The thirsty teens thrust forward. Before them were two tunnels and they paused to study them. One stayed level. The other sloped downwards and clearly bore the sounds of a brook. A large hole marked the ground between them, with a few feet on either side. "I seem to remember that we should go right," he announced, "but let's find the stream first."

Seth skirted around to the left of the hole, stopping to look inside it. A steep drop led to a pit of water. Evan stepped beside him.

At that moment, the ground gave way underneath Seth and Evan's feet. They plummeted down before landing in the murky water. As they came to the surface of the pool, the young men noticed that the area was lit by the luminescence of the plant life below and the snail-like creatures clinging to the

Xsardis   143

lower wall. Both in vain attempted to scale the slimy sheets of rock before them.

"Are you guys okay?" Max shouted down from a careful distance. Vaylynne dared get even closer, her stature tense in case she needed to run.

"We're fine!" Seth yelled, kicking to stay afloat.

"We'd be better if you got some rope and got us out of here!" Evan called out.

Vaylynne slipped a coil from her bag and stretched it out.

"What's taking so long?" Seth questioned.

"The rope's too short," she shouted down to him. Taking Katarina's in her hands she tied them together quickly.

"Did you kick me?" Evan glared at Seth. "Is now really the time?"

"What are you talking about? I didn't touch you!" Seth promised. "Oh, so you retaliate by kicking back? That's real mature."

"I didn't touch you!" he emphasized. Evan rolled his eyes as he felt the movement again. "Come on!"

A sudden dread set over Seth as he realized that neither one of them was touching the other. He looked below him and let out a cry of surprise. A giant worm—twice his own size-- circled below them. "Oh, that's not good," he said in a low voice.

Evan's brief look into the water told him all he needed to know. In unison they hollered urgently for the rope, but it would take too long. Vaylynne was tying yet another coil to the others.

"What are we going to do?" Evan inquired.

"You looking to me now, prince? I thought you wanted me to stay silent."

"And I thought you were the man with the plan!" Evan reached for his weapon, "We can fight."

"I don't think we can fight that!"

The worm charged to the surface of the water, grappled onto Seth and drew him down. He desperately reached for his dagger or sword but could get to neither. The creature's body was wrapping around him and the pressure was squeezing the life out of him. In the odd blur of the water, he tried to find some avenue of escape, but the worm's grip was tight. Seth wasn't getting free.

His eyes fell shut. The worm writhed in pain. Feeling the lessening grip, Seth opened his eyes. Sword drawn, Evan was fighting. Again the prince slashed at the beast; it released a murky tan color and let Seth go. The prince pulled him to the surface. As soon as he was clear, Seth gulped at the air. They both knew that they did not have much time before the worm attacked again. "There's a tunnel down there," Seth informed him. "The worm won't fit."

From above, Rachel heard his words. If the tunnel did not lead quickly to an opening they would run out of oxygen. "Hold on for the rope!" she cried, getting closer to the hole.

"There isn't enough," Vaylynne spoke. The warrior's eyes showed her own understanding of the risks, but that there was no other way.

"Let's try it," the prince decided.

Taking steady breaths, they readied themselves. The two pushed off the wall and deep into the water. They slithered past the worm, dashing out of

the reach of its strike. The thing was wounded, but it was angry. If it got a hold of one of them, it wouldn't let go, no matter what.
They reached the tunnel. Seth went in first. Evan was quick to follow him. Seeing nothing in the darkness, they pushed forward. Almost a minute past. Evan's heart thumped in his ear as his lungs longed for oxygen. A light showed to their left. More shining plant life. They swam toward it and toward the surface it promised. They came to the top of the water and swallowed the air. "Land," Evan choked. They swam hard and fast toward the gray mass, pulled themselves onto it and collapsed.

Stewart threw his cloak on his bed and pulled off his boots, dumped out the rocks and put them back on. Before he had even been allowed to do such a basic thing after his long travels, he had had to bow to Sasha and listen to her rant on and on about something. He couldn't remember what. Stewart was tired of taking orders from her.
Sasha claimed to be the ultimate power, but rumors circulated that one called Kate was even more skilled. And perhaps Kate did not have the weakness Sasha showed. Not only did Sasha take pity on Edmund (something Kate did not do in the least), but she had little control any more of her own powers. Under strong emotion—Stewart knew from provoking such a thing—she would change form unexpectedly. Often, she would leave the palace for a flight through the air and was prone to changing her skin color to match her surroundings. She flinched at the croak of a frog. He took great pleasure in mimicking the noise. Sasha was weak, past her prime. It was time for a new ruler.
With a kingly posture, Stewart stepped out into the courtyard of Maremoth, where once prisoners had abounded. Without the slaves to grow their food and the wages that had been weeks in coming, the soldiers that were left were close to deserting. He had to hold onto his forces—either by bribery or by fear.
Bribery was so much easier, but he had little to offer. Fear? The idea sent a chill through him. If he punished a deserter, publicly and brutally, no one else would dare leaving. He simply needed the right one.
"Lord Stewart," a captain stepped beside him.
"Yes, Devar," Stewart replied, roused from his thoughts by the fierce warrior.
"All but my men think of deserting this place."
Annoyed and curious, Stewart asked, "Why not your men?"
"They fear me." Devar eyed Sasha's second-in-command before speaking again. "And I have promised them a dangerous thing. Something that I think lies in your mind as well."
"What is that?" Stewart turned to face him.

"To rid ourselves of Sasha. If you will lead, I and my men will commit ourselves to your cause," his tones were deep and low so as not to carry to the balcony where the empress was ever listening.

Stewart would not have risked seeking out Devar. His long service to Sasha and his competence for leadership had made him a formidable force in the shifter's dwindling army. Surprised that he was willing to turn, Stewart knew that Devar would offer much credibility to his plans if they worked together. "I think we can reach an agreement."

"Then perhaps it is time you capture the army's loyalties as I have captured my men's."

As Devar spoke, Stewart could not help feeling like he was being led somewhere in a carefully woven plan. Even so, he said, "Go on."

"Are you aware of a former guard by the name of Brooks? He helped a prisoner escape."

"I am," Stewart nodded.

"He's in our custody and coming here. Perhaps a public demonstration of your power is at hand."

"Hah!" Flibbert laughed. The dice rolled in his favor and he won the game. A disappointed human groaned. "Play again?"

The human shook his head and left. Flibbert scanned the camp for another challenger. He was with a wood-side platoon of twenty, meant only to keep Sasha from using the road. A few men were on guard; most were sleeping in the late night hours. Then a minotaur stomped toward him and took a seat on the stump opposite the frog. "I'll play," he spoke in gravelly tones.

"Joeyza," Flibbert greeted with more honest warmth than he had thought he could ever have for a minotaur. At first Flibbert had loathed the concept of bringing all those minotaurs along on an untried journey from Issym to Asandra. Joeyza, however, had proved the good intentions of himself and his kin. On the voyage, he had been the one to stop the sound sprite who had turned the crew on itself. The frog hated to admit it, but under her influence he and Galen probably would have killed each other, had not Joeyza stepped in.

"Are you ready to lose, Flibbert?" Joeyza questioned, all too glad to quash a frog's pride.

"I'm ready to win!"

As they began their game, Flibbert stayed focused, not willing to allow a minotaur to best a frog at anything, let alone child's play. Downwind, he was assaulted by the smell of Joeyza's matted fur. His onyx coat masked all but his deep eyes and his glinting horns in the shadows. Even for a minotaur, Joeyza had an impressive build.

During the first part of the game, Joeyza stayed still and silent. Flibbert fidgeted enough for the both of them. Despite the rivalry between their

Xsardis

146

two races, Joeyza counted Flibbert as a friend. Finally, Joeyza came to the point: "Really, Flibbert, why did Galen send you? Should we be expecting a fight?"

"We should always be expecting a fight!' Flibbert responded. He took his turn before answering further, in a much lower voice: "Galen suspects some new enemy is rising. I was sent to keep all our troops at the ready."

Joeyza completed his turn, mulling over the frog's words. "A new enemy is often an old enemy."

As the game progressed, Flibbert's focus dwindled. He sensed something dangerous in the air. Joeyza did not pick up the dice for his next roll. "That's a dark presence…" he spoke.

The minotaur rose to his hooves and picked up his ax from the ground beside him. Flibbert wrapped his fingers around the sword that lay in his lap and slowly stood. The feeling was like nothing he had ever sensed before—an inky darkness that sent a deep cold through him. One by one the men in the camp sensed the evil and woke. They did not need Joeyza's growl of "Attention!" to stand ready.

Flibbert's eyes looked toward the stormy clouds. A heavy wind had blown them in suddenly. The gusts threatened to knock even the frog's fine balance off. "Airsprites," Flibbert realized before anyone else, due to his close connection with the sprites of Issym.

"Dark sprites," Joeyza renamed. These were so unlike the beloved airsprites of their home continent.

Figures were dropping from the sky, but Flibbert and Joeyza locked their sights on only one. The woman's dark skirt was of clouds and her straight, white hair was pulled up. The wings on her arms retracted as she landed, but the sword in each hand remained. Her white, sinister eyes locked on Flibbert.

The frog charged toward her. She easily blocked his first attack and with her powerful arms sent him flying. The sprite moved to finish him. Joeyza ran toward the dark sprite with a shout almost inaudible in the din of battle. As she turned to face him, a gust of wind in her control knocked him back.

Flibbert hopped to his feet as rain began to pour from the sky. The thick sounds of battle surrounded him. In the little torchlight left, he discerned the woman's right sword blocking his blow while her left slid toward his legs. He hopped them out of danger just in time. Her eyes glowed with anger and hail poured from the heavens.

"God, help us," Joeyza prayed with sincerity as another sprite attacked him. The first of her powerful kicks drew blood.

Flibbert jumped behind the dark sprite he battled, but she spun and blocked. The force of her movement and the slickness of the ground drove him to his knees. Joeyza was at her back again. This time a bolt of lightning shot through his horn and he fell to the ground, unconscious. Flibbert lunged with his sword for her legs, but the blade went right through the mist. Her eyes flashed with brutality. Knowing that he was at her mercy, Flibbert's last thoughts were for the others in the camp. *If a minotaur and I cannot defeat one sprite, how will anyone survive?*

The dark sprite before him brought her weapon down on his head.

Chapter 19

From above the watery death pit, the five teens listened for sounds of Seth and Evan, but none came. "They must have gone into the channel," Katarina spoke to keep herself sane. Her brother…

Rachel slung her bag over her shoulder and headed down the sloping path.

"Wait," though Vaylynne spoke softly, her command stopped Rachel. The warrior threw down the useless rope and moved to Rachel's side. "What do you think you're going to accomplish?"

"They fell down; this tunnel leads down. If they're injured or lost, I've got to help them," Rachel answered with a calm in her eyes.

"*If*," Vaylynne emphasized. "And it's very doubtful they are alive. Seth told us to go right. He and Evan would have prioritized the mission." The rebel-leader would not lecture her on how important it was; Rachel knew that.

"I won't give up on Seth again," Rachel replied. "But we can't afford to waste the time searching. We'll have to split up."

"And what if the Valean rock separates us?" Reesthma questioned.

Katarina hardened with skills learned in six months of acting strong. Her worries about Evan and Seth were put on hold. She spoke clearly and with the authority she possessed. "Even in such vital times, we must hold to the right course of action. That is to never leave a man behind. Rachel, you're right to go after them. I will go the other way."

Rachel's respect for the princess grew exponentially in that moment. She knew that with all her heart Katarina wanted to find her brother, but she chose to bear the burden of her position and stay behind.

Max moved to stand next to Rachel. "I'm going to get them back."

"Reesthma and Vaylynne will come with me," Katarina decided. "We'll fill our canteens, then head back here. Let's move."

Rallied by her attitude, the group followed her instructions. The water skins brimming, Max caught the princess' elbow as she turned to follow Reesthma and Vaylynne down the other tunnel. He could have asked her if she was going to be okay or encouraged her with some bold speech, but he knew that she needed to focus, so he moved to the point. "The mission is still paramount—to us both. If Vaylynne gets in your way…"

"You don't have to tell me what to do," she returned confidently.

"Whatever happens, destroy that artifact."

"I'll make sure it happens. And Max?"

He stopped and looked back at her.

"Despite my speech, if it comes to a choice between Evan and Seth and the artifact…"

"You don't have to tell me what to do," he spoke with solemnity.

Katarina made to catch up with Vaylynne and Reesthma with the unhappy knowledge that without Seth's guidance, if they came to a turn, they would have to guess which direction to go. Long hours they marched, Katarina and Vaylynne's determination pushing them on and Reesthma's agile body barely struggling.

Only when they stopped did Katarina speak in tones she was certain Reesthma could not distinguish. "You need to understand something."

Vaylynne knew a threat was coming. "What's that?" she mocked the princess with her eyes.

"I may not be as talented a fighter as Seth. I may not have the imagination of Rachel. And I may have played submissive princess in front of the others. But know this: I will not put Xsardis or Reesthma in danger for *any* reason. If you try anything you will see a new Katarina—and that's a promise."

"I applaud you Princess. Your little threat was actually intimidating."

Kat's eyes narrowed; her voice stayed low, "I am not like the others. They might not carry it through, but I will."

Vaylynne nodded. "Fair enough. I am warned."

Still shivering from their soaking, Seth and Evan were determined to find a way back to their fellows. Seth knew he should have been grateful to have escaped the water, but all he felt was grumpiness. He was covered in the murky liquid, separated from the others, and wasting precious time.

"How big is this place?" Evan wondered as he realized that they were in a network of caverns below the ones they had just walked through. "Certainly Issym must have had help in carving it."

"I think there are more important things to worry about," Seth returned.

Evan glared. Walking to the wall, he pulled off a glowing snail. It was one of many lighting the room. With their torches lost in the fall, the snails might be their only choice for illumination.

Seth followed his example. The creature had a tough exterior and a slimy body, but it let off a considerable amount of light. Together, the teens walked down the only path left to them. Narrow ground; high, cold walls. When they came to their first choice Seth, once again, directed, "We go left."

Evan stared down the tunnel. "How can you possibly know that? You're just guessing."

"Do you really want to imply that I'm a liar right now?"

"A show-off."

"And the only person on Xsardis who knows how to find the artifact," Seth pointed out. "You're welcome to go right. I'm following my memory."

Evan hesitated, feeling the confrontation brewing with Seth, and then joined him.

Bound and pulled along by the rough commands of his captors, Brooks recognized now that it had been foolish to leave the safety of Saphree. Of course Sasha would take pleasure in making an example of one who had helped the first prisoner escape. When he arrived at Maremoth, he would count the days to whatever glorious execution she and her current minion would plan for him.

Though he might have been justified in regretting ever helping Bridget, Brooks didn't regret it. If given the opportunity, he would aid her again without hesitation.

Bridget had proved herself to be more than a blind believer in her God. With a constant smile and a true trust, she had survived both prison and the whirlpool that should have ended their lives as they made their escape from Maremoth in a boat. When they had woken up on Issym, Brooks had begun to wonder if maybe her faith was not misplaced. And the unnamable void in his life, something had filled for her.

A pang of unexpected sadness filled his heart as he recognized that he would never have another chance to ask her what had filled that hole. For so long he had cared for no one but himself, but now he counted Bridget a true friend. Was she angry at him for abandoning her to Saphree? Could she see why he had had to leave?

None of that matters now, he knew. Before long he would be hung in Maremoth—if Sasha was merciful.

Despite the rush his escorts possessed to get him back to Maremoth, they were forced to take a long route back to the fortress. It seemed that Sasha had more enemies than her army knew what to do with.

Brooks caught snatches of conversations about fantastical creatures. He did not doubt that their origins were the creatures of Issym, who, for all their wonder, were nothing like the tales told. King Galen and King Remar's forces seemed to have spread themselves out effectively and quickly. Over every bush, Brooks' guards feared they would spot their mighty forces.

They would have made better time if Brooks had been their only prisoner, but he was one of many. The large group would be easily spotted. Careful time was spent to ensure this did not occur.

At least, even if he did die, Asandra would survive. He believed that without doubt until he heard the soldiers whispering about some strange new enemy from the skies. Their descriptions were useless, but the fear was evident. Some said they served Sasha. Others thought they had no master.

Like you can do anything about them, Brooks reminded himself. He was a prisoner now and would be until he died. There was no point in regret or sorrow. There was no hope. There was no one coming for him. He just had to accept it.

"What's the plan? To knock on the front gate?" Drainan asked, admittedly struggling to keep up with Bridget's pace. At this rate they would get to Maremoth earlier than expected. He could tell by the way her ankle would twist or she would wince that the fast gait was hurting her, but she showed no signs of slowing.

"Brooks defied Maremoth," Bridget answered, panting at the top of a hill and waiting for Drainan and Caleb to catch up. "From what I gleaned of Stewart, his vengeance on the traitor will be hard and swift. We have to save Brooks before that."

Reaching her side, he stopped until she told him more. "But how?"

Her eyes flicked away as if she would not answer, but Bridget declared, "You're going to lead me into Maremoth as a prisoner."

"I'm what?" Drainan's brain jumped as she started down the hill. He looked back at Caleb in surprise. Who was this woman? "Wasn't getting you out of Maremoth what Brooks risked himself to do?"

Walking backwards, she said, "Once inside, I know enough to get us out."

Only after shouting, "You're crazy!" did he follow.

When he caught up to her again, Drainan protested, "It took you fifteen years and a guard's help to get out the first time. What do you really think you can accomplish? Besides getting yourself captured and hung next to him?"

"Look," she spun on her heel, "you don't have to come. You don't have to try. But I'm going to. I *wouldn't* leave Maremoth before. I knew the weaknesses and Brooks was not the first guard to offer to help me. But I also knew the punishment the other prisoners would have received for my leaving.

"Now they're safe and I'm ready to do what must be done. If you want to help, then come and trust me. If not, leave me alone!"

Drainan gave up trying to argue with her. He waited for Caleb to run down the hill and held onto the lad's arm before he could continue. "When I encouraged you to come with us, I didn't realize how crazy she was. Are you sure you want to go all the way?"

Caleb wasn't sure. Not at all. He had barely known Brooks a few days, but he had liked him. The two had been planning on traveling together until they found either a place to call home or somewhere they were meant to serve.

It was not that Caleb was afraid of Maremoth or lacked the resolve to follow through. He worried that he would do more harm than good to Drainan and Bridget. He had never done anything right in his life. Not entirely certain he could risk Brooks' life on whatever part he would play in his rescue, Caleb wondered if he should turn back.

Brooks had been the first person to accept Caleb for who he chose to be and see him for what he longed to be. Not a bumbling fool, not a hero, but someone trying with all his breath to do what was right in a very turbulent time. Brooks had encouraged him not just to find some place to blend in, but a place to serve. Together, he had believed they would find that place. And now Brooks was in danger and Caleb refused to put him at greater risk. *Brooks would have trusted me to try.*

"What do you think?" Drainan pressed.

Caleb looked back to him. "I'm coming. But do me a favor."

"Tell me what it is first."

"Teach me to fight. I only had a few lessons with Seth."

"That we can handle. If Bridget ever slows down, that is."

"My lord, something terrible has happened," a man ran into Galen's room.

The high king rose quickly on his booted feet. His premonition of danger had become reality. "What?"

Rushing to a makeshift infirmary tent, he found Flibbert wildly angry and shoving fairy doctors toward a minotaur. Galen squinted at the figure and recognized Joeyza's massive profile. As soon as Flibbert saw the king, he demanded, "Won't you tell them I'm fine? Joeyza needs their help, not me!"

Galen put a hand on the nearest healing-fairy's shoulder and nodded. The man moved to the minotaur's side. Only when the fairies had cleared away from Flibbert did Galen realize how injured the frog was. His posture was slumped, his movements were jerky, his pupils were dilated, his green skin was lighter than normal. Cuts and bruises covered him.

Flibbert had seen enough battle in his days that little affected him visibly, but whatever he had seen on the last battlefield was now marking his eyes. The frog had lost his prideful arrogance. He was muttering something, shaking his head back and forth.

At that moment Flibbert did not need sympathy or comfort. He

Xsardis   152

needed an authority figure to debrief him. Only then would he be able to rest. "Tell me what's happened."

The command from his superior snapped the frog back to reality. "It was a normal, quiet night. Then the sky grew dark; the wind changed; and the next thing we knew we were surrounded by dark sprites. They were mightier than any warrior I have ever seen. One alone brought both Joeyza and I down, Galen! They called wind and rain and with their own unshakable power, they decimated us. We never stood a chance. Only Joeyza and I made it back alive."

Carefully processing the information, Galen tried to glean what threat had descended upon Xsardis. He doubted that hours of conversing with Flibbert would truly let him understand the danger. What was so horrifying that it had shaken the brave warrior frog?

The king's eyes drifted through the healing fairies to their motionless patient on the table. "You dragged Joeyza here?"

"He saved my life. I could not leave him."

Ordering a fairy of the blue back over, Galen exhorted Flibbert, "Let the medic do his work, then come join me in the palace. We will need your knowledge and your full strength to plan."

Flibbert nodded and lay back down on the bed. Galen started out of the tent. "Galen," the frog called. His friend stopped and looked back. "There is no defending against them. And they'll be back. We were just the beginning."

Chapter 20

"Max, look," Rachel whispered in the mysteriousness of what she saw. It was the first time they had stopped that day. Four hours rest last night had been as long as they could keep themselves still. Lost friends offered a strange invigoration. They pushed themselves because they knew they could and pulled on each other's energy when their own ran low.

"Such strange markings," Max replied, stepping beside her and bringing the torchlight closer to the wall. The rocky surface held a few carefully painted runes.

"I've never seen runes on Xsardis," admitted Rachel. "I don't think I even imagined them."

Max readjusted his bag. His muscles were stiff. "The runes wouldn't have been painted on Valean rocks. These walls must have been carved, like the path that Seth was trying to follow. Maybe we're on the right track after all."

"Have you noticed that the air has changed? It's getting mustier."

"Well, we've clearly been heading down."

Having spared the few moments for talking, the teens began their fast clip again. Max glanced at Rachel as he felt some wave of emotion sweep over her. "What's wrong?"

"It's like I forgot something about Asandra," she answered him though she knew it would not make sense. "Like I left them to fight some unknown variable."

"Don't we have enough of our own unknown variables to worry about?"

Rachel smiled. "You're right."

They fell silent as they conserved their energy. Max's thoughts drifted back to the runes. They captivated more and more of his thoughts as they pressed on. It was nearing the time for their morning rest when Max saw another set of runes. With growing intensity they consumed his mind and he ceased walking.

Rachel immediately noticed that the steady rhythm of his feet was gone and turned to see him staring dumfounded at the wall. His body leaned towards the runes, the torch dropping from his hands. "Max, come on," she pressed. He didn't react. "Maybe we *should* take a break."

Max's ears heard her words but his mouth ignored them. His mind flashed, giving him a small glimpse of other runes. He had seen them before. His heart beat wildly.

Flickers of a scene began to play in his mind's movie theater. With each new development his body twitched. At first, all he saw was darkness and he felt numbness. It was as if his mind was disconnected from his body. He distinguished the shape of a tunnel, dark and dusty. Voices filled his ears. They were yelling. He looked down at his hands as he felt a heavy, rough weight in them.

In reality, Max looked down at his hands; they were shaking.

The medallion and the key! The medallion was illuminated with its various runes that suddenly glowed brilliantly. He had used the medallion to cause the earthquake on Issym in order to save… "Arvin!" he shouted in present time as he fell with his back against the wall.

Max fought to regain control. Was the vision of Arvin real, or Rachel's arms gripping him? Max so longed for Arvin's presence to be true, but he was fading. Rachel was shouting, "Snap out of it!"

Reaching for his canteen with hands that felt swollen, Max could not bring it to his lips. Rachel helped him and the drink fell down his burning throat. "What's happening?" he locked onto her for long enough to ask.

Then Max's eyes rolled back into his head and he crumpled to the ground.

"Which way?" Evan inquired. The snails they had brought for light grew more brightly the farther they went from the others of their kind. Both clung to the bags of Seth and Evan, offering a colorful glow to the wet walls.

"They're both Valean detours," Seth replied unhappily.

"Then I suppose it doesn't matter." The prince moved to go left.

"Wait. The air is lighter to the right. And we know we have to go up."

Evan growled. Seth would have said the opposite if Evan had wanted to go right. He was sick of bantering around the problem. There were no referees now to keep them from duking it out. "Did it ever occur to you that *you* don't need to find the others? The others will find you."

"What?" Seth stopped, equally weary of the game.

"If you would let them, the others would lead. And succeed! I know Rachel. She'll find us."

"You know her, huh?" Seth's anger rose. "Just how well?"

"Better than you, apparently. Rachel knows we went down. She's coming down. She'll find us."

Seth got in his face. "Don't make the mistake of thinking you understand me. I trust Rachel more than anyone to find us. I believe she will. But I'm not going to sit around waiting for her to rescue me. We need to move fast. There *is* a war going on."

"Like I don't know that? I have thought of nothing but my country since birth!"

"You have thought about nothing save *controlling* your country since birth."

"So that's it!" Evan triumphed. "You don't want me to be king."

"I want you to stop getting in my way while I try to get you on the throne! Your people want my help and I'm giving it to them." Seth kept walking.

Evan was not about to give up now. "I need to know, Seth."

"Know what?"

"You're leading Asandra right now. Fine. I can take a secondary role. But when this is over are you going to keep your dominating hands on my country, or are you going to back off and let me do my job?"

"Can you do it?" Seth challenged.

"That's not up to you to decide."

"You needed me to step in before. You came to Earth seeking my help."

The prince let out a breath and the anger with it. He spoke more gently, but just as boldly, "I appreciate what you did for Katarina and Asandra while I was gone. Now, I'm back. I'm willing to follow if you are willing to stay and lead. And I'm willing to lead if you are willing follow and leave. But if you won't make the decision, I can't do either one."

Seth shook his head. "I can't believe we're wasting valuable time on this."

"You better think about it, because sooner rather than later we're all going to need that decision."

"What is she doing?" Reesthma asked in muffled tones to Kat as they sat tucked in the corner of a wider corridor of the tunnels.

Eyes closed and breathing steady, Vaylynne performed a series of movements that had the precision of a dance but the power of a fatal attack.

"I think she's honing her skills," Katarina answered.

Some part of the princess ached for the abilities this woman possessed. They had been born out of years of dedication. She once might have followed in a warrior's steps, but not now. Now she was the ever-polite and diplomatic princess.

"How does that help?" Reesthma wanted to know, her hands resting gently on her knees.

"Watch," Katarina mouthed. With a quietness that permitted not a sound, she stood and made her way to Vaylynne's side. She moved to punch the warrior, but Vaylynne caught her fist in midair. Her eyes shot open and the rush of battle filled them until Vaylynne forced herself to back off.

"That was incredible!" Reesthma clapped.

"Just training. Nothing incredible about it. You could do it too," the warrior closed her eyes once more.

"I could?" Reesthma whispered, as if realizing the possibility for the first time in her life. She stepped forward with a new hope. "Do you mean it?"

Surveying her, Vaylynne knew the answer. Reesthma was sharp, surefooted, and completely in control at all times. If she would allow the smile to fall from her face she might even scare her enemies. The strong figure; the graceful power. Vaylynne replied, "Yes; you have the build and the energy."

"Teach me," Reesthma decided eagerly.

An apprentice. The thought excited Vaylynne. For a long time she had been searching for such a blank canvas. None of her troops had been suitable candidates, but Reesthma would make a fine warrior.

There would be difficulties. Clearly and for some unknown reason, the girl had been shielded from learning how to fight. Even if Katarina would permit the battle training, she would never allow Vaylynne to instruct the girl's mind. Without that teaching, Reesthma could never truly be her apprentice. *I like a challenge,* Vaylynne reminded herself. She spoke, "Alright. I'll teach you."

"Oh no," Katarina knew too well what Seth had promised Joppa and suspected the rebel's motives. "That's not going to happen."

"That you can't learn with your flopping movements is no reason for you should deprive the girl," snipped Vaylynne unfairly. Katarina, too, had a form of grace.

"Come on, Kat!" Reesthma burst. "Would Joppa have me so far from battle that I cannot defend myself? We've already lost four members of our party. I need to be able to stay alive!"

Kat recognized that once Reesthma began her training there would be no stopping her. She would have a constant thirst to learn more. But her point was undisputable.

"I'm not the one who will have to explain it to Joppa," Vaylynne bowed to Kat's authority because she knew it was the best way to manipulate the princess.

"*I* will explain it to Joppa," Reesthma responded.

"We don't have much time to waste on training," Kat dashed Reesthma's hopes before adding, "...so made it quick."

Xsardis   157

"We'll have to rely on what charity is offered us," Bridget sighed.

Unable to find the manna that grew by the water or any other source of food, they had run out of supplies. It seemed that despite Sasha's withdrawal, Asandra was still short of food and had picked over the abundant manna too frequently.

The three companions had made their way to a town inside a small wooden fortress. As they approached, they saw that the gates were sung wide open. Even from the distance it was evident that some kind of commotion was developing inside.

"Can we risk going in?" Caleb inquired.

When Drainan heard the shouts of battle, he glanced at Bridget and Caleb. "Stay here."

"Where are you going?" Caleb tried to stop him, but Drainan was racing to the gates.

Ducking behind a post, Drainan judged the condition of the fight. A dozen young men and women battled angry villagers. Children huddled in the windows watching. The attackers had poor weapons but fine skills. It would not end well. Drainan knew who these youths were and he knew he had to act.

"Ah!" he yelled, distracting an older boy before he could do any harm to the mother bearing a stick. A swift blow with the butt of his sword to the kid's head sent him to the ground. Locating the young warriors' leader, Drainan ran straight for him.

The youth was barely sixteen, but he smiled when he saw the fight coming his way, relishing battle. Drainan determined to teach him a lesson he would not soon forget.

The leader attacked first, throwing his full weight into a lunge. Drainan easily side-stepped and brought his blade down on his opponent's. The youth tipped, but regained his footing. Wildly he called as he charged the man twice his age. Drainan parried several times before slicing the boy on his right arm, knocking his sword out of the way, and grabbing him by his shirt collar. "You are going to call off this attack right now and then tell me who gave you orders to harm a helpless village!"

"And who are you to say that?" the boy protested with all that was left of his cockiness.

"Drainan, Vaylynne's cousin."

The color fled from his face as Drainan dropped him to the ground. "Stop!" he ordered his troops. "Stop right now!"

"Call them to you," Drainan directed.

The youths gathered around their fallen commander, and the townspeople surrounded them. Bridget and Caleb joined the crowd. Drainan kept his sword point at the sixteen-year-old's neck. "Tell me who you are."

"Jugan," he said, glad that Drainan allowed him to stand and regain some of his honor. "I command one of Vaylynne's caves. She's been missing; so we did what we had to do to keep her name alive."

"You think Vaylynne would want you to attack the people she is trying to liberate?" Drainan snarled. How could his cousin both recruit kids so young and then leave them on their own?

As Drainan's sword moved closer to him, the young rebel saw the flaw in his logic. "No."

"No," Drainan repeated. "But you did it anyway. And now these good people have been hurt." He looked around him. "Anyone seriously injured?"

A man stepped forward, the self-appointed spokesperson for the town. "No. We owe you our health."

"That's good for you," he spoke to the youth. "Listen carefully to what you're going to do. First, publicly apologize to these people. Then you will spend the next few days working for free for this town. And after that you are going to make it the highest priority of your cave to keep this place safe. You will repair the name of Vaylynne. Understood?"

It was not simply his cousin's name; it was his.

"Yes," Jugan sheepishly replied. All bloodlust had evaporated.

"What?" he barked.

"Yes, Sir."

The spokesperson took over the instructions from there as he put the youths to work. Drainan marched toward Bridget and Caleb, ears red with frustration. "I warned Vaylynne that anarchy would follow her rebellion. She wouldn't listen."

A grateful family pulled the three inside their house for lunch and packed them enough food for many days. While Drainan and Bridget conversed with them, Caleb stayed in the realm of his own thoughts. He was beginning to realize that a true leader did not look like Vaylynne, but like Drainan. Caleb was even more glad to be trained by him.

From his seat on the steps of the castle of Saphree, Galen watched the way men and women from Asandra interacted with their king. On the voyage from Issym, Bridget and Brooks had been honest about how the country had viewed Remar. They had cautioned that the king was little-respected. Yet this was not what Galen perceived.

Flute to his lips, Galen recognized that the people of Asandra related to King Remar as if he was a new man. Perhaps he was. Even so, Galen was glad Remar recognized that he did not have a gift for battle strategy. He left the planning mostly to The Brothers and those Galen trusted.

Jeff had been in Illen when Flibbert and Joeyza had returned to Saphree. Immediately, Sphen had sent for him but had not held back his planning with Elimilech and Flibbert.

Galen was grateful Joeyza would live, but the joy did not seem to penetrate his heart—despite the cheery tune he was playing. The dark sprites were a formidable enemy, but they warned of a greater danger: deceit in Issym's camp. Already tension between the fairies and the shifters was ratcheting. Now it seemed the airsprites had kept some part of their history from Galen and even Flibbert. The king mulled over how to confront their

Xsardis   159

young queen Danielle. Maybe she had not known about the dark sprites, but Galen doubted that was true.

"What I have to say today I do not relish," Kate spoke as she alighted the steps and sat beside him.

The busy stairway was as private a place to talk as any. The multitude of noises would obscure their voices. Galen set his flute down on his lap and waited for Kate to say more.

"The dark sprites frighten both our troops and the troops of Asandra. In the time of crisis people search for a strong leader—the kind you were when you led a makeshift army up Mt. Smolden with your unstoppable passion. This is the reason we made you our king."

"What are you asking of me, Kate?"

"Though you were once that leader, now you dance around Remar as if he was made of glass. His recent decisions should engender more respect from his people, but he seems to be a relic of a time that nobody wants to remember. If you do not lead until Remar's children and Seth and Rachel return, the army will disintegrate in this grave time. You must bear both countries for a short while."

"We did not come here to control the war. We came to help."

"And we're going to lose!" she spoke forcefully. "It seems that the creatures and gifts and curses of Asandra are a mystery even to those who have lived here. Look in these people's eyes, Galen. Don't you see the defeat there? They are not strong enough for the decimation I know Sasha is planning."

"Can't you hunt her down, Kate? Can't you stop her?" Galen hoped. He trusted in both her wisdom and her abilities.

"If I could have I would have put a stop to this a long time ago."

"What is it that you want me to do?" he asked, returning to their first subject.

"Don't overexert your power, but you must lead where Remar stays silent. Both armies need you now."

"Asandra has Jeff and Sphen."

"And in battle, few rally men in the same way. But in the daily grind, it is your persistent hope that keeps the troops believing they'll make it home."

"What if I can't bring them home?"

Xsardis

Chapter 21

"If only we had Max's music contraption," Reesthma sighed, staring at the dead-end room they were about to enter. Its floor was made of hand-laid stones.

"I doubt the builders of this maze would have bothered with the same trick twice," Katarina answered. Being the sole watcher of Vaylynne was more wearying than she could have expected.

"Seth said we should have come this way," Vaylynne insisted. "There must be something we're missing."

They swept the room with their eyes. Bricks scattered the floor. Someone had built up a pile in a kind of tower. The bricks reached halfway to an open space in the ceiling. Invigorated by the sight, Vaylynne put her sword in its hilt and pulled a brick into her hands. "Let's finish this tower."

Katarina moved to help her, but hesitated. "Why didn't somebody else complete it?" she questioned.

"Maybe they were taller than we are. I don't know!" Vaylynne returned.

The pieces were coming together in the princess' mind. She called, "Wait! Stop!"

"What?" Vaylynne turned, holding the brick above the pile. "We can do this; no problem. We can still finish our mission. We can save Asandra!"

"The only instruction we had was to follow hard the Word," Katarina began to explain.

"This reminds you of the Tower of Babel, doesn't it?" Reesthma asked. "The people who tried to build that were scattered because of their pride."

Seeing Katarina's agreement with the girl's words, Vaylynne returned, "We don't have time for this. It's no wonder your parents lost their throne. You depend more upon your legends than on common sense!"

The princess boiled but checked herself. "Come on, Ree. We're going back."

The two started to move away but Vaylynne went on unhindered. She placed the large brick on the pile.
Instantly the ground began to tremble. Dust fell from the ceiling. The stones beneath them cracked and fell. Katarina and Reesthma ran for the exit. Vaylynne tried to catch up. The floor gave loose before her feet and she was sucked into the pit. Katarina turned back, costing herself a precious second. She too fell. Reesthma screamed for them before being pulled into the opening chasm herself.

Max's eyes flicked open and he realized how badly his head hurt. He patted the damp cave floor beside him and smelled the soggy air. He groaned. Whoever said that adventure was fun deserved to be shot.
He sat up and spoke to Rachel. "How long was I out?"
"A couple of hours." The relief in her eyes was evident but she joked nonchalantly, "If you wanted to rest, there were easier ways to tell me."
He squinted at the runes on the walls and felt none of the strange sensations of before. Head throbbing, Max struggled to his feet, "I think I'd feel better if we got out of here."
"Yeah, we should get you back to the surface."
"No," he focused on her. "I don't want to turn around. What if Seth and Evan need us? I'm fine!"
She could have fought with him, but she knew she would lose. They began a slow walk. Rachel waited for Max to regain his clarity before asking him, "What happened back there?"
"Honestly, Rachel, I don't know," he answered.
"It was as if you were seeing something…" she probed.
Max's eyes flicked to the left as they always did when he was thinking more than he was saying. "What did you see?" she pressed.
"It was like I was back on Issym, in the underground. Arvin was in front of me and I was holding the medallion. I didn't know which perception was real and which one was false. Now I have this strange feeling, like we're getting close to the artifact."
"You can't know that…" Rachel was unsure what she was hearing.
After waiting a moment, Max went on, "The medallion was marked with the runes we saw on the wall."
"Are you sure you want to go on?"
"Why wouldn't I? It was just some fluke memory," he brushed it off.
"With acena I kept pushing forward and it was almost too late by the time I stopped," she glanced at the fairy dust around her neck as she spoke. If not for that gift she would have died, but she had nothing to offer Max if he lost consciousness again. "If you go on…"
"I know the risks," he replied. "But Kat and Reesthma took the risk

of traveling with Vaylynne so that we could find Seth and Evan. I don't want to let them down."

The day passed, according to Max's watch—the only real way to tell time in the cavern. Already, after only a few days, they longed for sunshine and fresh air. They enjoyed a meager amount of food, saving all that they could. Rachel wanted to stop early that night for Max's sake, but he insisted that they push on.

For the next two days, Rachel had to force Max to stop. With each passing moment he felt that they were drawing closer to the artifact and the excitement pushed him to go faster and faster. She almost forgot about him passing out as he grew stronger than ever.

Finally he stopped of his own accord as they came into a wide tunnel with ten distinct passageways leading off before them. "This doesn't bode well for us," Max muttered.

"No, it doesn't," Rachel shook her head.

Above each passage was a number accompanied by a single word: plague.

Seth and Evan's path was blocked by large roots that grew thicker as they continued. The two walked as far apart as they could, each cutting away their own barricades with their swords. Their glowing snails provided the only light they had in the form of an eerie glow and they were so turned around that not even Seth could boast that he knew where they were going.

Their progress had slowed as each teen grew weaker. Their food had been ruined in their drop into the murky pit. Evan had lost track of how long it had been since he had eaten and how long they had been walking. At least streams of water were abundant.

As Seth tried to cut off a thick root, Evan got ahead of him. The young man's form was masked by the roots. Not worried in the empty tunnels, Seth kept cutting steadily to clear his path.

"You'll want to come look at this," Evan's voice called back.

Seth abandoned the massive root and went through the hole that Evan had already formed. Soon he was free of the roots and was standing before a passageway marked with the number two and the word *plague*. "That's not good…" Seth murmured. The hole looked dark and foreboding. The snails' small glow offered little to dent the cavernous darkness.

"We could backtrack," Evan commented. "Maybe find a safer route."

"It's possible the writing is just to scare us off. We won't make it much longer if we don't find some food and I don't think we have time to backtrack."

"We'll have to risk it." Evan extended his hand, "Let's call a truce for the time being."

Seth shook it. They plunged into the darkness.

"Empress, your dark sprites have sent terror throughout Asandra. They have attacked and destroyed two outposts of Issym's army already. Your fame spreads throughout the land once more." Stewart was coating her with flattery, but each word he spoke left a bitter taste in his mouth. He had to make her feel confident so that she would leave.

Something had changed in Sasha. She was supposed to be growing weaker, losing control of Asandra as she had been for months. Instead, she was regaining both her power over the continent and her power over herself. He could not afford to have the strong empress leading. His recent alliance with Devar against her would find its way to her ears if she stayed.

Thankfully, Stewart still knew how to make her jealous rage erupt. The sly smile she wore across her lips would soon be gone. He opened his mouth and coaxed her, "It is just a pity that people say you trusted Edmund to do your job for you. It makes you look weak."

"Whelp!" Sasha cried, rising from her chair and growing several feet. "How dare you?"

"I have never even thought such a thing," he bowed. "But others do…"

"Silence them, then!" the shifter shouted.

"I fear only that Edmund deceives us," Stewart replied. "How easy it would be for him to turn back to Seth's side! He has proven to be a traitor."

Sasha descended her steps, having grown to the ceiling's limits. Stewart doubted that she noticed. He stayed low, recognizing that he had put her in a volatile mood. There was no telling what she would do. Stewart kept spinning his web, "I have tried to silence the ignorant fools who dare insult the Empress of Asandra, but I am simply an ordinary human. It would take a remarkable show of force to truly silence them."

"My dark sprites are force enough," she assured. "Their power will soon finish all those who dare oppose me. As for Edmund… have we heard from him since he left for Noric?"

"No, Empress," Stewart replied, glancing up. She was shrinking again, gaining control.

"Then I shall see to it that he has not betrayed me. While I am gone, you will ensure that all continues according to my plan. Do not make the mistake that your predecessor did."

Stewart waited until she had left the room to allow the smile to form on his face. He could taste the power. He was in sole command of Maremoth.

His gloating was cut short as Sasha returned. With a whimsical voice she threatened, "Oh and Stewart, try to stay away from the dark sprites. Without my protection they would easily and happily destroy you…"

Flibbert leaned on his cane as he stepped toward the council room, his left leg bothering him with each step. He would soon regain his strength, and then he would beg Galen to send him to the battlefields. Until then, he carried heavily within him the knowledge that he was one of few to have survived the dark sprites.

Settling into his seat, the frog put his top hat on the table before him. He, Elimilech and The Brothers had talked long about what would be decided in this meeting. Their opinions were not the same. Jeff was convinced that the only course of action was to call back the soldiers to the protection of Saphree. He believed the dark sprites would not attack helpless villages. Sphen was sure that the second Saphree called its troops back, the villages would be subject to slaughter and slavery again. Even as they sat at the table, Sphen and Jeffery argued around and around, each unable to change the other's position.

Elimilech wanted to bring Issym's forces back. Though Flibbert disagreed heartily with the fairy, the frog knew it was because he was battle-anxious for the sake of the men who had already died, not necessarily because he was right. The more he tried to calm his aggression, the more determined Flibbert was to keep the men on the battlefield and fight beside them.

Joppa took a seat at the head of the table. He was uninvited but no one sent him away. The old man opened the meeting, "Speak, good frog, of what you have seen and I will tell you what I know."

As Galen, Elimilech and The Brothers had already heard what he had to say, Flibbert looked alternately between Remar, Juliet and Joppa as he spoke. When the frog was finished, Jeff leaned forward on his powerful arms and spoke, "The dark sprites attacked another of our small outposts. Again, there were only a handful of survivors. We cannot afford to keep our men in the field any longer."

"My informants tell me the dark sprites work for Sasha," Sphen added. "If we pull our soldiers back, the villages will be at her mercy again. This is unacceptable."

"What kind of sprite are they?" Remar cut off the argument that would have ensued between the two brothers.

"They are Airsprites."

"Like those you brought?" Juliet's voice was dangerously low.

Flibbert responded, "They are similar, but they are not the same."

"Have your sprites been in contact with these dark sprites in the past?" the queen questioned.

"No," Galen assured. "Not in my lifetime."

"How can you be sure?" Remar asked, distrust rising. "Do they not live in the clouds? Could you really control their movements?"

"I have been a protector to our airsprites and I know them," Flibbert informed. "These dark sprites are not affiliated with them."

Xsardis 166

"Even so…" Juliet was not satisfied.

"Perhaps your airsprites should return home," Remar finished for his wife.

Galen looked to Flibbert and Elimilech before replying. If they sent the airsprites away, soon the fairies would want to send the shifters back and the frogs would long to get rid of the minotaurs. "You can trust them. And more importantly, you *must*," Galen decided. "Because Issym is one. We fight as one or we do not fight at all."

In the silence and heat of the room, Galen and Remar met each other's eyes. Galen's features were etched solid, unmoving in a way Flibbert had seen only rarely. He remembered the days when the king could never look serious. He had always been jovial. What had they done to him in making him carry the weight of a country? What had Kate done in asking him to carry the weight of two?

"What does Joppa say?" Remar looked to his historian, caving for the time to his fellow king's unyielding proclamation.

"The dark sprites' story is one with sorrow, betrayal, loss, and joy— as any other," the man began. "The airsprites of Issym and Asandra were once one, living above us. It was a time of great peace in the clouds. But one young sprite correctly sensed a danger growing below her.

"She and a small group trained secretly to defend their clouds. When the attack came, they saved their community at great cost. She longed to be looked at as a hero and finally accepted, but the airsprites could not see what she had done for them. Only that she was a warrior. They feared her.

"A close friend died in that first battle. Rejected and alone, something changed in the warrior airsprite. A darkness began to numb her. Her people recognized this and refused to listen to her further counsel to be ready for the next attack. Anger and rage consumed her.

"Perhaps with the good intent to send the airsprites somewhere they could live in peace, she cast all noncombatants from their home above Asandra. The elite warriors whom she allowed to remain, she controlled through fear and an iron fist. Over time, they honed their skills and the girl gave evil reign inside the clouds.

"These emotionless, ferocious warriors, once full of light and now full of darkness are the creatures that Sasha has awakened from their long latency above us. The bitterness that has lain dormant now rages. The dark sprites will destroy all to avenge the war of centuries ago. They will succeed if we do not stop them."

"You have allowed such sleeping monsters to lie all this time and have said nothing?" Juliet questioned the historian.

"I have prayed that they would remain so removed from us," answered Joppa.

"It seems that they have not," Sphen snapped. Ignoring the old man, he spoke to the kings, "What if we used the old maxim? Cut off the head of the snake and the body dies?"

"Kill Sasha and the sprites will stop?" Remar clarified.

"She did summon them. Maybe we can send them back to the clouds if she's dead," Jeff agreed with his brother on this rare occasion.

Xsardis   167

"Sasha may have awoken them, but we cannot simply send them back to sleep. They do not view her as their head," Joppa spoke.

"Are we truly more afraid of the dark sprites than we are of Sasha?" Elimilech perceived.

"With the stones, I stand a chance against Sasha. Against the dark sprites, there is little hope," Flibbert trembled. "We must find their weakness."

"As their anger and pride is their strength so it is their weakness," Joppa returned.

"Instead of drawing our men back, we increase our troop deployments," King Remar declared, intending for his words to be followed. "We keep better vigilance. This is our only option. If we draw our men back, Sasha will have free reign of Asandra. And we know that neither she nor the dark sprites will spare the villages."

"No," Galen returned. "I will not leave my men out there to be massacred."

"I have made my decision," Remar retorted.

Galen felt the pull between protecting the land of Asandra and putting his soldiers at risk. "And I have made mine. Your men should return as well."

As the door opened, Kate stepped in. "This is a private meeting," Juliet told her.

"Forgive my intrusion," Kate offered.

"What is it?" King Galen's permission made sure the counsel would listen to her.

"You are right to bring the troops back," Kate said.

"How did you hear that?" Remar was indignant. The room was supposed to be safe from prying ears.

"Your words may not carry through the door to the average hearer, but to my ears they were as easy to distinguish as a shout in an empty room." She looked to Galen again, "Bring the soldiers to Saphree, yes, but allow me to distract Sasha. We must ensure that she leaves the villages alone."

Galen explained for the benefit of those from Asandra. "Sasha and Kate have a long-standing rivalry. Kate will be able to draw her attention." He turned back to her, "I thought you said you couldn't track her?"

"All I have to do is distract Sasha. That I can manage."

But the high king knew there was more to her plan than that. "Are you sure you want to risk going after her?"

The shifter nodded. Even Flibbert understood what she sacrificed. If Kate stayed away from Sasha, her youth and her power would grant her long life. Yet she sacrificed the bright future and accepted the duel with a rival who would long to make her suffer.

"Thank you," the frog said as he took her hand in his three fingers.

"And what of the dark sprites themselves?" Sphen returned to the main point.

"Elimilech, call our men back," Galen commanded, standing. "Meanwhile, I will seek out the information we need to defeat the sprites."

"This is a half-witted plan," Remar protested. "We are not done here, King Galen."

"Yes, King Remar," Galen remarked. "We really are."

Xsardis

Chapter 22

Galen sent for Danielle, queen of the airsprites, and waited with Flibbert in Issym's war room—a large space that felt small with the many people moving in and out at all times. A map with their troop deployments was set out on the table before them. Already they had drafted reassignments to most of them. Everyone was to pull back to Saphree in the next couple of days.

"We're going to tax the food supplies of this area too heavily with all these extra men," Galen spoke with concern as he looked out the many windows at the land beyond Saphree. "Have one of the fairies command a group of our fastest riders and flyers. They'll have to assume the duty of the mushnicks in gathering food. I don't want to put the others at risk."

"I'll assign the mushnicks to cooking duties then?"

The king nodded. Men and women brought in weapons and armor that had no place else to go. All of Saphree was busy making room for the hundreds of extra soldiers that would be returning. "This place is hardly big enough for what we're trying to do with it," Galen went on. "Assign someone to coordinate the placement of tents. We need to maximize every square foot of this place."

"You realize that there is every possibility the dark sprites will see our rallying as a challenge. They may bring the fight to us," Flibbert voiced.

"Yes, I know. Instruct some airsprites to watch the skies. We need as much advanced warning of an attack as possible."

The two put aside their conversation as Danielle entered the room, her dress reminiscent of spring and her youthful face not belonging in the war room. Flibbert emptied the space of all others, despite the protests.

"Is this about the dark sprites?" Danielle probed as she was shut in with a tense Galen and Flibbert.

"It is. Did you know about them?" Galen investigated.

She answered honestly, "I did."

"How could you say nothing?" Flibbert demanded. He had spent his life protecting, serving, and trusting the airsprites. This felt like betrayal.

Xsardis   170

"Before we left for Asandra, I asked you specifically about sprites," the king declared. "You said nothing."

"They are our enemies and our disgrace," Danielle replied. "But they are also legends from centuries ago. I could not dishonor my people with their memory."

"So for your pride you did not warn us," Galen chastised. "You could have prevented this!"

Flibbert questioned her, "What possessed you? Your mother would never have lied to her king."

She pushed back, "My mother would never have bowed to a land-locked human. But I have followed you in all ways, save risking my people for the mention of a rumor."

"Danielle, your silence was the action of a foolish child. Now it is time to see that," Flibbert beseeched her.

"My actions were those of a ruler seeking to protect her people. Have you not seen how Issym has treated the disgraced races? The illuminescents and the shifters are outcasts. The minotaurs barely even made it on the ship for Asandra. I kept secret a legend that only the airsprite royalty knew because if I told Issym, Issym would have cast us from its courts. For all I knew, the dark sprites had died off."

"I cannot believe…" the frog began.

Galen's heart broke to see the disrepair under which Issym continued to suffer. With a voice emotionless, he said, "Flibbert, no more. There is time to discuss her decisions later. Now, I need information."

"If I could give it to you, I would. But we are a people of peace; they are a people of war. I know little but that they exist."

"You must be able to tell us something of value!" the frog croaked.

"They loathe us," Danielle cried. "Do you think they shared with my ancestors their greatest secrets? I know nothing about them!"

Though Galen had to look up at Danielle, she was still a young woman to lead her people. He relented from the harsh words of discipline that would have been fitting. "Are they fighting us because they know you're here?"

"It's entirely possible," the airsprite queen responded.

Flibbert answered a knock at the door. Seeing Jennet, he allowed her entrance. She stood beside her queen and friend. "Excuse me," she said softly, "but I rarely leave Danielle's side."

Her steps were soft in her simple shoes; her dress was cut off at the knees. The sleeves stopped at her elbows to allow room for her silvery wings to retract. Jennet had her brown hair pulled up in a ponytail with shimmering jewels placed throughout the strands.

Flibbert marveled at how she had transformed since Danielle had become queen. Once Jennet had been a boyish child, unable to think about growing up. When Danielle's mother had died and the new queen had begun to rely heavily on her friend, Jennet had chosen to grow. Almost overnight she had transformed into a lovely young woman, bearing counsel worthy to be heard by any ruler.

"If the dark sprites are angry with us," Jennet had learned much of this history from Danielle already, "then we must reason with them. Perhaps we can bring peace between our two societies."

"It's too dangerous for anyone to go to their territory," Danielle tried to dissuade her friend.

"I am not afraid. I will go."

The day after Sasha had left Maremoth, Stewart began enacting his changes. He distributed the food liberally. He coated the guards in flattery. He promoted the soldiers with too much intelligence to positions outside Maremoth and replaced them with men that possessed minds more malleable to his purposes.

He gave it another day before he called together a council of his nine captains and revealed his treasonous plans, with Devar by his side. A banquet was laid out before them. Stewart layered the captains with compliments, showing them how good the good life could be. At the end of the meal, he stood at the head of the table and announced, "Gentlemen, I have called you here because I believe in your skills as leaders. Our Empress has only ever treated you as servants; that's all you'll ever be under her reign."

Pacing the length of the table, he went on, "I would never have spoken out against our Empress, but she is not the leader she once was. Anyone with eyes has seen her strange behavior in the last few months."

In fact, few had seen Sasha's behavior. She had become more and more reclusive to hide it. But no one would go against such a statement.

"Not only that," he continued, "but she lied to us about killing Rachel. How hard have you worked for her? It is time to help yourselves."

"What is it you want from us, Stewart?" asked an older captain, less convinced by his show.

"Devar has already agreed to fight with me. In name, still serve Sasha, but answer to me. I will keep our power and add to it. We will never live under Remar's rule again!"

The bellows of agreement rose throughout the table.

Vaylynne groaned as she opened her eyes. Everything hurt. She moved slowly, aware of the black outlining her vision. When she finally made it to a sitting position, she scanned herself for injuries. Her left shoulder burned, but the arm moved normally. Blood trickled from each of the many holes in her

Xsardis

172

pant legs. Putting a hand to her head, she felt for the lump that would warn of a concussion, but found none.

Only when she was sure that she was alright did she allow the memories to come back into her mind. Vaylynne had set one brick down on a pile and the whole floor had crashed deeper into the underground. The jagged walls around her drifted up well beyond her reach to the room from which she had fallen.

Katarina had been right. *Kat. Reesthma.* She scanned the room for her companions.

The princess lay face down on one side of her. Her breathing was steady and the blood was clearly from scrapes, not deep wounds. Nearby lay Reesthma's twisted and pale form. Vaylynne's heart beat faster as she rolled the girl onto her back and touched her clammy forehead. Opening the bag of herbs she wore at her belt, she put some into Reesthma's mouth. Then Vaylynne bunched her own cloak and put it under the girl's head before forcing some water down her patient's throat.

Knowing she could do no more, the rebel leader stood once again. The unconsciousness of her companions gave Vaylynne the opportunity to scheme. Where was Edmund? After he had approached her in the tunnels, the plan had been for him to follow her. Why had he not come to help? She rotated her sore left shoulder again. A crunching noise filled her ears.

Gripping one of the many handholds on the wall, she pulled herself a few feet off the ground. Her muscles trembled. Vaylynne dropped back in frustration, no other holds within reach.

Her eyes fell onto Katarina and Reesthma again. As they lay asleep from the fall, she could see in their faces the peace absent from her life for so long. Had she ever had it? The two were not oblivious to danger like so many were. They knew pain, suffering, and loss, and understood the evil that threatened to consume Xsardis. They were fiercely determined, yet peaceful.

While Vaylynne tried to make a compromise with evil in her fight, they were committed to turning away from it completely. Was it possible? *No!* snapped her mind. *No,* she repeated. And she was going to show Reesthma that.

A squirrel descended nimbly down the wall and landed before her. Vaylynne scowled at it. "A little late, don't you think?" she whispered to Edmund.

The animal cocked its head at the two unconscious girls. "They should be fine," she replied. "Have you seen the others?"

The squirrel shook his head.

"Well, I can take care of these two. You go and watch Rachel and Max. We don't want them happening upon the artifact without one of us there to stop them from destroying it."

The squirrel nodded. Vaylynne used all her self-control not to kill it as it scurried up her leg and tapped her sword. She grabbed its tail and held it before her eyes, "Yes, I'm ready to do whatever it takes. Now get!" She dropped the creature.

Scurrying to safety, Edmund climbed the wall and disappeared from sight. Vaylynne closed her eyes, sighed and used her practiced skill to banish the emotions which would have kept her from completing her mission. It was time to find the artifact.

The air was humid and putrid. The overwhelming smell of fish and stale water filled Seth and Evan's noses. The sign at the opening of the tunnel had warned they were heading toward a plague, but what kind? Uncertain of their surroundings, the two teens stayed quiet and kept their hands above their sword hilts.

They heard the croaking of frogs long before they saw them; hundreds of frogs. Breathing through their mouths, Evan and Seth kept their pace steady. It only made sense that the warning on the passageway had been of a plague of Egypt. More specifically, the plague of frogs.

"Oh…" Evan moaned as he lifted his foot off a frog that he had stepped on. Seth looked down. The creatures were already littering the pathway. They were not like the man-sized, sentient frogs of Issym, but like the frogs of Earth.

Upon rounding the corner, they saw a massive pond. Every inch of the water and the floor beside it was covered with frogs piled on top of frogs. The chorus of their croaking was deafening. The air offered little clean oxygen.

On the far corner stood a hallway leading out. Seth and Evan did not wait to exchange a glance. They both ran for the passage, stepping on helpless, slimy frogs as they made their way. Seth slid on the mucous and toppled. He was immediately covered in so many frogs that he had to fight their weight to sit up.

Evan turned back to help him, pulling Seth to his feet. Frogs clung to their boots and Seth's shoulders. Throwing the amphibians from them, Seth and Evan rushed through the passageway out. Even once they had put the pond behind them, it took time to get away from the frogs. The noises diminished; the air began to freshen; and then they were alone again.

Seth scraped mucous from his skin. "I officially hate frogs," Seth groaned. He looked to Evan, a prince he thought was arrogant and selfish. But stopping to help Seth had been neither. And it hadn't been required. Seth hadn't been being threatened by a life-sucking leech or dueled by a shape shifter. He was just in trouble and Evan had become a servant and helped. Seth knew what he had to say. "Thanks."

"Don't mention it. Really. Please, don't ever remind me of this place."

Xsardis   174

"Rachel, don't move," Max commanded from behind her.

She stopped, aware that he was not joking. "What's going on?"

He groped for an explanation, then ran his sword gingerly down her cloak. Holding perfectly still, Rachel trusted him until he had put the weapon away. Then she turned and saw the floor littered with grasshoppers. Her eyes fell shut as she groaned, covering a roll of her eyes. "Where those on me?"

She instructed Max, "Turn around."

He too was covered in the many creatures. No more than two inches tall, the brown bugs had six long legs, two wings and distorted faces. Unclasping his cloak, Max scraped them off the garment himself. "I guess we were right about the plagues being the plagues of Egypt," he said almost nonchalantly. He was not nearly as bothered by the bugs as Rachel was.

"We could have chosen a worse tunnel," Rachel tried to make the best of it, but the thought of entering the plague of locusts was repulsive.

The two pressed forward. Grasshoppers began to cover the floor and hover in the air. Then suddenly a rush of locusts sped toward them, seemingly attracted by the lights of their torches. Rachel and Max began to run.

Rachel flailed her hands to make a path in sea of locusts. The farther they pressed forward, the more dense the population became. The air grew black with locusts flying from ceiling to floor, barely any space left between their thick lines.

Holding her breath for fear of the grasshoppers flying into her mouth, Rachel kept a straight course. She could see little until the thickness of the locusts began to decrease. Able to see again and without the fear of running into a wall, Rachel picked up her speed. She rubbed off scores of grasshoppers, finally trusting the air enough to take in deep breaths. "Any on me I can't see, Max?" she looked back.

Max was gone.

In the haze they must have gotten separated. Was he still trapped with the locusts? "Max!" she called. "Max!"

In an instant she felt very alone. She was buried underneath layers of rock with no allies left to her. What if Max had passed out again? She determined to head back into the plague and find him. "You have to go toward the locusts," she steeled herself.

"Thankfully you don't." Max's voice trailed to her from the direction opposite the swarm.

She spun around, never having been more happy to see him. "I thought you got lost."

"It's you who got lost," he returned. "I found a door and got out of the locusts much sooner than you did."

"How did you find me again?"

"There were a few different ways I could have gone. I guess I happened to choose the right one. Come on," he jerked his head in the direction he wanted her to go. "I found a tunnel with more of the runes. I figure they must be leading us toward the artifact."

"You're luck with selecting tunnels seems to be pretty good. I'll follow."

Alerting Rachel to the few grasshoppers still clinging to her, Max

Xsardis 175

asked, "How do you suppose a swarm of locusts survived in an underground hideout with no vegetation?"

"I'm not sure," she replied. "Why do you ask?"

"We're running out of food. If they had a source, I would have liked to find it. I'm worried about the return journey."

"We should be worried for more than one reason," Rachel understood.

"I know," he nodded. "I seriously doubt that Sasha is oblivious to us being here or unable to stop us. She'll be closing in on our trail—blocking our exit."

Glancing at him, Rachel spoke with appreciation, "You knew that before we left Asandra."

"I think we all did." He pointed to give direction when they came to a fork in the path. "So, aware that this was a trap, why did you risk it?"

Rachel considered the question. "After thinking that Xsardis was gone, and finding out that they thought we were dead, my life just felt borrowed."

"You and Seth were always glass-half-full people. I'm still hoping to live. I intend to have a very lucrative life."

Rachel laughed. "And how do you plan on accomplishing that?"

"I can't tell you my secrets!"

Max seemed distracted after that. When they came to another set of runes, his eyes focused on them. Rachel could instantly tell that his mind was drifting. She tried to distract him, "What do you think about the locusts again?"

"I don't know…" he murmured, before allowing the dream-like state to completely consume him. The runes filled up his vision, then danced before his eyes. He could almost remember something.

Pain seared through his leg. He gripped it. The same pain stabbed through the other leg. "Ow!" he hollered.

His hands were shaking; his head was throbbing; his breathing was sharp; his stomach began to churn. Max did not want to stay conscious. "What's happening to me?" he gasped, collapsing against the wall.

Rachel searched her imagination, longing to answer his desperation. "I don't know," she whispered.

The flickers from his fallen torch lit up his wild eyes. "It all started on Issym with Issym but it came here!" he persisted.

"How do you know that? What do you know?"

He stared at the floor, unable to speak as the pain clawed through his system. He met her eyes once more, then passed in unconsciousness.

Xsardis

Chapter 23

What's happening to me? Rachel recalled Max begging before he had passed out.

I don't know, she had answered him.

It all started on Issym, with Issym, but it came here!

What did that mean? Covered in Rachel's cloak, Max lay asleep. He had stopped trembling, but his eyes kept flicking as if dreams plagued his subconscious. When he woke up he probably would not remember what he had said and she would never know what he had meant.

No disease that she could think of acted like this. Was it only that the stress was too much for Max? It could not be the runes themselves. They had no power. They were simply an archaic form of writing—a secret code she and Seth had developed, as she now remembered.

The dank smell of the tunnels grated on her and she longed for fresh air. Without her cloak, the chill penetrated through her. Rachel determined that when Max woke up, regardless of what he said, she would take him back to the surface. Seth and Evan would have to find their own way out.

The tap of footsteps crept into her ears so slowly she at first did not recognize it. Waiting motionlessly, she made out sounds of breathing. She could hear two people coming her way.

Rachel rose in anticipation. Her sword slid effortlessly from her hilt. There were two choices: it was friend or it was foe. There was nothing she could do to anticipate which. She could not drag Max to safety and she would not leave him exposed. Rachel waited.

The forms rounded the corner. Seth and Evan. Relief rushed through her and she could have run into Seth's embrace, but she checked her emotions. Her eyes fell to Max; Seth followed her gaze. Seth dropped beside him, wordlessly processing the situation.

Rachel reported, "This is the second time he has passed out. There doesn't seem to be a reason. Both times he grew dazed as he looked at the runes on the wall. He was wracked with pain."

Xsardis   178

"Did he say anything?" Seth looked up at her.

"Something about the medallion on Issym. And this: *It started on Issym, with Issym, but it came here.*"

Seth focused back on his friend lying unconscious on the floor and ran through his memories. The medallion had been given to him as a boy by a fairy who told him it would divide the land. It had caused the earthquake on Issym, but what could it have to do with Max passing out?

While Seth thought, Evan asked Rachel, "Where are the others?"

"We split up after you fell down the hole. You guys okay?" She picked up his glowing snail in her hand and examined it. "You got resourceful, but you smell awful!" Rachel stepped away.

He knew she was right. He let her get some space. "I was almost hungry enough to eat that thing. The food we had was ruined in the fall."

Instantly Rachel checked their supplies and handed him a small piece of now-stale bread. "We don't have much left ourselves."

"None of us anticipated this trip taking days," Seth sighed. "We're going to get very hungry before this trip is over. We'll have to ration our supplies even more carefully."

Seth's cadence changed as he planned, "Reassessing where we are, it's pretty clear someone needs to wait for Max to wake up, then make sure he gets back to the dwarfs. The other two have to keep looking for the artifact."

"What if Kat has already found and destroyed it?" Evan inquired.

"It's possible," Seth replied.

Rachel did not want to ask her question. "But what if Max doesn't wake up?"

Seth studied his unconscious friend, then announced, "Then he has to be left behind. Max understood the risks. We don't have enough food to sit around for days waiting. This is all we can do."

Rachel rubbed a hand through her hair. Nobody should be forced to make decisions like this about his own friends. It was no wonder that Seth had changed. The moments when she saw the boy with whom she had played or the teen for whom she had fallen were few and far between. They had been replaced by a man, weathered from battle and capable of doing whatever it took to accomplish good.

"If we keep going, we don't have enough food to get back to the surface," Evan recognized.

"You're probably right."

"This is a stupid plan," Max groaned, sitting up.

"How long have you been awake?" Seth demanded, more relieved than he could say that his friend was conscious.

"Long enough to know that you want to leave me behind. Not going to happen." Before Seth could protest, Max went on, "More than likely, Sasha is guarding the exits to this place. If two of us go back, we don't stand a chance. And nothing has changed since I signed up to come on this mission back at Saphree."

"You're sick, Max," Rachel pointed out.

"If I pass out again, leave me behind. But I'm not backtracking."

Accepting bread from their small supply, Seth studied Max's eyes.

"Okay."

Stewart fretted nervously as he stood on the empty forest road, waiting for the wagon to arrive with his precious cargo. A box of gold tucked under his shoulder, he paced the path as his bodyguards remained motionless. Though he should have felt more powerful than ever since taking control of Maremoth, he had never been more afraid. His blatant power seizure would earn him no mercy if Sasha returned unexpectedly. He was willing to give every last piece of gold he possessed to gain protection on that day. Half of his gold he did carry with him, ready to trade without hesitation.

Finally he made out the shape of the old wagon coming toward him. He glanced at his bodyguards, and hoped that he was not about to be ambushed.

The wagon rolled to a creaking stop and a single man dressed in dark robes hopped down.

"Do you have my items?" Stewart questioned.

"Money first," the man grunted.

Reluctantly, Stewart handed over his box. The seller nodded to the back of his wagon. Greedily, Stewart peered inside. A broad smile spread across his face. The already legendary armor of the frogs. The gray stones loosely tied together stared out at him. "Excellent, excellent," he grinned, unaware that he was spending his money on stones found by the roadside.

The man in the black robes waited until all the armor had been moved, then set himself on his own wagon and headed back to Saphree. He knew that Philip would be pleased that his plan had worked. Even if Stewart found out that he had been sold fake merchandize, the much richer seller and Philip would be untouchable within the walls of their fortress.

Edmund was having a hard time controlling his impatience. For months he had spun a web of lies for his ignorant sister and borne all her snide remarks, working up to the journey he was now taking. That journey had surprised even him. The ever-united teens had become disjointed, somehow dividing into three separate groups. He had been too far back to hear or see what had happened.

He doubted they had had a fight. Edmund remembered all-too-well Seth's shocked face when he had punched the teen. Seth was clearly not accustomed to fighting amongst his team. He should have seen the fist coming.

The shifter could still feel his anger rise when he thought about how Seth had cast aside months of their work and risked Xsardis with his pretty speech to the dwarfs. He had even won Kate to his side.

Edmund had spent a lifetime catering to other people, but no more. Either he was setting things right—with himself and Kate at the top—or he was going out trying. As for his alliance with Vaylynne, they both knew it was short-lived and born out of desperation, but it would hold at least until they had the artifact in their possession. Of that he could be sure. After that... with the way she had ordered him around after he'd found her fallen through an obvious trap, he doubted they could survive in each other's space.

Suddenly he heard the shuffling of boots. Thick, dwarf boots. He had spent so much time alone in the last several days that he had forgotten what it felt like to be the one being chased instead of doing the chasing. He tried to change into the form of a mouse, but he had allowed himself to get too close to the stones in front of him. *What a mess you've made!* he chastised himself.

As the dwarf grew closer, Edmund had no choice but to turn and face him. "Lotex," he greeted. Of all the dwarfs, did it have to be this one?

"Edmund," Lotex peered at him uneasily from under his bushy brows. "What are you doing down here?"

"Making sure that Seth stays out of trouble. You?"

Lotex was out of breath, as if he'd been running. He must have been down in the tunnels for days. Why was he only now beginning a run? *We must be getting close...*

"Same," Lotex answered. "But I don't think Seth needs *your* help."

"He won't want it, that's for sure," Edmund replied coolly.

"You haven't changed shape," Lotex put together. "You *can't* change shape."

"Fight me and find out," Edmund bluffed.

"Just stay out of my way." Lotex pushed past him.

The shifter stared on. What had so distracted Lotex that he could not see the danger Edmund represented? He picked up his pace and followed.

Katarina allowed a wince as she kneeled beside the stream flowing toward the edge of the wall. She put her hand in the cool liquid and watched as the blood and grime from the fall washed away.

The princess closed her eyes, a massive headache causing even the small light from her torch to hurt. With a gentle pull, she moved the mass that was her hair and felt for the lump she knew was there. Rinsing every part of her hopelessly-scraped self, Kat tested every muscle to make sure they still worked.

It was not merely the immediate pain of the fall that bothered her. She would have no time to rest or heal and would be running on low energy for the remainder of their quest.

Vaylynne and Reesthma seemed to have no trouble bouncing back. The three of them had been walking for several hours and while Katarina rested, the two were practicing sword fighting. Reesthma had an unnatural glow in her eyes, as if this was the first time she had ever truly come alive.

Kat wadded her cloak into a ball, put it under her head and was off to sleep in seconds. She ignored her own last thought, *Now would be the perfect time for Vaylynne to make a move.*

"There isn't time for coddling you," Vaylynne barked to her new apprentice when the girl had stumbled on Vaylynne's outstretched foot. "You need to learn."

"I am trying," Reesthma informed, knowing that Vaylynne had meant to send her to the ground, but she had kept her feet.

After almost an hour of practice, the instructor allowed her pupil a rest. Reesthma reached for her bag and pulled out some bread. "We're running out of food," she pointed out.

"There's nothing we can do about it. We can't turn back. We fell, remember?"

"You want me to ignore that we'll be without food soon?"

"In battle, as in life, if you focus on the negative, you will not survive," Vaylynne returned. "Now stand and fight me."

"Count my blessings then?" Reesthma rephrased.

"Blessings are easily taken away," Vaylynne answered her. "Don't let your opponent know where you're weak. That's how you'll win."

"So what do I focus on?"

"Your next movement. That is all."

Sasha's aquatic form jumped free from the water, turned into a dwarf and landed on the beach of Noric. She had had to skirt her own continent and take a water-route to Noric in order to avoid the stones. Her mood would have been foul if she had not been distracted by the presence of the artifact. It was on this forsaken land. How had she not sensed it before? It would be hers.

If Edmund had betrayed her, she would cut him from her grace forever. If he had not, she would use the time offered by her victory to retrain the little brother for whom she hoped it was not too late. The thrill of conquest energized her weakened body. Seth and Rachel were going to lead her right to the artifact. Just a little longer and nothing would hurt her.

Had anyone thought conquering the world would be easy? She had never wanted it to be! Sasha had a thirst for battle and a craving for disaster. *Soon. Soon. Soon,* the voices in her head chanted. So many forms, so many goals, so many pressures.

The nausea filled her as she began to morph back into the form of the sea that she had possessed since leaving Maremoth. It was happening again.

She had no control. Beached on land, Sasha struggled to breathe or to change back to a human form. Finally she managed to shift into a dog. Breathing, she gained enough strength to take over a dwarf's persona.

She was grateful no one had been around to see it. It was a horrifying experience and it made her all the more desperate to have the artifact.

Gaining control, Sasha entered the mines and walked right past the guards. Sometimes the frailest forms could be the best. She had taken on that of a dwarf named Blowen. The shifter marched right to his quarters and pounded on the door.

The real Blowen opened the door. He was dumbfounded when he saw himself and patted his head as if to ascertain his own identity.

"Let me in, fool," Sasha's dwarf voice commanded.

"Sasha?" he questioned, eyebrows rising. The glare he received changed his words, "Empress."

He bowed and stepped out of the way. This dark alliance with Sasha had him worried. To be sure, the dwarfs did not deserve his loyalty, but Seth had talked of a certain side to the shifter queen that made Blowen worry. Was his promised reward worth his treachery? Was that reward even coming?

As if she perceived his thoughts, she spoke, "You would not hide anything from me, would you Blowen? You know what I think of liars."

That made up the dwarf's mind. "No, no, Empress. I would never keep anything from you. What an honor…"

She silenced him with a wave of her hand—which looked exactly like his. "Then tell me, have Rachel and Seth come this way?"

By this point, Blowen could keep nothing back. "Yes, and I know where they're heading."

Kate's thoughts remained with the turbulent counsel at Saphree. She was growing weary of the role she played: the never-invited, always-needed voice of reason. She had held up her own rebel shifters for months as she had grieved the loss of her fiancée and her homeland. She had supported Issym in its early years—more than any of the others realized. Now Asandra looked to her as the last great defense against Sasha. What choice had she had but to pursue the shifter? Sooner or later they would have asked her to go after Sasha anyway.

Did they not realize that before the war on Issym, the shifters had never before hurt their own kind? And they could not imagine the difficulty and pain required to shift into those hundreds of forms. Only Sasha really could.

Kate's thoughts carried her over Asandra quickly and she arrived at Maremoth before she even realized it. She knew Sasha was not within. Her presence was distinctly lacking. Not willing to turn back to Saphree after such a small attempt to find Sasha, she determined to learn what she could of

Xsardis

183

Maremoth's plans.

Disguising herself, Kate entered the fortress and carefully made her way through it in a multitude of forms. She listened to the sounds of conversations throughout the palace and felt the wickedness contained within it. The brutality shown to the prisoners, the black hopes expressed by the leaders… She felt dizzy.

Destroy this palace of darkness before Sasha returns. End it now! spoke a voice in her mind.

I am tired of war, she replied. And there was something about Maremoth. She had to admire the architecture. If Kate could have built it for defense she would have constructed it no differently. The high walls; the open space for the growing of crops; the large palace. There was an unusual grandeur to the castle. The stone walls; the fine tapestries. This place would make a fine home for her.

Sasha deserved to have it taken from her. Her mindless servants would call out for Kate to be their master if they could understand how she would lead them. There was something better for the lost souls within.

This center of evil power… somehow it still called to her. These could be her minions. This could be her world. No one could stop her. She was not like Sasha—weakened and wild. Controlled, skilled, powerful; there was nothing Kate could not accomplish for the good of Xsardis.

No more death under her. She could make sure. No more famine, no more tragedy. Edmund would see and turn back to her. Maybe he had been right all along.

Kate fell back against a wall in the shadows of a hallway. Her stomach clawed from the inside and she rocked with pain from her own thoughts. *What am I doing?*

Xsardis

Chapter 24

Edmund followed Lotex carefully and silently. Lotex did not hesitate as he chose between different tunnels, going steadily downwards. The shifter endured the insufferable locusts by becoming one of them. The dwarf was not as lucky, but it did not slow his pace in the least.

As they drew closer to the stones Edmund had a choice to make. Would he hang back and risk Lotex ruining his plans or press onward and be found out? The way Lotex had just pushed past him earlier made Edmund wary. All he could figure was that the dwarf was going to try to stop Seth; he could not let him succeed. The shifter morphed himself into a dwarf and followed.

Lotex knew Edmund was following him, but he did nothing. There were more important things at stake. *More important than your friendship with the boy?* his heart questioned him. *After all he did for you?* The dwarf remembered clearly how Seth had saved his life. It was not a debt he could easily set aside.

Do what you need to do or I'll do it for you, Beatrice's voice filled his mind.

I have a responsibility. Seth will come to understand that, he attempted to convince himself. Never in his life had he had trouble making decisions. Everything was black and white; his judgment never failed. From the time Seth had first set foot on Noric, Lotex had known that he was going to help the lad. But for hundreds of years the dwarfs had been given a charge that now passed to him. He could not fail—not even for the imaginer of Issym and the warrior of Xsardis.

Before he could lose his certainty, Lotex barged around the corner and moved straight for Seth. The boy's face held a pleased confusion until Lotex drove the butt of his ax into his head. Seth slumped to the ground, unconscious.

"What was that?" Rachel jumped to her feet and demanded before Max and Evan could even draw their blades.

Xsardis   186

"He'll be fine in an hour," the dwarf assured. "I would never hurt him."

"You just hit him with your ax!" Rachel shouted. She knelt beside Seth and checked to ensure that his breathing was steady. Despite what she had witnessed, she could not think of Lotex as their enemy. Deluded, perhaps; but he would do no more harm.

"I know Seth would never turn back, but the way he spoke of you," Lotex addressed Rachel and ignored the two teens who were very close to engaging him in battle, "I hoped you would listen to reason."

Holding out her hand to restrain the others, she ordered, "Speak quickly, Lotex."

Rachel had only met him for a short time on the way to Maremoth and had barely seen him again at Saphree. Seth's conversation had been full of respect for the dwarf. That alone was keeping her from returning the blow he had given to Seth.

"This island was given to the dwarfs," Lotex began. "It is forbidden that any outsider should go down here. This is our sacred land. You have to turn around."

"You know about our mission," Prince Evan tried diplomacy. "You know its importance!"

"And even so I ask you turn back. Surely that means something."

His eyes shone with sincerity. Rachel could not comprehend how his actions met the honest goodness she saw there.

"Tell us what the secret is," Max declared. He comprehended that even secrets kept for the best reasons could be destructive. Seth's crumpled form attested to that.

"I can't. You'll have to trust me."

"Trust you?" Rachel was losing her patience. She drew her blade. "Seth trusted you. Look what happened to him."

Lotex gripped his weapon. "I don't want to hurt you, but I have to protect our treasure."

"Treasure?" Max scoffed. "That's what this is about? It's not worth it, believe me!"

"A treasure more valuable than you can imagine," the dwarf chanted.

"The artifact? Gold? What?" Rachel questioned.

"Just go," Lotex pressed, his eyes now heavy. "It's the last time I'll ask."

Evan determined, "We are not leaving."

"Then I have no choice," Lotex sighed. He lifted his ax.

Evan expected to see the blade swinging towards him, but instead there was a loud thud and the dwarf's eyes rolled back in his head; he fell over, unconscious.

Another dwarf stood behind him, clearly responsible for the blow that had knocked Lotex out. "Who are you?" Rachel asked.

Edmund responded, "There's no time to explain. Get your friend and go! The others will try to stop you."

Max picked up Seth's legs as Evan grabbed his torso. With Rachel leading the way—sword in one hand, torch in the other—they carried him

Xsardis

187

deeper into the tunnel. They stopped not long after the dwarfs were out of sight.

They waited for Seth to wake. "What would cause a friend to knock unconscious another friend?" Rachel pondered.

"Treasure can have a terrible draw," Max spoke from experience.

"Do you really think it was about money?" she inquired.

Max shook his head. "No. That's not what I saw in his eyes."

"Tell me that did not happen," Seth sighed as he woke.

"It did," Max confirmed.

It took Seth several moments to find the balance to sit up. "What happened?"

"Another dwarf helped us get away. He said there were others who would try to stop us."

Seth buried his eyes in the palms of his hands, the torchlight increasing his migraine. A large red welt was developing on his brow. "Did he just let you go?"

"Another dwarf came up from behind and knocked him out. Told us to run."

"Did Lotex say anything?"

"He was muttering about treasure," Rachel kept nothing from him. "Drink this," she commanded, handing him her water bag. When he had complied, she knelt by his side and looked over the wound.

"Am I going to live, Doc?" he joked.

"Not with that attitude," she returned, keeping the smile from her face.

His tone dropped as she leaned against the wall. "It doesn't make sense. Lotex never cared about money."

"People change," Evan replied, offering him a hand up.

Seth accepted it. People might change, but Seth wasn't sure which shocked him more: getting hit in the head by Lotex or getting helped to his feet by Evan. Spots crept around his vision as he stood, but with a hand on the wall he kept his footing.

"Are you okay?" Rachel put a steadying hand on his arm.

He nodded gently. "If the other dwarfs are coming, we need to move."

As they started along the path, Rachel watched as Max once again seemed to be stronger than before he had fallen unconscious by the runes. What was the strange energy that flowed through him?

Seth did not know how long they walked. His injury, hunger, fatigue and concern for Lotex blurred the time together. He focused his mind as they entered a spacious room filled with chests and bags.

Max's heart skipped a beat. A treasure room. They could destroy the artifact, but what said they had to leave the rest of it?

A torch hung on either side of the entryway. Rachel lit both with her own torch. Evan took one in his hand; Max the other. In the light they could see that runes marked the walls. To the far side was a huge suit of armor—fit for a giant and complete with a helmet. "Shouldn't there be a pedestal where this artifact is sitting?" Max asked, thinking of the Indiana Jones movies.

Evan looked to Rachel and then to Seth. Though they had said

Xsardis   188

nothing, it was clear that they were not remembering anything about this room, yet. Rachel knelt beside a chest and gingerly opened the lid. Reflecting from the light of her torch were scores of fine necklaces. Rachel ran her fingers across them.

Max kicked the top of another chest off. The thud echoed around the cavern. The gold of coins shown on his skin. His eyes widened.

Rachel stood and returned to Seth's side. He had not moved. "Do you recall this place?"

"No," he shook his head. "But I know I should."

Max opened yet another chest full of gold. He laughed to Rachel, "Suppose it will matter now that we can't get into college?"

Even in the circumstances, Seth's mind caught on the words. "What do you mean 'can't get into college'?"

"Well, not good ones anyway. Not with suspicion of kidnapping and murder..." Max replied casually. He was completely invigorated by the sight of the gold.

"What? They thought you guys were responsible for my disappearance?"

Rachel rolled her eyes, frustrated. "That's not our problem right now."

Seth would not let the conversation go, "Did they really suspect you?"

"What were the cops supposed to think?" she returned forcefully.

"We'll set it right," he promised her.

"It doesn't matter," Rachel shook her head. She meant it. "Seth, you and Xsardis are here. That's all that counts."

Max was still oblivious to the problem he had opened up. He said, "This room is just a distraction."

"A distraction?" Evan asked.

Looking to Seth, Max explained, "It's how you've been thinking all your life. Fake a jump shot and pass me the ball. Even as a kid you wouldn't have made it easy."

"It makes sense," Seth agreed. "Give the treasure hunters enough loot and they wouldn't keep pursuing the thing of real worth."

"There must be a trap door," Rachel scanned the room with new eyes.

"Do you hear that?" Evan inquired. Echoes of voices were coming towards them. "It's Kat's voice."

He started back up the passageway and soon found Katarina, Vaylynne, and Reesthma had joined them. They were covered in dirt and scrapes.

"You're okay!" Katarina wrapped her arms around her brother quickly. Her nose wrinkled at the smell.

"I know," he replied. "Have you looked in a mirror lately?"

She punched him. "We fell down into a pit."

"And we endured the plague of frogs."

Katarina gave him a quizzical look.

"You have a surprising talent for staying alive," Vaylynne nodded to Seth. "What happened to your face?"

Xsardis

189

Seth felt for the bruise he had forgotten about. "Long story."

A natural smile filled Reesthma's face as she saw her friends again. Seth could tell from the way she held herself that Vaylynne had been training her. He said nothing.

Kat took in the room. "Have you found the artifact yet?"

"We're looking for the trap door," Max responded.

"We're assuming, I take it," began Reesthma, "that the armor represents some parallel to Goliath."

It suddenly seemed so simple to Seth. "Nice job, Ree."

He picked up the out-of-place slingshot he had seen resting on the ground and the few stones beside it. "Anyone a better shot than I am?"

Katarina took it from his hands. She felt the weapon, tested the stone, then sent a practice shot toward one of the runes. It hit very close to its mark.

"Where'd you learn to do that?" Reesthma asked.

Blushing, Kat answered, "Annoying Sasha's soldiers was one of the few joys I had as a kid."

"It got us into plenty of trouble," Evan added.

"I told you it would come in handy someday," she returned.

Aiming for the nosepiece of the helmet, Katarina hit her mark. At first nothing happened. A disappointed sigh came from all parts of the room. Then the helmet came down, followed by the armor itself. The walls began to move, shaking the cavern, as a passageway was revealed.

The stone corridor was no longer than a few body lengths. As each of the teens passed through it, they fought their way through water that was pouring down from the ceiling and into water that was half-way to their knees. A strong current pulled that water down a steep drop off into a large body of the salty-liquid. Rachel observed from as close a position as she dared. The ledge on which they stood was thin. "What now?" Katarina shouted over the noise.

The passageway closed behind them. On the other side they had barely felt it. Now, they were nearly thrown from the ledge with the force.

"An invisible bridge?" Max probed half-sincerely.

"Not to my knowledge," Seth returned.

"Maybe the Valean rock shifted and blocked our way down," Reesthma forced her voice to carry.

"So we can't get to the artifact?" Katarina questioned.

Vaylynne and Seth were exchanging concerned glances. "What is it?" Rachel perceived.

Vaylynne's eyes drifted to the water below. At first Rachel noticed nothing. Then she realized. The huge gray mass her eyes said was just a shadow was, in fact, swimming. The pitara.

Something began to ram the wall behind them. Was it the dwarves or something worse? The pitara heard the sounds and slowly began to rise.

None of the teens cried out. They simply stared at their fate as it rose.

The first thing to come above water was the pitara's long, sharpened fin. Next the bulging shoulders rose, followed by its head, which thankfully was still turned away from them. Time slowed as the creature spun toward them. Its bumpy left arm and clawed fist showed. The muscular face came into view. Horns stuck out of the sides like a mane. Its eyes were almost as big as the teens' heads. Its nose projected but was overshadowed by its mouth. Opening the vast empty cavity that was its mouth, the pitara roared. Suddenly long, sharp teeth descended.

Half its body was below the water. *Its three-pronged tail,* thought Max. He punched Seth's shoulder.

"What?" Seth shouted at the strange aggression.

"We should go with the pitara," Max stated.

"Are you crazy?" Seth demanded. "It wants to eat us!"

"Think, Seth; its Jonah and the big fish."

"I thought that was a whale," Vaylynne ascertained herself that she still possessed her voice. The pitara horrified her.

"The Scripture never said what kind of fish," Max bickered. "Please, trust me."

Seth put both his hands on his friend's shoulders as the creature stared on. "Keep your sanity for a few more seconds."

"Who imagined it?" Max cried as he broke Seth's hold.

"I can't remember," Rachel replied, the salty water getting into her mouth as she spoke.

"Maybe neither of you did. Maybe you don't know all there is to know," the bitter words tore out of Max in that moment. "I have *always* trusted you. Now you trust me!"

The pitara moaned. The teens covered their ears in pain. The beast lowered itself so that its mouth was level with the rocky ledge. The teeth sucked back up and they were able to stare right into its purple-tongued cavity.

Max turned to look at his friends. Katarina understood what he was thinking. She took a step forward, pleading with her large green eyes, "Please, don't."

He saw her lips form the words. Even though he could not hear them, they tore through his system. Max met her gaze. "I know what I'm doing."

Then the teen stepped into the pitara's mouth. The chasm closed around him before the pitara dropped back into the water and was gone.

Hovering over his new stone armor Stewart could not have felt more secure. Then a figure stepped out of the shadows. He opened his mouth to call for his guards, but clamped it shut again when the mysterious woman before him spoke, "Don't bother. If I wanted to kill you, you'd be dead."

Stewart gulped. Assassination attempts already? "You're a shifter…" He could tell. "This armor of mine will stop you!"

The woman laughed. "That has no effect on me." To prove it, she morphed herself effortlessly into a tiger, then returned to her human shape.

"Sasha?" A new fear coursed through Stewart's veins.

"Kate," she introduced herself.

"What is it you want?" he cowered.

"We can start with information," she began, sitting down across from him. "Where is Sasha?"

"She left a few days ago for Noric."

"And why did you think this pathetic armor could have any effect on me?"

"A traitor in Saphree's camp sent it to me," he replied without thinking.

"Name," she demanded.

"I can't..." Stewart protested despite his fear. This woman's calm demeanor was more terrifying than Sasha's bursts of rage, but he would not give up his spy. He needed Philip.

"Name," Kate repeated.

He did sell me fake armor, Stewart reasoned. "Philip."

"Good. Now, would you like to hear why I came?"

He bobbed his head.

"There is a simple fact that has become exceedingly clear in my head: that I could rule better. I know you are trying to fight against Sasha. I will aid you. In return, you will aid me."

"And what would I get out of this?" Stewart braved.

"You have no children, no one to rise up after you. And you humans have such short lives. I will allow you to rule Asandra while you live. Currently my focus is Issym. When you die, I will spread my empire."

"Can you guarantee me I won't die any unnatural death at your hands?"

"I don't kill my friends," she returned.

Stewart felt the rush of the plan. With Kate on his side... "It's a deal."

Jeff on one side, Sphen on the other, Jennet rode. She had determined to leave Saphree behind her before she rose to the clouds. When her presence drew the dark sprites, she did not want to risk bringing them to the fortress.

Danielle had been furious that she had determined to converse with the sprites. With good reason. Born only a few days apart, Jennet and Danielle had been close since birth. They both understood that if the dark sprites did not accept Jennet's offer of peace, she might never return. But if they were not going to offend their fellow airsprites, someone prominent had to speak with them. The queen could not risk her life. Jennet could.

"Are you sure you want to do this?" asked Jeff as she called a halt.

"No one expects you to," added Sphen.

The three had grown close in their brief ride. The Brothers had decided to be her escorts, unwilling to allow such a sacrificial effort as Jennet's to go unsupported. They already knew what her answer would be.

"Thank you for coming with me." She smiled at them and took one of each of their hands. "Go now." As she spoke, she rose, her fingers touching theirs until the last moment.

When she was gone, Jeff praised, "She's brave."

"Far too brave to die so easily," Sphen completed.

Jennet rose into the darkening clouds with apprehension. The orange streaks offered little promise. The presence of the dark beings alerted her that, if anything, she had underestimated their evil. They wore black clothing and hid themselves in the turbulent clouds.

The young airsprite took a deep breath, rallying her courage. Her mind played scenes of her beautiful enchanted clouds, the laughter at Danielle's side, and the sweet Flibbert who had always defended them. That others could have that life, those memories, was worth fighting for.

Holding onto those thoughts, she spoke, "I am Jennet, right hand of Queen Danielle of the Enchanted Clouds of Issym."

She let each phrase sink in. "I know our history has not been easy. Your warrior queen saved us and we rebelled against her. But now our worlds are separate and what happened so long ago should not affect us now. We are sorry and we wish for reconciliation. We want to fight beside you; not against you."

Six dark sprites encircled her, stepping out from orbs of light. They showed no sentiment and offered no response to her words. They surveyed her and remained silent.

A dark skirted, white haired sprite landed before her. "You come to fight with us?" she repeated Jennet's phrase.

"Yes!" Jennet replied wholeheartedly.

"You cannot fight. You never could. You have come here for our protection."

"No, that's not true," Jennet tried to convince her. "We want to be your allies."

The look in the dark sprite's eyes showed that there would be no joint cause, no change of heart, no reconciliation and no mercy. "It's too late for that."

The bear snarled as it entered the damp mines and saw five passageways before it. It scratched its nose with a fury, clawed hand. Its thick coat and its previous heavy gait forced heat and smell to radiate from the animal.

Sasha shifted from the bear into five human shapes, all exact feminine duplicates. They surveyed each other, then set out into each of the five passageways. She would search every inch of the mines until she caught up with Rachel and Seth.

Xsardis

Until proven otherwise, she would hold onto the belief that Edmund was doing his job. She would assume that he was following the teens until they discovered the source of her future invincibility. She was simply on Noric to ensure that all happened as she needed it to.

Sasha could not afford to take any risks. Her future, or lack thereof, rested on Noric alone. Forget Asandra. She just wanted to survive.

No, she wanted more than that. She wanted to destroy Rachel and Seth and their gang of foolish teenagers who had already ruined her plans twice. Sasha was going to get her revenge.

Xsardis

Chapter 25

"Max!" Katarina screamed as the jaws closed around her friend. Evan held her back from charging the sea monster.

"You'll only bring it back," he spoke into her ear.

The sounds of the waterfall still pounded, but could not drown out the banging on the passageway behind them. Someone was desperate to get in. It could have been an army of dwarfs, but Evan guessed that Sasha had finally caught up with them. Trapped between two monsters.

"Max would have leapt into the pitara's mouth on one of our crazy whims," Seth's voice was monotonous and steady. "We should have trusted him."

Rachel could not yet process what she had seen. "He would have followed our imaginations. His actions were based on a hunch."

"Were they?" Seth pressed. "Max did imagine the orb that brought you here."

"Maybe," she returned.

"And he's been obsessed with sea monsters for as long as I've known him. Is it so farfetched that he could have imagined the pitara?"

Unmoving, Reesthma stared into the water that was tugged down the falls. Either Max was dead or history that told of the pitara's cruelty was false. The chill from her soaking clothes filled her.

Vaylynne drew her sword as the wall behind them lifted for only a moment and fell back down again. The enemy on the other side would break through soon. She looked to Seth to lead the fight, but his blade still hung by his waist. She knew what he was thinking. "Don't."

The pitara rose slowly again from its watery hole and sets its mouth before the ledge. Seth stared in the open chasm. "You were always the girl who believed in the impossible," he reminded Rachel.

Fear slipped from her face and was replaced by youthful confidence. "Together?" she asked.

"Together," he nodded as he entwined his hand around hers.

Xsardis   196

Rachel and Seth stepped into the pitara's mouth.

Darkness surrounded them as its mouth shut. A deep, saturating heat consumed them. As the pitara plummeted into the water, Rachel and Seth rose, then fell back onto the sticky tongue. The ride was smooth until the beast came to a sudden halt. Its mouth opened. Without hesitation, Seth and Rachel stepped onto the solid ground offered. The pitara met their eyes and was gone.

Letting out a breath, Rachel exclaimed, "I can't believe we just did that."

"I'm surprised you followed me," Max confessed.

After surveying the solid door before them and determining to wait with the hope that the others would join them, Seth and Rachel dunked themselves in the salty water around them. Seth abandoned the bag that now had nothing but ruined supplies left, removed the cloak that was far too wet to offer warmth, and readjusted his sword. As ready for battle as he could be, he addressed Max, "First the orb, then pitara. Did you really imagine it?"

"I wasn't sure at first, but when I got a better look at the pitara, I knew. I called it Jonah. It fit. How did my imagination start affecting Xsardis?"

Seth commented, "You've always thought pretending was childish."

"Yeah, well, I *did*. But after seeing Xsardis go up in flames, all of the sudden I missed imagination."

"I like your style." Ringing her hair out, Rachel asked, "Can you sense the artifact, Max?"

"It's not far beyond this door." He put up a hand. "Don't ask me how I know that."

With a splash, the pitara surfaced and released Evan, Katarina, Reesthma, and Vaylynne. Snorting, it swam away.

"Did you imagine that thing, Max?" Kat demanded.

Max nodded.

The princess glared at him. "You didn't have to make it so gross inside."

"It's a fish. What did you want me to do?" Max retorted, hiding a smirk.

The newly-released teens washed themselves off. Reesthma was the first to be done. Her attention was fixed on the door before them. It had been carefully crafted of a shimmering, white bark. A handle of a curved branch from the same tree rested on its right. Though the door was clearly aged and surrounded by water, it had not fallen into decay. "What is this wood?" she asked herself.

"It's wood," Vaylynne was not impressed and not interested in wasting time dissecting the composition of a door. All she wanted was to be on the other side, the artifact in her hands. Then the hard work would begin.

Reesthma went on unhindered, "It's not from Noric or Asandra. I've never seen it before."

Rachel stopped and examined it. At first she had thought the door to be made from birch wood or some similar tree, but now she recognized it for what it was. "This comes from Issym," she said, smiling at the memory of when she had first seen the trees.

His focus captured, Seth recognized the wood. "From Valinor?"

Xsardis 197

"Valinor exists?" Reesthma's eyes widened with wonder.

Evan inquired, "What's Valinor?"

"A place of restoration on Issym," Seth answered him. "Mostly, Rachel's imagination, though I had my part in it. I imagined a grove of trees. They had shimmering bark that could withstand almost anything. And blue leaves more rugged than most trees, but soft to the touch."

Rachel picked up where he left off, "The fairies harvest one tree each year. They use every part of it to build dwellings like their meeting center."

"Very interesting, but what does this have to do with anything?" Vaylynne questioned.

Despite Vaylynne's tone, Rachel returned peaceably, "When Max passed out the second time, he said that the artifact started on Issym, with Issym, but it came here. This wood is the first proof—beyond Seth's memory—we have that someone from Issym was ever here."

Assured that they were close to the artifact, Seth stepped toward the door with determination, but turned to face his fellow teens. "I doubt I need to remind any of you how important it is that we destroy the artifact as soon as we find it. There may be traps in place. Don't waste time; don't hesitate. If our enemy from the passageway is heading here, we don't have much time."

Wrapping his hands around the bark of the handle, Seth pulled the door open.

The high-walled cavern that they entered was large. The rocky mass on which they stood had broken apart. Scattered islands of the rock jutted from the water. To get from one side of the room to the other would take large leaps. On the walls facing them hung fine armor and weapons: glistening swords, bows with a strange shape, arrows tipped with silver, chainmail, staffs and more. Bowls of fire on each of the islands lit up the room brightly.

It took only a second for them to absorb the room and their focus to fall on the woman standing on a rocky floor connected to the far wall. A look of deadly determination marked her face. Her curly brown hair was pulled back. She wore long black boots and a simple blue dress slit at her knees. In an instant, she had drawn a sword from the wall and was running toward them. Without even a battle-cry, she hurtled over the islands.

Vaylynne and Seth jumped to two of the platforms before them, ready to intercept her.

As the woman flipped from one island she pulled a dagger from her boot. She landed before Seth, with her knee, foot and the hand with the dagger touching the ground. Her eyes never left him, ever searching for his weakness. She rose to her feet, the dagger forward, the sword ready. There would be no conversation. Seth hesitated, though he did not know why.

The warrior drove her blade towards his stomach; he pushed it aside with his own. Her dagger thrust for his throat; he twisted it from her wrist with his free hand. Seth had to duck to avoid her next blow toward his head. In the small second her balance wavered, he aimed for her stomach. She jumped back.

Katarina and Evan wordlessly determined their action, than leapt to a platform to Vaylynne's left and moved toward the far wall, encircling their opponent. Max was a few seconds behind them.

Vaylynne leapt onto Seth's island. The warrior blocked both Seth and

Xsardis   198

Vaylynne's attacks with one movement of her sword, then kicked the rebel back. Vaylynne fell into the water. Seth's eyes were diverted to her sinking form.

Seizing the opportunity to jump to the wall beside her, the warrior pulled down two throwing axes. She threw them at Seth. He fell to the ground as he dodged.

The warrior reached for a long white staff and used it to propel herself onto Kat's island. Aiming her foot for Katarina's throat, she sent the princess to the ground gasping for breath. Evan made the mistake of bending by his sister's side. Picking up Katarina's sword, the warrior lunged toward his head. He barely defended in time and fell flat on his back. It was Max that saved him. His sword deflected her next attack. He thrust toward her shoulder. She blocked, but jumped to the next platform.

Pulling herself up from the water, Vaylynne was almost trampled as Rachel rushed past her and ran for their enemy. A blinding light emanated from the warrior's staff and Rachel clutched at her eyes. Seth moved swiftly to her side, working from memory as he kept his eyes closed. As soon as the light receded, Seth opened his eyes and fought to see through the spots that covered his vision. He was just in time to stop a cutting sweep that was meant to sever Rachel's head.

Time slowed as Seth gulped down facts like air. He could not fight this woman on instinct alone. She was far too skilled.

In a second he replayed her movements thus far. She seemed to be equally capable with her left and right hands. She was fighting with the fervor of a last stand, holding nothing back. She had the upper-hand on terrain she knew. Replaying several of the blows, Seth knew she could have killed his friends. Why had she held back? It was as if she was determined to kill them but found herself unable to do so. Seth studied her face more carefully.

The warrior did not share in his hesitation. She swept her staff under his legs and he fell to the ground. Standing over him, she brought her sword down. Seth moved his arms in a futile attempt to defend his chest.

Reesthma tackled the woman to the floor, then rolled out of the reach of the warrior's weapons. In an instant the warrior had her footing, but by then so did Seth. Rachel was by his side. Together they parried her blows. "This isn't right, Seth!" she yelled. "Can't you see who she is?"

His eyes lingered on his adversary's face once more. She slit his leg and brought him to his knees. "Ethelwyn?" he finally perceived.

The warrior hesitated, doubt covering her face.

"Why are you doing this?" Rachel whispered, stepping forward. Of all the friends to have to face as the sprites had predicated, did it have to be this one? Ethelwyn was a woman of honor, someone Rachel truly trusted. As Universe Girl, she had watched over Xsardis well.

"How can I know it's really you?" Ethelwyn replied.

Rachel moved to bind Seth's wound, but Ethelwyn barked at her to stop. "He's bleeding!" the teen protested. "Shifters don't bleed. It's us, Wyn. What has happened to you?"

A rush of color came to Ethelwyn's cheeks and the look of grace and beauty that only she possessed reclaimed her, but she kept her sword up. "For a

Xsardis 199

thousand years this place has been safe. Why have you come?"

"Sasha seeks an artifact that will give her eternal youth," Rachel answered, though unsure whether to fight or to speak. The others stayed back, waiting for her or Seth's direction. "We have come to destroy it."

"This is what I feared," Ethelwyn cried, her voice laden with sorrow. She spun back to the far platform. "I won't let you hurt the child I guard."

"You know us better than that!" Seth shouted.

"And we thought we knew you," Rachel added. "But you'd attack us without hesitation!"

Ethelwyn stared at them with heavy eyes, then nodded. "I will offer you one opportunity to discover what you lack. Seth and Rachel, alone, follow me." Drawing in deep breaths, she held open a door almost indistinguishable beside her.

Rachel, you will fight a person you honor and cherish—a friend—to accomplish your quest. She will lay down her life if she must to stop you...

The prophecy kept Rachel back. If Ethelwyn was ready to die to stop her, how could she be trusted even for a few moments? Recognizing that loyalty was unlikely, Rachel remained motionless for a moment. Lotex had turned against Seth. What was to say Ethelwyn would not turn against Rachel? She refused to give in to the doubt. Unwilling to allow the sprites' words to come true by her reluctance to listen to Wyn, Rachel moved toward the door. Seth eagerly joined her, motioning for Vaylynne to be patient.

The room into which he and Rachel followed Universe Girl had low ceilings, but it appeared even smaller than it was because of the tree piercing the ceiling in the center of the room. Seth recognized it as the tree he had once climbed. Ethelwyn closed the door behind them without a word and locked it. Rachel glanced at Seth uncomfortably. "I distrust you as you distrust me," Universe Girl remarked.

"You did try to kill us," Seth returned.

"I hope to make you understand why, if you are who you say you are," she informed them, taking a seat against the trunk. "Please sit."

A small brook of clear water trickled to the left. Rachel bent beside it and took a drink before leaning against the door. Around her were bags and chests, bearing what she could only guess was treasure. Was this what Ethelwyn was protecting? "Where did you learn to fight like that?" Rachel asked, eyes locking on Wyn again.

"A thousand years of training can make anyone excellent in battle."

"A thousand years…" Rachel repeated the words.

Universe Girl met the teen's gaze with the weary eyes she had hidden so well at their first meeting on Issym. Light from one of the bowls of fire reflected off her hair. Rachel had never before noticed that amidst her dark locks were strands of silver hair. "What is going on?" Rachel insisted.

"Oh, I think it truly is you," Ethelwyn groaned. "If it is not, let Issym forgive me! I will tell you all."

Putting aside her sword, she continued, "There was a time when I was the happy child you meant me to be, Rachel. After tragedy, I found a better existence than what I had lost. But one creature's hatred destroyed that life forever."

Xsardis   200

She gestured with her hand for someone to come to her. A girl who appeared to be ten years old rounded the tree. Her wavy brown hair fell above her shoulders. Her keen blue-green eyes peered out with a depth of understanding unusual in children that young. Though her pink dress hung loosely about her childish figure, it could not diminish the beauty derived from the pure radiance of her nature. "This is Nadine, my sister. Nadine, greet Seth and Rachel."

Nadine's delicate lips parted as if she was going to speak, but she remained silent and erect, soaking in the picture. Rachel was instantly and overpoweringly drawn to the girl.

"This is who I protect," Ethelwyn explained.

"I see why you would have done anything to defend her," Rachel professed.

As Nadine took her place by her sister's side, Universe Girl began her tale, "You may remember parts of this story, but so much has been hidden from you."

"By whom?" Seth investigated.

"By me," she confessed. "In the early days of Issym's wanderings, he happened upon a young dragon: Santana. Issym became his older brother—like a father to the leviathan—and taught him to speak. He gave him a family and a purpose. The two would fly over the land. Though Issym would drop from his back before Santana could be seen, the two made a powerful pair.

"Issym was wise enough to know that people fear what they cannot understand. They would have killed Santana had they known about him. This is why Issym kept him a secret. Santana's jealousy rose," her voice was so low they strained to hear it.

"Not taking money for his services, Issym remained poor. The dragon's thirst for gold began to grow. He could not comprehend Issym's love of the people of his homeland. Santana craved attention. When Issym agreed to take Asandra to her palace, Santana refused to help him.

"Seeing the love Issym offered Asandra, the dragon turned his back on his brother and allowed selfishness to consume him. He began to wreak a secret havoc over the land. When he claimed Mt. Smolden, he took that name and gathered evil men to himself. His attacks grew more bold and less satisfying.

"King Shobal learned of Issym's connection to Smolden and sent for him. Pushed by his bride, the warrior returned home. With the help of two children, he banished Santana to the unground.

"Even in light of his victory, Issym was grieved at the destruction he saw and the knowledge that it was his brother's hatred of him from which it had stemmed. When he met a girl orphaned by the dragon's cruelty, he could not leave her. Adopting the child, he brought her back to Asandra on a ship filled with treasures granted by a grateful Shobal. That child was me."

Rachel blinked rapidly. "You're a thousand years old?"

"As is my sister. Nadine is Asandra's true daughter."

Rachel stared at Nadine, the child of the woman she had spent much time pretending to be. Her beauty was reminiscent of Asandra's. The soft manner, the gentle spirit, the wild life in the blue-green eyes… Rachel's heart

Xsardis

201

swelled as she realized the truth of what she was hearing. Nadine looked back at her, unaware of the awe she was inspiring.

"Issym had no descendants," Seth protested.

"None that ruled," Ethelwyn corrected. "Asandra grew sick—very sick. In his rage, Santana had poisoned her." Her desperately beautiful eyes watered. "I cared for Nadine as our mother grew worse and worse. We were closer than blood sisters could have been." Wyn ran her hand through Nadine's angelic hair. "Like Asandra and Issym, she was an incredibly curious child. One day, a suitor came to the palace to see me. I was not with her.

"Nadine loved stories. She wanted her maid to take her to the vault where we kept the treasures from King Shobal and tell her of her father's exploits. The woman was distracted by the guard at the door. No one noticed as Nadine swallowed a small pearl."

Shaking her head, Ethelwyn lamented, "I should have been there!"

"What happened to you, Nadine?" Seth asked softly.

"At first nothing," Wyn answered for her sister. "I went to wake her one morning and she was no longer five, but ten years old. I was stunned, but I knew my own sister."

"She had grown five years overnight?" Rachel made sure.

Universe Girl bent her head in answer. "A few nights later I found her to be fourteen. She continued to grow until she appeared to be an elderly woman. Issym was so broken. Every day we expected to find out that Nadine was dead. With Asandra's worsening condition, it was more than any of us could bear.

"A violent earthquake shook the ground one night. I raced to get Nadine and heard a baby crying. She had started her life over. Growth, too, was different on the land. Other children weren't aging. Food would sprout overnight and then wither in the morning. With a grave perception, Issym knew that if he did not move his daughter, she would unwittingly destroy the world. He had a terrible choice to make."

Seth and Rachel remained silent. This was not just history to them. The people in the story were the family of their childhood.

"He commissioned the dwarves, Asandra's elite and respected citizens, to go to Noric and oversee her protection. They were experts in Valean rock—possessing more than anyone knew—and built this entire network of caverns. Issym imported the finest gifts he could to this underground chamber—all that King Shobal had given him. Bags where food would replenish overnight. The softest blankets they had. Staffs that would offer light when the cave grew too dark. Carousels that played songs he had sung to her. Books—scores of highly prized books. Yarn and thread and wood so that she would have things to do.

"With great agony, he took her and put her in the cave. When she transformed, she would hurt no one else. And in this shelter of Valean rock, the earthquake that occurs with her recycling ceased and the land replenishes itself as Nadine's body does. Even so, Issym could not leave her alone. He was going to stay. But Asandra was dying and the world still needed him. I begged my father to let me stay with Nadine. With increasing pain, he assented.

"Issym bound the dwarfs with oaths of loyalty that would last

Xsardis

throughout the centuries. He gave me the orbs that made me Universe Girl, in order that I could still see the sun from time to time. When he left us, I thought it was the last time I would ever see him. But he came back once more. I recognized a look in his eyes. It said he would never give up searching for a cure for her to free us both. He never came back.

"Over the years, Nadine and I decided it would be better if I kept an eye on the world to watch for danger or a cure. I established myself on Issym—every generation as a new woman, most commonly a warrior."

"I understand how Nadine has lived for a thousand years," Seth began, "but how have you?"

"As she made the growth on Asandra change, she also changed me. I will stay young forever. I possess the eternal youth that Sasha searches for. The dwarfs, living above us, also receive long life—though not eternal."

"Do they know you're here?" Seth thought about Lotex, willing to do anything to protect their treasure: Nadine.

"Only a few, and they are tasked with our protection."

Remembering how she fought, Rachel said, "Seems like you don't need them. Why did you attack us?"

"I had no choice. I didn't know if you were shape shifters, or if you had been perverted somehow. I could not risk Nadine falling into Sasha's hands. Nadine would unwillingly give her eternal youth and, more than likely, invincibility. Sasha seeks the pearl Nadine ate, but once she knows all that you know, she will claim Nadine. This I could not let happen."

"Why didn't you come with the others to Asandra to fight?" Rachel probed.

"When Nadine is an infant I must be here to care for her. Seth, Rachel, you must help me guard Nadine. She is a treasure that Sasha will seek not only for what is inside her, but also for what she knows. By the time she is old, she remembers all that she has learned in her thousand years of life."

Seth and Rachel sat there, letting the lore of Xsardis sink in. Everything—all they had ever imagined or done on this world—boiled down to the words Ethelwyn had just spoken.

Rachel stood, "We believe Sasha is right behind us."

Ethelwyn rose to her feet. How had Seth not noticed before that she carried herself as a warrior? He had seen the burden of knowledge on her, but not this. They had thought she was merely a twenty-year-old girl with some mystical orbs. How wrong they had been!

"I will fight Sasha here if it comes to that. Since rumors first came of her I feared she would be the one."

"What one?" Rachel inquired. She longed to do something for Nadine and Ethelwyn other than ask questions, but until she knew more, it was all she could do.

"Issym warned me that one day a shifter utterly consumed with self would push beyond the bounds of reason and grasp for eternal youth, not comprehending any cost," Universe Girl reported. "That is why I went to Issym—to watch for this danger. And I commissioned men like Joppa to be watchers of Asandra. This is why I have trained for a thousand years. If the day to make this stand has come, then so be it."

Seth looked to Rachel. They both recognized that their own fates were now tied to Nadine and Ethelwyn's. "We brought Sasha to your door," Seth determined. "We will not abandon you to the consequences."

Rachel agreed, "We must prepare ourselves to fight."

Caleb stumbled back to their small camp bearing a load of sticks to keep his fire alive. It was hardly after dark, but his fatigue was overwhelming. For days Drainan had been pushing him in weaponry, in making fire, in finding shelter, in hunting and in anything else that came to the man's mind. A rabbit roasted over the fire, the trophy of Caleb's successful hunt. Though he was weary as he sat down, the youth also felt invigorated and competent for one of the first times in his life.

They were nearing Maremoth, and although Caleb was still concerned that he would do more harm than good in attempting a rescue, he was beginning to feel hopeful. He leaned back against a tree, listening to Drainan and Bridget bicker about when to leave the next morning. Drainan continually put his will against hers. He seemed like the kind of man who rarely lost a fight. She seemed to be a submissive personality. Yet, if Bridget disagreed with him about their strategy, she would say, "I'm doing it this way. If you don't agree, you don't have to help me." That usually ended the debate.

As their conversation waned, Bridget and Drainan allowed Caleb to take first watch. He was unable to sleep anyway. For hours he stared into the dying embers of his little fire. He had a decision to make.

Bridget still did not want him to go into Maremoth. She said it was too dangerous. Would he back out or stick to his determination to follow them into the belly of the beast?

Caleb tried to discern what Seth would have said had he been there. But Seth was not there. He was off doing something important. Someone had to stand up for the individuals that the heroes of Saphree could not yet free. That was why he had joined Vaylynne's movement in the first place. He could not back down now!

Yet when Drainan took over watch for the evening, Caleb remained unable to sleep. By the time the dawn had risen, he was no closer to a decision or to being rested.

"How could you have just let them go on?" Beatrice demanded. She

Xsardis 204

held a drink of water in her hands for her weary brother, but he would receive no more care until he offered answers.

"Leave me alone!" Lotex barked.

His customary growl did not set his sister back in least, "You should have taken help down with you! But your favor for the boy clouded your judgment."

The dwarf lowered his voice in a rare moment of truthful interchange between himself and his sister, "I had no right to stop them."

She hesitated, then shouted, "You had every right! For a thousand years we've kept Issym's greatest treasure. Not even Seth has the merit to break that tradition."

"Sometimes traditions need to be thrown out," Lotex replied meekly.

"Yes. And sometimes brothers need to be thrown out too," she half-teased.

Chapter 26

"We're going to assume that Sasha is coming for Nadine." Seth had explained to the others what Ethelwyn had told Rachel and him. Now, he carried the formal tone of their leader. "Obviously, our pact to destroy the artifact is not an option. Our only course is to stay and protect a child that must be protected at all costs. We have the stones; we have a chance. Even so, I cannot ask any of you stay. Sasha's desperation will test us in ways we cannot prepare for. I will fight."

"As will I," Rachel agreed.

Katarina looked around at the group, then questioned, "What did we come down here for if not to stop Sasha? I'm not going anywhere."

Max glanced across the room at Nadine, then stood. "Neither am I."

Evan looked at her. The daughter of Issym and Asandra, both pure and beautiful. "That girl is what we have been fighting for since the very beginning. I will not leave her."

Reesthma glanced at Vaylynne, then determined, "I will stay."

Vaylynne asked, "Have I ever turned down a fight?"

Ethelwyn nodded gratefully. She might have said something, but Nadine whispered to her. The two moved to the next room and shut the door.

Katarina spoke softly to her brother, though all could hear her, "What do you think is happening on Asandra?"

"There's no way to know, but I hope we can get back to them soon," he returned.

The sounds of a water splash filled their ears. Katarina turned to see what had happened. Max was missing. Leaping to the signs of where he had fallen into the water, Kat saw his limp form. She reached for his head and floated it above water. Seth was there in a moment. He dove into the salty water and pulled Max ashore. Seth's features turned stony as he quickly scanned his friend for breath or injury.

Ethelwyn opened the door and moved to their sides in an instant. "Is he hurt?"

Xsardis

206

"He passed out again for no reason," Seth answered.

"Has this happened before?" she investigated, her mind suddenly focused.

"Twice," Rachel replied. "As we've been getting closer to this cave."

Ethelwyn bent over Max, sweeping Katarina out of the way. The girl waited beside her brother. Universe Girl eyed Max with wonder. He was shaking.

Seth demanded, "What's happening to him?"

Taking another moment to be sure, she informed him, "He is tied to Nadine's transformation."

"How?" Seth and Rachel asked in unison.

"Only he can tell us." Clearly, Ethelwyn craved the knowledge herself.

"Is there anything we can do?" Seth inquired.

"Blankets and a fire to keep him from catching cold. That is all."

Seth and Evan lifted Max to the fireside that Vaylynne had already built up in a stone pit made for the blaze. Then they waited.

Vaylynne moved to a distant platform and began her dance-like routine. Reesthma made her way to her mentor. "You're doing that now? While Max is in trouble?"

Sighing, Vaylynne told her, "A routine like this is meant to help you stay grounded when the rest of the world is chaotic." She paused, then added, "And it is meant to be done alone."

The warrior longed to think in peace, but her apprentice would not be dissuaded. Reesthma began to mimic the moves she had been learning.

Seth studied them and guessed, "Vaylynne is training her, isn't she?"

Katarina shrugged, staying close to Max's form. "I didn't know what else to do when the group was separated."

"You did the right thing."

Standing, Seth moved to the door to which the pitara had brought them. It was still open, providing a view of the empty water before them. How long would it be before Sasha came? He did not doubt that it was her approaching. Maybe it had even been her who had taken on dwarf shape and stopped Lotex. It would make sense if Sasha had meant to follow them to the artifact all along. If only it had been an artifact! He could not comprehend how Ethelwyn and Nadine had had the heart to survive for so long.

When Max's shaking stopped, Evan drew Katarina to play a hand-game in the corner. They passed the tension as they so often had done in the underground. The princess' untimely laughter brought some life back into the cavern.

Nadine opened the door to her chamber and stepped out, practically unrecognizable. The same watery blue-green eyes and soft skin were all that was left of the child they had seen only a few minutes ago. Her hair had darkened and now fell below her shoulders. The dress fit the curves of her new figure. Though she walked without pride, her gait showed confidence. An anklet of bells rang as her bare feet graced the rocky floor.

She might have been as young as fourteen, but the maturity that had claimed her spoke of a young woman. Though her attire was not adorned, her

Xsardis

207

fingers bore rings the likes of which the teens had never seen before. Their large, colored stones possessed deep colors.

Discerning the stares of all those in the room, Nadine spoke, "Yes?" It was the first time they had heard her voice. The inflection was perfect. One word set them all at ease.

Taking Ethelwyn's long, white staff, she propelled herself over the islands with strong arms. At Max's side, she knelt beside him with her hands on his chest. "How are we connected?" she whispered with anticipation. Only Evan heard the small words of a girl desperate for answers.

Standing, Nadine addressed them, "Thank you for your willingness to protect me. I would try to dissuade you, but Ethel has assured me there would be no point. If you are to win this battle, you need rest and food and weapons stronger than you now have. These things I can offer you."

The simple thought of food made Seth weak in the knees. He *was* hungry.

Nadine perceived the group's needs easily and took over as host, allowing Ethelwyn to sit with Seth and Rachel to talk further. She returned to her room to gather supplies. Evan followed wordlessly to help.

As he rounded the tree, he saw her shoulders shaking with emotion. "Are you alright?" he asked quickly.

She turned, her face flush, but her eyes clear. "I am fine, Prince Evan."

Ethelwyn had introduced them only once, but Nadine had no trouble remembering the names of some of the first people she had met in a thousand years.

"Can I carry that for you?" he offered, extending his hands for a bag full of food she had picked up.

"Thank you." She gratefully handed it over. When he stayed unmoving, Nadine told him, "There is nothing wrong. It is just that when all of this started, Ethelwyn used to tell me that someday someone would come and set me free. She would never say 'us free,' though she is as much a captive as I am. After a few hundred years, she stopped saying it. I stopped believing it. And then you and your friends came."

"There is still hope," he promised her.

"I am not the naïve young child I once was," she responded. "Though I have confidence you may stop Sasha, there is no exit for me from this place. I would not risk Xsardis for anything. And yet," her eyes watered, "my very life puts Xsardis at risk. That *is* unbearable."

"Nadine," he stepped closer to her, longing to give comfort to one such as this, "we won't let that happen."

"Those stones that hinder Sasha now will have no effect if she takes me. Ethelwyn is not easily injured. With Sasha's power, she may not be able to be hurt at all. That is why I weep. I cannot serve to destroy Xsardis."

Evan could not blame her for her concern. If there was a cure, would it not have been found in a thousand years? Suddenly a great longing to find that remedy lodged in Evan's heart. He could not leave her trapped down here for another thousand years. "Have you never come out?" he asked.

"No," she shook her head, filling a canteen. "Sometimes a dwarf will come and visit here. Only when Ethelwyn is absent. She does not approve of the risk. I'm not sure I do either, but it gets very lonely down here. I would not risk going to the surface. It is better if I fade from memory."

Nadine looked anything but faded. With each sentence a color came to her cheeks and a strength grew in her eyes. She carried a weight, but Evan could see a freedom lurking behind this girl's eyes. If the day came to throw down the chains that locked her in this place, she would put her life to remarkable use.

Conquest is no easy thing, Stewart remarked as he rode toward the sprite nest. Was Kate deceiving him? Would the dark sprites destroy him as Sasha had warned? Was he tying his own noose in setting himself against Sasha?

After all, Stewart had never been credited with an overabundance of ability or intelligence. But from an early age he had recognized in himself two far more powerful assets: charm and motivation.

The most brilliant men in the world often never had their abilities recognized because they either lacked the attractiveness to get people to notice them or they had no drive to complete their work. Stewart had dreams of power and riches and he had set about to conquer those dreams. He had charmed his way up the social latter of Sasha's empire—skipping all but the meaningful levels. He had kept her favor so far, too. And now he was charming his way through Asandra, winning allegiances that Sasha had cast aside or forgotten.

The shape shifter had become too absorbed in hunting Seth down and finding her eternal youth. Once she had had powerful alliances. Now she let her once-servants become strong. *An estranged ally is a great risk.* He'd thought of that one himself. And they said he didn't have brains!

Stewart's horse trotted toward the sprite nest. This quest would require more diplomacy than any other. His flattering tongue would have to work hard to woo these young children from their old mistress. Perhaps romance for the ladies… He slicked back his hair. He always had been a flirt.

Admitted to the nest, Stewart was glad they had received word that he was coming. No dramatic pyrotechnics for him. He was simply led down a hole and into the caverns. The sprites hovered in the air, hundreds of them. There were many varieties—none of them appearing powerful—but all of them looking selfishly and wondrously evil. Scrawny creatures, they bore more resemblance to teenagers than to the legends that abounded about them.

The large room in which he waited breathed excitement. There had been a commotion not long ago. Stewart cursed his timing. He was supposed to be the light of their boring lives.

Their ruler, Golesha, had been expecting him. So why was he just standing there? Why had she not yet sent for him? A true king of Asandra would not wait. Finally, two fire sprite girls and an earth sprite boy flew to him and led him to a separate room.

Sitting on a boulder was Golesha. Around her were a dozen other sprites. They were laughing, sharing a drink, having some glorious moment that had nothing to do with him. It didn't bode well for his speech. And he had never been a favorite with Golesha.

When her eyes landed on him, she sat up straight and smiled. "Ah, Stewart! How do you like my palace?"

"It's lovely." He caught his derogative tone and said with more enthusiasm, "I like how you run things."

"I hear you're running things differently now, too. I didn't think you were the type to stand up to Sasha!"

Stewart cast his eyes about the room. Though food abounded, few touched it. Every sprite there looked anorexic. It would not be a surprise. They were an especially vain group. "What has caused all the excitement?" he asked.

"You are not the only important person to have visited us!" she boasted. "The shape shifter Kate came only a few minutes ago."

"Kate?" Stewart's face dropped. "Are you sure?"

"Yes. Do you think I cannot tell one shifter from another? Kate does not see us as weak children. She seeks our aid."

Grimacing, Stewart evaluated the situation. Had Kate come to the sprites to advance *their* cause? Or was he every bit as much a pawn of hers as these foolish sprites were? "Did she prove her loyalty to you, Lady Golesha?"

The fire sprite grinned, "She told us of an enemy sprites' post. We will destroy it soon enough."

"Could it be a trap?" he suggested.

She flew toward him. "I don't like you, Stewart. I don't trust you. I think you believe we're useless kids. But Kate has made an alliance with you and I believe in Kate."

Her voice deepened, "That is why I will permit you to turn around and go back to Maremoth. When Kate calls on our services, I'll support you. Until then, stay out of my way."

The Brothers had returned to Saphree with heavy hearts. They had waited hours for Jennet to return. They would have waited days, but a single bracelet had dropped from the heavens. She had told them it was one of a set that she and Danielle had been given. It never left her wrist.

"She's gone," Jeff had whispered, moved despite all the death he had seen.

The two men entered Issym's counsel room to inform the others. Danielle gleaned all she needed to from their faces. "Galen, how could you?" she exclaimed.

Xsardis 210

The king bowed his head, taking the impact of the grief. Queen Danielle dashed from the room, all ceremony abandoned. Galen felt Flibbert's three fingers grip his shoulder. He looked up, "Why did you put me on the throne, Flibbert? I can't save their lives."

"But you'll try. That's all we ask."

"When Jennet went up to the clouds, they turned suddenly dark. A few hours later this dropped from the sky," Jeff informed, handing Flibbert the bracelet.

"I will send men back out to search for a body," Sphen declared.

"Don't," Flibbert replied. "Airsprites disintegrate when they die."

Sphen nodded. He hesitated to report more to Galen before he had spoken with his king, but went on, "I think it is clear that we must not wait for the dark sprites to pick us off one by one. We must bring a decisive battle… And quickly."

"At what cost?" Jeff retorted. "We still cannot defeat even one of the creatures!"

Galen looked between the two men. "We cannot wait and leave the villages helpless. Speak with your king; make sure he agrees."

Sphen marched from the room. Jeff held back just a second longer. "Surely *you* wish to speak to King Remar," he suggested to Galen.

The discord between Remar and Galen had been growing. It could cost them much in battle and it was already costing them support with the soldiers.

"I would," the high king responded, "but it would be more effective if you did."

By the time Jeff had regained his brother, Sphen had reached the king's throne room. It was now more of a war room than an audience chamber. Long tables stretched out. Men in armor moved about the space. King Remar and Sphen stood in the doorway. "We must fight this enemy in our full strength," Sphen finished.

"What are they?" mused Remar in Jeff's direction. "How can they have lived above us for so long without us ever knowing?"

Jeff exhaled before answering, "They are a powerful enemy. We must learn about them. I will go to the historian as soon as there is time."

Remar searched The Brothers' eyes, looking for some other option but drawing out a battle with the dark sprites. Finally he nodded.

Chapter 27

Rachel finished sewing a couple of the stones Seth had brought with them onto her new leather vest. She put it on over her long sleeved, white blouse. The armor was not much protection, but it might save her life.

They knew the battle could come at any moment, but they still moved sluggishly. "It could have been Lotex," Rachel offered to Seth.

He weighed the chainmail, then picked up the leather armor. Nadine had offered him his choice. Though the chainmail was lighter than any had had before felt, he knew speed would offer him greater defense than armor in the fight to come. He pulled on the leather. "Maybe. But I've been thinking about the noise. One creature—a big creature—made it."

The cavern was filled with the sounds of Vaylynne and Reesthma sparring. The ground almost gave Reesthma the upper hand. Her balance allowed her to jump from island to island with ease. In the din, Seth found the opportunity to talk to Rachel out of the others' hearing.

"I thought," he started, "that when we came to Asandra, we were waging a different war than the one we fought on Issym. I figured we had won one battle and we simply had to win another. But this is the same fight that Xsardis has been waging since the time of Issym. We keep learning things that we didn't know; that we couldn't have helped with.

"Smolden poisoned Asandra. I feel like that just happened! He probably put the pearl on the ship with Issym to cause trouble... Now Nadine has been a captive for a thousand years and we might not be able to aid her. We might not set Xsardis right."

Rachel leaned closer to him, "And what if we do finish our work here? What then? We're not the same people we were when they brought us here for the first time. I was a dreamer with no sense of cold reality. I can't just be that person again, even if we got things figured out on Earth."

"I don't want to be the person I was before I came here," he returned. "Would it be so wrong if we stayed? There's a lot left for us to learn about Xsardis; a lot we might be able to help with."

Xsardis   212

"I didn't want to hope that you were thinking about staying. Seth, you know my life is totaled at home. I don't want to go back."

Seth felt Vaylynne's eyes on him—drawn in by their quiet conversation. When they moved on from him, he spoke to Rachel, "I think Vaylynne is about to do something dangerous."

"For us or against us?"

"Probably against us. I shouldn't have brought her along."

"Maybe not. But you did. And I'm not sure you were wrong."

Ethelwyn knelt beside them, her face turned from the others. "I have communicated with the dwarfs above. I believe you know Lotex, Seth."

Nodding, Seth wondered what could possibly come next.

"He informed me that the dark sprites have risen." Her voice was soft, but in the lull without the sounds of Vaylynne and Reesthma's practice it carried around the cavern. "They need your help on Asandra."

Katarina plopped to the ground beside the still-unconscious Max and pulled on a new pair of boots. Her previous clothing was ruined from the fall, and what she wore now was all new. Her auburn hair was already pulled out of the way. Her vest was waiting for her to slide it on. She tried not to focus on her sick friend and how if battle did come, he would be in the most dangerous position. She dodged thoughts about how much danger Asandra was experiencing. She did not know anything about the dark sprites, but the way the warrior Ethelwyn's face paled, she understood that her country was in grave danger.

"Mountain Dew," Max whispered. "I want Mountain Dew."

His eyes popped open as a sly smile spread across his face. Katarina's gleaming eyes were his first sight. "We're nowhere near a mountain," she replied, missing his reference to an Earth drink.

Max sat up. "Did I pass out again?"

"Yes. But now we have an idea why."

Max did not need to hear. His eyes were locked on the older form of Nadine. "I'm tied to her."

Kat snorted.

Staring at her across several platforms, Max felt as if he knew Nadine. She skipped across the islands and alighted before him, her eyes never falling from his. He rose to his feet as she greeted him in her soft tones. "Hello, Max."

"Hello."

"I'm sorry my transformations are hurting you."

"I don't know how you go through that every time."

"You get used to it. I have a lot of questions for you."

"I hope I can answer them."

Nadine put a delicate hand on his arm and steered him toward the far wall. Katarina had been the one sitting there when Max had woken up. How quickly he had moved on! She couldn't discern what Nadine said, but it made Max laugh. Kat turned to her brother and spoke forcefully, "We can't hope to protect Nadine. We need to take stronger action."

Her brother told her, "I don't like where you're heading."

Earning Vaylynne's approval, Reesthma sheathed her weapon and

Xsardis   213

jumped to their platform. Her breaths came in the steady rhythm forced by exercise as she explained, "History is full of aggressors who were determined never to stop. We've exposed Nadine, not only to Sasha but to anyone who hears of our mission. We can't make one stand and think it is over."

"We have to seal the cave," Princess Katarina finished.

"What?" Evan's mind caught on his sister's words. "No!"

"Evan," she lowered her voice, "this is the only way to make sure Nadine is safe. She'll live another thousand years in peace."

"Peace?" the prince rebuffed. "She's a captive and she deserves our help."

Kat assured, "If we could, I would do anything for her. But we can't. This is for her good."

"Her good? She is not in the least danger. Anyone who comes after her will want her alive. Still, she stays here for the good of the rest of us. Doesn't that merit more?"

Agreeing with him could not change Katarina's certainty that there was nothing they could do but close her in the cave. She pulled Seth and Rachel back with a look. In a few moments, the entire group was huddled on a small platform, discussing the ramifications of their decision.

"Are we really talking about hiding like cowards?" Vaylynne questioned.

"We won't get off this island without fighting Sasha," Seth knew. "We're not hiding anywhere, but we are hiding Nadine. I don't want to risk her."

The daughter of Asandra stood without offering her opinion. She did not beg them to search their memories to find an escape for her. She did not beseech them to save her at any cost. She did not offer a tear at the prospect she was being offered. Nadine waited. It hurt Rachel more than her weeping would have. The last thing she wanted to do was to forever condemn this beautiful child to life in this cavern. Prayerfully, she voiced, "Issym already made this decision. And it was for a day such as this that he gave Ethelwyn the orbs."

"If we are talking about making a final seal, I would choose to remain here with my sister without surfacing again. It would be better if nothing happened to arouse suspicions that she had survived the sealing. Let all think we are dead," Ethelwyn decided.

"But you would still have the orbs if you discovered a way to heal Nadine," Reesthma offered.

"I would," the elder sister nodded. "And I would use them for only such a time. Though I assure you, if I was capable of saving my sister, I would have done it long ago."

"This is ludicrous!" Evan decried. He challenged Seth and Rachel, "Come on! You are the people who scaled Mt. Smolden, destroyed an invincible dragon, saved me when I had been mortally wounded with a poisoned dagger, defied prophecies of evil sound sprites, and discovered the lost location of Issym's daughter! Now you are just going to give up? Figure it out! Seth, if this was Rachel, would you give up so easily?"

In frustration, Vaylynne shook her head. "Nadine has been here for a thousand years. What's changing?"

Xsardis

214

"Hope," Evan answered simply, his eyes falling on her still-silent form. "That is exactly what we have been fighting to keep!"

The prince implored his sister, "Kat, remember what it was like to live in the underground, with little optimism that we would survive. We didn't have the heart to fight. We didn't have the heart to go on. And now you want to close Nadine in forever with no hope? Even if someone finds a cure, they won't be able to give it to her. What would that do to you?"

"I see all points here," Max added his opinion to the chorus as Katarina reeled from her brother's words. "I can't stand the thought of leaving Nadine down here, but I know it would torture her more to be the reason Xsardis fell to Sasha."

Evan and Seth began to argue the points again. Rachel's focus fell on Ethelwyn. She was barely holding herself back from launching into the bickering teens and making the decision that was her right to make.

Nadine silenced them for her. The daughter of Issym and Asandra stepped forward and made her voice heard, "Listen to me now! This is not your choice to make. It is mine. I have the right to sacrifice myself for my people. I exercise that right. Seal the cavern."

At the protests from Evan and Max, she added, "Don't waste precious time. Asandra needs you heroes back on its mainland. The dark sprites are an enemy too great to trifle with. Please, defend my homeland. This is the favor I ask of you. If you do this, my captivity here will not seem as bleak."

Prince Evan nodded. "There is another choice we must make. As we've already been told, to defeat the dark sprites we will need strong warriors—like Ethelwyn."

"No…" Ethelwyn knew where he was going.

"If I'm not mistaken, you're not only a bodyguard. You are The Legend. A female warrior who has arisen at every terrible time in Xsardis' history to defend the good."

Universe Girl nodded. "I am."

"Then Asandra needs you now." His words bore the weight of his choice, "Can you defeat the dark sprites?"

She spoke with honesty, "I stand a greater chance than the others."

"I will take your place guarding Nadine, if you will take mine guarding Asandra."

"Evan, no," Katarina pleaded.

The prince rubbed his shoulder. "The one thing I know is that I must protect my country. I can't fight until I am healed. Nadine's youth should be able to take care of that. In a few days I will be able to defend her. But Asandra can't wait. It needs you all back now. It does not need me."

"Of course we need you, you idiot," Katarina began. "You're the heir to the throne!"

A glance passed between Evan and Seth. Seth still could not answer whether he would stay on Xsardis or not, but he could guarantee to watch out for the country if Evan remained with Nadine. Seth nodded. The prince stepped back from the group. "You will lead, Katarina. Seth and Rachel will aid you. Under your guidance—and Ethelwyn's—Asandra may see a new time of peace. This is worth any cost. Least of all staying with one such as Nadine."

"How can you do this to me, to our parents, to our country?" Kat demanded.

Ethelwyn could contain herself no longer. "I won't leave Nadine."

Her sister put both her hands on her arm. "Ethel, you've been with me a thousand years. It's time to say goodbye."

"I've trained a thousand years to defend her," Universe Girl rebutted to the group.

"Maybe you've trained a thousand years to defeat Nadine's biggest dangers: Sasha and the dark sprites," Max suggested, finally coming to terms with Evan's determination to stay.

"Be free now," Nadine pressed.

Ethelwyn held out, then nodded. She succumbed in an instant to duty, as she had all her life. "Issym thought we might one day have to seal the cavern. He gave us the tools required."

"I hate fighting dirty," Flibbert acknowledged, "but we don't have much choice. The dark sprites are vulnerable at only one time."

"Which is?" Sphen was eager to glean.

"Right after a rain. Most of their cloud cover will be gone, and with it, their power."

"He is right. Although, it won't take them long to blow in more clouds." Queen Danielle, her face washed out and her form limp, moved into the room and took a seat.

Hesitantly, Galen looked at her. Danielle addressed him, "I am sorry for my anger and my secrecy. Let me help stop the damage my silence caused."

"What do you suggest?" he queried, trusting her again.

"Draw the fight here. We can use the fortress of Saphree to protect us from much of their power over the weather. The dark sprites fight best in the freedom of the skies, not the confines of man-made walls. I must admit that though they are few in number, they are great in power. I cannot guarantee that we can best them."

"How do you suggest we bring them here?" Sphen probed.

Her eyes lifted for the first time and Flibbert discerned a fire still in them. "I will challenge them."

"And what if they kill you first?" Jeff recognized the probability. "Why do you think you would have a different outcome than Jennet?"

"They won't touch me," the airsprite queen replied. "They'll want to meet me in battle—where they can kill me in front of my people. And they'll want to prolong my suffering at Jennet's death." She met Galen's stare. "I can do this."

"Danny, no," Flibbert spoke quickly.

"You haven't called me that since I was a little girl," she smiled

Xsardis   216

faintly. "But I am not that girl anymore. You need only set a time, High King."

Galen thought about seeking Remar's counsel, but with The Brothers present, he had the authority he needed to make the determination. He could not afford to waste the time Remar's endless debates would require. "One week from now."

The meeting concluded, Galen and Flibbert moved towards the kitchen. The afternoon meal would be their first of the day. Flibbert masked his concern as he said, "I don't know if it was wise to send Danielle."

"It would have been more unwise not to send her," Galen pointed out.

Flibbert scooped out a bowl of soup, grabbed a piece of bread and took a seat at one of the few small tables in the kitchen. Galen took a sip of his cider and spoke, "Can we avoid the topic of war for a few minutes?"

His own thoughts rested with Andrea. Sweet Andrea. Had their child been born healthy? The draw to return and protect his bride and infant was too great. Fear grew inside him every day that Sasha was not on Noric hunting for the artifact or at Maremoth hiding, but was on Issym terrifying his land.

Flibbert raised a subject he knew Galen would not relish. "There is something we have to talk about. You may find this surprising, but I have come to respect Kate. Still, there are rumors developing."

Galen abandoned his spoon and his soup. So much for dinner. "What rumors?"

"That she may have turned on us." Flibbert would not say anything further until Galen sought more information. It was a dangerous topic.

The king leaned forward. He strongly doubted the accusations were accurate, but he could not afford to turn a blind eye. "Is there reason to believe this is true?"

"I don't know," the frog admitted. "She has been missing. Elimilech has searched for her with his scouting fairies. He cannot find her. There are uncertain reports of her near Maremoth."

Unconvinced, Galen reminded, "We sent her there. And Kate's always kept me in the dark about her true plans. Her disappearance could simply be part of her attack on Sasha."

"But there is one thing we cannot explain. The enemy fire and earth sprites are boasting of a massacre of our sprites at the Gratuk Lake."

"Kate's overseeing the sprites, isn't she?" Flibbert's large eyes told Galen the truth. "And you can't think of anyone else who would have told the enemy where our troops were stationed." The king paused. "I thought we called our troops back. Did Remar have sprites at Gratuk?"

Flibbert sighed and slapped his spindly leg. "I don't know! I wouldn't put it past the king to leave soldiers on the field and not tell us."

Galen knew the frog would already have confirmed the rumors or he would not have brought them up. One of the many things he appreciated about Flibbert. "What did you find at Lake Gratuk?"

Flibbert finished his soup before replying, "Evidence of battle. No bodies. This will only increase the distrust between the shifters and the fairies."

Galen rubbed his weary eyes. "I refuse to believe ill of her until we know more."

"Agreed," Flibbert responded. "But by then, it might be too late to stop her."

"Who else do the shifters look to? Anyone we can trust?"

"Kate's second is Nevel. Even I like him."

For Flibbert to like a shifter, Nevel must have been impressive. "Delicately," the high king emphasized, "let's bring him into our circle. Transfer power to him until we know more about Kate. Maybe he can even earn the fairies respect."

"We have to wait until tomorrow, Bridget," Drainan forced.

"It might be too late by then. What if his execution is at dawn?" she countered.

Despite their difficulties finding food, Bridget was looking less and less malnourished as time went on. No one had been able to refuse her honest face when she had asked for a small loaf of bread and anything was better than what she had gotten in Maremoth. Her skin was a perpetual tan from her time at sea and their constant walking. Though her dress was muddy from their journey and a twig stuck out of her long hair, Bridget still looked strong. Muscle earned from Maremoth and a brave spirit led to a healthy glow and fiery determination to rescue her friend.

Drainan refused to be distracted. "*Our* executions will be at dawn if we look conspicuous as we enter."

Bridget looked forward at Caleb, pressing on towards the fortress despite his stumbling legs. Drainan had trained him well in the short time. She saw enough improvement that she was not entirely opposed to him attempting the rescue with them. They all needed sleep if they were going to succeed. "Okay. We'll wait until tomorrow."

They dropped amongst the trees. Caleb was asleep in an instant, not even possessing enough energy to eat. They did not risk a fire that close to Maremoth.

Storing up his energy, Drainan wrapped his cloak around him and leaned back. He was going to stay awake with Bridget, just to make sure she didn't do anything stupid. "You sure you want to do this? I know Brooks wouldn't expect it."

Close to Maremoth again, her plan held a new reality. "I can't leave him." Bridget bent toward her companion, "You don't have to come."

"Still trying to get rid of me?" he scoffed, but he was thinking the same thing. He didn't have to enter Maremoth. He didn't know Brooks. Except for the journey, he did not even know Bridget. Yet, he was risking everything.

"I am more grateful for your help than I can say," she told him. "I guess I'm not very used to other people taking care of me. But thank you."

All Drainan's doubts vanished. "If what you're doing for Brooks is the way you treat all your friends, I'm glad I'm on the list."

Xsardis 218

"What makes you think you are?" she teased.

"Very funny." Restlessly, he took a long swallow of water. "Isn't there some better plan than me taking you in as a prisoner?"

"I've got to find Brooks," Bridget explained. "They're not just going to have him sitting around. I have to get into the dungeons."

Drainan put a rough hand to his sword, eyes darting around the forest. Bridget sat up swiftly, whispering, "What is it?"

Their eyes drifted to the skies. Blackened clouds had blown in. The wind, suddenly turbulent, swept Bridget's hair about. Through the strands she saw figures falling from the sky and catching themselves on wings that shot from their arms. One's pure white eyes landed on Bridget, as if she could see her in the darkness.

The winged-woman swept over them, bringing two others with her. They flew inches above the three. Caleb awoke with a start. Drainan recognized their first flight as reconnaissance. Their second would not be so merciful. Quietness abandoned, Drainan led Caleb and Bridget forward into the night.

"What are those things?" Caleb practically shrieked.

"I've never seen…" Drainan's words fell short. There was no extra energy for talking and it would only draw the creatures to them. Maybe, just maybe, they would choose not to bother following. What were three humans anyway against the power they represented?

The panic stayed in them as the clouds expanded as far as the eye could see. The winged men and women could be seen dancing in and out of their territory in increasing numbers. By the time they reached the bottom of the hill overlooking Maremoth, Caleb was drenched in sweat. "We're trapped," he moaned and drew his sword.

Bridget made to get over the hill.

"Stop!" Drainan cried, desperately wanting her to be safe.

"I have to go!" she returned.

"Don't you know where we are?"

"Yes."

"Why do you care so much about this?" Drainan refused to let go of her arm. "Those things are going to destroy you. They're heading for Maremoth. Anything inside is probably going to be dead in a matter of minutes. We're going to die if we go up there."

"They're sprites. They're probably working for Sasha!" she reasoned, but the unreasonable passion was in her voice.

"Bridget, this is insane," he pleaded. "Listen to me."

"Come down," Caleb added his voice.

"These are the moments that decide our fates," she spoke clearly. The force of her weight was already up the hill, but Drainan's strong arm held her back. "The war that gave Sasha Asandra in the first place wasn't a single battle; it was a million little battles where people chose not to do the right thing. Now is the perfect, distracting opportunity to get into Maremoth. I won't waste it."

"But how can you be sure that this is the right thing?" he demanded. He had chosen God at an early age, before the turbulence overtook Asandra, but time had pushed religion to a backdrop in his life. Was he ready to allow God to have all of him? That's how Bridget was living. That's what she was

Xsardis

219

asking of him if he ran down the hill into the clutches of the enemy.

"I know it," energy filled her words. "This may sound crazy, but it's not. This is the same commitment that gave me the strength to stay alive in Maremoth. Trust me. Trust God." She put her free hand on the top of his. "Please Drainan, you have to let me do this."

He met her eyes finally. "Not alone. I'm coming with you."

Xsardis

Chapter 28

The sounds of water splashing drew Vaylynne's attention to the door. She had recognized who had been pounding on the passageway above the waterfall. While Seth was convinced it was Sasha, she knew it was Edmund coming to finish what she had agreed to when they had made their uneasy alliance.

But things had changed since then. The artifact was not an artifact after all. While those she traveled with were, no doubt, slightly psychotic, they were not what she had been expecting. Though all save Seth had limited talent with a sword, they had managed to steal both Asandra and Issym from Sasha's grip. They fought with faith, commitment, love, and a passion that matched—if not bested—her own. Could those weapons be more powerful than the sword?

She glanced at the location where Rachel and Reesthma were preparing to seal the cavern. A certain kind of powder, made from the slimy secretions of glowing snails, would cause the Valean rock to shift. When it did, the entire support of the cavern would collapse. Carefully, Reesthma planned it so that the outer room would seal, but the inner room would remain intact.

Seth and Rachel could have claimed the power of deities. After all, it was their imagination that had designed Xsardis. Yet, they trusted in God? That was the insanity she saw in them. Their unwavering trust would make them do foolish things.

Even so, she longed to throw down her self-propelled war and join wholeheartedly with a group that could protect Xsardis. *This is a temptation to stop a movement that will succeed. You were chosen for this because you have the strength to hold on.* Her projection of what Tahath would have said steeled her resolve. She could not let Asandra's freedom slip through her fingers.

A form came onto land. Bearing Edmund's general appearance, the shifter had gills on his neck. *His powers are already inhibited,* Vaylynne recognized with a sigh. The stones were more powerful than she had anticipated.

Hoping he could not see her uncertainty, Vaylynne met Edmund as he

Xsardis

222

entered the cavern. Together they stood. All eyes fell to them. Still several platforms away, Seth demanded, "What are you doing here, Edmund?"

"Good to see you too, Seth," Edmund replied smoothly to irritate him.

"How long has this alliance existed?" Seth probed Vaylynne, his sword drawn.

"You sound surprised," she returned with an unsteady voice. Could she truly go with Edmund against Seth and the others?

"Not surprised, but disappointed," he answered her.

Vaylynne felt the loss of fellowship. Even at that moment, she admired Seth for the warrior and leader that he was. She attempted, "We can both accomplish our goals here."

At Ethelwyn's direction, Nadine entered her chamber. Her sister and Evan guarded the door. "What's going on?" Edmund questioned.

"Vaylynne, you and your gilly friend had better get out of here before I decide not to let you go," Seth ordered.

Edmund put his hands up, "If I wanted war I would have come in a vicious form, but I am human to show you my sincerity."

"Sincerity. You've always been good at that," Max answered sardonically.

"Then allow me to offer a peace offering," Edmund replied. "A piece of information. Sasha is on Noric, in the tunnels, on her way here."

"You led her to us!" Katarina charged.

"No; no I didn't," the shifter stepped forward, aware that he was losing his audience. "Months ago I told her about the artifact to win you the time for Issym to arrive. I was helping you. When I did not report back quickly enough, she followed me here."

"Just tell me what you want and get it over with," Seth decided.

"This isn't about me," Edmund explained. "I'm not following you to stop you. Kate needs your help."

"Kate?" Subconsciously Rachel lowered the bow and arrow she had aimed for Edmund.

The shifter addressed Seth, "You can say whatever you want about me, but you know I love her. I've given up thinking I can win her, but I have to protect her." That wasn't exactly true, but then again, nothing he was about to tell Seth would be exactly true.

"Explain quickly," Seth directed.

"Sasha seeks the artifact not only for extra power, but for her life. She's sick and dying. As is Kate. Both of them pushed themselves too far. The artifact you have come to destroy is the only thing that can save my Kate from an agonizing death. Give the artifact to her. You know she'll put it to good use," he implored.

"You don't understand," Vaylynne informed him.

Seth cut her off from explaining, "What do you have to gain, Vay?"

Energetically, Vaylynne enlightened him, "To destroy a source of such power is a waste! Kate has had a master. Do you think she'll make Asandra live under one? Edmund has assured me that she will help to liberate us."

Xsardis

223

Passing a look to Seth, Rachel spoke, "We would help Kate if we could, but the artifact isn't what you think."

"What do you mean?"

"I'll explain it." Vaylynne turned Edmund and told him all in tones that could not carry. "What do you want to do now?"

"Nothing's changed."

"How can you say that?" she challenged. "It's not an artifact. It's a living, breathing child—one that causes earthquakes! You let her out of here and Sasha will have her in a second. Are you thinking of Xsardis' good or just Kate's?"

"You are starting to sound like the others. They have been influencing you too greatly." He surveyed her new apparel, clothes that were neither as black nor as practical as what she had once worn. "Are you willing to take risks for Asandra's freedom or not?"

She grilled him, "Then what are you suggesting?"

"I need you to steal Universe Girl's orbs. That will give us access to this chamber after they close it."

"Yeah, well, in case you haven't noticed," she replied, with a glance at the staring eyes behind her, "my helping you didn't win me a lot of favor."

"You'll find a way, Vaylynne. Isn't that what you always do? I don't care how you steal them, but get the orbs."

"You want to kidnap Nadine, don't you?" she realized.

"You said that Ethelwyn is leaving. It should be easy!"

"This is different. I don't know if I can do this. Maybe we should trust Seth."

"I tried that," he spoke with steely eyes. His gills flapped as his frustration grew. "Are you going to do this or not? Because if you don't, I have to warn you: I'll turn back to Sasha and I'll make sure that you never get independence. Your fighters will be the first people to die."

"You're threatening me," she seethed. "That's a mistake."

"Get your job done," he snarled. Having underestimated her fury, Edmund added more gently, "I promise you we'll take good care of Nadine. Nothing will change for her. We'll give Kate the orbs and sole access to this chamber. Once she's invincible, she'll be able to kill Sasha. Slowly, the power will corrupt Kate just enough that she won't work with Seth and Rachel anymore, but with us."

Vaylynne nodded, convinced. "I'll use Reesthma. Did you see the sorrow on her face when she heard about Kate? I think I can get her to help."

They turned back to the others. "Edmund and I have discussed it. With Sasha so close behind us, we are willing to set aside our goals for the time being."

Katarina rolled her eyes. "That's what you said back at Saphree…"

Despite everything, Seth could not hand them over to Sasha's mercy. "I'm not letting you off that platform. Stay put."

Evan entered Nadine's room, Max a few steps behind. She sat a desk. The legs were made from the wood of the Valinor trees. Judging from the leafy, blue top, he guessed that it too came from Valinor. Nadine turned when she heard him, revealing a sketch book in which she had been drawing. Her eyes

Xsardis   224

searched him for information.

"Edmund and Vaylynne are still outside, but the others are watching them. You're safe."

"I believe they will guard me well until the cavern is sealed."

"You're very trusting of people you don't know."

Nadine stood. "I know much about them."

"From stories?"

"No," she laughed. "From their actions in this place. They could stay with me. In their grasp would be the wonders of Xsardis, long life, and the company of those they care for. Xsardis would be safe from the danger I pose and they could enjoy a well-deserved rest.

"But they don't stay. They chose to keep fighting a battle that for some of them was never theirs to begin with. That is why I trust them."

"You are a good judge of character."

"Well, she is a thousand years old. Even if she does not look it," Max remarked, peering at her drawing. His heart beat fast, "What is that?"

Nadine picked up the book. "This is the pearl inside me." Recognizing that Max was beginning to remember something, she pulled the paper from the book and handed it to him. "Take this."

"Thank you," he accepted the drawing and slipped it into his pocket. He returned to the outer cavern and took a seat beside Reesthma on the cold rock floor.

"I miss the sun," she commented.

"As far as undergrounds go, this is pretty nice," he assured her.

Reesthma chuckled and glanced at him. "What are you thinking?"

"Can I pick your brain?"

"What kind of a question is that?"

Max groaned. Sometimes the smallest cultural barrier could make it seem like you were talking different languages. "Sorry. Can I use your knowledge?"

She resettled herself so she could look at him more easily. "Sure."

"What do you know about what Issym did when he left Asandra's country after her death?"

"Well," Reesthma gathered her thoughts, mentally pulling the appropriate books from the shelves, "he was King Shobal's army captain for a time and then he was king."

"But what did he *do*?"

"His first task was to climb Mt. Smolden and re-purge it from evil men. Then he traveled throughout the land, learning and building an army. He trained them hard and well for years. And when he became king, he made it his sole goal in life to eradicate Santana's influence from the land."

Max shook his head, not having found what he was looking for yet. "How did he die?"

"From what Joppa and I could tell, he and his finest men traveled into the underground on some secret mission. They never returned." She paused and looked at him, "Why?"

"I don't know yet."

Vaylynne's hand beckoned Reesthma to her. The girl held back, her thoughts muddled. Was Vaylynne a traitor or wasn't she? She had lied to them from the beginning, but it was her concern for Asandra that led her. She went to her mentor, still uncertain. "Why didn't you tell me that you were working with Edmund?" Reesthma questioned.

"Because I didn't want to make you keep a secret from the others. *I* didn't even want to keep the secret."

"Then why did you?"

"Reesthma, sometimes things aren't clear. We have to work against our friends in order to do what's right. Seth is smart, but he's not seeing the whole picture. Kate needs our help."

"You don't even know Kate."

"Does that mean I shouldn't help her? Edmund came to me and asked me to save the woman he loved. And Kate can help heal Asandra. Don't you want that?"

"How could she?"

Vaylynne kept spinning her deception, feeling more guilty but more determined with every sentence. "Kate is a mighty warrior—one who can stop Sasha. And she is a great leader. But not if she's dead.

"And what about Nadine?" Vaylynne went on. "Nadine could save Kate. Kate could protect Nadine. She could go into the real world again."

"If that was true wouldn't Seth…"

Vaylynne cut her off, "Seth won't listen to Edmund or I because he doesn't trust us. He feels like I betrayed him, and maybe I did, but what choice did I have? Two peoples' lives were on the line! Do you trust me, Reesthma?"

Reesthma's brown eyes bore into the floor as she thought. Vaylynne almost had her. "But Seth's the hero…"

Vaylynne shook her head, "He's the leader, but we don't know who the hero is. It could be you. I've trained you and I can tell you would be a strong warrior. Seth and Joppa will never allow that. They won't listen; just like Seth won't listen now. Seth can be wrong. You can be right."

"I can be!" Reesthma stood straighter, epiphany striking her. "All the time in history it was the people who weren't noticed who changed the tide of battle. Maybe I'm that person."

"Then it's up to you to save Nadine and Kate."

"How?"

"We need the orbs."

"I can get them."

In the short time it had taken Bridget and Drainan to catapult across the divide between them and Maremoth, Drainan's entire personality had changed. He hardened his face; straightened his shoulders; swung his arms; assumed a gruff air—taking on the persona of a soldier of Maremoth.

Xsardis 226

To look like a prisoner, Bridget did not need to widen her eyes with fear. In the open space, the dark clouds, terrifying thunder, and sweeping movements of the dark creatures in the skies caused terror of their own. She was only a few steps behind Drainan and struggled to bind her wrists as she moved. She waited for the deafening roar of thunder that would accompany the brilliant strike of lightning. Then she shouted at him, "Here."

He caught the lead of the rope she tossed and made the final few stumbling steps to the door. A glance over his shoulder showed that Caleb had decided not to follow. Drainan was surprised and perhaps disappointed, but he knew it was for the best. If the dark sprites did not end Maremoth, Maremoth would probably end Drainan and Bridget.

Drainan turned his eyes to the high doors of Maremoth. In the dark, the fortress was all the more terrifying. He pounded on the gate.

Slowly it began to pull up. The two pressed under it and instantly the gate was set down again. Drainan stepped under a small awning to his left, shielding himself from the rain. A rough tug to Bridget's rope both pulled her under the shelter and ascertained that it was realistically tight. A form pounded down the steps, barely discernable in his soaking black clothes. "Who are you?" he demanded.

"This one tried to get away," Drainan spoke without mercy. "I pursued and was separated from the others. They back yet?"

"The group with the prisoners?" the man asked.

"Who else?" Drainan snapped with a sneer.

"They got back a couple of days ago," the man replied.

"Where are the prisoners?" Drainan was quick.

The guard was slow, "Why do you want to know?"

"To put her with them." Drainan's look accused the guard of being a fool.

The soldier gave up and tilted his head to the castle. The violent storm kept him from being thorough.

Drainan jolted the rope forward for show and made for the castle. Even when they were out of view of the guard he had to drag Bridget. She was spellbound by the sight of her old prison. All the soldiers they passed eyed the clouds with fear, but they did not make ready for battle. Maybe the sprites really were serving Sasha.

Escaping into the shelter of the fiercely guarded and cruelly built castle, the two felt the sound of the door thunking shut behind them. It took a moment for the dimly lit corridor to become clear to them. Only then did Drainan press on, Bridget following wordlessly behind him.

When he came to a turn, he asked her, "Which way?"

She directed him down. Better timing might have allowed their rescue to succeed, but as they descended the high stairs to the dungeons, a man was shutting the door to one of the cells. Rubbing his knuckles and with a grim look of disgust on his face, he almost did not see the two waiting helplessly on the stairs. When he looked up, his eyes fell on them with a piercing gaze.

Bridget recognized him. His hideous desires seeped from him like the vilest of marrings. Drainan saw the air of authority. He bent his neck in a bow, then straightened.

Xsardis

227

"Who are you?" the man demanded.

"Kurin," Drainan lied. "This prisoner escaped the others. I brought her back."

A flash of lightning lit up the room brightly and, for a moment, they were blinded. The man took a few steps forward when his vision cleared and studied Bridget's face. "I know you," he recalled.

She stared at the slick guard, who had taken pleasure in tormenting her fellow prisoners. Now he was the lord of Maremoth. "Stewart..." she breathed.

Stewart knew the stories about her too. About her escape with Brooks... Was that why Bridget was here? To rescue him? The thought caused Stewart to move down another stair and look at Drainan's features. "You've done well," he finally declared. "Bridget is quite the catch. Bring her to my throne room. Now."

His throne room? Was Sasha so completely distracted that she would allow him to talk so?

Drainan reluctantly led Bridget from the cells. So close to Brooks and yet so far. They ascended through the passageways with bare stone walls and into those with loud décor. When they reached the throne room, they saw the grand, mismatched decorations, chosen only to show off the loot Maremoth still possessed. Bridget trembled as she entered the room where she had been sentenced to death.

Stewart took a seat on the elevated throne, stretching out his legs before him and slouching in the chair. Drainan was aware of the guards moving to block the door. He and Bridget moved closer to Stewart's chair. Bridget fell to her knees.

"Where did you say you found her?" Stewart interrogated.

"She ran from the other group of prisoners. We found her first at Ganetiv, where Brooks was captured."

"Excellent story," Stewart clapped his hands together, then leaned forward. "There is only one problem. I recognize you too."

Drainan had never seen Stewart before in his life—of that he was sure. "Sir?" he questioned, maintaining his character. Surely this was some kind of test.

"You have Vaylynne's jaw; her jet hair; her mannerisms. You're related."

"She may be family," Drainan admitted, "but I serve you."

Maremoth's leader descended his steps, "You're the cousin Sasha spared when she made the deal with Vaylynne to capture Rachel and Seth. Drainan."

Drainan's face washed out. There was no retelling this tale.

Stewart enjoyed the moment, then went on, "What was the plan? Just to waltz out of the front gate with Brooks?"

His eyes were drunk with power. Drainan stumbled back a few steps. Stewart said, "You know, I have to thank you, Drainan. My men need to see how powerful I am. When I kill the two that started the escapes from Maremoth, they will start to believe. But when I kill Vaylynne's cousin and she does nothing, they will truly see how powerful I am."

Jeff knocked outside Joppa's room. He was one of the few in Saphree to have his own space—though as Jeff opened the wooden door, it looked more like the scrolls possessed the room than like Joppa did. From floor to ceiling, on every surface, on the floor, and on the bed, scrolls and books were piled around endlessly. Joppa's eyes moved speedily across the page of the book in his hand, not stopping to meet Jeff's form.

When clearing his throat won none of the historian's attention, Jeffery put a hand on his shoulder. "Joppa, I need you tell me a story."

Now Joppa raised his eyes. "And what story is that?"

Skeptical of the peculiar man who could possess such quarters, Jeff almost remained silent. At that very moment, Sphen was planning the defenses for the war against the dark sprites—assuming that Danielle would succeed. He should have been there, not pursuing clues lost in the mind of an aging eccentric. But without those clues, the dark sprites might well massacre them all. "Have you not heard?" Jeff inquired.

"I have been busy," Joppa opened his hands wide to the chaos. "Heard of what?"

"The dark sprites killed the first representative we sent to them: a young airsprite, Jennet. I want to know why they would kill a girl who went in peace. I want to know why they decimate our troops with a cold fury. I want to know what you've kept from us in your tale of the airsprites."

Joppa's face dropped. "There are two versions of the story. I told you what the airsprites of Issym themselves believe."

"Which is truth?"

"I don't know," the historian admitted unhappily. "Perhaps we should ask Danielle."

"We can't," Jeff responded. "She's gone to challenge them to battle."

The book slipped from Joppa's hands, "She'll die."

"What do you know, Joppa?" Jeff demanded.

"It is a dark story," the old man answered somberly. "One that ought never to have happened."

"Just tell me."

Chapter 29

The sky swirled around her. When allowed admittance, vibrant orange light blinded the young Queen Danielle. Disoriented, grieved, broken… It would have been easy to let her mind slip. If she did, she would plummet to the ground.

Danielle was so tired of war. She had never even had the time to mourn her own mother's death or come to grips with the kingdom she had inherited too early. Had she been wrong in keeping her limited knowledge of the dark sprites from Galen? How severely would it cost her people and his?

"You killed my sala," Danielle called. Sala—a forgotten word. No, a dead word. Abandoned when the airsprites had separated. For reasons few knew. But Danielle knew, or had guessed from what her mother had left out.

"And your people killed mine," came a heavy voice.

Out of the haze emerged one dark sprite. Their leader. White eyes; white hair; misty skirt; beautiful and deadly. She spoke her own name, "Feyah."

"You still live?" Danielle questioned in surprise.

"I know the secret of Noric…" came the reply. "I have kept my people alive with it, while you have let yours die."

"Are not our hundreds of years enough?" Danielle queried, gauging this woman. "I have grieved enough in my short years not to want to live for eternity."

"Not for eternity," Feyah answered. "We could only extend our years. I will die after I destroy your kind."

"You are our kind!" Danielle reminded her. That Feyah had appeared alone meant she would be granted life.

"I was once," she chuckled lowly. "Tell me, youngling, do you know the truth?"

"In the days when all was well, you were the daughter of a respected airsprite," Danielle prompted.

"But I was not like the others," Feyah cut in. "I knew something was

Xsardis

230

wrong. I learned to fight and I trained a small group in the ways of battle. The others detested me for it. But not my sala, my Tanya. She followed me into battle. And my love, he doubted me but supported me. I was right and battle came to us."

"And you defended our people," Danielle interjected, wanting Feyah to recognize that she knew. "You and your troops are the only reason any of us are alive. I am familiar the story."

"You know a false tale!" Feyah took the telling back. "At first things went well after that. We were hailed as heroes. But we no longer belonged among such delicate creatures. Our perspectives were too strange. We might still have lived in harmony," her voice shook with rage, "but your people would not have it. They tried to cast me out. They won over my love with their deception and lies. He left me." She fell to a whisper. "I grew angry. They said that was why they did not want me.

"My sala, she tried to protect me. They pushed her aside. Too hard. She fell unconscious. And she slipped through the clouds. They were on top of me. They would not let me catch her. I watched Tanya plummet and die. My sala... Just like that."

The white in her eyes shone wildly. Though she had suspected this, Danielle had never heard the story before. The tragedy of it hit her hard. The airsprites were a people who up to that point in history and from that point until now had never hurt each other.

Feyah was far from done, "That was the day our peoples split. I took the best fighters and made them my subjects. I promised them safety and life and vengeance for Tanya—she was well-loved, not like me.

"Did your people ever come back and seek forgiveness? Did you even love these clouds enough to fight for them? No, you ran. And as we lived for years past our time, our hatred of you grew," Feyah sputtered, "as did our abilities."

"If you know the pain of losing a sala, how could you take mine from me?" Danielle challenged.

"Your sala with her gentleness was too much for us to bear. Nothing has changed. She did not recognize her part in Tanya's death."

"She had no part in it!" Danielle fought back. "She didn't even know about it."

Feyah smiled. "If you had been here when our peoples first separated, I would have asked you to stay. You could put that anger to good use. You could become like me."

"I don't want to be like you," the queen answered dryly. "Jennet and Tanya would not have wanted that."

"It did not happen overnight, youngling," she replied. "Your upbringing will not allow you to see. I will take pity on you in battle and kill you mercifully. Did you come for a fight?"

Danielle forced herself not to shake. "Yes. But not here and not now."

"Set the time and the place. Give yourself the advantage. You'll need it. But one condition I hold. All your sprites on Asandra must be there. I seek to destroy your kind at once. Then we may die and end this horrid legacy of ours."

"We're not as easy prey as you think we are," Queen Danielle promised her.

The rumors of Kate's treachery spread. The massacre of the sprites at Lake Gratuk had done much to promote them.

Some doubted. Where were the bodies? Which sprites were missing? Unanswerable questions made for un-sustained gossip—uncontainable and un-provable.

Kate had been said to be seen with Vaylynne's troops, with Edmund, with Stewart… The rumors were so thick there was no hope of discerning the truth.

Queen Juliet appealed to those who had been under Kate's direct command. None of the shifters would say that their leader had betrayed them, but some wondered if her ideas about what was right had changed again. Once she had been happy ruling by Edmund and Sasha's side. Then she had turned on them, but her love for Edmund had been deep. Had he somehow turned her back?

Remar and Galen had already had several confrontations about her. Remar wanted Kate to be labeled a rebel; Galen would not have it. Issym's leader knew the damage such a determination could have among his troops. The already strong conflict between the fairies and the shape shifters had led to the shifters moving their tents near those who still trusted them: illuminescents, and some sprites and minotaurs who were wise enough to keep their opinions to themselves. The others sprites held the shifters responsible for the death of their fellows at Gratuk. The fairies, humans and frogs easily fell in with them. The armies had been taking sides before Kate's loyalty had even been questioned.

Saphree might have split completely had not Nevel intervened. The greatest fear was that in light of Kate's choices, the shifters might return to Sasha's service. Nevel's strong leadership abolished that concern. His life beyond repute, the fairies and sprites accepted his good intentions. Though toleration was all that could be hoped for between the various races, it seemed that Saphree might stand together until the battle against the dark sprites.

"You must take action," Sphen said to Galen.

The high king was sitting in his window sill, one leg dangling out, the other bent on the sill itself. His back and head rested against its frame. Galen surveyed The Brother's face. The scar earned from Vaylynne added to the heavy air he bore. To Sphen it was easily discernable that the makeshift peace Saphree had managed would not last if the leadership refused to make a decision about Kate. Sphen was right.

Elimilech and Flibbert leaned over the blueprint of Saphree, formulating a plan of best defense. The fairy caught his king's eye. Straightening, he offered his own opinion, "I agree with Sphen. More and more

Xsardis 232

reports come in that Stewart is relying heavily on Kate as he readies an army. My fellow fairies are not blind to this. They will not take the risk of the shifters forever. Even I cannot hold them back for long."

Sphen apprised, "Even if we declare her a traitor that will change nothing for Kate. She's not here; we can do nothing to her. But it will stabilize our armies."

"Will it?" Galen turned his gaze over Saphree. "Or will it cause the shifters to rebel?"

Jeff and Nevel made to the enter the room at the same time and collided. Nevel stepped back. Jeff moved through the door frame and stepped beside his brother. "I just talked to Joppa. There are two stories about the dark sprites. Most of the differences are minor, but there is one foundational variance. The dark sprite leader had a dear friend. The airsprites were responsible for her death," Jeff explained.

"It's a blood feud between the two sprite groups," Sphen surmised.

"You must consider sending the airsprites back to the safety of Issym," Jeff told Galen.

"We've awakened the battle now," Flibbert replied. "There will be no safe place for the sprites."

"More than likely, if you send them away, the dark sprites will decimate us for hiding them," Sphen added. Discarding the idea, he resolved to use the information in their favor. "This will change how we do battle. We'll know how to distract them."

"And who we need to protect," Jeff completed.

Nevel stayed by the door, waiting with a heavy look. Galen called him forward. "What is it?"

"I have to talk to you about Kate."

Returning to their initial conversation, the king asked him, "What do you think we should do about her?"

"I trust Kate," Nevel began. "Long have I respected her. But the proof against her is too great for the leadership of Issym to remain silent. Let us call her deeds what they are. We may still hope that we are mistaken and offer her the opportunity to explain if she returns."

Realizing that Galen was waiting for him to speak, Flibbert lamented, "If only I could speak with her!" The frog made his determination, "Somehow I don't believe she's guilty even after all the evidence, but we don't have a choice but to assume she is."

Galen nodded. Accepting the decision he had to make, he declared, "I label the shape shifter Kate a traitor."

Sphen and Jeff left to inform their king. Nevel and Flibbert approached Galen. "Is she to be captured or killed?" Flibbert queried.

"You think you'll be able to arrest her?" Nevel shook his head, awareness in his eyes. "I doubt that. You have no idea the kind of power Kate has."

"I won't have her harmed until I talk with her," the king ordered.

Nevel assured, "Then you won't talk with her."

With Seth as her fellow watcher for that shift of the night, Reesthma was easily able to enter Nadine's room and find the bag of orbs. Seth did not suspect her deception in the least. Had it been this easy for Vaylynne to betray them? It almost did not feel wrong. Yet it did. Reesthma hesitated.

She picked up one of the milky white balls and held it delicately in her hand. So much history had happened because these orbs had allowed The Legend to travel across the land. But what was history? The pitara was not what she had been taught it was. Scrolls that said Issym had had no children had been falsified. And there was so much more to Universe Girl than she had seen. The world felt upside-down. Reesthma put her trust in the mentor who had seen value in her and placed the orbs in her own bag.

Carefully she stepped over the sleeping bodies before her. Ethelwyn's arm was draped over Nadine. The Legend had stayed up late, instructing Evan how to properly care for his new charge.

The group rose only an hour later, unwilling to rest for too long. The caves had to be sealed before Sasha arrived. Though Edmund had assured she would not be coming for a few more hours, they refused to take any chances.

"Never believe that our father left you here," Ethelwyn counseled her sister as she looked down at her. "I know he searched for a cure until he had used up his last breath."

"I try to believe that," answered Nadine. "Tell Flibbert I always wanted to meet him. And please, Ethel, don't worry about me for the rest of your life."

"I know you'll be fine."

The sisters stepped back from each other, a bravery consuming both of them. Nadine took Max's hand, "I wish I could have known how we're connected."

"I'm sorry I couldn't tell you more."

Katarina lingered in her brother's hug. "You shouldn't do this," she attempted one more time.

When his sister had moved away and he knew she would not be able to look his way again, Evan grabbed Rachel's hand. "Are you mad at me for staying?"

"No," she shook her head. "It makes sense. The sprites said we wouldn't all walk the path a second time. At least you'll live on. But I can't believe I'm never going to see you again." Rachel hugged the only friend she had allowed to be around her during her time on Earth.

"Go," Ethelwyn pushed Evan, Nadine already waiting in her chamber. "We don't have any more time."

Evan nodded and entered the smaller cavern. Ethelwyn let out a long sigh and led the others past the door. The pitara began to take them to the waterfall. Edmund, Rachel and Reesthma went up first. As Max moved to

Xsardis   234

follow Seth and Vaylynne on the monster's return, he held himself back. The drawing in his pocket felt like a heavy weight. Suddenly the pieces fell together in his mind. Seth saw the look. "What? We don't have time."

"I just need a second with her," Max swore.

Ethelwyn looked between them. "Go," she told Seth. "I'll wait for Max."

Max jumped and ran the distance to the chamber. Evan, in full protective mode, grabbed the scruff of Max's shirt as he entered the room, thinking it was Vaylynne or Edmund.

"Whoa," Max let out as he put his hands up in defense. "Nadine," he called for her help.

"Let Max go," she ordered Evan.

"What if it's not Max?"

"Let him go!"

Evan grudgingly released him, but did not admit him to the room. Max spoke anyway, leaning around Evan to communicate with Nadine. "He didn't abandon you," he told her with energy. "Issym, he didn't."

"Most likely, you are right," she agreed as she knelt and waited for what would come next.

Max knew he was not being clear. He tried again, "Did your cycle of growth change almost two years ago."

Her face lost its color. "How could you know that? Only Ethel knows that."

"It did change." His eyes glowed in triumph.

"Yes; it slowed down."

Max smiled victoriously, "After Issym placed you here, I believe that he spent the rest of his life searching for a cure. If he's anything like Seth, he went to his home continent to find that remedy—not to escape Asandra's memory like everyone believed. And I think he found it."

"Then why didn't he come back?" Nadine stood now and spoke over Evan's shoulder.

Even the discomfort of what he had to say could not silence him, "He went to the underground to look for it; and I think Smolden killed him."

Nadine's eyes widened with the realization of Max's words. She groped for a phrase or a question, but she could find nothing.

"Look." Finally, Evan dropped his arms and allowed Max to enter. He pulled her drawing from his pocket. The pearl was covered in small runes. "These runes I've seen before on a medallion in Smolden's underground. It was concealed in a wall, as if someone hid it when they were discovered. I turned the key that was with it and the medallion caused an earthquake that split Issym in two. That was over a year ago."

"It does not make sense," Nadine denied.

"Yes, it does," Max was certain. "You and I are connected. The medallion and the pearl have the same runes. The pearl came from Issym. I found the medallion in the underground. Your father died in the underground searching for something he was willing to give everything to find. Nadine, that medallion can cure you."

"You can't know that," Nadine protested. She could not allow herself

Xsardis

235

to hope. "And even if it could, what if the medallion causes another earthquake?"

"Where is this thing, Max?" Evan queried. His excitement was rising.

"In the underground of Issym—buried. I'll help you look for it."

Nadine allowed the joyous news to fill her. The smile lit up her face. "Let's go!" She bent down for the orbs that would carry them. "Oh no." Circling the tree, Nadine realized they were gone.

"Maybe Ethelwyn couldn't leave you and took them with her?" Evan suggested.

Max tuned him out. He sensed the evil behind him. With a slow turn, he looked into the water beyond the doors. A pitara stared at him—this one even more hideous than the first. "Sasha," he breathed.

The pitara ripped through the doorway. The force set off the already primed Valean rock. Explosions boomed around them. Evan pushed Max back with all his strength, sending him into the water and saving his life. Rocks fell around Max, the walls changing shape on all sides. The youth held his breath and stayed under water until the worst of it was over. *I just told her about a cure and now she's locked in a room with no way to get to it...* Max realized as he broke the surface.

Half in the water, half dragging itself on land, the hideous shape was moving toward Nadine's door. The water rocked Max in violent waves and he was pushed against a newly-broken, rocky platform. He held on and pulled himself to land. The pitara did not even look at him. Sasha's claws were ripping for the rock-encrusted door leading to Nadine and Evan. He had to do something.

A white arrow whistled through the room and buried itself in the back of the pitara's shoulder. Sasha howled, held in form by the few stones on Max's armor. He searched for the origin of the shot. Ethelwyn stood in perfect form, another arrow already braced in her bow. Her eyes blazed with her commitment to and love for her sister. Those terrifying eyes landed on him for a second, ascertaining whether he would fight or flee.

Max took a second to get his bearings in the room. Most of the armor and weapons that had been left outside Nadine's chamber had plummeted into the water. Hopefully, he looked for his companions, but they had all returned to the waterfall. It was Max and Ethelwyn against Sasha in a pitara's form. The odds were not good. His eyes fell on Nadine's door and his thoughts to her smile when she heard about the medallion. Max drew his sword and wiped back his hair. He was not running from this fight.

The Legend loosed three more shots, each angering the pitara more. Sasha locked her focus on Ethelwyn and lunged for her with her hand outstretched. Ethelwyn vaulted herself away, barely escaping the behemoth's movement. Sasha swept for her with her other claw, but Ethelwyn escaped again. The beast was not fighting with the intelligence of a sentient being. It was fighting as an animal. But with nowhere to go, The Legend was knocked against the wall by Sasha's next strike. Ethelwyn clutched her ribs and fell.

Max reached for the dagger wedged into a nearby rock. He threw it and it lodged in the pitara's side. Sasha turned on him with rage. When she saw his face, she hesitated.

Max met her eyes. Once he had thought she was beautiful and her power had lured him. Now he shuddered and felt not the minutest compulsion to spare or side with her. It was not just her form; it was Max's awakening. She was holding back for the memory of his near-turning. "Remember me?" he called and charged the evil with a mighty bellow.

Her hand landed a few steps from him; the other was coming toward his head. Max ducked under the moving appendage as he jabbed his sword into the other and used it to propel himself to a farther platform.

The danger was a thrill; his freedom from her charisma was exhilarating. Max had no idea what happened to him as he rolled, dodged and lunged at the mighty pitara.

Ethelwyn rallied her strength and ran past Sasha, slashing with both her swords at the creature's fleshy, three-pronged tail. One of the blades slipped from her hand as the pitara bellowed.

When The Legend had made it to his side, Max suggested, "How about a plan that doesn't include death?"

The next time the hand came for him, Max lodged his sword up into it. Unfortunately that left him without a weapon. Ethelwyn had only her sword and she was still gripping her ribs.

Jonah the pitara returned with a roar of force. His head knocked Sasha into the wall, causing rubble to fall from the ceiling. Jonah turned quickly and without hesitation picked the two humans up in his mouth.

From inside, they felt his jerky movements. Max tried to stay upright, to be glad that they were alive. Then Ethelwyn's voice destroyed any calm that he had left, "We're being pursued."

Bridget had known that the likelihood of success in storming Maremoth had been slim, but even so she had not prepared herself for the terror she felt in being discovered. Stewart had ordered Drainan to be thrown into the dungeons. Watching him be dragged away was enough to send tremors through her. She would have rather gone with him than stayed alone in Stewart's throne room. He was just staring at her. Bridget shivered as a bolt of lightning struck not far from the fortress.

"The dark sprites do put on a show, don't they?" Stewart's tone was level, "Bridget, I have control of Maremoth. The soldiers look to me now. I have the power to crush or rebuild Asandra."

"No, you don't," Bridget disputed. "Saphree is too strong for you."

He took her arm and pulled her to the balcony. "The sprites will soon take care of that old regime."

The dark forms dropped from the sky, catching themselves on wings that shot from their arms. They were clearly powerful. Could Saphree stand against them? "What do you want, Stewart?" she probed.

Xsardis

237

He released her and Bridget stepped back from the terrifying scene lighting up the sky. Stewart enlightened her, "I want to give you the power to save Asandra."

With effort she swallowed. What would this cruel man ask of her?

"On 'The Day' Maremoth lost more than prisoners and soldiers. We lost the element of deception. I don't care what Asandra thinks about Sasha, but I do want them to recognize me for the benevolent leader I am. I need someone to proclaim that I am a good ruler. Someone respected by all the prisoners who told of Maremoth's cruelty... you."

"I don't lie," Bridget returned.

"I'm not asking you to lie. I am asking you to prophesy—a self-fulfilling prophecy."

"You want me to be your figurehead?" she questioned, hardly believing her ears.

"I'm offering you a chance at life. And you hold Asandra's fate in your hands. Think about it. On the one hand, you die and life continues in Maremoth as it always has. Miserable for the prisoners. And Drainan hangs because you brought him here.

"But, on the other hand, if you tell the world how benevolent I am, then I have to prove you right. You live, and all the prisoners still in this place begin to eat and rest and receive medicines again. I might even send a few of them home—like Drainan. If you won't do it for yourself, do it for them, for him."

"And how long should I expect this mercy to last?"

"Long enough," he smiled. "I'm not Sasha. I don't wish to destroy Asandra. And Bridget," he stepped towards her, "a figurehead is well-cared for. Anything you could wish for would yours. You could intercede for anyone you thought I was mistreating."

A servant entered, in ragged clothing and bent low. He carried a tray with a pitcher and two goblets. Stewart poured and offered Bridget a cup. "Join me. Save these miserable souls. It would be such a waste for one such as you to die. You don't realize your own power."

"And Brooks?" she asked, holding back her hand.

Stewart took a sip before answering, "He has to die, Bridget. I'm sorry. It's justice. He disobeyed orders. But think of yourself for once, dear. I'm not only offering you life. I'm offering you power and comfort. Don't you want to feel safe?"

"I do," Bridget replied and paused. "But I'd never feel safe working for you."

Her eyes showed that she would not be moved. Stewart was disappointed. "You are certain this is the fate you want?"

Bridget nodded.

Stewart finished his drink, then ordered the servant, "Get her to the dungeons!" He called melodiously to Bridget, "I'll see you at your execution."

When the servant straightened, Bridget instantly recognized him as the most antagonistic of prisoners. He had loathed her from the start. "Josiah."

"Why'd you come back?" he questioned as they moved to the lower levels.

Xsardis

238

Bristling, Bridget found that she had no more patience to offer him. Not only had he treated her with contempt, Josiah had alerted Stewart to Brooks' friendship with her. Now, he was Stewart's errand boy, trusted enough to lead prisoners to the dungeons. "I came to rescue the man you condemned for no reason."

"He did help you escape," Josiah pointed out.

"Only because he was going to hang anyway."

"You were manipulating him."

"I wasn't."

"You were manipulating all of us. Here we were thinking you cared. Then you took your opportunity for escape. You left us behind, Bridget. And you come back for a guard?"

"They were going to execute me," she answered sharply.

"That's what happens when you play both sides against the middle. Of course, now that Asandra needs you to play both sides you won't. Why won't you aid Stewart? I want to go home! When all the others escaped I was trapped. I have another chance, but you refuse to assist me."

"I can't help Stewart gain power!" she exclaimed.

"Perfect little Bridget, too good to help Stewart…" he rolled his eyes.

"Josiah, more than our comfort is on the line. All of Asandra would suffer if I helped him. This isn't some strategy of mine. I'm going to hang for my choice!"

"I have a wife and a child. They probably think I'm dead. How have they survived without me?" he appealed to her. "I have to get back to them!"

She stopped, surprised. They were approaching the cells. "I didn't realize that." Bridget softened with a sigh, "I wish I could help you."

"Then do!" he challenged and unlocked her prison. "Please do."

Bridget stepped inside and dropped to her knees, her hands shaking from her conversation with Stewart. The door banged shut as Josiah locked her in. Brooks and Drainan were sitting on the hay-filled floor. "I can't believe you were stupid enough to come," Brooks said, but his face was filled with gratitude.

He was bruised and bloody, clearly beaten. From the way he held himself, Bridget figured that he had cracked a rib. She moved closer and began to examine his wounds. "Forget it," he returned. "It's too late to matter now."

"Some rescue attempt…" Bridget muttered, sitting back.

Taking her hand, he made sure she received his words, "Thank you for trying."

"Sorry I got you into this, Drainan," she turned to him.

"I'm the one whose face got us caught," Drainan replied. There was an anger about him, but it was not at her. It was against the cousin who perpetually ruined anything he tried to do.

Brooks closed his eyes, accepting sleep out of pure fatigue and injury.

"What did Stewart want with you?" Drainan questioned, protective even in the cell.

"He asked me to be a figurehead for his new regime. Apparently Maremoth no longer serves Sasha, but Stewart."

"That's good for Asandra," Drainan hoped.

Xsardis

"But bad for us…."

Xsardis

Chapter 30

Jonah the pitara shot out of the water and held himself still just long enough for Ethelwyn and Max to leap out of his jaws. "What's going on?" Vaylynne demanded.

"Sasha... pitara," Max panted.

Ethelwyn was more clear, "Sasha has taken on the form of a pitara. She was trying to get to Nadine's room."

Below them, Sasha's pitara pushed Jonah aside. She showed no mercy as she raked her talons through the ever-faithful creature. Jonah slammed Sasha back, but was not strong enough. A final blow to the head sent Jonah below the waters.

Sasha's shoulder rammed into the wall, knocking them all off balance. Her second blow sent Rachel falling off the side. Seth had seen it coming. With a speed brought about purely by adrenaline, Seth flung himself to the side of the wall and extended his arm. Their grips met.

Rachel felt his muscles strain as she forced her fingers to stay locked around his forearm. Her body collided against the rock wall. Her vision shook.

Seth wouldn't let go. She trusted that. He would pull her up. But would it be soon enough? The pitara roared beneath her and she could feel the steam of its mouth as it jumped to swallow her. Her other arm reached for a hold.

Urgently, Seth planted his feet. He felt Max's arms around his waist, helping to keep him steady. Seth yanked his arm with all his strength and put his free hand under Rachel's shoulders, pulling her to safety. Her shaking arms wrapped around his neck.

The danger had not passed. They rose to their wobbling feet and raced from the edge.

Ethelwyn took the lead as they entered the passageway. When she could, she still held her ribs. Her eyes flicked to where the sister she could not help remained, and then she turned away for the last time.

As her hand found just the right placement on the wall, it began to

Xsardis   242

lurch back. Vaylynne was the first one through. A human-sized toad was
running for her. This was why they had brought Vaylynne along. Ducking
underneath his first and only blow, she rammed her sword into the shifter's
chest.

Moving ahead of her, Max punched his fist in a human projection's
face before bringing his sword down. There were no moral quandaries or
hesitations when he knew he was not truly killing anything.

Recognizing Ethelwyn's injury, Katarina probed, "How bad is it?"

"I will be fine," The Legend replied.

"How bad?" the princess repeated, putting an arm around her waist to
offer some support.

"I do not think anything is broken."

Enemies began pouring towards them. Ethelwyn urged, "Do not stop
and fight. Run. Defend yourselves only."

Edmund blocked an attack from a woman who looked like his sister's
preferred human form. "You betrayed me!" she accused him.

"You betrayed me first," he returned, stabbing his blade into a heart
she did nothing to protect.

"You already broke my heart," said a frog with the feminine voice.
"What's one more?"

Edmund ran the frog through. His anger burned. How many times
had Sasha threatened to kill him? How many times had she said that he had
failed her? How many times had she used him? Now she wanted to be the big
sister? He was not about to feel sympathy for her. He had his own plans to
worry about.

Reesthma had the orbs, but was too distracted to hand them over.
Vaylynne seemed to be in no hurry to take them.

Sasha's duplicated forces were not skilled fighters. She had too many
to control. Yet the sheer numbers of their attackers slowed the group. "We'll
never get out of here like this," Vaylynne knew.

"Then we need to play off of Sasha's weaknesses," Ethelwyn
answered.

"She doesn't have any," cried Reesthma, blocking an attack from a
frog with her sword. For the first time she engaged in battle. Her kick knocked
him back. Max saved her from the next blow and sent the toad to the ground.

"Yes, yes, Sasha does have flaws," Edmund spoke quietly. "But we're
not going to talk about them here."

Seth silenced the conversation and entered his battle mode. He
pushed away the fear he felt for the lives around him and the concerns he had
for the now-vulnerable Nadine and Evan. The only way any of them were
going to escape was for him to control his mind. A certain Scripture always ran
through his head before battle. Psalm 44:6-7: *I do not trust in my bow, my
sword does not bring me victory; but You give us victory over our enemies, You
put our adversaries to shame.*

Save us, O God, he prayed, and then he charged. Sword in one hand
and dagger in the other, Seth swept through versions of Sasha with a deadly
precision. The others followed in the path he had carved, placing Ethelwyn and
Katarina in the more-protected middle.

Xsardis 243

The group found corridors where Sasha's forms were absent, followed by scores of enemies whom they should never have been able to escape. Vaylynne and Seth fought in synch. Rachel marveled at how they anticipated each others' movements.

How much time past, they could not say. Every member of the group was out of breath and sweating, longing for a rest they could not afford to take.

In the empty hall, Edmund moved to Seth's side. "We all need rest." When Seth did not push him away, the shifter went on. "Sasha is losing control. With her powers maxed out like this, she won't be thinking clearly. Use her fears and she will waver."

"What's your plan?" Seth turned to him. It was easier to temporarily trust Vaylynne than Edmund. She had never pretended to be anything but what she was.

"Sasha was a fly once. It makes her terrified of frogs."

If he had had the time, Seth might have doubted Edmund's words. After all, Sasha had been coming at them in the shape of frogs. But with no other recourse, he nodded. "The plague of frogs isn't far."

Ethelwyn stepped toward them, no longer accepting Katarina's support. "There is a hidden room near the frogs' pond. Sasha will not be able to find it. *I* know where it is and often overlook it. If she is too scared to be thorough, we may be able to rest for the night."

Ethelwyn led again. The others followed her into the right corridor while Max lunged for a minotaur in the left one. The strong creature did not slow when Max's sword went through its shoulder. Max fell to the ground as an overpowering absence filled him. He fought to move.

The minotaur leaned over him with his ax. Max's mind flashed back to the menacing creatures of the underground, then to the face of Samson. When Flibbert had fought against that minotaur, his most powerful hit had been to the beast's nose. Max drove his fist up into Sasha's snout. Roaring, the minotaur fell back. From nowhere, Katarina returned and finished him. She offered Max a hand up. "Nadine…" he whispered. "I can't feel her anymore."

Sasha's forces were thinning. The familiar croaking filled the teens' ears. "I hate frogs…" Seth murmured, remembering the mucous-covering he had received earlier.

A pang of guilt filled him as he recalled how Evan had helped him in this place. All the prince had wanted was for Seth to make up his mind about leadership. His inability to do that was in part what had led Evan to stay behind with Nadine. If Max's 'feeling' was right, Evan might now be dead because of that choice.

They entered the frog-filled cavern. Reesthma held a torch for Ethelwyn, shining it against the wall. Hurriedly, Universe Girl reached her fingers into a crevice. The wall shifted back, leading into a small room. The group entered swiftly and fell to the ground, panting.

The door closed behind them.

As the pitara's force sent the Valean rock into its shift, Evan pushed Max into the water, never expecting to survive himself. But Nadine kicked the sturdy door shut and pulled him away from the falling rubble. A newly-formed barrier of Valean rock settled right where the prince's body had been.

Putting a hand on the wet rock, Nadine was grateful for the protection it offered. "That was close," she breathed. "Are you alright?"

He nodded with a mix of gratitude and discomfort. It was horrible to think that Nadine finally knew about a possible cure, but the orbs had been taken. Without them, she would never be healed. His eyes focused on her still-peaceful persona. "Nadine," he suspected, "is there another way out?"

Nadine informed him, "My father left me an exit as a last resort, in case something happened to Wyn while she was away. But Evan," she stopped the excitement that was claiming him, "we can't go. We would have to excavate an underground demolished by an earthquake to find that medallion. Without Max's help I would recycle long before we could find it. Issym would rupture with the earthquake I would cause to its already divided land."

"Then I'll go," Evan determined.

Stepping toward him, she tried to make it clear, "Look at what's happened. We can't risk leaving this place now and drawing more attention to me."

Protests died on Evan's lips. She was right. Nadine settled herself on the ground and offered, "I hope Max is okay."

The penetrating sound of claws scraping on the rock that separated the two rooms filled their ears. Nadine froze. "Nothing can get through that," Evan hoped, dropping beside her.

For minutes the two sat looking at the barrier and listening to Sasha's desperate sounds. "Remind me again why they did not leave us with the frog's stones," Nadine voiced.

"They thought we'd be safe once the cavern was sealed."

"Right…" A crack etched into the wall. "I think they were wrong," she said, her voice monotone.

"We have to go," Evan snapped to his feet.

Nadine passed two canteens to him to fill. She pulled a dagger from the wall and stuffed several books into an already full bag. "Do you need that stuff?" he asked quickly.

"I don't want Sasha reading everything about me," she explained.

The crack got bigger.

The daughter of Asandra put her hand on the tree. As she circled it, only her middle finger remained touching. When she stopped, she pushed with both her hands and all her strength. The bark fell in, revealing a hollow space. She turned to him. "Come on."

"You first." Evan put himself between the tree and the wall. Cracks filled the Valean rock. He could make out the pitara's form between them.

Nadine moved swiftly up the hollow trunk, propelling herself upward with her nimble arms and legs. She reached the next doorway and escaped to less cramped spaces before calling for Evan to join her.

The prince jumped into the hole and replaced the bark a mere second before Sasha forced the upper half of her pitara's form into the room. With a silence that he had practiced hiding with Katarina in the woods, he climbed the tree and joined Nadine.

"Did she follow?" Nadine whispered.

"She will soon."

The ceiling was low. Nadine and Evan crouched through the tunnel. They could see nothing in the darkness, but with her fingers enclosed in Evan's, Nadine led him with confidence. When she could stand again, Nadine reached a torch on the wall and lit it. The illuminated cave walls looked no different from the various tunnels the prince had already seen. "Does this connect to the other passageways?" he asked.

"No," she replied.

Swiftly they walked, putting distance between themselves and Sasha. Evan assured Nadine, "Sasha can't follow us until Rachel and others with the stones get far away. We can get ahead of her."

The prince glanced at her in the torch light. The way she had led him in the darkness told of her familiarity with these corridors. "How much do you remember from previous cycles?"

"Bits and pieces. I have an idea of what my father looked like, and I have this horrible sinking feeling when I recall how sick my mother was. I can remember this path and I already know everything about Ethel. As soon as my second transformation I can read. And I know general things—like that Seth and Rachel imagined Xsardis and that I was never going to leave that place. By the time I am an old woman I can truly regain everything from every cycle—or so I think." Her voice dropped off before she spoke another question, "Do you think Max was right... about the cure?"

Her face was turned down as if she was trying to get away from his answer, but her eyes were locked up at him. The childlike purity and intense desire he saw there seemed to stop all other thoughts in the prince's head. "I hope so."

It was a strange feeling. Near Rachel and Seth, Sasha was stuck in the forms she had already created. But now that they had distanced themselves from Nadine's chamber, Sasha could shift her pitara's form into that of a human woman.

Creating an extra version of herself just so that she could gloat over her ever-nearing victory, Sasha taxed her mind as she focused on her various

Xsardis

246

versions. It hurt, but she felt stronger than she had in months.

Pent up in her forlorn castle, all she had had were reminders of her previous failures. Sasha must never again forget that the surest way to renew her energy was to use her energy. With every ounce of fear she drove into Seth and Rachel, and with every step she took closer to the child who held her powers, the shifter was stronger.

The easily manipulated Blowen had revealed not only Rachel's location but also the fact that the artifact she sought was no longer an artifact but a child. Sasha had sent a dwarf messenger back to Stewart to prepare a room for her future guest. The girl would be hers!

Finding the exit in the hollow tree, Sasha attempted to climb it. She burned with pain. She could not spread herself over the entire island! She had to choose: to follow Rachel's crew or the girl?

Her heart felt a throb of pain, strong and steady. Edmund was running with Rachel and Seth. Maybe he was only acting. Certainly her own family would not betray her again! Yet he destroyed her versions without hesitation. Stewart had been right. She should never have trusted Edmund.

Edmund and his new allies were running towards the room of frogs— slimy small frogs, all hungry for flies. *They'll sense I once was a fly,* breathed her subconscious. *I can't go in there.*

He's exploiting my weaknesses, she knew.

The choice had been made for her. She would follow the girl and the prince. Then she would destroy the others.

Chapter 31

    For hours Nadine and Evan had been able to stay ahead of Sasha with their fast pace. The two had settled into a steady rhythm. "Are you okay?" Nadine looked at him with her green-blue eyes. "Your shoulder is sagging."
    It was true. Evan's old wound, inflicted by Sasha, burned. He knew he would be fine if he could rest it. His solemn nod said more than words would have. An encouraging smile spread across Nadine's lips, breathing new life into Evan. Just in time.
    They heard speeding steps behind them.
    Nadine broke into a full-out run. Evan kept a few steps back. His sword came from its sheath with a perforating sound. He passed the torch to Nadine. As she took it, she glanced past him. "After a thousand years of hiding…" she breathed, seeing Sasha. Her black pants; her blood-red blouse; her crooked grin; her pursuing eyes.
    "Oh," Nadine groaned, clutching her stomach.
    Evan brushed his hand against hers. It was cold and clammy. Nadine took a few more steps but stumbled to her knees. "No. Not now…" she muttered. Her ashen face clearly betrayed the intense pain she felt.
    "You're transforming, aren't you?" he stooped down beside her when he could not raise her to her feet. Sasha was several dozen steps behind.
    The daughter of Asandra nodded, her pupils dilated. She pushed him, "Go Evan. No heroics," she panted. "Go."
    The prince swept her up in his arms and ran. Her head rested on his shoulder, with a clear view of Sasha as the shifter closed the distance between them.
    Nadine's breath was shallow; her form went limp. In Evan's own hands he felt her spine lengthen and her shoulders straighten. "Look!" she managed desperately, fighting to maintain consciousness for him. Her jaw was clenched with the pain. Her eyes threatened to roll into her head.
    Spinning to face Sasha, Evan set Nadine to the ground with all the speed and care he dared.

Xsardis   248

"Prince Evan," the shifter smiled ruthlessly. "We meet again."

Evan's shoulder seared with the memory of her attack. "I seem to remember you failing to kill me last time," he said, attempting to maintain his courage. It was fading fast.

Evan was not fooled by her simple form. He had no idea how long Nadine's transformation would take, but she had no strength left to help him. And there were no stones. What did he think he could accomplish?

"Now I can finish what I started," Sasha taunted.

"Come and try it. You may find I'm stronger than you expect. I won't let you touch Nadine."

She laughed. "You do not disappoint. The chatter I hear says that you were the only thing standing between me completely crushing what little resistance there was. You rallied people's spirits. Do you think that makes you invincible?" she whispered for effect. "Did you really believe that an eighteen-year-old whelp of prince is going to stop me? Did you really think you could protect her?" She pointed her sword at the breathless Nadine, who was still reeling in agony.

Stunned, Evan could not speak. *He* had rallied people? *He* was the reason for the resistance? It was as if his mind had opened for the first time.

Sasha provoked him, "That girl will watch you die and then will see Xsardis' destroyed because of her!"

With the desperation very few are ever called to reach, Nadine struggled. She gripped at the walls, trying to get up and cutting her hands on the rough rock. Her tears for Evan stung from her eyes. "Please Evan, go. Go!" She fell back to the ground, groaning in an agony unlike anything she had felt in a thousand years of life.

"No," Evan's voice was low, but firm. His sword went through Sasha's gut; the shifter did nothing to deflect it. He pulled it back out and the blade was clean. The hole that should have been in her skin and blouse were not there.

As he drove it through her again and again, Sasha cackled. When Evan at stabbed her a fourth time, she brought her arm down hard on his wrist. When he jumped back, she pulled the weapon from herself. Her original sword turned to dust. "This is far too easy," she grinned, testing the blade's balance as she whipped it through the air.

Evan glanced back at the girl he was so futilely trying to protect. Her eyes never stopped asking him to go as another wave of the change began to take her. Her hair lengthened and deepened in color. Her cheek bones rose. Her stomach flattened even more as her torso grew.

Turning back, the prince saw Sasha lunging for him. Evan ducked past her and her weapon. The shifter spiraled around, only toying with the boy. To kill the heir to Asandra's throne!

Evan threw his fist towards where her head should have been. It disappeared for a moment, then reappeared as she punched him twice in the eyes and once in the chin, knocking him over. As he struggled to his feet, blood pouring from his nose, her foot kicked into his gut, sending him back down. She drove her boot right into his injured shoulder. Evan groaned as his vision went black. He was pouring with sweat. The wound throbbed as it had not done since its initial injury. He was fighting to stay awake.

Lifting her foot, Sasha bent over him. He could feel her breath. His sword she cast away. Her own dagger materialized. "What a disappointment! Just like your family. A royal legacy of failure. It ends now."

With the tenacity of Issym and the resolve of Asandra, Nadine pulled her bag off her shoulder. It snagged around her neck. Barely, she silenced a cry of pain before finally forcing it off. She dumped its contents on the ground and rubbed her hands over the items, searching for what her heart longed to find. She could barely see, but she made out a white sphere with a long sharp point coming from it.

Nadine clawed her way over the few short feet separating her and Sasha. The cold ground seemed so inviting. *Lie down. You'll never make it,* it cried. The pain was too great to bear. The change was still happening. She felt her skin spreading out, felt the muscles stretching. Her whole body shook.

She was at Sasha's feet. She meant to aim for her heart. Just a little farther.

"You'll never win this…" Evan promised Sasha with his faint voice. "Goodbye, Prince."

Sasha raised her arm. Nadine drove the sharp point of the object deep into the shifter's calf.

Nothing happened. Sasha did not cry out. She did not turn around. She did not bring the dagger down. She did not breathe or even blink. It was as if she was frozen.

Evan waited for the killing blow. It never came. "Move, Evan," Nadine pressed the words out, then flattened to the ground and accepted sleep.

It was then that the prince noticed the object sticking in Sasha's leg, and the form of Nadine sprawled against the floor. He crawled toward her. Sullied liquid poured through his shirt. He made it to her side, then collapsed beside her.

"Regardless of whether or not you believe me that I can't feel her anymore, Nadine and Evan don't have the orbs," Max addressed the cramped room. Although not a single version of Sasha came near the frog-filled entry to their hideaway, no one was sleeping yet. The adrenaline was too much. "They were missing."

"So they're stuck down there?" Katarina inquired. Her cheeks were flush with color; her skin marred by various wounds; her voice carried more loudly than it should have.

"Not forever," Ethelwyn replied softly, her ribs already bandaged. Her eyes glanced around the small space. "*Someone* has the orbs."

Max focused on Seth and Rachel, recalling how hesitant they had been to believe him about the pitara. It was one thing to give Nadine hope with

Xsardis

his theory about the medallion. Her bright eyes would never have mocked him. "What is it, Max?" Rachel perceived his look.

"I think I know why Issym died and how to save Nadine."

Reesthma inched forward. "Go on," she bid him.

"The medallion that caused the earthquake on Issym's pearl had the same runes as Nadine's pearl. Her cycles changed around the same time I put the key in the medallion. Issym died in the underground searching for it.

"I remember how desperately Smolden wanted that medallion, and now I understand why. It was the last battle he was still fighting with an archenemy long dead."

Is Smolden dead? Seth wondered, but would not say aloud. The other two prophecies of the sound sprites had come true. What about their words that he would face the dragon again?

"Right now we have more important things to worry about," Ethelwyn shook away information that she had been searching for all her life. "Why has Sasha not come to look for us? Surely the frogs do not frighten her that much."

Edmund slid his fingers into the crack and pulled open the sliding wall. "I'm going to find out why."

"On your own?" Seth tried to stop him.

"You're concern is touching, but I'll be fine." Edmund shut the door as he exited.

Seth rubbed his sore neck. "I don't know if we should bring him along. He's too great a risk."

Vaylynne did not come to his aid. Reesthma did. "We need his expertise on his sister."

"We don't need him that much," Katarina disagreed. "And we don't need the traitor either."

Vaylynne did feel very much like a traitor. That was why she had not yet asked Reesthma for the orbs. She did not want to feel the weight of her deception of the people beside whom she had battled. "I've got to give you all credit. You certainly know how to work as a team. If not, we'll all be dead by now. Sticking together is the only hope we have."

Edmund returned to them shortly. "She's nowhere."

"Sasha gave up?" Max doubted.

"I haven't sensed another shifter for a while," Edmund admitted.

"Great," Seth sighed. "Now we have deadly, missing shape shifter."

Galen was awoken from a dead sleep by a sudden rush through his door. Jeff's feet crashed into the room, a lantern in his hand lighting up his wide eyes. "What is it?" the king questioned, already alert.

"Kate's in your council room waiting for you," Jeffery reported. "I

Xsardis

251

have it surrounded. Now I must go tell my king she is here. He will arrest her. Speak to her quickly."

With haste, Galen pulled on his boots and raced to the council room. The guards let him through and he shut the door behind him, unafraid for himself. Kate turned to face him from her position by the window. She wore the same simple clothing. Her tired face possessed less serenity than usual, but he still could not seriously think that this trusted woman had turned on them. "Do you have any idea what people are saying about you?" he asked.

"People say many things," she answered cryptically. "I am more surprised that you have believed them."

"Tell me where you have been. I want to defend you, but the accusations are too serious to be overlooked."

"I went to Maremoth as you instructed. Sasha was not there."

Galen interrogated, "Then where have you been all this time? Do you know how this seems?"

She looked straight into his eyes with a determination he recognized. He had seen it in her face many times. She replied emphatically, "I'm no traitor, Galen. How can you even think that?"

He told her more fully of the rumors. She shrugged. Growing disquieted, Galen opened wide his hands, "Give me something to work with."

Kate turned to the window. "I don't feel the need to justify these accusations with my response."

"I can't help you if you won't help yourself," he reasoned. "I need an explanation."

"Explanation for what, Galen? Where I have been? Whom I have been seeing? The hypocritical bigots condemning me don't have a right to know that."

The anger in her made the king being to doubt her. "Sprites have died from actions put on you."

"This wouldn't even be a question if I was anything but a shape shifter!"

"But you are! A very powerful shape shifter."

Kate stepped closer to him in frustration. "Despite all I have done, you have never trusted me or my people. I will not play into your hand any longer. While the world was still ignorant of the danger, I was the first to fight against Sasha. I have already proven myself. I refuse to be treated like this any longer. Without me, your kingdom would not exist."

"Kate," he put both hands on her arms, trying to reason with her. "*Please* tell me where you were. We have barely seconds before King Remar arrests you. I cannot stop it if you will not confide in me."

"I can't, Galen."

"Kate!" King Galen snapped. He looked into her eyes and he did not see a traitor, but he did see a hidden truth, a burden within her. She had always hidden things from him. How could she ask for trust?

Kate was out of the castle in seconds and in the air.

Galen's heart sunk. Not even he could hold out hope now. Kate was their enemy.

The shifter only pretended to leave. In the form of a simple peasant

Xsardis

252

woman, she slipped back into Saphree. Returning to the kitchen, she found Philip sitting at a table, munching away. At first he paid her no attention, but he felt the presence of her power. Squinting at her, he asked, "And who are you?"

She came into the light. "I need your help."

"Why I would help a traitor?" he returned with a cocky voice, recognizing Kate.

"One traitor to another I thought we could work something out. I know about your deal with Stewart."

He dropped his bread into his bowl of soup and gulped, "That's a heavy charge."

"Yet true. I could name you as my fellow conspirator."

"Don't do that…" he entreated.

Kate bartered, "Then you will help me."

Intrigued, Philip stood. "What do you need?"

"I want the stones gone."

His jaw dropped, "Do you know how hard that would be? Every frog in this place is prepping his armor for the battle with the sprites a week from today. I'll never get the stones."

"And if there is even one left, you will have failed."

"Even if I wanted to, I couldn't," he tried to make her understand.

The shifter held up her hand. "I have a substitute, prepared by Sasha for such a day as this."

"You truly have been to Maremoth then." He moved toward her. Philip was skilled at pegging the evil in people. He was rarely surprised. "I thought you were loyal."

"Did you really think someone of my power was just a pawn in this war?" Kate scoffed.

He bowed, realizing the glory of the alliance he was making, "I am your servant."

Chapter 32

Nadine awoke, the familiar warmth of an after-change sleep still clinging to her. She could feel the cold rock ground below her stomach. Her eyelids fluttered open. At first, Nadine remembered nothing. Wearily, she lifted her head. Sasha's still-frozen form held a sword ready to strike… "Evan," she whispered, everything now coming back.

Quickly, she forced herself to sit up. Too quickly. Her vision faded, then returned. The prince lay beside her, still asleep. Pushing him onto his back, Nadine pried the now-sticky and soaked vest from around his shoulder wound. "Evan," she spoke and brushed her hand against his forehead. "Evan, we have to go."

More loudly she called him back to reality. He tried to focus on her, tried to say something. His pupils were dilated. Blood still seeped from the wound. Nadine did not know how long they had lain there, but if she did not get help for Evan soon, he was going to die. She supported him as he sat up.

Evan's gaze drifted to Sasha. "What did you do to her?" his speech was slurred.

"She's stuck in time."

"For how long?"

Nadine shook her head. "I don't know." She pushed him. "Get up."

He put pressure on his shoulder. "There's no point. There's nothing we can do down here."

"I have a plan. You'll have to trust me."

"But if you drag me, Sasha may wake up before you get to Issym. That can't happen."

"Then don't waste my time. Come on," Nadine commanded. She wrapped her arm around his good side and pulled him to his feet.

She supported him as they moved. The more they walked, the more Evan slumped. Nadine began to practically carry him. Finally he fell into the wall, taking her with him. "Evan," she snapped to grab his attention. "See that?" He looked up. "That room right ahead of us is where we are going. We

Xsardis

254

are so close."

Searching for strength, Evan finished the walk with Nadine. She sat him against the wall in the cavern they entered. In the prince's fevered mind, he was not sure what he was seeing. The whole room had a blue-ish glow that seemed to emanate from the various colored gems that hung like fruit from the five trees that filled the room. With proportionate width and height, full crowns of leaves, and just enough gems on each one to make them look beautiful, the trees were perfect.

Nadine approached the trees, caressing the gems. Their shadows seemed to begin a steady swaying. Buzzing filled his ears and his arms began to tingle. *I'm sorry, Nadine. Sorry I couldn't help you more,* he thought.

Evan's mind saw fairy wings sprout from Nadine's back and a shimmering halo crown her angelic head. When she turned to look at him all he could see were those outstanding eyes. The shadows on the walls turned into figures he knew—Rachel, Katarina, his father, Jeffery, Sphen. The trees themselves began to dance.

A bright red figure, very like Zara, flew before his eyes and stayed there, staring at him. *Ruby?* his mind wondered.

What was the point of staying awake? He might as well be dreaming. Evan slid into the realm of unconsciousness.

Nadine wanted to run to his side, but she refused to allow herself to move. If Evan was going to survive, she had to finish. She rubbed her hand against a blue gem. "Wake up now, little one," she spoke with her melodious voice. The gem fell from the tree and shattered on the floor. The small blue figure of an illuminescent rose from the pieces.

It looked at her inquisitively. She pointed one of her slender fingers at Evan. The illuminescent was barely hovering above the rocky floor. It began a flight to him, then sank to the ground. Nadine looked to the red illuminescent, whom she knew to be Ruby. Ruby had come through Nadine's chambers to hide amongst the sleeping others of her kind. "Help," Nadine whispered.

Ruby sped to the newly-hatched illuminescent. The impact of her touch sent the blue creature into the air, now alive with energy. He raced to Evan and under Ruby's quick, buzzing instructions began pouring his light into the prince.

The sparks filled the room. Nadine waited to see the outcome. When they had cleared, she fell by the prince's side. Evan's eyes flicked open.

"What is this place?" he asked softly. His whole body was warm, but the pain around his shoulder was fading fast.

"The last resort my father installed, for both the illuminescents and me," Nadine replied.

It took another hour for Evan to surface enough for him to press for more information. She went on to explain, "The illuminescents were a dying race. The adults chose to flee to Issym's land in an attempt at life. Few thought they would succeed. They entrusted their children—the gems—to my father. He placed them here to sleep until the world was a safer place, and to offer a last support to me.

"Over the years," she spoke, fingering her rings, "I have woken one at a time to be my companion. Three have passed from the wear of life. I did not wake another until you needed help that I could not give."

"So we ask an illuminescent to take us to Issym?" Evan gleaned. "How was this place safe for you if the illuminescents can just come and go as they please?"

"These illuminescents keep others from being able to transport here. Even Ruby had to come by flight."

"I'm not sure I understand," he straightened, "but I am grateful."

"As soon as you are well we will go."

"I don't want to wait for Sasha to wake up. Ruby, are you going to take us to Issym?"

"I thought… you were… dead," the illuminescent stammered.

"He almost was," Nadine remarked.

"Not here. On the tower," Ruby clarified. "And Rachel and Max too."

Evan was glad to give good news for a change. "It was an illusion of Sasha. Rachel, Max and I all live. Thanks to you, Sasha had to get creative to get rid of us."

Flying into his face, Ruby inquired, "Where is Rachel?"

"In the tunnels, running from Sasha."

"Then I cannot take you to Issym. Wake one of the others. I must find my Rachel!" a note of triumph filled her sparking voice.

When morning came and Edmund still could not feel Sasha, the small band of heroes decided to cover as much ground as they could before the shifter returned. With breakfast finished, they began their brisk walk again, making up much of the time lost yesterday to battles.

The group had plunged into a melancholy spirit. Evan and Nadine filled their minds; Sasha's disappearance added to the worry; no one knew how Asandra was faring under the attacks of the dark sprites. One concern outweighed all the others: they had a traitor in their midst. Someone had taken the orbs. Vaylynne and Edmund had not gone near the room where they had been kept. With grim reality, the group understood it was one of their trusted number that had taken them.

Rachel might have suspected that Ethelwyn had kept them to maintain her access to her beloved little sister, but The Legend would never risk Xsardis or Nadine for her own pleasure. Who of the others had the motive to steal the orbs?

"Why didn't you tell us the truth about Nadine and yourself long ago?" Seth inquired of Ethelwyn. "Or at least Flibbert and Galen?"

"I am a thousand years old," Ethelwyn replied, deciding to answer. She had almost remained silent. "Do you think there is someone I can easily seek for counsel or understanding?"

"Surely you trust Flibbert," Rachel pondered.

Xsardis   256

"I care for this generation," The Legend assured, "but I have cared for many generations." Her voice was steady and calm, but it moved its hearers. "I have seen many good men come and go. I have seen bad men become good and good men become bad. And I have seen good men make very bad decisions for the right reasons. I could not trust even Flibbert with the secret of Nadine."

"Why did you keep it from Seth and Rachel?" Katarina pressed.

Ethelwyn considered the question, then decided to be blunt. "I had to wait for them to be ready. They were children the last time they came.

"Flibbert said that you stuck up for us when he doubted our age," Seth responded. In truth, he was irritated. Ethelwyn did not believe them to be too young to fight a dragon and a shape shifter, but she did think they were too young know a secret they had imagined.

"I did not spend enough time with you to discern whether or not you were ready for this knowledge. It's not as if that was your first visit to Xsardis."

Rachel was dumbfounded. It seemed that every sound the group made was amplified: the shuffling of feet, the harsh breaths, the trickle of the stream… "What?"

"Did you just say what I think you said?" Seth asked.

Universe Girl smiled at them, a familiar twinkle in her eyes. Her skin had lost the summer's tint and adapted to the darkened cave. Her armor covered the youthful figure she still possessed after so much life. "Does that surprise you so?" she inquired. "You remember the story we tell of the two children who found the gem of light. You did not *act* that out on Earth. You lived it, here. You helped Issym put Smolden in the underground.

"That was not even your first visit. Once you came only for a day. You brought us the Word of God—in a pocket edition."

Seth felt the memory of having lost a small Bible given him by his grandfather. He had been so frustrated with himself. It made sense. That was how Xsardis could have the exact Scriptures he read from at home. "How could we not remember that?" he was stunned.

"To your childish minds, your imagination was as real as your lives on Earth," she answered him. "But understand that I had no way to know how much you had grown. Would you forget your work on Issym as you had forgotten before? I knew you to be capable. I also knew you to be a thousand years younger than I was. *I* do not feel equipped to carry Nadine's secret."

Rachel felt electricity run up her spine and she shivered as it touched her face. "You okay?" Seth inquired.

"I don't know what that was," she replied, turning behind her to look for a cause. A bright illuminescent was sweeping towards them. "Ruby?" Rachel called. The illuminescent rubbed against Rachel's cheek, sending new energy through her system.

"Where have you been?" Rachel investigated with excitement. "Seth said they hadn't seen you since Maremoth!"

"Oh Rachel!" Ruby shouted in her buzzing language. "I thought I had failed you. I was so miserable. I came back to Noric to hide."

Ruby did not need an invitation to continue, "There is a special cavern in this place where many illuminescent gems lay waiting to hatch. I searched for them when I came here with Seth, but did not find them. I came

Xsardis

257

here again after the battle at Maremoth—longing to hide myself. This time I found them."

"I'm glad you're back."

Ruby did not move. That was enough to show that she had something important to say. "Prince Evan and Nadine came into the cavern with the illuminescents. They're going to Issym."

The expressions the company held were mixed. It was good that Nadine and Evan were not trapped, but very dangerous for them to be out of their hideaway. Everyone knew the truth. Sasha had found a way into the cavern.

Ruby flew lower, "But Rachel, Seth, there is something terrible I must show you."

"Show us?" Rachel asked. She could tell that something was different about Ruby, but she could not place what it was.

The illuminescent bobbed her body up and down. She flew to the ceiling of the cave and showered sparks until what looked like a projection appeared before them. Edmund did not move from his distant seat, but Vaylynne drew closer to the image.

Before them flashed truly frightening scenes. The dark sprites' attacks. A bloody Flibbert dragging Joeyza. Sphen pounding the table in a frustration they could never have imagined him possessing. Jennet's death. Queen Danielle mourning. Remar and Juliet's troubled faces. Fires and battles that they could not discern. Many tears. The images fizzled out.

The information made one thing clear: Asandra was in grave danger.

"What has happened?" Katarina trembled with concern and fury.

"The dark sprites." Ethelwyn looked fierce, as she first had when they had entered Nadine's chamber. "Long have they slept. I have dreaded the damage they would do to Xsardis if they awoke. No doubt this is Sasha's doing. We must return to the mainland."

"What about Evan and Nadine? We can't just leave them here with Sasha!" Katarina lobbied. "Nadine is what this whole mission has been about."

"We can't do anything for them. They're on their own now," Universe Girl knew her duty.

Reesthma clutched her bag, in which the orbs rested. *What if they could help? End all this?* she questioned herself. *Surely Vaylynne would want me to give them back now!* Her eyes flicked to the warrior. "Seth," Reesthma began to confess.

Vaylynne's mind spun. Her eyes flicked to Edmund: he was confident in his plan. He offered victory for her independence movement. He was selfish. She looked to Seth: strong, capable, selfless. The way his team worked together showed how pure their motivations were. But joining them would cost her everything.

Seth caught the look and stayed motionless. Whatever decision she was about to make, she had to make on her own.

Can I really give up my movement? she inspected herself. Vaylynne already knew that she could not see any more battle like what the illuminescent had showed. Seth and the others could help Asandra. Once more her eyes fell on Edmund, then landed on Seth. "Reesthma, show them the bag."

Xsardis   258

Gratefully, Reesthma opened her leather satchel and pulled one of the orbs out. Seth took it from her hand, disappointed that it was her that had betrayed them. "Do you know how much trouble you could have caused?"

Tears welled in the tender girl's heart. "I never meant for anything bad to happen. I was trying to help. I'm sorry."

"They're yours now Seth," Vaylynne spoke calmly, despite the storm that had just swept through her. "I lied to Reesthma. It's not her fault."

"Vaylynne, what are you doing?" Edmund barked, his mind unable to process the scene before him. He had expected Vaylynne to possess a passion unshakeable.

Reesthma slipped the bag off and put it in Seth's hands. He passed it to Rachel as Edmund approached. "Give them back. I have to save Kate!"

"I have to save Asandra. I will help Kate in any way I can—any way that she would approve of," Seth assured.

"You arrogant boy! You know nothing!"

The shifter gripped his shirt. Seth leaned back and asked him, "Why must you hate so much?"

Max was quickly in between, separating them.

Edmund turned to Vaylynne, arms flapping wildly. "You betrayed everything you held dear! You betrayed me!"

"I did," she agreed. "But I was fighting for things that didn't matter. I'd lost sight of what did."

Unwittingly, Vaylynne took a step backwards into the protection of the others. For the first time she had sacrificed her own will and gained defense against the blows life had been throwing at her for years. It felt good. "Join us," she offered, though she already knew what his answer would be.

"I'll help Sasha destroy you!" Edmund promised and darted away.

Acquiring the orbs, Ethelwyn decided, "There's no time to waste. Max will to go to Issym. He'll have to find the medallion quickly, then return to the cavern to reach Nadine and Evan. The rest of us must press on to Asandra."

For only a moment Max's mind hesitated. To leave the group in danger; to go to Issym on his own where Sasha might be heading. He was not sure which thought he minded more. But doubt gave way to decision. He straightened and was ready.

Reesthma quickly repacked his bag with the rations and water he might need. Max's goodbyes were short. Katarina yanked him by his wrist until he was sufficiently removed from the others. He was already looking past her, trying to go. "Kat…" he tried to get in.

"Look Max, I'm not a good leader. I work better alone or following orders. When I try to take over… well, just look what happened between me and Rachel."

His eyes laughed and his attention waned. The princess grabbed onto his shoulder and wrenched his attention towards her. "But you're not like me. You *can* lead. And when you do people will follow. You've been following Seth, but God is sending *you* to Issym because you are needed there. I don't know what political situation you are going to get yourself into; I don't know what danger you'll face, but you need to have the confidence to command the situation, whatever it is. I know what happened last time you were on Issym, but you are ready for this now."

She wrapped her arms around him and whispered, "And then come back to me!"

The young teen in the over-sized black uniform of Maremoth walked quickly with a tray in his hands. The urgency in his face almost mirrored fear. Entering the throne room as if he had been beckoned, he offered the liquid he bore to Stewart.

"And who are you?" Stewart asked, not yet accepting the drink.

"Caleb, Sir. A new recruit."

Stewart sipped confidently. New recruits meant his power was growing. "Welcome to my service." His attention returned to Devar, "You say the dark sprites have ceased their attacks?"

"Yes, and Saphree has withdrawn all its troops."

"What could have…"

His question was cut short as Kate swept in through the balcony. The wings left her back. Her tall, graceful form landed before him. He might have seen her as a beautiful flower but for his recognition of her thorns as she demanded, "Is your army ready?"

"For what?" he stepped toward her.

"Battle."

"I figured that," Stewart returned. "But against who?"

"Saphree has challenged the dark sprites. In less than a week, they will war. The loser will be decimated. The winner we can finish off while they are still weak."

"You want to fight the dark sprites?"

"Surely you see the danger they pose to your kingdom."

Stewart directed Devar, "Move the executions up."

Caleb wanted to drop the tray and run, but the training he had received kept him steady. Waiting for Stewart to dismiss him, Caleb kept himself from arousing attention and then moved directly to the dungeon. Knowing time to be short both for himself and for the others, he refused to look back or hesitate. When he approached the guard at the top of the stairs, Caleb straightened himself. Seth's words rang through him, *Act like you know what you're doing and you're capable—even if you are not. Make your opponent afraid of you and you've won half the battle.*

"I've been sent to relieve you," Caleb informed the soldier before him.

"I have another hour on watch," the large man returned.

Keeping his confidence even though he knew this man could snap him like a twig, Caleb replied, "Stewart sent me personally. If you have a problem, take it up with him."

The guard wavered, but decided, "Then we can both stand watch."

"He wants you in his throne room." Caleb paused, then barked, "Now."

The youth was amazed as the man handed him the keys to the prison and walked away. Descending the steps, Caleb unlocked one cell and tugged the door open.

"Caleb?" Bridget's voice was full of surprise.

He smiled and pulled her to her feet, accepting a hug. Though he had grown much, her motherly embrace made him feel like a small boy. "We've got to go."

"I didn't think you were coming," Drainan met his eyes as he helped Brooks stand.

"Bridget suggested you might need me as your backup plan," Caleb explained.

"You had said no," she reminded.

"I thought things over. I would have told you before, but I didn't have time with the dark sprites overhead."

Bridget put Brooks' arm around her and followed Caleb out of their prison. Her eyes hesitated on the other cells. "We don't have time," Caleb informed. "They've moved up your executions. Stewart is about to go to war against the dark sprites and against the combined forces of Issym and Asandra."

"Is he crazy?" Drainan wondered.

Bridget was still focused on the doors that locked countless prisoners inside. "I left without them once. I can't do it again."

"She won't be dissuaded," Brooks slurred.

"Caleb, get Brooks out of here. I've got to help Bridget," Drainan determined.

"I'm staying," Caleb resolved.

Offering his sword to Drainan, Caleb helped Bridget to free the prisoners while Drainan stealthily knocked out the many guards on the floor. They made a run for the surface, Drainan and Caleb each with a sword.

"I can't believe it," Josiah spoke to Bridget in amazement.

"I didn't have to leave you this time, so I didn't," she answered.

Their dash to the gates had good timing. Devar had called the soldiers to stand at attention while he gave them their new orders. It took only a few well-aimed blows to the remaining guards to escape into the fresh air of Asandra.

It was an odd feeling, being frozen in time. Sasha could not move a single muscle, not even her eyes. To be unable to shift was like a grievous wound. It was that wretched daughter of Asandra. But how? Sasha craved the knowledge the girl possessed almost as much as her powers.

Xsardis

261

The shifter might not have been able to move, but she could brood. And to her that was just as strong a muscle as she could wish for. Whom did she hate more? Nadine, Rachel, or Edmund? It was clearly Rachel. But before she could deal with the girl, she had to finish her pursuit of Nadine. Dealing with Edmund would be her reward for conquering Xsardis.

Though the daughter of Issym had slowed her plans, Sasha knew she could still execute them with her hard-earned skill. It would take time for Rachel and the others to escape the tunnels. Sasha would close in on them before they could. With Nadine in her power and Rachel dead, Xsardis would be mere days from falling. Her new power would make even the dark sprites bow.

Then suddenly Sasha was free. As the bonds fell from her like ice and shattered on the ground, she tumbled to her knees. Without wasting time the shifter ripped the small pick from her leg and observed it for only a second before casting it from her.

"What exactly happened to you?" Edmund's voice filled her ears.

Sasha turned in violent anger. "You!"

"Don't bother looking for Nadine and Evan. They're long gone. I checked myself," Edmund informed her. "They used the illuminescents to get away."

"You have betrayed me for the last time," she swore, rising to her feet.

"I didn't betray you!" he returned.

There was something about his posture and the cadence of his voice that showed an unusual emotion for her brother: defeat. It caused her to pause. "Explain."

Edmund was focused on one thing, and it was not saving Kate's life, or gaining power, or helping his sister. It was vengeance. Vengeance on a group that had cast him out one too many times. If he had to use his sister to get it, he would. "I had gained their trust. I had the orbs and the girl in my fingertips. You're the one who ruined that!"

"No," Sasha protested. "You failed me."

"You failed *me!*" Edmund knew just how to get under her skin.

"No," she put a hand up to deflect his meaning, suddenly feeling weak.

"And you started failing me a long time before that."

"No!" she shouted. How could he always make her feel so weak? She was the most powerful creature on Xsardis and he made her feel like a pouting child. Her body, unable to shift for so long, was on the verge of changing against her will. It made it difficult to focus.

Edmund knew he was close. "But there is still a chance to finish this mission. To destroy Seth and the others for good."

"I've sent many versions of myself after them. It's a waste of time until I find Nadine."

"Seth is beating you because he trusts fully in his God. Take away that trust and you can stop him."

"I'm listening."

Xsardis

Chapter 33

"What about the rest of us?" Reesthma asked, in her mind already describing what Max's disappearance by the orbs looked like. Someday she would include this in the book she longed to write about this adventure. With displeasure, she knew she would have to be honest about her own actions.

"My orbs cannot take us to Asandra. The journey is too short and the risks too great," Ethelwyn responded.

"Ruby, what about you?" Rachel searched for the best course of action.

"I can't." Her whole body moved from left to right quickly. "I'm too weak."

Recalling the sickness that had once almost killed the illuminescent, Rachel allowed Ruby to land in her cupped hand and offered a word of encouragement. "You have already done much for us, my little friend."

With renewed resolve, they marched towards the surface. Memories of the attacks Ruby had shown them on Asandra were fresh in their minds. Ethelwyn called halts sparingly and only let them stop for the night because she recognized that they would move more quickly with even a little rest. The weary group simply leaned back against the wall or curled up on the floor and sought sleep. Even Seth felt it grip him, adrenaline's affects fading.

He did not know how much time passed, but he was suddenly awake. Seth heard the claws scrape and recognized the all-too-familiar panic fill his chest. His eyes shot open, his body not far behind. "Go, go, go!" he ordered his companions.

They groggily stumbled to their feet. Ethelwyn had sat on watch. Her eyes were wide; her color pale. She had seen what he feared so deeply. They were running now. Seth felt himself drawn to be at the head of the pack. He could not face this monster again, but he would not leave his friends to its mercy. Seth forced his feet to stop. Katarina spun around. "What are you doing?"

His expression told her all she needed to know. He was making a

Xsardis   264

stand so that they could escape. She wanted to fight with him, to make him come, but his eyes showed the stubborn determination that refused to be reasoned with. The princess would have gone back to him, but Vaylynne's fingers were on her arm. "Get out while you can." Without waiting for an answer, Vaylynne backtracked to Seth's side.

The scraping of the monster's claws was almost drowned out by the thudding of its paws. Seth glanced to Vaylynne, grateful for her sword beside his but understanding that their only purpose was to buy the others time. Sweat covered him as he anticipated the beast with a fear he thought he had long ago conquered.

"The dragon?" she prodded.

He nodded. A bend in the tunnels obscured his view, but he knew. He would have known without the prophecy. Seth forced himself to take the steadying breaths that would keep him alive. Try as he might, he could not separate his panic from his rational mind.

A taloned hand slid into view on the wall in front of them. "God, let this be a dream!" he hollered. The paw seemed to be smaller than he remembered. It would have had to be to fit in the tunnels. The slick, black scales were the same. The head rounded the corner, obscured in a puff of smoke coming from raised nostrils. A forked tongue, red as the fire it would soon be breathing, slid from its mouth.

Vaylynne took an involuntary step backwards. The fear leached onto her, sucking courage along with air. There was no defeating this monster. There was no gem of light, like in Seth's stories. No sword; no army; only death.

As the smoke dissipated, Seth looked into the face of the creature and knew that it was not Smolden. That was some relief. The dragon's form came into view. It was more serpent-like, less bulky, but every bit as full of hate. Sasha.

The silent stare passing between Seth and the dragon had no effect on Vaylynne. She jabbed her blade into the only part of it she could reach: the flesh surrounding its talons. Blood poured from her wound, a vibrant stain to its midnight scales. "We can kill this thing!" Vaylynne triumphed in a giddy voice. They did not need the gem sword to defeat Sasha's dragon.

Sasha's other paw swept toward them angrily. Seth and Vaylynne dropped to the ground, just in time. As the shifter's bleeding appendage stomped toward them, Vaylynne performed a back flip and dodged.

She and Seth evaded Sasha's movements several more times, before he succeeded in slashing his sword across her nostrils. Full of anger, Sasha drew in a breath. "Get back!" Seth bellowed to Vaylynne.

Together Seth and Vaylynne ran around the bend, barely escaping the flame from the dragon's lungs. The heat poured round the corner, threatening to cut off the oxygen. When the wave of heat rolled past and left only a fragment of what had been present, Vaylynne straightened. She said lowly, "Let's finish this."

The beast came toward them. Vaylynne ran past its legs and jabbed at its belly. Sasha growled, but focused on Seth. Her eyes never moved from the teen. He could feel them. His fear was ratcheting.

After the dragon destroyed him and Vaylynne, it would go after

Xsardis   265

Rachel and Katarina and the others. Then Sasha would rip through Xsardis, destroying everything in her path. Because he was not strong enough to defeat her. He could not do it. She was too powerful.

"Isn't this where your God is supposed to help?" Vaylynne shouted at him, half out of a sincere searching and half to wake him from his stupor.

Seth suddenly felt energy rush through his body. This was where he let go of his competency and trusted his Maker. *Okay Lord. Whatever it takes. Just don't let it go after the others.*

Seth lunged onto the dragon's leg. It swung wildly to get him off. He mounted its torso, scaled its neck. He swung his blade at its eye, but he was wrenched away. A swing of her neck sent him flying. The dragon snapped at him. He felt the teeth go through his leg. The pain that seared through him covered the jolting of the fall. With the command of a warrior, he forced himself to roll over and stab up with his blade. As Sasha's mouth lunged for his body, his sword found its mark in the soft flesh of her exposed pallet. The head of the dragon fell on him, dead.

"Whoa!" Vaylynne hollered with joy. She ran towards Seth. "We did it! Seth?"

The warrior dropped to her knees beside the dragon. Its head was draped over Seth's legs and chest. His eyes were glazed and stared at the ceiling. His breaths were shallow. "Seth!" she attempted to call him back to reality as she pushed his hair back from his brow.

He passed out.

No! her heart cried. This stirred her more than all the others she had buried on the field. *Not like this. Not when victory should have been his. We need him!*

Vaylynne had finally found a team she trusted—a family. She wanted to search for a pulse, but she had to get the dragon off of him first. Tears stinging from her eyes, she called to him. "Hold on, Seth. Hold on!"

She pushed at the dragon's head, kicked it, and pushed again. Finally Seth was clear. But below the knee of his right leg was nothing. "No…" she called. To a fighter like Seth this would be a worse fate than death. "Not him!"

Rachel was running to them, her movements swift and her concern evident. Her eyes fell to him, but for several long seconds she could not process what she saw. A desperate cry escaped her lips before she fell trembling on her knees beside Seth and put her hand in his. She felt for a pulse and found one. "Thank You, God," she whispered. Examining the amputation, she saw that while the skin was maimed and dark red, little blood came from it. "Why isn't he bleeding?"

Ethelwyn put a hand on Rachel's head. The teenager looked up for some words of consolation. Universe Girl could only offer, "The dragon's saliva sealed the wound. It saved his life."

Katarina leaned against the wall, too shocked to speak. Reesthma's form shook at the agony of battle. The princess held her.

"We won't be able to move him for a few hours," Vaylynne declared as she stood. Ethelwyn took her place and began to examine the cut. "Sasha will send her forces here. We need to be prepared. Katarina, you take that entrance. I'll take the other. Ethelwyn, whatever you need to help him, you'll have it."

Allowing Vaylynne to take control, Rachel brushed her hand through Seth's hair. He had always been an athlete. He had been the warrior all of Xsardis looked to for help. His life would never be the same again. And in the war-torn land where he had so many enemies, a missing leg was a near death sentence.

Ethelwyn assured her, "He's lucky to be alive."

After a breath, Rachel replied, "I know. But what are we supposed to tell him when he wakes up?"

Max closed his eyes on one side of Xsardis and opened them on the other. The rush of being transported was like nothing else. It left him feeling like gel when he came out on the other end. He touched his skin, looked at his hands. There were always risks with teleporting—he knew from too many movies— but he seemed whole.

The wind blew across his face, still holding the bite of night air. The sun was just rising. It cast its orange rays on a ground littered with fallen trees. Max had gleaned from Ethelwyn that Issym had been racked with smaller after-quakes, following the Great Quake. The land around the initial quake had become practically useless. Any homes too near had been rebuilt at a safer distance. Ethelwyn had thought it best not to risk transporting Max too close to the rubble; she had sent him to a place near Prince Aldair's castle. Arvin's home.

Taking in his surroundings and grateful for the light of day after so long in the tunnels, Max moved swiftly in the direction of the castle. He could faintly make out the traces of what had once been a clear path to the mighty palace. It did not take long for the high white walls to come into view.

Aldair's castle was a testament to the architecture of the olden days. It had aged, but aged with grace. The walls still offered solid protection. They did not have the menacing look of Saphree or Maremoth. This was a place of learning and distinction—just like Prince Aldair had been a man of learning and distinction.

Max's chest throbbed. It had been years since his friend's Arvin's death, but it felt like it had happened yesterday. He could still feel the pressure of the man's dying grip on his shoulder and hear his hoarse voice as he gave him a commission. Arvin's sister had embraced him with trembling shoulders after hearing the news. Princess Valerie's tears had fallen onto his shoulders unchecked. Before he had left, she had offered her own challenge to him.

Shaking himself, Max put away his grief. He needed a horse and he needed to get to the medallion. The youth marched to the gate without slowing.

"Max!" a voice hollered a surprised welcome to him from the guard house.

Xsardis 267

"Kesh," Max greeted. This guard had admitted Arvin and him into the castle after the earthquake. Though Kesh was desperate for battle, he was always left behind. The young man stared at Max for several moments, before Max asked, "Might I come in?"

"Of course!" Kesh's face disappeared from the window and with a grind the gate pulled up. Kesh slapped Max on the back as he entered. "Good to see you! Where did you come from?" He put up a hand. "No, don't tell me. Tell the princess. She'll want to see you. Go on!"

Kesh pushed him into the palace. The whole castle seemed oddly empty, but as regal as he remembered. The teen instinctively looked down at his muddied clothes, his tattered boots and his dirty hands—one of which he ran through his greasy hair. He was in no condition to talk with a princess, or anyone for that matter. He started for the door, but a commanding voice drifted down the steps. "Max."

The freckled teen turned to stare up at the form of Curt. Finding no words in his throat, he offered a respectful bow and remained silent.

Curt was great battle leader and had been a true friend to Arvin. As captain of his guard, he had done much to help Valerie and all of Issym after Aldair's death. This he knew from Galen's high praise.

"You have come a long way," the captain spoke, reaching the bottom stair.

"Where is everyone?"

"Issym is not what it once was, now that King Galen and his army have left. Many of Princess Valerie's excellent citizens have gone to the high king's castle to help in this grievous time."

"Grievous? What's happened?"

"Much. Too much to tell a traveler, who has come for some set purpose," he responded. "What is your purpose?"

"I need a horse."

"And a bath," Curt replied.

"I don't have time for that."

Curt sniffed. "Make time."

The shuffle of feet above them brought Princess Valerie into view. Her cheeks were flushed. Her long brown hair was all that spoke of her brother or her former self. She wore a slim white dress and carried herself with a new confidence. One look at her set eyes and Max knew that she had continued her brother's standard of fine leadership. "Max," she spoke with delight before descending down the stairs. "You look exhausted."

Her words reminded him of that truth. He could barely stand. How long had they been running and fighting and desperate? "Come," she ordered.

Wordlessly, he followed her through several grand chambers, before coming to a dining room. A table was laid out with food. Max dropped into a chair as she poured a drink from a silver pitcher. The princess sat beside him and wrapped the chalice in his hands. "Drink."

Max drank, never taking his eyes from her. The teen felt the heat of the sun and he was transported to the battlefield where Arvin had said, *Tell Valerie that she will make a great ruler of the castle.*

He had had so much love for his sister and she had had so much love for him. It was for Max that they had been separated forever. Prince Aldair had given his own life to save Max's.

The princess assured him, "No one blames you. My brother was determined to die a hero. Thanks to you he did."

Straightening, Max focused. "Xsardis is in trouble."

Valerie leaned back, instantly a ruler. "What do you need?"

"A horse and some food for the journey."

"Of course. But where are you going?"

"Back to the underground. I need to find the medallion."

"The one that caused the earthquake?"

He nodded.

"You don't intend to use it again…"

"It's complicated." Max did not want to explain. It had been hard enough ensuring it made sense to friends who had imagined the medallion to begin with.

"Try to tell me," she pushed.

"There's a girl who will empower Sasha if I don't turn that medallion and stop the artifact inside her."

"What?" the princess struggled to understand.

"Please, trust me. We don't have time to waste. Sasha may already have the girl in her clutches."

"I'll do more than trust you. I'll come with you."

"What? No!" Max stammered. That had been the last thing he had expected her to say.

"Do you think that my brother would have hesitated for a moment to go with you? I will do no less than him."

"Valerie," Curt growled. "Your brother was a warrior. You are princess. I cannot allow you to…"

"You are needed back at Galen's castle, to give them a report of Max's arrival," she commanded, standing. "And I will go with Max. He will protect me."

"I don't think this is a good idea," Max protested.

"I agree," Curt added, arms folded in front of him.

"Well, I think it is a good idea," she replied. "And since when have you known anyone in my family to be deterred once we get something into our heads?"

Evan, Nadine and a red illuminescent landed in the middle of the woods. It was sheeting rain and Evan immediately searched for what cover he could find. "Over here!" he called, spotting a thick overgrowth that would shield them.

Nadine hollered back over the heavy droplets, "There's a path this

Xsardis   269

way!"

The illuminescent faltered under the fall of rain and made the decision for them. They hid under the overgrowth.

"Where are we?" Nadine questioned, ringing out her hair. The trees offered a surprising amount of shielding from the rain.

"Issym. That's all I know," answered the still-young male illuminescent. His red color was faltering.

"If there's a path we at least know we're not completely lost," Evan replied.

Nadine stretched out her hand and the illuminescent landed. She clasped her fingers around him, offering warmth and protection. Again, Evan's gaze fell to the vibrant rings on her slender fingers. "Can the illuminescent get us back to Noric?" the prince investigated.

"He doesn't seem strong enough," Nadine answered sadly. Her eyes had lost any gleam.

Water dripped down Evan's face and into his mouth as he asked, "What do you mean?"

"Illuminescents don't live for a set number of years. They survive until they use all their energy. Some are born with more than others. I have had three such companions in my lifetime. After the last one died, I swore I would awaken no more."

"The rings?" he figured.

"When they die, it is possible to preserve some memory of them," she confirmed. "Other than Ethel, these three have been my only constant companions."

Lightning lit up the sky. Nadine's eyes were absorbing everything. She tilted her head to the heavens and enjoyed the rain. It was her first time feeling the wind since before her father had died.

"If he can't get us back and we don't find another illuminescent before your cycle ends…"

She looked at him, the realization painful to her as well. "Then Issym is going to suffer a larger earthquake than before." The thunder resounded around them, befitting her statement.

"We have to get out of this rain!" Nadine eventually decided as more lightning flashed and the downpour intensified.

Their rescuers came in the most unlikely forms. Four short, plump men with fluorescent hair and colored skin advanced through the rain. Their high boots and wild cloaks were comical. From Rachel's stories, Evan knew that they were mushnicks. And mushnicks meant shelter, warmth and creatures they could trust.

The mushnicks gestured for them to follow. Despite their short appendages, the men moved quickly. Nadine and Evan struggled to follow but were soon in the shelter of a cozy dwelling.

"I dreamed about a place like this," Nadine breathed, entering the home and releasing the illuminescent. Wooden walls. A fire blazing. Well-used table and chairs. The smell of food in the air.

Evan smiled at her, then addressed the mushnicks, "Thank you. I am Prince Evan of Asandra. And this is Nadine." He did not hold back the truth.

Xsardis 270

Rachel had assured that mushnicks tied themselves to fairies and both races could be trusted.

Nadine studied the quizzical creatures as they introduced themselves. "My name is Freddy," offered the first. His hair was brilliantly white and fluffy. His skin was white with purple triangles on it.

To Freddy's right stood one that was slightly taller than the others. His face was lime green with six vertical orange lines on it. The wild multicolored hair stuck out on every side. He leaned forward and almost toppled over as he announced, "And I'm Simmy."

The next man in line was the shortest of the group. His body was blue. The spots of red on his chin and forehead matched his curly hair. "Clarence. And we are so glad to have a prince here!" He pumped Evan's hand up and down.

The last man stepped towards Nadine. "I'm Cobby. Such a lovely lady is always welcome." His whole body was a deep purple and brilliant large, yellow circles scattered his skin. His hair was bright green.

Nadine sneezed from the cold.

"Oh no!" exclaimed Simmy.

"You're sick!" added Freddy.

"Soup!" called Cobby.

"Right away!" finished Clarence.

The green haired mushnick hurriedly tossed a bowl to the white haired one who handed it to the curly haired one who filled it with soup before passing it to the one with the multicolored hair who put it in Nadine's hands. The process was repeated for Evan.

The two teens took several sips of the hearty stew before a door opened and a fairy entered. Her simple white dress descended to her ankles. The blue sparkles on her wings and eyes caught Nadine's eye. "You're a fairy," she stated. She had seen more in one day than she had in a thousand years.

"I am Esther. And you?"

"Nadine," she answered, captivated by the look of peace and purity in the fairy's manner, but recognizing the solemnness of one who knew much. Nadine believed she could tell Esther anything. "Daughter of Issym and Asandra and Sasha's most desired prize. I have only days to return to Noric or Issym will rupture."

"Well," Esther began. "Is that all?" She looked to Evan, "Do you have an equally exciting tale?"

"I am Prince Evan of Asandra."

"You never know what you'll find in the rain," she smiled. "Why are you both here? I assume you would not have come unless the danger was too great elsewhere."

"We seek a medallion," Evan explained. "It will cure Nadine and stop Sasha's plan to use her."

"You are not the only one who searches for it."

Standing in the puddle of water that had dripped from him, Evan queried, "What do you mean?"

"One called Max and Princess Valerie are searching the underground also for this medallion."

Xsardis

271

"Max is here?" Nadine was surprised, but her mind pieced things together. "He must have had my orbs!"

"Your orbs. You mean Universe Girl's?"

"One and the same."

"Then you know Ethelwyn? Perhaps you know where she is now. We have been searching for her."

"She is with Seth and Rachel—on Noric."

Though it was clear she was deep in thought, Esther moved on quickly, "You need dry clothes. Mushnicks are always prepared."

Excitedly, Cobby opened a chest by the door. Simmy selected clothes for Evan, while Clarence chose for Nadine. When the travelers had emerged from changing, Esther had retired to her room again.

Nadine sat down by the fire, her knees pointed to it and her new chocolate brown skirt draped over her legs. Her arm rested on the chair seat and her head in her hand, the wavy brown locks flowing past it. Her cheeks glowing in the warmth of the fire, Nadine's welcoming persona drew the illuminescent and the four mushnicks to gather around her. She smiled as they fidgeted, not certain what to say. She asked them, "What are you?"

Cobby jumped up and down. "We are mushnicks!"

They looked at each other as if timing something and then began singing:

> *Long ago the mushnicks*
> *Were thought to be stupid*
> *And then there was a battle*
> *A mighty, mighty battle*
>
> *Smolden and his army*
> *Were crushing everybody*
> *And all of Issym rallied*
> *In our land*
>
> *We fought alongside Rachel*
> *And stopped Sasha*
> *Supporting our fairies,*
> *We tended the sick*
>
> *We helped stop Smolden*
> *And became heroes*
> *Because we saved the mighty Flibbert*
> *And finished his quest*

The enthusiastic song was accompanied with dancing and badly timed clapping. Her smile won them over forever. "Those last two lines are about us!" Simmy informed.

"That's wonderful!" Nadine praised. "Who wrote the song?"

"The greatest poets of every generation," answered Cobby.

"Yes, the greatest, most awesome poets," added Clarence importantly.

Xsardis   272

"They started writing it in the early days of the world," Freddy put in.

"Those are the newest four verses. That makes 155 in all," finished Simmy.

"Well I think it's excellent," Nadine complimented, ignorant of what she was getting herself into.

"We'll sing the others for you," decided Simmy.

"Oh!" she exclaimed. "You know them *all*?"

"We do! Every mushnick does."

"Evan and I need to talk to Esther, though. I fear we will not have time."

That diplomatic answer might not have worked, but the fairy entered the room on cue and sat in a chair opposite Nadine. "Clarence, Freddy, Simmy, Cobby," Esther addressed each one directly, "perhaps you should show the illuminescent your rooms. He should enjoy your treasures."

The mushnicks joyfully rushed off to serve. Evan moved to stand behind Nadine, his hands on her chair. "There is something on your mind you wonder if you should tell us."

Esther took a breath, then said, "Issym's high king is gone. So are most of the land's officials. Those who lead us now are frightened of doing something wrong. Their concern has often led to poor choices. They have apprehensions about using the medallion. My fellow leaders have summoned a council to decide whether it should stay buried, be destroyed or be used."

Nadine's face dropped. Evan did not have to see it to feel it. She shut her mouth for fear of the words which would proceed. They would be pleas, and she was not sure if the pleas would be selfless or selfish. Refusing to interfere with the government on Issym and its decisions, she determined to accept her fate—whatever it was.

Evan could not find the silence Nadine did. "With all due respect, if Max is looking for this medallion then Seth and Rachel sent him. The same Seth and Rachel who are representatives for both Asandra's king and queen and Issym's king. If you are in doubt as to what to do, then you should trust their judgment."

"I agree," proclaimed Esther. "And, under normal circumstances, our rulers would as well. But already the Great Quake has left homes and farms destroyed. The land of Issym has split. The effects of the medallion are uncharted. To those who lead us, that is more frightening than knowing the danger."

Nadine locked her eyes on the fire as she voiced, "I would not have come if I did not believe that Xsardis will be in greater danger if I do not use the medallion, but I defer to your wisdom."

"It is not my wisdom that shall make this judgment. Both of you have spoken calmly, rationally and without bias. I wish the others could have heard you. But if I understand you correctly, there is not enough time. I fear this decision now rests with me. I may send you on or hold you back."

Esther stood stiffly and walked to the fire. Evan and Nadine waited without saying another word. The fairy called, "Cobby." Turning, she spoke to the teens, "I, myself, will fly to Queen Andrea and explain that I sent you on. I will bear the consequences of this decision. But be warned. Once the council

Xsardis

273

makes its decision, they may come to stop you."

Cobby's bright face appeared out of the doorway and waited expectantly. Esther addressed him. "These two need to find Max and Princess Valerie at the underground. Can you make sure they get there?"

He saluted with great ceremony. "Of course."

Esther had to warn him about the danger he was stepping into. "This may not be a good thing, Cobby. Many people will not like this."

Another colorful face appeared beside his, and said, "If our fairy wishes it, it will be done!"

Xsardis

Chapter 34

Max halted his regal, white horse and stumbled down onto the rubble-filled ground. His eyes surveyed the earthquake-caused hole before him. He turned back to Valerie. The princess was still sitting on her own horse, waiting for Max to decide whether she should bother getting down. She had exchanged her dress for more practical pants, riding boots, a belted blue tunic and a thick cloak. "Well?" she asked.

He moved past her and looked down an entrance a few feet from the dividing chasm. Piled rock created a set of natural stairs leading into the pit. Max shrugged. "As far as I can tell, this is above where I dropped the medallion."

The princess jumped agilely from her horse and removed her riding gloves. She surveyed the stairs. "Seems promising."

Max tied their horses to a fallen tree before lighting the torch they had brought with them. It was almost dark, but he would not wait for the morning to explore. He planted his left foot, then put his right in place. The ground wobbled and Max worked to maintain his footing.

"Careful," the princess warned. "Several of these openings have collapsed."

As he moved farther down, Max could hear her footsteps behind him. It took almost ten minutes of steady climbing to reach the bottom. He was able to take three full steps before his way was barred by rock upon rock.

The obstruction sent more than the typical dose of frustration through Max. He had hoped to grab the medallion, save Nadine and be back with Seth and the others before they had made it out of the tunnels. Right now they were fighting for their lives. Before he could help them, he would have to oversee an excavation project that would take far too long. Did Sasha already have Nadine? "No!" he groaned.

Valerie placed her hand on his shoulder. "Maybe it's better this way. The medallion might be too great a risk."

"You don't get it, do you?" he replied. "If we don't save Nadine, she'll never be safe. It's only a matter of time until Sasha finds a way to get to her. She may already have her. We need to get a force here and dig this place out."

"If even one dishonest person betrays us…" she contended. "The medallion is more than a cure for Nadine. Look around you. It caused this earthquake. Issym won't be able to handle a second impact that strong. And we don't have time."

"What do you mean?" he was suddenly aware that the air was thick.

"Once Curt delivers the message to the castle, we won't be allowed to continue." Before Max could insult the entire castle, Princess Valerie went on, "Our queen is ill. Others rule in her place. They don't take risks. They don't allow dissension. And they won't listen to a teenager. When they hear about you, they'll make sure you never find the medallion."

"And you sent Curt with that message anyway. Why?" he demanded.

"I am subject to authority just as you are. My fellow rulers may make decisions I disagree with, but they are good, honest creatures. How could I make a choice that would affect all of us without consulting the council?"

Angrily, Max began climbing to the surface. "I can't believe this!" Of all the things he had expected to go wrong, he had not expected Issym to fail him.

"Max!" she called after him.
"I can't fail her!"
"And I can't fail Issym."

"Life couldn't have been as difficult as you describe," Nadine spoke. "You had the sun!"

"When I was on Earth I forgot how blessed I was," Evan responded. "I forgot when we were in the tunnels, too. You have a way of making me remember."

Evan wondered if this was what the storytellers meant when they said that Asandra was loved by her people. Did she have the same perceptive, peaceful spirit that Nadine possessed?

Nadine was in her twenties now. At some point in the night she had transformed. The change had been less radical than the last time, but she carried herself differently and had a uniquely adult air about her.

The mushnicks were running ahead, singing another verse to their song. Stumbling upon a pair of horses, they began to pet the white steeds. Despite their loud voices and quick movements, the animals began to neigh happily.

By the time Evan and Nadine had caught up with the fast-paced creatures, Valerie and Max were coming out of a chasm. Excited to see them alive and free, Max met them by the horses. "Reesthma took your orbs. How did you get here?"

"Nadine had an exit route," Evan replied. "Reesthma took the orbs?"

"It's a long story."

"Is the medallion here, Max?" Nadine asked hopefully. She was breathing hard.

"It's buried underneath layers of rock." Nadine sat down on a boulder, her face growing pale. He tried to encourage, "We'll get it out, I promise."

"What you see in me is simply my change about to take place again," she reported. "We must find the medallion before I recycle. That is when the earthquake will occur."

"We'll dig it out!" Freddy promised.

"And fast!" Cobby put in.

"Very, very, very fast!" Simmy shouted.

Nadine gave her hand to Clarence. "Thank you, my friends!"

The mushnicks pulled shovels out of their large bags and descended into the pit rapidly. Nadine wondered how much else they had carried with them over the distance as she moved to the shelter of the woods. Out of sight of the others, she aged years in only a few minutes.

After watching her go, the prince turned to Max, "How were things when you left the tunnels?"

"Ruby showed us images of the war on Asandra. It had everyone shaken up. Our armies are in real danger."

Seth's eyes opened. Without waiting to gather his bearings, he tilted his head. He already knew what he would see, or rather what he would not see. "Oh…"

Rachel whirled around. It was clear she had not left his side. Her quick initial reaction slowed for her question, "How are you feeling?"

Though his leg was not bleeding, the shooting pain sent rolls of nausea through him. He could feel the hurt in the limb that was gone, his nerves and mind unaware of what to do with the loss. Seth was not oblivious to how it would change the rest of his life and the group's ability to make it back to Asandra. Leaning his head back, he answered "I've been better."

Seth did not know how they had saved him. It could have been an illuminescent; it could have been surgery. At that moment, he didn't care. "Has Sasha come at us again?"

"She has sent some tough forces our way, but nothing as tough as what you faced. Are you okay?" Rachel pressed.

He closed his eyes, resolving himself. With a sigh, he sat up. His whole balance was different. "I've already cost us time Asandra cannot afford. Ethelwyn should make a run for the ocean."

The Legend disagreed. "If we don't stand together, do you really expect we'll survive this?"

"I can't walk. I can't fight. I'll slow us down too much."

"Don't even think about that," Rachel returned forcefully. "We'll find a way. We always do."

"Rachel, come see this," Katarina's voice called to her.

Rachel moved to the princess' side. The fluffy purple feathers made it clear what was approaching. "Firil?" she questioned.

"We can't know if it's really him," Katarina mentioned. "Why would it be him? We left him on Asandra and he was afraid of the sea. He's probably a trick of Sasha's."

"He must have heard Rachel's cry for Seth," Reesthma believed. "He's very loyal. It would have brought him across even the ocean he so feared."

Rachel brushed past Katarina to make a determination. Surveying him carefully, she approached the bird. Firil was smaller—yet again. Otherwise, he might not have fit in the tunnels. His big eyes stared at her with watery concern. He squawked his own name and ran to her. Rachel wrapped her arms around him, listened to his beating heart, and knew it was truly her Firil.

"I am so proud of you for braving the ocean. I'm alright," she assured him. "But I need your help. Seth's been hurt. He needs you to carry him very carefully to the water's edge. Can you do that for me, Firil?"

How much he understood, Rachel could not be sure, but he nodded his cumbersome head with such a look of sincerity that she could not doubt he would do whatever she asked him.

"Firil!" He wrapped his neck around her.

Rachel looked back to Seth. "I think we found a way to get you out of these tunnels."

"Won't you come with us all the way?" Stewart questioned Kate as he rode in the glory of the morning. Soon power would be theirs. The thought invigorated him.

"You know that would be foolish. We would lose our opportunity to place your men inside the fortress."

"Yes, of course," he returned. Forty men would do much inside Saphree.

He glanced at the magnificent shifter, full of youth and control. Sasha was a shrunken form in comparison. How had darkness corrupted the light inside Kate? "I would love to hear your history."

"There is not a person on this planet who yet understands it. You think you will be the first?"

Xsardis

Stewart laughed. She made him feel mighty.

Kate glared at him. He treated her like some captive lioness. "Where are the sprites?"

"They sent word that they will meet us at Saphree. Golesha likes to do things her own way. She doesn't seem to trust me."

Kicking her horse forward, Kate forced Stewart to catch up. He asked, "Kate, you are sure the dark sprites will attack Saphree?"

"The words came from the mouth of *your* spy."

Not unaware of the dangerous being with whom he traveled, Stewart pressed for reassurance, "You're not deceiving me?"

"You have already decided to trust me and thus have determined your fate. Accept it. Now, Stewart, stop delaying me. Allow me to take your men and place them in Saphree."

"Fine, fine," he assented, not at all sure he could trust the cryptic shifter, but with no choice but to follow through.

Xsardis

Chapter 35

Evan knew that their time had run out as soon as he heard the sounds of a large group of horses coming their way. He hopped out of the hole, sweaty as he was, to try to be the diplomatic prince that changed the mind of whoever it was in charge.

Two full days of digging and still nothing. Max was certain they were looking in the right spot and the mushnicks dug with a persistence and coordination that astounded, but even so, who knew how long things would take?

Nadine met him as he returned to the hot afternoon air. She was now in her forties. Though she was still thin as ever, her skin was not as soft, nor her hair as radiant. The eyes and lashes were the same—deep, long and attractive. Her manner had also matured. She no longer radiated incredible child, but a powerful adult to be listened to. As she handed him a canteen, Nadine scanned the group approaching them. A dozen frogs and humans, all dressed in armor. She spoke calmly. "I will try diplomacy but if that fails, let them do what they have come to do."

Evan was willing to listen to her words. It was Max that protested. "They have no right to do this! Seth and Rachel sent me here. Seth and Rachel have the authority of Galen. We can fight this."

Laying a hand on his arm, Nadine constrained him, "No."

The exuberant cry from the mushnicks could not have been more ill-timed. They proceeded to the surface with their great joy, the medallion passing through each of their hands. The golden circle was attached to a leather strap, an old key hanging with it. The runes etched into the medallion's surface drew Nadine and Max's eyes. They knew those runes well.

An official frog in fine stone armor hopped off his horse and landed before them. He extended his three fingers for the medallion. "I have orders from the council to take this medallion and have it destroyed."

The mushnicks, still and somber, handed their prize to the frog. He jumped onto his horse. Nadine stepped towards him.

Xsardis   282

"Noblefrog, please listen to me," she began. He did not seem to want to stop, but her presence held him there. "I only want to ensure that you know all you must know to make this decision. Destroying that medallion will have irrevocable consequences for all of Xsardis."

"You are the girl! I know that you will cause a second earthquake if you stay here too long. That is why you must not stay on Issym." At the snap of his fingers, two other frogs descended and moved towards her.

"But if you send me to Asandra, I'll destroy it. Please!" she resisted against the strong arms that now held her.

He shook his head, "Then we'll send you to Noric. I have strict orders."

"Think beyond your orders!" Evan cried. Noric was the last place she should be sent. That was where Sasha now lay in wait for her.

"Valerie!" Max summoned her help. When the princess shook her head, Max moved towards the frog. "Sir, I am Max. I have come from Seth, Rachel and Universe Girl's side. They sent me here to find that medallion and give it to this woman. Heed their orders!"

The frog drew his blade unsure of Max's intentions. That brought Max's hand over his own weapon. Nadine called, "I accept your decision. Where am I to go?"

"To the illuminescent wood. They'll send you back to Noric. Unless that illuminescent before you can do so."

Nadine looked at the low-flying, red creature and determined, "Take me to the forest."

"Release her. We'll come of our own will," Evan stepped forward and was heard.

Valerie met their eyes and promised them, "I'll see what I can do."

"You've helped enough," Max criticized, standing back. To be mere feet from the medallion and unable to seize it.

"I did my duty," Valerie snapped to capture his thoughts. "But it is also my duty to try to find a way out for her."

Max resolved, "I'll go with you. Maybe someone will listen to me."

Nadine and Evan were set upon horses in the middle of the group, in case they chose to run. Dark was only a few hours away. The urgency with which they rode led Evan to doubt that they would rest. But when the evening came, the group did stop and make camp. The reddish glow from the fire lit up Nadine's face that no longer possessed youth, but still retained its beauty. She had changed again. "I'm glad for one more night with the air upon my skin," she spoke to him, her eyes not leaving the blaze.

Evan looked at the lead frog. "Why did we stop?"

"In these woods are bandits. It's not safe to go on," he answered. "Now get your rest. We'll leave early in the morning."

"Bandits?" he searched for more information.

"Go to sleep."

The domineering voice with which he spoke was too much for Evan. "I'm not some prisoner to be tossed around. I am Prince Evan of Asandra, commissioned by your high king to put a stop to Sasha's plans. Why will you not listen and give us the medallion?"

Xsardis

283

"I have orders."

"Forget the orders!" he shouted.

"I don't care who you are," the frog expanded his chest to show just how large he was. "If you don't sit down, I'll make you sit down."

Morning revealed a few grey hairs in Nadine's long tresses. Their 'escorts' were unusually silent. The closer they grew to their destination, the more tense they became. As they approached a forest of tall trees and rich dirt, Nadine instantly liked the look and feel of the place, but it set the others on edge.

The horses whinnied and started to pull against their reins. They were not ignorant to their riders' alarm. There were audible whispers of fear amongst the guards of Issym. Evan started to get nervous too. What was this place that had so unnerved the trained soldiers? "What's going on?" he questioned, but he was firmly ordered to be quiet.

Illuminescents of all sizes and colors poured from the trees and moved toward them as a pack, encircling them. Nadine smiled. Evan relaxed. There could be no danger that a group of illuminescents this large could not handle.

The illuminescents buzzed to them. Evan and Nadine understood the short words, "What do you want?" None of the others seemed to be able to translate as they sat in the shadows of the mighty trees.

"Illuminescents, these two must be sent back to Asandra. Can you understand me?" the captain hid his shaky voice under the irritability with which he spoke, but Evan perceived it. He was afraid of the illuminescents.

The creatures spoke not another word. They averted themselves from the soldiers, who were recoiling in fear, but landed freely on Nadine. "Why are you so afraid of them?" Nadine inquired of the captain.

A guard near her answered under his breath, "They took many captives before the war. If we anger them, they may do so again."

The illuminescents insisted, "Why are you in our forest?"

It was echoed several times, "Why?" "Why?" "Why?"

"Take these two to Asandra, please!" The captain backed up his horse, anxious at the noise.

Evan rolled his eyes. "You don't even speak their language, do you?"

"No!" panted another guard.

"Do *you*?" the captain asked with eyes of fear.

The prince spoke, receiving an instant migraine as he mimicked their buzzes. "Will you take this woman and I to the island of Noric?"

The whole of the guard stayed nervous, but they were in awe of the prince's strange tongue.

"Who are you?" the creatures wanted to know.

"I am Prince Evan of Asandra. This is the lady Nadine—a more noble heart cannot be found."

The illuminescents bodies bobbed up and down. "We will take you."

"They'll get us there," Evan informed the frog.

The leader gripped the medallion in his hands to ascertain that these two had not somehow deceived him, then signaled his men to move out. He would not remain in these woods a second longer than he had to. Evan and

Nadine stared at the medallion until it was out of sight. The prince's heavy sigh returned their attention to the illuminescents. "Do you want to go now?" inquired a blue creature.

Nadine looked to Evan. "We're safe here, right? Why hurry back? I want to enjoy the sun."

"It's better if we wait anyway," Evan informed. "The longer we stay here, the greater the chances the others will have stopped Sasha."

Nadine translated their decision to the illuminescents. The colorful group led them deeper into the woods, to a breathtaking spot overlooking a lake. The crystal waters glistened.

"It's so beautiful," Nadine remarked. Her now almost-black hair fell to her knees, but had stayed smooth and untangled. "Do you ever get used to such wonder?"

"When we lived in the palace—before Sasha—I was never much of a woodsman," he admitted. "I took after my father in that regard. My mom, she loved the beauty of nature. And Katarina hated confined spaces.

"So when we went to the underground, Kat was going stir-crazy and I had to get used to a new style of living. All of the sudden I loved the sun and the moon and the trees and the fresh air. I blamed my sister every time we escaped to the surface without informing our parents, but I wanted to go just as badly. The underground reminded me how much I loved nature."

She perceived a look in his eyes. "What do you miss now, Evan?"

"Kat," he answered. "I thought I couldn't lead and that she could. But Sasha said I was the reason Asandra still had a fighting chance. Instead of realizing that when I should have, I left Katarina bearing the weight of Asandra. I don't regret staying with you. I still believe Xsardis needs Ethelwyn, but I wonder if my choice was fair to my sister."

"Sometimes," she confessed, "I'm glad that I wasn't able to be Issym and Asandra's heir. I doubt I could have continued their legacy."

"You could have, Nadine. You would have been brilliant on the throne."

"You say that after I've had a thousand years to grow up," she smiled.

The two walked on, followed by half a dozen illuminescents enjoying the fearless company of two humans. They did not receive that fellowship from most of the creatures on Issym.

Together Nadine and Evan discussed the past—both the broad events of history and the small events of everyday life. They enjoyed more than a day in the quiet of the forest. Then Nadine's wrinkled skin convinced her heart she had to return to her uncertain home.

Seth rode upon Firil, his arms keeping him balanced. Everything was different without his leg. Not to mention the pain coursing through his body or

Xsardis   285

the realization that he could no longer protect those he loved.

Sasha was pursuing them with a new vengeance. Ethelwyn had taken the lead, slashing at anything in her way. Vaylynne was in the rear.

"The exit!" Ethelwyn called back to them.

"We'll make straight for the boats," Rachel returned with excitement.

Katarina stopped moving. She spoke the determination she had already come to after days running from Sasha's brutality. "We can't go back to Asandra. They're weak enough as it is. We'd bring Sasha with us." The motionless faces of the group told her they recognized the validity of her point. "They need The Legend. She can go back to Asandra."

"And the rest of us keep Sasha's focus here," Reesthma finished, her hand on Firil.

"We won't survive that," Vaylynne cautioned.

"But Xsardis will," Rachel knew. "Maybe a miracle will happen and we will defeat Sasha."

"Sasha has been able to find us because she knows where we are heading," Seth pointed out from his perch on Firil. "When we begin to change our strategy, it may not be as easy for her to surround us."

"There's really not much chance we'll hold out, is there?" Reesthma said.

"No. Not really," Katarina responded. She looked them each in the eye, "None of you have any responsibility to stay, but I do. Asandra is my country now and I will do whatever is necessary to save it. I'm not going anywhere."

"I don't have a movement to go back to anyway. I'll stay," Vaylynne asserted.

"Reesthma, I want you to go back with Ethelwyn," Seth determined.

"Seth…"

"You will tell this story."

"You're hurt. You should come back with us," Reesthma prodded.

"A big purple bird is going to draw her attention. If Sasha sees me, she will follow. There's the chance that if Ree and Wyn are spotted, she'll let them go."

"We shouldn't hold this position any longer," Vaylynne stressed.

"If we don't see each other again, rest assured that I will get word of your deeds to your parents." With that, Ethelwyn pulled Reesthma away.

As they darted for the shore, Katarina, Vaylynne, Seth, Firil, Rachel and Ruby moved toward the dwarf mines. Sasha's wolfish forms ran after them. A searing pain slashed across Katarina's back as one raked its claws against her flesh. She cried out and stumbled. Rachel stabbed the beast, then helped Kat to her feet. Heat radiated across the princess' skin as blood filled up her tunic.

Rachel might have continued to support Kat, but her blade was needed to defend against the wolves. As one jumped for Seth, he sliced it with his sword, then clung to Firil. When the bird saw how alarmed Rachel was for Seth, he changed his stance. Three wolves were coming toward them. Keeping two feet on the ground at all times, Firil kicked and snapped until the wolves lay motionless. Rachel's smile was all the praise the bird needed.

They made it to a dense part of the forest and lost Sasha. Katarina fell

Xsardis   286

to her knees. Rachel bent beside her. There was no choice but to find the time to bind her wounds. Vaylynne paced the space, ready to swing her sword at whatever came near. At that moment, she was the only defense the group had. How far she had come from being the traitor!

"How bad is it?" Katarina probed.

"You will be hurting for a while."

"I can handle that," boasted Katarina.

"Good." Rachel looked to Vaylynne, willing to keep following her lead—for now. "Can we afford to give her some rest?"

Vaylynne nodded. "The second I see Sasha, we're moving."

Though she did not explain it to the warrior, Rachel believed that Sasha might abandon her pursuit for a short time. They had destroyed many of her forms. The pain of that would be wearing Sasha out. Eventually she would have to relent, even if not for long.

"I will help you keep watch," Ruby hovered by Vaylynne's side.

When Katarina thought no one was watching, she winced. The claws had torn through more than the skin.

Though they sat for almost fifteen minutes, none of them closed their eyes. They waited for the next signs of Sasha. Vaylynne spun around when she heard a branch snap behind her. Rachel's bow was already drawn and pointed in the direction of a barrel-chested figure striding toward them.

"Wait," Seth commanded.

Strained, but compliant, the group did nothing.

Using the tree beside him to hoist himself to his leg, Seth questioned, "What do you want, Lotex?"

"To help you," the dwarf replied, looking at Seth's injury for only a second. "I've been searching for you for a while, in order to bring you back to the mines. I know you shouldn't trust me after what happened."

There did seem to be regret beneath those bushy brows.

"No, we shouldn't," Katarina answered for Seth.

Lotex appealed to them, "I was trying to keep an old oath to Issym."

"Asandra is so bitter that it can't even see the point of things anymore," Seth rebuffed. "Issym never wanted that child to be locked in the caverns for centuries. He wanted someone to rescue her and he would have trusted me to do it. If you had told me, we might not have brought Sasha to Nadine's door. But you couldn't recognize that. You could only see how outwardly it would be breaking an oath you didn't even make, not that it would be fulfilling the purpose of the oath: keeping Nadine safe."

Lotex's sigh almost came out as a growl. That was how Seth was sure it was Lotex and not Sasha. "Are you coming or not?" the dwarf demanded.

"We're coming," Seth determined. "We don't have a lot of options."

Resettling himself on the bird for whom his affection was increasing, Seth realized that he was very close to forgetting that Lotex had ever knocked him out. It did not seem to matter anymore. With Lotex and Vaylynne cleaving the way, they pushed through the bears and coyotes Sasha formed to chase them.

"What does she think she'll gain?" Reesthma wondered. In every story she had ever learned, she had never been able to grasp the warlords'

Xsardis

287

motivations.

Seth grabbed the dwarf's attention. "You need to get your people off this island. Sasha isn't going to leave anyone alive."

"I knew that long ago," Lotex stated. "It's just Beatrice and I left now."

By the time they reached the mines, Katarina was leaning on Rachel again. Her tough attitude could not mask all the pain she felt. Firil balked at entering the mine, but followed Seth's instruction. He recognized that he was getting sleepy, that the amputation felt strange somehow, but he attempted to keep his focus. They were so close to a safe place to rest.

Recognizing his glazed eyes, Vaylynne slapped his arm and drew his focus. "Don't start resting on me now!"

He tried to revive himself. Seth was not sure that he could. "Need to get checked out."

"Stop whining," she replied, more concerned than she would say. Sweat poured from Seth's brow.

They rested not in one of the apartments but in one of the spacious rooms meant for the dwarf meetings. Lotex soon had a fire stirred and blankets and drinks for the band of travelers. Beatrice, anger brimming inside her, came into the room with food which she plopped on the floor. She then moved to Katarina, who was lying on her stomach, and not so gently began to tend the scratches in her back, muttering, "I don't see why we're helping you. This is all your fault anyway!"

Despite the anger she displayed, Beatrice made Rachel realize that the dwarfs had lost more than their purpose. Sasha was destroying their ancestral home.

"Take care of Seth first," Katarina was adamant, pushing the dwarf woman away.

Vaylynne was kneeling above Seth's head. He was asleep already. She felt for the fever that she knew was there. Rachel bent beside what was left of his leg and peeled away the bandage that had bled through again.

"What happened to him?" Lotex moved beside her.

"Sasha turned herself into a dragon," Rachel reported. What had happened in the tunnel, she left in the tunnel. She needed Lotex's aid now. "We think the saliva sealed the wound, but not anymore."

"Did he lose much blood?" Beatrice was drawn to Seth's side.

"Not as much as he should have," Vaylynne recognized.

The dwarf woman examined the amputation quickly, growing stiff. "I've seen wounds like this before. The sealant has been rubbed off by his movement." She added, "We breed reptiles with the same kind of saliva for injuries like this."

"We can put more on?" Reesthma prayed it could be that simple.

"If we had it. But we sent everything of value to Asandra with the others."

Pressing a new cloth firmly over the wound, Beatrice recognized they were dealing with an injury far beyond her skill. "I don't know if I can save him." The bandage was already soaked.

Katarina rose to her elbows despite the pain. "That's not acceptable."

Xsardis
288

Ruby flew before Rachel's eyes. "Seth takes good care of you?" she spoke in a low tone unfamiliar for the chipper illuminescent. Only Rachel made out her buzzing words. The others were talking to each other.

Seth's eyes were twitching. Rachel could feel the danger growing for him. In a matter of seconds the wound was opening. An hour from now? With emotion, she spoke to her illuminescent companion, "Better than I deserve. I don't want to lose him, Ruby."

The illuminescent's voice was steady, "I can create the saliva."

"Oh Ruby," Rachel smiled brightly. "Thank you!"

After rubbing against Rachel's cheek, the creature rose. Sparks fell from her, vibrantly red at first. As their color faded, Ruby fell. Soon she was barely hovering above the ground. A glass jar filled with the gel-like, yellow saliva appeared through the haze.

Beatrice snatched it quickly and began applying it liberally to Seth's wound.

Falling into Rachel's extended hands, Ruby's color was more of a pink than a red. "Ruby?" Rachel discerned that something was not right.

"We only have so much energy," the illuminescent spoke softly. "When it is gone, we are gone. I have moments left to be with you."

"Why didn't you tell me?" Rachel lamented.

"I couldn't protect you anymore. He can."

A tear slipped out of Rachel's swelling eyes. Ruby found enough strength to flutter up and rub against Rachel's cheek before falling back into her hand for the last time.

A few clear sparks filled the red fog that rose from Ruby's form as it disintegrated and flew before Rachel's eyes. The fog was swept downward into the clear gem ring that Rachel wore.

"They come from gems," Rachel remembered. "And they can return to them."

Rachel stared down at the ring on her finger, recalling Nadine's rings. Illuminescents were entirely devoted creatures—selfless. It hurt more than Rachel could say to lose Ruby.

"Seth will recover now, but he must rest," Beatrice informed.

Looking back at him, Rachel wiped away the water in her eye.

A flash of sparks engulfed a space to their right. Evan and an elderly woman barely recognizable as Nadine emerged from the light along with a red illuminescent. "I brought you to the illuminescent I felt…" the creature explained.

Evan and Nadine took in the scene. The daughter of Asandra recognized Rachel's somber face and the shining ring on her finger. Bending beside her, Nadine took her hand in her own withered palm.

Though she would have hugged her brother, Katarina was forced to lie still as Beatrice re-bandaged the wounds. The princess craned her neck and asked, "Did you find the medallion?"

"We found it," Evan told her. He was concerned for the entire group. Where were Edmund, Ethelwyn and Reesthma? "But they wouldn't give it to us."

"What?" Rachel questioned in disbelief. Issym had refused them?

Xsardis

"I thought you would all be gone by now," Nadine spoke, fingering her long white hair, which still glimmered.

Evan identified her tone and turned to her with concern, "What are you planning, Nadine?"

"I was going to send you back to Asandra. There is no safe place left for me to cycle. Sasha has destroyed my hiding place."

"What are you saying?"

"Over time the effects of the earthquakes that I have not allowed have built up. With nowhere to contain the shaking, Noric will be destroyed."

"You're going to die," he stumbled back.

"There is nothing left to do," she returned, still peaceable. "But my death will mean something. If Sasha is on Noric, she'll be destroyed along with me."

Xsardis

Chapter 36

The urgency that had clutched Max's heart was fierce. He knew that every moment he spent on Issym could mean the difference between life and death for one of his friends on Noric. He would not waste time. Xsardis could not afford it.

"Issym is disoriented," Valerie tried yet again to make him understand. "Queen Andrea fell ill after giving birth. She may not survive. The third-in-commands left behind were absolutely unprepared for leading this way. They won't unmake their decision about the medallion easily."

Max covered his eyes to block out the sun. He was tired. Every movement his horse made sent a new pain through him. He did not respond to the princess, his thoughts too muddled to speak.

Faced with a moral quandary, he thought about what Katarina—even the newer version—would have done without hesitation. Seth and Rachel would have made a different determination. Yet what was God's answer?

The fact was that Galen would have ordered the rulers of Issym to give him the medallion. There wasn't time to wait for his return. Max could try to convince illuminescents to discuss their top-secret abilities and find a way to get Galen's opinion across the seas, but he doubted that would yield anything. Perhaps he could convince the council to listen to him, but that would take far too long. There was always another option...

It made his stomach turn. He had never been a thief, really. Even before Christ. But Max realized he had the mind for stealing. He had always known exactly where the flaws were in any security system simply by looking at it. Deviousness still held a certain charm. Knowing that he could steal the medallion back was far too tempting.

Would it really be wrong? he questioned.

You so sure that using *the medallion would be right?* a second voice inside him shot back.

Max was certain that the medallion would cure Nadine, but turning it might well cause destruction. The daughter of Asandra and Issym deserved to be saved. The risks of Sasha finding her were high. Using the medallion would help not just Nadine and Evan, but all of Xsardis.

Yes, it's worth the risk, Max decided.

"But it's not my decision to make," he muttered grumpily. He would have to find another way.

"Did you kill him?" Edmund had to shout to get his sister's attention. With her shifting forms spread out across Saphree, she struggled to focus on each one.

Her human figure flicked her attention to him for a moment. Edmund waited with an emotion he could not distinguish. He knew he would feel guilt, and, yes, even loss if Seth was dead. The boy should have thought about that before he turned Edmund aside.

"I claimed his leg," Sasha answered.

Edmund took a sharp breath. Certainly not of relief.

"You were right," his sister went on. "As long as I had him scared, I could touch him. Did you do as I asked?"

"Yes." Edmund had returned to Asandra to discern what had progressed while they had been on Noric. "As you anticipated, the dark sprites have spread fear throughout Asandra. Both Issym and Asandra's armies are hiding out in Saphree. Stewart has attempted to cross you."

She waved her hand in dismissal. "That I expected. It's why I chose him. He can be easily ripped from his perch."

Edmund was not sure how easy it would be, given the alliances Stewart was making. Sasha recognized the shadow that crossed his brow. "What?"

"Kate is helping him—working against Issym."

Sasha stiffened. She was comfortable with Kate working for the cursed light, but if she now served the darkness she could exert her control over Xsardis in a mighty way. Perhaps she already had while Sasha had been distracted on Noric. "Do you believe the reports?" Sasha spun on her brother. He would know the truth. She would see it on his face.

"I wouldn't have," Edmund shook his head. "But they seem to be accurate."

His concern for Kate was growing. Everyone in his life had failed him, including Kate. But she had lost herself in a lie and he did not blame her for it. If Kate had turned from Issym maybe that lie was falling from her eyes as she grew more and more ill. He had to have Nadine. He had to save Kate, win her back.

Thinking for several moments, Sasha's realization dawned on her slowly. Kate was a greater enemy than Seth and Rachel. Even the hope of her great prize Nadine could not keep Sasha on Noric any longer. "Edmund, change of plans. We're going back to Asandra."

"My transformations have never been consistent," Nadine spoke. Seth had awoken and his attention never left her. She could not read his expression. Would he allow her to do what she must? "I do not know how long we have. There is still time for you to get off this island."

"This can't be the only option," Evan was sure there must be another way. He searched his thoughts again and again.

"I must go deeper into the tunnels to assure that the earthquake does what it must. The further I go, the more impact it will have. If I am unprotected by Valean rock, Noric will implode as I recycle." She added the technical details for Seth and Rachel's consideration.

Rachel and Seth's shoulders rested together. Ruby's sacrifice chilled Seth. Rachel was grieving. They both looked to the daughter of Issym and Asandra. It was one more casualty, but not just of anyone. Nadine was a true child of their imagination, a representation of the value of purity, a woman who had given much. In silence, they searched their minds for anything they could do.

"We'll have to spread out the stones across the island to ensure that Sasha cannot shift. If even one version of her survives, all of this will have been for nothing," Seth decided, coming to terms with the fact that he could not find a way out for Nadine. When he was finally allowed the time, the list of those he would grieve would be far too long.

"Can you truly not think of any escape for Nadine?" Evan stepped toward Rachel.

"No." Rachel shook her head.

"How are we going to get the stones across the entire island?" Katarina asked. She could not bring her eyes to Nadine's aged face.

Lotex stood. "Beatrice and I can scatter them here in this mine. It spreads all of Noric."

Ripping the stones from their armor, the teens handed them to the dwarfs. Lotex gently held Nadine's hand in his own. No words came for the charge he and his fathers had protected for so long. Beatrice and Lotex moved away.

Nadine addressed the others, "I must go deeper now. Goodbye, friends."

Evan followed her as she moved away. She expressed, "Please, Evan. Don't fight with me anymore."

"I won't," he assured. "I just want to say how sorry I am that we came looking for you. If we hadn't, Sasha never would have found you."

"These few days have been filled with more life than the previous thousand," she answered. "I would not trade them, and the chance to destroy

Xsardis   294

this vile Sasha, for a thousand more. Thank you, dear Evan."

He embraced her, then watched her walk away. Head held high, Nadine was more radiant in her age and sacrifice than she even had been in her youth.

The fast steps of Vaylynne carried her back from her scouting above the mine. "We have a problem. Sasha is leaving the island," the words whipped out of her mouth.

Rachel snapped, "Now?"

"Now," Vaylynne repeated breathlessly.

"We have to keep her here until Beatrice and Lotex are finished setting up the stones." As Katarina sat up with haste her scabs reopened. If she could have, she would had walked right up to Sasha and challenged her—earning even a little more time. She refused to let this entire journey be in vain. Nadine and Ruby dead; Sasha alive. It couldn't be.

Rachel moved past Vaylynne, determination marking her thin features. Seth struggled to get to his leg, calling after her, "Rachel, don't!"

"I have to!" she replied. Her face turned to him, but her body was still turned the other way.

"Give us a minute," Seth ordered the others. They complied quickly, disappearing into the other tunnels.

Rachel walked back to Seth, her features softening. "We don't have time for this. You know that I can slow Sasha down. Even if I don't know why, she hates me. She'll make the duel last."

"She's going to kill you," his voice was coarse.

"But Lotex and Beatrice will be finished by the time she does." Rachel took another few steps towards him. "And at least it won't be you she kills."

"I would go if you'd let me."

"Smolden was your enemy; Sasha is mine."

There were a thousand more things they could have said, but time was slipping by. He put his arms around her and drew her close, whispering in her ear, "How can I let you do this?"

Rachel hesitated; if she let herself feel his embrace, she was not sure she could sacrifice herself. For only a moment she put her hand on his strong shoulder, wrapped her arm around his waist, and put her head on his chest. "I don't want to do this," she admitted under her breath.

At that moment, Seth recognized the power he wielded. He could keep her here, but he would not. He freed her to do what she had to, "You can do this."

Looking into his confident eyes, she knew she could. Rachel pulled away and ran. Blood rushed through her ears, her breath grew strained, the impact of her steps shocked her body, energy poured through her system. She broke into the daylight, moved from the mines and called through the air, "Sasha! Been looking for me?"

Her white bow lay in the palm of her hand, an arrow ready in an instant. The branches of trees scratched against her soft skin. Her hair blew wildly before her.

Catching her first sight of a human version of Sasha, Rachel stopped

Xsardis

for only a second. She aimed and fired. Her arrow plunged through the woman's heart.

A frog ran toward her, bearing remarkable resemblance to Flibbert. Rachel knew it was not him. Another arrow went through his heart as she forced herself to keep Sasha's ploy out of her mind.

Two men lunged at her from either side and one from behind her. She stuck her arrow into the one to her left. The tipped points of her bow jabbed through the others and they fell. "Come on!" Rachel hollered and kept on.

She was nearing a small cliff's edge overlooking the water, maybe fifteen feet from the ground. It was clear of trees and full of flowers. A single version of Sasha stood there, dressed in regal garments, standing tall, with a long, curved blade in her hand, hair whipping in the wind. Her hideous figure did not fit the beautiful surroundings. "Today, you die," the shifter promised.

"Don't count on it," Rachel rebuffed.

Sasha smiled. "When you feel my blade plunge through your gut, remember your cockiness."

Rachel took steadying breaths, her body brimming with momentum. Her eyes fell closed, then opened. "Why do you hate me so much?"

Sasha twitched, taken aback by the question. "You don't know?"

"No."

The shifter's answer came out clearly, "You dared limit me."

Rachel's brain spun. She had not expected a real answer.

"You imposed restrictions on my powers," the figure continued. "You created the bounds we shifters—who should have been gods—had to live under. You are the reason I am sick. You are the only thing standing between me and immortality. And now you will die!"

Seth held Firil back from following Rachel. A hand on the bird's neck, he waited. The second Lotex and Beatrice returned from placing the stones, Seth jumped onto Firil's back. Together they charged out of the mine.

Madly he urged the bird on and wildly the bird ran. Never before had Firil exerted himself with as much precision or speed. Past the tree branches, over the stumps, they moved, following Rachel's scent. Nothing was going to stop them. Seth's sword gleamed in his hand. His brow furrowed with determination. His heart lodged on the hope that he could still save her.

Xsardis 296

Sasha jumped at Rachel, her blade bearing down on the girl's own. Rachel's feet dug into the grassy land, but she found enough strength to the push the blade away and spin backwards. The next move was hers as she lunged for Sasha's middle. The hilt of the shifter's blade bruised Rachel's back. She turned in time to deflect the next strike.

Rachel's fist landed on Sasha's face, the impact probably breaking the shifter's nose. Held in form by the stones, Sasha winced with pain and aimed a hard kick towards Rachel's stomach in retaliation. Rachel stumbled back, clutching her stomach as no air reached her lungs.

Sasha's blade barely missed her shoulder. Her next move disarmed Rachel. A slash against her leg brought Rachel to her knees. The imaginer's eyes looked up defiantly for Sasha's last taunting remark. A flash of color lit up the corner of her eye. Firil rode from behind Sasha. Seth launched himself from the bird and brought Sasha to the ground. Rachel rolled toward her sword and drove it through the woman's heart before any of them could regain their footing.

"We don't have much time," Seth urged. The others would have, he knew, taken a shorter route to the water. They had probably already put the island behind them. And the howls of Sasha's animal forms coming for them already filled his ears.

Supporting Seth, Rachel felt his breath. It steadied her heartbeat and gave her a reason to move with haste. With their permission, a nervous Firil took to the water and swam rapidly to the deep.

Lotex had promised there would be a boat nearby—that he had left one near every possible exit, anticipating the need for a fast escape. He did not disappoint. Down to the bank they hurried as Seth leaned on Rachel. They jumped into the sturdy vessel that should carry them to safety. Rachel shoved the boat off.

Seth rowed, perspiration dripping from him. Rachel's eyes were locked on Noric. Had they lingered long enough? Had they lingered too long? They could just make out the other three boats, already free from the danger of the island. Rachel's attention fell to the single frog stone that Seth still bore. He was planning as if Sasha would survive the earthquake. *Oh God, please give us victory,* she prayed, grateful to be alive.

A flash of light poured from the center of Noric. The ground sunk. Trees fell. The cracking of the land resonated in their ears. Water poured from the island like a tsunami, capsizing the small craft.

Long seconds passed before Rachel grabbed a breath. She was instantly pushed down by another blast of the chilly water, whipped around as if she was a doll. Again she came to the surface and was plunged down. Finding the surface a third time, she grabbed onto the floating pieces left from their boat.

Her eyes searched for Seth, still lost underneath the water. "Seth!" she shouted. Rachel dove deeper, searching through the wild sea for him. He broke the surface not long after she returned to it and gripped the driftwood.

Their eyes fell to the island that was left. Most of it was submerged and sinking into a watery grave. What was there was covered in fallen trees and collapsed cliffs. Nothing could have survived. "Did we do it?" Rachel panted.

Xsardis 297

Seth could not answer her. There was no way of knowing.

The other boats made their way to them. Though the vessels were intact, each of the occupants was soaked. Rachel was pulled up into the boat with Evan and Vaylynne. Seth climbed in with Katarina and Reesthma.

Lotex and Beatrice stared at their now-destroyed home. Everyone's thoughts were with Nadine, mourning her loss; and with Sasha, hoping she was really gone. None of the group noticed as a figure moved toward them. It pulled Rachel from the boat with its human-half and held a dagger to her neck as it kicked with its tail.

"Edmund," Seth recognized, despite the shifter's merman form. He must have already been on his way to Asandra when the island imploded. "I'm sick of this." That Rachel's life could still be in jeopardy after so much; that Edmund could truly be so deceitfully wicked… Anger and concern rose inside Seth. His voice turned fierce as he commanded, "Let her go."

"I'm sick of it too, Seth," Edmund returned. He held Rachel's waist firmly and his dagger to her throat.

Rachel's mind flashed back. This was not the first time Edmund had held a blade to her neck. Then, Seth had barreled toward her on a futile rescue mission. Now, she knew he would act only when he was certain of his plan—a plan she could already see forming in his mind.

Evan had his hand out to make peace. "Slow down, Edmund. What do you want?"

"Stay out of this, Prince. I could have taken any of you, but I chose Rachel for a reason. You killed my sister, you killed the cure for Kate. You crumbled my whole world. Now I'll crumble yours, Seth."

Suddenly, Seth realized from Edmund's hazy green eyes and spiteful tone that he was actually willing to harm Rachel.

"I thought you hated your sister!" Kat pointed out. The irrationality Edmund was using to make his decisions had been hers not so long ago. Maybe she could get through to him.

"I thought that she was the cutthroat," Edmund jerked back, the blade pressing closer to Rachel's exposed throat. "But you killed Nadine! And you condemned Kate. You never trusted me. At least Sasha looked out for me! She was only the true family I had!"

Seth looked back at Lotex and Beatrice. They were motionless, leaving the action to him.

Katarina kept talking, if only to give Seth more time. "You've broken every alliance you have ever had, but there's still a chance for you, Edmund."

"Shut up! Shut up! You little preachers!" he decried.

Glancing everywhere for help but from the one place he knew it would come, Seth kept Edmund's attention from Vaylynne. The once-rebel had strung Rachel's bow and notched an arrow without looking at it or allowing it to be seen. Now in one swift motion she raised the weapon and fired.

It would have struck Edmund's skull, but a fellow mermaid propelled itself out of the water and took the wound through the shoulder. "No!" Edmund screamed with an agonizing horror. He dropped Rachel and caught the slumping figure.

Rachel swam from them, accepting Evan's hand back into the boat.

Xsardis 298

She looked at Vaylynne with a new appreciation, then glanced back at the two figures. *Don't let it be Kate...*

"This wasn't your last form, Sasha. Tell me I just can't feel the others," Edmund begged with a childlike necessity.

"I didn't expect the explosion," Sasha breathed heavily. "I'm sorry to disappoint you. I never was..." her voice faltered, "what I should have been for you. I should have seen... this coming."

This was no illusion or prearranged scene. This was real. The emotion, the pain, the sacrifice of one who had never sacrificed anything in her life.

The elder sister reached up with a hand and stroked his hair back, "Family." Her hand fell. Slowly, the body turned to ash and slipped into the sea. Edmund's cry gurgled through the water as he followed after the dust.

A strong wind blew suddenly throughout the lands of Noric, Asandra, and Issym sending chills through all who felt it.

"She's gone..." Seth could barely believe it, yet it was so breathtakingly true. It was the most certain feeling they had yet had on Xsardis. "She's gone."

They could have shouted. They could have celebrated. They deserved it. Years of battle finally over. But there was no strength left in them. And death, no matter how terrible the person, is still death.

Their silence lasted a long time. Then they saw scores of illuminescents flying toward them. "Nadine must have woken them before she cycled," Evan smiled at her last living act of mercy.

Katarina said with longing, "Let's go home."

Chapter 37

Stewart halted his troops close, but not too close, to Saphree. The heavy clouds testified to the dark sprites' approaching presence. He would not allow his stolen army to be destroyed by them. Let them first decimate Saphree and be injured themselves.

Kate had great confidence in the skill of Issym's army—certain that they should bring down most of the sprites, but be defeated themselves. Stewart had to trust her. He had made that choice long before. Risks made for rewards. That was all there was to it.

As the dark storm swept in with torrents of rain, lightning, and deafening thunder, Stewart's siting of Saphree disappeared in a shrouding mist. The horses stirred and longed to flee—the men only slightly less so. But they were held by their commanders' new-found admiration for Stewart and the chance for power untarnished by Sasha.

The army did not know that Bridget, Drainan, Brooks, and the other prisoners had escaped. It would never know. When he had discovered the truth, he had been outraged—especially to learn that an impotent boy had led the way. A simple act of deceit had covered his tracks. He had told his men that he was pushing the executions back as a celebration. By the time he returned as lord of Asandra the prisoners' freedom would not matter. He might even say that they had escaped while Stewart was away and kill some guard to make his point.

He was immersed in these thoughts when the cries broke out throughout his army. A terrible force was sweeping through them. In the dark it was indiscernible. It could not be the dark sprites. No, this was coming from the ground. A figure flashed before his eyes. "Kate." Too-late he understood.

"When you wake up this will all be over Stewart," she spoke as hundreds of her forms destroyed his army. "And you will hang for your crimes. As for your men, I will spare as many as will let me."

Stewart put his hands up to block her out. The flat of her sword slammed down on his head.

"We've had our differences," King Remar spoke as he approached Galen. "But today I have instructed my men to bow to you. You have given much to come and you lead with great wisdom. Forgive our foolish quarrels."

Galen offered his hand. "Clashing heads is how you spot a leader… Flibbert taught me that."

Galen looked out at the approaching storm clouds as he strapped on his armor. So many would die in the coming battle.

The darkness had almost been defeated, but it seemed to cling to Asandra—not ready to give up its own precious child. Well, the darkness could not win! Galen turned with certainty and, with the might of battle, ordered a guard, "Ready yourselves. They're coming."

The storm clouds blew suddenly closer. The gust of wind knocked him over. Another blast blew toward him. He struggled to his feet and hurried down the steps, bumping into Joeyza as he stepped outside. The minotaur grabbed him by the shirt collar to keep the wind from pulling him away as a third outburst swept through the fortress. Stones fell. Creatures were flung into the air only to fall again.

And then the world was calm. The sun shone forth past blue sky and fluffy clouds. "What's happened?" Queen Juliet's voice wafted toward them.

Setting Galen safely down, Joeyza's bulking frame turned outwards and his horns pointed to the sky, "That was a warning, designed to make us fear."

It was at that moment Galen understood the strange distress he had seen in Flibbert when the frog had returned from the first encounter with the dark sprites. He had seen a foreshadowing of what would decimate all Xsardis.

"What have we awakened?" cried an airsprite.

Danielle put a comforting hand on the man's shoulder, before stepping toward Galen. Though she carried a sword, she wore no armor as she bowed before the kings. "King Remar, King Galen, allow me once more to offer to give you time to flee. The dark sprites seek only our lives."

Remar shook his head. Galen answered for them, "We're not giving anyone over to their evil."

Accepting the decision as final, Danielle swept her gaze over Saphree. Men and women armed and ready for battle stood—tents packed away and fear having escaped into their eyes. Reinforcements waited inside the fortress. The bravest of men stood on the battlements. They would be the first ones whom the dark sprites would destroy.

"Galen!" a booming voice of alarm shouted from behind. The king turned to see Elimilech. "The stone armor—all of it—is gone."

"How can that be?" Galen questioned.

"A supplement deceived us. Flibbert discovered it only seconds ago."

Xsardis

301

"Kate," King Galen knew with finality that she had betrayed them. It must have taken days for her to slowly remove stones from everyone's personal possessions without raising notice. What spies did she have in Saphree?

"I just caught a group of enemy soldiers inside our gate, trying to blend in," Flibbert launched himself toward them, hopping with a fury and speed. "They wouldn't say much, other than that Kate let them in. I deposited them in the dungeons."

"We can't face both Kate and the dark sprites," Elimilech's face was pale. They would not only take staggering losses that day but would leave Xsardis without defense.

"No doubt the forces of Maremoth are on their way," Galen expected. "This powerful alliance explains why we have not heard from Seth and Rachel. We will not see them again."

"Don't say that!" Flibbert shouted, locking his fingers around his friend's shoulder.

Darkness covered the land again. Battle-hardened men stood in shock as ghostly creatures descended from the sky. They all had pure white or raven black hair that was long and pulled back, and eyes that bore witness to nothing but battle rage.

The battle had begun.

The dark sprite's long, curved weapons swept through the ranks. The terror of Saphree only made the troops more susceptible to the dark sprites.

Jeff and Sphen moved separately, but together. One would be the decoy; the other would run the dark sprite through the heart. Any other impact seemed only to injure them. And injury seemed only to make them angry. Again and again, Jeff would be caught with nowhere to go and the hideous eyes turned upon him, and Sphen would save his life. Then Sphen would be caught off guard and it was Jeff who killed the dark sprite.

Though the dark sprites were clearly more talented than their airsprite fellows, they fought independently while the airsprites battled together. Though one dark sprite might have destroyed one airsprite, the airsprites were ever at each other's sides. The dark sprites were falling, but not quickly enough.

The wind continued to rip through Saphree.

Danielle shot through the sky and met a dark sprite. They spun through the clouds, dodging each others' strikes with their quick movements. Then Danielle dove lower. Elimilech rose and finished the sprite.

Galen's mind reeled as he rolled from a dark sprite's attack and was lost in the tumult. He could barely see anything in the darkness, but he could hear the cries of his men. They were losing. Heavy rain pelted from the sky. Flashes of lightning began to claim his soldiers. Thunder deafened them.

Lilly, Lucas and the other water sprites began to fight against the dark sprites' power over the skies. They turned back the rain. It was not worth the dark sprites' efforts to hinder them.

Suddenly a figure appeared at the high wall of the fortress. A gleaming staff was in her hand and lit up her face. Creatures on all sides of the battle stopped and looked at her.

In response, a mass of clouds rolled closer, then dissipated, revealing the dark sprite leader—Feyah. Her eyes perceived the drawing figure as she

Xsardis   302

leveled herself with her human foe.

"Leave this place," the human commanded her.

The dark sprite studied her form, her determination, her words. The armies began to whisper, "The Legend…" "She's come back…" "I never thought I'd see the day…"

Feyah determined "Finally, a worthy opponent. Will you truly risk all for the cursed airsprites?"

Ethelwyn allowed her staff to plummet and drew her sword. That was answer enough.

Her weapon lunged for Feyah. The dark sprite circled behind her and landed a punch on Wyn's jaw before unsheathing her own scimitar. Forward and backward they swung. Feyah moved quickly, along the fortress walls, seeking a new avenue of attack. Ethelwyn ran after her, keeping a rapid pace.

All at once battle resumed over Saphree, as dark sprites turned again on the subjects of their torment.

Ethelwyn threw her sword at Feyah. The sprite woman barely dodged, then returned a punch to The Legend's jaw. "You're weak," Feyah taunted Ethelwyn. "You don't want to kill me. You don't even want to be here. You're no warrior."

A sudden feeling took not only Ethelwyn but all those in Saphree. To some it felt like a great cold blowing over the land. To others, a distinct joy. To others a sharp pain accompanied by a warm freedom. No one felt it in the same way. Some knew what it meant. Others were blind. But Ethelwyn knew. "Sasha's dead!" she rejoiced. Nadine was free.

Feyah took her distraction. She stabbed not with her scimitar but with a short stick she produced from her skirt. Electricity pulsed through it and sent Ethelwyn reeling to the ground. She held her stomach, weary of pain after so many years. *Nadine's safe. I am no legend. Why go on?* the thoughts slipped past her subconscious.

Images flashed through her mind. Of Rachel, Seth, Max. Of Nadine's willingness to do whatever it took to protect people whom she had never met. Of the brotherhood on Issym, defending each other. Of the new castle built by willing hands for a king they cherished. Of Galen and his family. Of Flibbert. This was not simply another generation. These were people worth protecting. Whether or not she wanted the responsibility to war for them, it had been given to her, and she would defend them.

Ethelwyn jumped to her feet and propelled herself off the fortress, grappling onto the dark sprite's waist. Together they plummeted to the ground. Feyah's wings slowed their descent. Wyn bruised on impact, but did not even feel it. She grabbed another sword and righted herself. Her eyes flicked to the nearby Flibbert and took in his smile.

Feyah perceived the look. Instead of running for Ethelwyn, she lunged for Flibbert. Her sword drew across his eye and then his leg. The frog stumbled back, open to her killing attack.

"No!" Ethelwyn cried. She grabbed Feyah in a chokehold. Flibbert jumped once more and landed on his good foot, then plunged his sword through Feyah's heart. She disintegrated into a burst of vibrant light.

The dark sprites reeled. Instantly, they ceased fighting. The good

Xsardis

303

creatures of Issym and Asandra held back their attacks, waiting to see what would happen. Their heads slightly bowed, the sprites looked to Ethelwyn for direction.

The Legend ordered, "Give me your word never to return to the land and leave!"

"You have it," they each said slowly, the dull drizzle of rain now accompanying their words. She knew their word would bind them. The sprites slipped back into the clouds already rolling away. The light of day was revealed.

Flibbert dropped to his knees. "Sasha's gone."

Ethelwyn fell beside him. "Thank you, my friend."

"You have some explaining to do," he spoke, only one eye on her. The other—that damaged by Feyah—was already a hazy darkness.

Breathing in deeply, she promised him, "All in good time."

Galen and Elimilech ran to their sides. "Ethelwyn, how did you get here?" Galen began.

"I come from Noric. Things there are not well."

Before she could go on, a messenger slipped in the mud before Galen. He went on undaunted, "My lord, you must see this."

Galen and Elimilech ran with him, The Brothers joining them as they went. They had to walk about ten minutes beyond Saphree before they saw anything. The army of Maremoth lay on the ground before them. Wearily, Kate walked in their direction. Galen kept his sword in hand and questioned her from the distance, "What happened here?"

It took her a long while to speak, but she replied, "I have brought you prisoners. Stewart's army is now in your hands. And the dark sprites?"

"They have been dealt with," Galen answered, waiting for more.

"They moved in more swiftly than I anticipated. I had hoped to deal with the army and join you for the battle. How did you rout them?" She spoke so calmly, as if she had not betrayed them.

Elimilech informed her, "The Legend resurfaced."

"I have also dealt…" Kate paused to draw a breath and her balance wavered, "with the mischievous sprites. They will cause no more harm."

"You would not answer me before. Will you now?" Galen inquired. He was inclined to go gently on the exhausted shifter, but he could not be certain it was not another deception.

"I will," she nodded. Her hair becoming blond as she approached. "I discovered we had a traitor in our midst. When I was certain Sasha was not on Asandra, I used him to remove the stones so that my shifters and I could fully use our powers to protect you. I allowed myself to be massacred at Lake Gratuk. If there were not even rumors of distrust among my own people, I could never have convinced Stewart that I was his ally. The battle would have raged much longer with Maremoth as a dominant stronghold. It is empty of both prisoners and soldiers now."

"And our enemies that you admitted into Saphree?"

"I myself made them known to Flibbert, but don't tell him that. Let him keep his pride."

Kate was a long time in reaching them. "I did…" she swallowed as

Xsardis 304

she stepped within feet of them, "my best to protect Xsardis. I am sorry it came at the cost of deceiving you, Galen. Was I wrong?"

Her eyes rolled back into her head and she fell forward. Elimilech caught the fatigued shifter and carried her back to Saphree.

By the time of their return, wounds were being tended, Flibbert's first of all. Fairies of the blue and blue illuminescents moved about freely. The other illuminescents would ensure the army of Maremoth stayed sleep until they could decide what would be done with them. Already a death toll was being taken. Galen ached to know what names it would contain. His eyes searched the land for the faces he knew well and those he had longed to know better.

"What do you think now?" Flibbert questioned, using his cane to strengthen his injured leg. His eye was bandaged. All other wounds had been healed.

The king stumbled to grasp the question, aware of his own fatigue. How bruised was he? "About?"

"About Kate!"

"There are many answers we still need," Galen replied. "But you were right. She never betrayed us."

"What of Seth and Rachel?" Flibbert inquired.

"We'll send someone to find out as soon as we can. For now, we have enough to worry about."

Saphree became a different place as healing began. Those who understood that Sasha was dead did not say a word about it—it was too indescribable, too unbelievable. Even those who could not comprehend it recognized a new type of peace in the fortress. They credited it to the defeat of the dark sprites and the army of Maremoth.

Power returned to The Brothers and Remar. Galen gratefully stepped back. Remar sent scouts to ascertain that no more danger approached Saphree. Sphen oversaw the making of a casualty list. Jeff, Elimilech, and other fairies of the green quickly found those trapped by the crushing rubble and lifted it from them.

Men who had been scattered in the storm returned to the fortress. The heat of day settled on them. Casting his eyes around the castle, Remar knew they would need to build a new home. The dark sprites had destroyed Saphree. Just as well. The fortress was a reminder of Sasha's power. They no longer had to live under that. *God, heal this land,* he prayed. *Grant me wisdom to lead.*

"What will you do with the army of Maremoth?" Galen asked him as he entered his tattered castle. "You cannot leave them asleep forever."

"Juliet and I must discuss it. It is her kingdom after all."

Galen cocked his head. "It is?"

"Her mother was queen. She had deferred to her husband. My wife followed her example." He did not say more as she came down the steps, her features etched with sorrow. The upper rooms where she had been were for the dying. Remar reached out his arms and held Juliet in them.

The kings moved back out and together worked their way through the troops, each knowing that a united front would do much for the weary souls. Juliet followed a few steps behind. "You long to take your soldiers home, don't you?" Remar remarked.

Xsardis 305

"I do," Galen answered. "It will be a long time before we receive the comfort of our families."

Juliet's gasp filled Remar's ears. He spun around, his heart knowing he was too late. Some young man dressed in black had pierced her. He was holding onto her unconscious form.

Remar did not need to be told that the wound would prove fatal. With a hand, the king held back the soldiers from charging the warrior. Unwilling to abandon the hope that a miracle might be done for his beloved wife, he would not risk more damage to queen.

"Who are you?" Galen questioned sharply, an intimidating figure.

"Tahath. Vaylynne's second," the man answered. "You have her kidnapped, locked in here. I have come to get her out."

"What should stop me from ordering your execution?" Galen queried. Remar was too stunned to speak.

"It was far too easy to get my men in here in the confusion. They lay in hiding by your prime leaders. Will you risk them? Give me Vaylynne, and we will leave."

"You have injured a queen," Galen returned, filled with sorrow at the course this boy had chosen. His handsome form and determined leadership could have led to better things. "Do you really think you're just going to walk out of here?"

"This queen is a symbol of a tattered age. I stand for Vaylynne and for freedom. If that means death, so be it. But let our leader go!"

"We don't have your leader!" yelled Remar. "She left of her own volition—went to Noric."

"You expect me to believe that?" Tahath chortled.

"It's true!" Vaylynne called, breaking into a run as she entered the fortress, despite her fatigue.

Her frame was racked with emotion. She knew how much she had changed since she had last seen Tahath, but he was the same. He would destroy himself and her army with him unless she stopped him. Vaylynne understood what that would require: betraying her goals even more and betraying him. "Let the queen go," she commanded.

"Vaylynne, you're injured." He was surprised to see her alive. He was happy to see her alive. It made her heart leap.

At his words, she realized how long her journey had been. Vaylynne must have looked like a ghost of her form, but she spoke with the authority he would recognize, "What are you doing here? Did I give this order?"

"You haven't given any orders. I had no choice!" he fought with her. Tahath was not blind to the change in her.

"Just let the queen go."

"What happened to you? Where's your backbone?" he challenged. "We have a chance here!"

The look in his eyes was so tempting. Her friend since childhood. The counselor she trusted. It was one thing to turn against Edmund, but another to turn against Tahath. "A chance to be slaughtered," she corrected, holding to her new standards. "This is not the way, Tahath. Listen to me, please."

The cost of this was too great for her! Vaylynne stepped forward,

anticipating his mind. He stepped back from her, still holding the queen.
    Seth rode in on Firil. Rachel was steps behind him. Katarina and Evan were moving together. They should have entered to a chorus of cheers, not to this. The princess was barely holding herself back, seeing her mother's life ebbing away.
    Recognizing Tahath would not listen, Vaylynne called to her men scattered throughout, "All of you! Stand!"
    They did as she ordered.
    "What are you doing?" Tahath's question was low.
    "What must be done. Trust me, as you have always trusted me."
    Disbelief marked his eyes, "Has some shape shifter replaced you?"
    "Tahath, there isn't time for this."
    As he had always done, Tahath reasoned with her, "If we do not act, this family will be on the throne."
    "Please. You were right all those years ago when you told me this cause was not worth the loss of life," her voice trembled. She had always appreciated the deadly determination she saw in his eyes, but now…
    He shouted to the men, "We're done."
    Maybe, he'll surrender, she hoped. Her dear friend.
    But instead, Tahath dropped Juliet and lunged for Remar. Jeff's swing cut him down. Her troops threw their weapons to the ground, an instant surrender. Vaylynne took several steps back and closed her eyes to the carnage. Dizzy, she stumbled toward Tahath's form. Closing his eyes, she whispered, "I'm sorry."
    A cry broke forth from Katarina as she fell over her mother's body. Juliet died a few seconds later.
    Remar stumbled backwards, caught by Evan's firm arms.
    No one spoke for a long while.

    Princess Valerie halted her horse and jumped down. Bending beside a small spring, she wiped away the grime of the day's travel. "Are we that close to the castle?" Max asked, unmoving.
    Nodding, she pushed him off his steed, "You should clean up too. You look like a disaster."
    "I feel like a disaster," he answered and poured the cool water over his hair and face. It refreshed him more than he expected.
    Their ride to the castle did not take long from there. Seeing the resolve on Valerie's face and knowing her well, guards moved aside and took their horses speedily. Max followed her footfalls throughout the castle.
    A frog woman leapt into their way as they moved toward a set of double doors. She planted herself firmly in front of them. "Not today, Valerie." Her voice held authority, but was marked by concern. It was then that Max

Xsardis

307

recognized her as Maria—Flibbert's sister-in-law.

"Is she very ill?" Valerie questioned.

"Very. She grows worse with every passing day. Please, we must let her rest!"

"If there was not so much at stake here I would not ask," the princess returned.

"I know all about the medallion," Maria replied. "But Queen Andrea can do nothing about it!"

Max's eyes darted about the stone castle. This place held such hope—hope that people had died to give; hope that Galen and the council had worked so hard to ensure; hope that the world might be whole again, not perfect but whole. From the looks in peoples' eyes, it was all disintegrating. This was why. Because everyone was too scared to do what had to be done.

Her eyes turned to Max, Valerie accepted Maria's words. "I'm sorry."

"Go back to your war," came a gruff voice of some unhappy fairy, clearly a member of the foolish council.

Max knew he had no right to speak. He had no allegiance to Issym and he had certainly not conducted himself well on the continent. Still, if everyone else was silent, someone had to find a voice. "The problems that caused Asandra's war started out the same way as this," Max suddenly cried, with a burst of energy that came straight from Heaven.

He stepped toward Maria with more civility, and explained passionately, "Nadine is a real person, a person who has sacrificed everything for all of us. And she came here, not to win her freedom, but to stop the destructive power she bears inside her. She submitted herself to the outcome, but we didn't help her. After all her effort, we banished her! We wouldn't listen to the truth. We wouldn't stop and think."

He stepped towards the fairy now, "Was it the safer decision for Issym to send her away? Maybe! But what about Asandra and our loved ones fighting there? We abandoned them just as we abandoned Nadine and we punish anyone who tries to speak up about it. Don't you see the path we are on? It will lead us right into Asandra's fate."

"What are you saying?" Maria asked.

"It all comes down to selfishness. I wanted power once so I abandoned my friends. Now you want a comfortable life so you abandon your allies! What I loved about Issym—what changed my life—was that it lived up to a call to risk everything to follow God.

"Don't you get that this is what life boils down to? We can run after the safe thing, the intelligent thing, the comfortable thing all we want. We can justify it with our great intellects. But God calls each of us, whether in a battle or an everyday war, to follow. To pick up our cross daily. I don't know about you, but I don't want to live life comfortably and intelligently at the expense of others anymore. I tried that and I hated it! I want to sacrifice everything to follow the One who sacrificed everything for me. He can take care of the rest. You must not be afraid to use the medallion."

Max was out of words and his arms were shaking. He had never poured out his heart so boldly in his life. He had never really meant the words before that moment. But now it was so clear to him, so very clear. And the

Xsardis

308

sacrifice of Christ was so overwhelming that he sunk into a crouching position. His body racked as images of Christ' betrayal and beating and death flashed in his mind. It was all because of people searching for comfort, money and power, like he had been doing all his life. He couldn't do his life for himself anymore. The emotion was like that of his first conversion. It was as if he was seeing the world through new eyes.

Maria, Valerie, and the fairy stared at him. The door behind Maria opened.

Queen Andrea stumbled out. White as a sheet, she had tears in her eyes. She clutched at wall for support. Maria braced her in her own arms and tried to bring her back to her bed. "You shouldn't be up!" the frog protested.

The queen dug her heels into the ground and refused to go backwards. "We're going to the council room. Nadine will have that medallion."

Max nodded gratefully, distracted. His eyes felt like someone had poured mint in them. So did his nose. And his lungs. Every sense was reading differently. Something had changed inside him, something big.

Chapter 38

Mourning for Queen Juliet swept through Asandra's forces. Even the stoic Sphen was plunged into sorrow, though it was only discernible to Flibbert and his brother.

Kate recognized that the only way to absolve herself of all guilt was to bring Galen to the stones, but Issym's king was reluctant to leave Saphree with their queen so recently passed. Prince Evan approached Galen, "You should go with Kate. I will lead my kingdom."

Galen turned to the young prince, soon to be king. He stood straight and tall, capable and with a compassion learned the hard way.

With a nod to Kate, Galen rode quickly with her on horses bred for speed. When the bramble blocked the animal's paths, they tied them to a tree and went on foot. The grim look of battle marked both their faces and kept silence between them.

The restrictions of the stones filled Kate's senses, an overpowering amount of nausea flooding her system. They were not close enough to limit her. No other shifter would have been able to feel them. But with her great skill came great repercussions.

She sensed a shifter beside her and turned to see Edmund. "I'm sorry about your sister," Kate offered, aware of the grief in his eyes. Despite Sasha's wickedness, it was a terrible thing for any family to have to face. Kate's love for Edmund was controlled, but ever present.

"I wanted to help you," he beseeched her to understand, ignoring Galen's presence. The king had drawn his weapon and stepped back. "That's why I did all I have done. I know you are sick like Sasha was."

"I'm not sick," Kate shook her head. "Sasha went beyond her limits, tried to take power she should not have reached for. I didn't."

"But you have more power than her…" Edmund could not comprehend.

"Who ever said that doing things God's way was less powerful? He's stronger than Sasha's master could ever have been."

Xsardis

310

Edmund's tone turned sharp, "Sasha had no master."

"You know very well, she did." Kate's memory rewound and she replayed what he had said: *That's why I did all I have done.* "What did you do, Edmund? Seth and Rachel?" They had mentioned little about him, but somehow she knew that he had attacked them.

"I would have killed that girl, had not that treacherous Vaylynne intervened! I will finish what I started."

"No…" Kate looked more fully into his eyes and realized that he had made a promise to himself that he would never relinquish.

"Yes. Join me. We can rule this world together. Don't you remember the life we dreamed about? Peace for our shifters? That will never happen under his reign!" Edmund pointed a sword at Galen.

Kate stepped back. "Will you be dissuaded?"

"You'll follow him, but not me? Did you ever love me?"

Her voice hoarse, she answered, "I loved the man I thought was inside you, but he's gone now. Isn't he?"

"He died with Sasha."

Edmund knelt in the clearing. His eyes looked up and met hers, then he spread his arms out wide with a horrible cry. She felt it deep in her soul. A second form, identical to the first, appeared beside him. "Oh no…" she whispered. The power would destroy him.

Galen's sword was drawn, but he did not move, waiting for Kate's guidance.

Both Edmunds stood, dark eyes boring into Kate. "Why?" she questioned him.

"My sister gave her life for me. What did you ever give me? I will give my life to finish her work. I will grow in skill—no matter the consequences. You have no more hold on me," Edmund promised as he lunged at her with both his swords.

Kate, weaponless, spun out of the way. "Edmund, don't," she begged him, emotion racking through her tone. "Please. Sasha's gone. Be saved!"

One version of Edmund moved behind her. The other stayed in front. They attacked with precise timing. She threw herself to the ground to avoid the impact. She would not draw a blade, not yet. Hope refused to be dislodged. "This will consume you!" she cried out. "As it consumed her! I won't fight you."

"Then I'll fight him!" Edmund charged Galen.

The king parried, then began to duel. But Edmund had unleashed the terrible power of hate. Galen ran for the stones he prayed were close. Could he even hope that Kate would chose to protect him over the man she loved?

"You think the stones scare me anymore?" Edmund challenged Galen as he felt their power limit his. "They don't. I have nothing left to live for."

His other form thrust his sword at Galen. Kate threw her body at his feet, pulling him to the ground. He whipped his sword toward her. She plunged his dagger into him and he fell back. When he did not rise, Kate knew the stones restricted them now.

Standing to face the last form of her once-beloved, Kate's whole body shook with pain. "Don't make me do this, Edmund."

Xsardis 311

"You fight for him, but you wouldn't fight for me. I hate you."

He brought his sword toward Galen again. Kate shielded the king with her own blade. Edmund's body ran through it and fell.

The king said nothing as Kate fell over Edmund's body and wept for what could have been, for his soul. She turned to Galen and asked for his counsel for the first time. "Why, Galen? Why would he choose this? God, I, you, Seth offered him everything and every chance. Why?"

"Jesus would have granted him life to the fullest, but Edmund would have had to sacrifice his love of sin, his love of self. He couldn't see the better things God was willing to give."

The coronation was simple. Evan bowed before his father in the throne room. There were only a few witnesses as Remar placed the crown upon his son's head. When Evan rose, Remar bowed. That was all.

But such a simple ceremony changed everything. Evan knew that the whole nation, no less his sister, would need time to grieve. He recognized that the best way to do so would be to work hard at rebuilding Asandra. He pulled Katarina into service as his second authority and together they began to make plans.

Seeking out the counsel of King Galen, who had been charged with a similar task of governmental rebirth, King Evan decided to enact a formula similar to Issym's. Even Vaylynne found it to be a satisfactory arrangement. He pardoned her and all the other rebels.

The Brothers were set as the military commanders. Together with four men from each region of Asandra, with Abigail and Lucas as sprite representatives, they would guide him in his decisions.

As days turned into a week, Galen began to make preparations for his return journey. "You're welcome to come with us," Galen offered Seth in the early morning hours. "We have some master craftsmen who could rig something for your leg. We would welcome your counsel and your presence among us."

Galen added, "There are many mysteries you and Rachel would discover. Information about your past. Look at what you've learned from Ethelwyn already. Maybe it would give you direction for your future."

The king could hardly believe how Seth had aged since they had first met. No longer was he some cocky youth uncertain and unwilling to struggle for the right. He was a warrior—despite his missing leg—a leader, one who understood grief and still possessed joy.

"I don't know what I'll do," Seth admitted. "I appreciate your sincere offer."

Looking out the window, Galen smiled, "Max has returned."

Seth moved with effort to Galen's side, the crutch already having

Xsardis   312

rubbed his skin raw. Max's lanky form pressed through the crowd, enjoying the attention. By the time he had made it to the castle itself Rachel was down the stairs and waiting with Galen and Seth.

Max's eyes slowly fell on Seth's missing appendage, but his relief that they had survived covered the loss he felt for his brother. "Kat?"

"Nadine died and saved the rest of us," Rachel answered.

Nadine's passing was devastating to all of Xsardis, even if the world did not know what it had lost and Max's connection to her made the grief sear through him. It felt as if someone had sucked all the energy from Max's body as he processed those words. "How?"

"Her implosion killed all but one version of Sasha. Vaylynne took care of the last one."

Galen could not contain his questions for long—both those concerning his wife and those concerning the people he had left behind. He let Max absorb the news and then asked, "How's Andrea? Issym?"

"Andrea has been sick for a long time, but your baby is doing fine." Max glanced at Seth, "She named him after you." He looked to Galen again, "She seemed to hit a turning point while I was there. I think she'll recover. Issym's been struggling without her, but it will pull through."

"Did they give up the medallion?" Rachel inquired.

Max nodded. "After several days, Andrea convinced them. I set out in a little row boat with Princess Valerie and turned the key in it. The water levels changed. I assumed it had worked. I was apparently too late."

Seth offered information to break him from his reverie. "Ethelwyn stopped the attack of the dark sprites. We have Sasha's army in hibernation thanks to Kate. Evan has ordered them to be woken slowly and given the choice to rejoin Asandra or leave it."

"Evan?" Max questioned.

Rachel's face was suddenly downcast, "Juliet died."

Max's eyes flicked to the steps behind him. "Where's Kat?"

Directed to the council room that had become her and Evan's temporary headquarters, Max moved quickly. He found Katarina, in a slim white dress and her hair brushed back, already heading for him. Max opened his arms as she took his hug. "I'm sorry," he whispered.

Katarina did not linger long before she stood straight and tall in front of him. There was a radiance of womanhood about her. "And I'm sorry about Nadine. I know that can't be easy on you. You seemed... connected."

"We were..." Max replied. "I'm really glad you are okay. I was worried about you. Your brother's running the country now?" he asked with mock skepticism, breaking the emotional conversation that neither of them really wanted to be having.

"Not without my help," she returned confidently.

"We always did make a good team," Evan spoke, joining his sister. "The Brothers need us."

Max watched them go. They would lead Asandra well. He walked back to Seth and Rachel. Obstructed by the corner, he heard their conversation long before they knew he was there. Not that he was eavesdropping.

"So," Seth was saying and Max could just envision him pulling her

Xsardis

313

close. "We made it."

She was probably leaning back against him, closing her eyes and sighing. "I didn't think we would." Rachel would straighten after a few moments. She said, "What do you want to do next?"

"What do we have if we go back? A whole lot of work getting back lives we won't fit into anymore."

"But if we stay, we'll get in their way. Evan and Katarina need to lead without us causing them problems." That was Rachel's voice.

"I want to make sure we talk with Max about this. It's all of our choices. Galen offered to take us back to Issym. I think that's a good option." Seth paused, then added. "But would that just be running away?"

Max hesitated, wanting to hear more before he voiced his own opinion about what they should do.

Rachel responded, "I don't want to go back, but I can't escape the oppressive feeling that it's the right thing to do."

"I know…" Seth sighed. "I can't either."

"I'm not saying we shouldn't come to Xsardis for visits. But if we ran from our entire lives on Earth, it wouldn't be right or fair to everyone we left behind. I did a lot of damage by my secrecy. I have to set that right. I think we have to be honest and bring our parents here."

"Agreed."

"You're going to bring them to Xsardis?" Max could hardly believe his ears as he came into their view. "The risks…"

They weren't surprised to find he had heard them. Seth replied, "We'll deal with those."

Max stared at his friends, hand in hand and heart in heart. He would have done anything for them. But their roads suddenly, joltingly, seemed separate. He thought about Arvin. About Nadine. About the others who had fought beside him. Katarina, Reesthma, even Flibbert. It was here that he could use his voice like he had used it before Maria and Andrea. It was here that he could live up to Arvin's challenge. Max shook his head. "I think I'm staying."

"What are you going to do?"

"Kat needs a friend right now. And I want to help Reesthma learn all she can about Nadine and tell her story. I'll be in and out of Earth, but this is where I belong now."

Seth studied his face, then accepted the decision. He offered his hand. Max shook it, then clapped him on the back.

"But you're right about one thing," Max went on. "I do have unfinished business. I want to wrap up a few things before I make the move."

"I'm ready to go home," Rachel spoke. "Sasha's dead. The war's over. We've done all we can to help Xsardis heal. Soon Issym's army will be leaving and Ethelwyn with them. I don't want to use up any more illuminescent energy than necessary." She could not bring herself to look at the ring on her finger.

Seth nodded his agreement before sweeping his eyes out over Xsardis. It would take a long time for the land to heal, but heal it would. And it wasn't because Sasha was dead or because the dark sprites had lost their leader. It was because the people had turned back to God.

Xsardis

Asandra understood that it was their own slumber that had allowed Sasha to take power. They had chosen to turn a blind eye to her evil and given up their rightful king and queen. They had placed their own townsmen in her clutches. It had not simply been their kinsmen's release after 'The Day The Whispers Became Trumpets' that had woken them. It was the sacrifice of Max, Evan, and Rachel on the tower. It was Zachary's preaching from village to village. It was the Word of God they were reading and longing for again. And Asandra was resolved to walk steadily toward that Light.

Seth felt an overwhelming surge of love for these creatures. Love had been what had driven him all these years to keep going. Love for Xsardis derived from a love for God—a love that had made it unbearable to do anything but his best. An all-consuming love. The same he now had for Earth. People there needed to know what he had learned here. He might not be waging war against an army on Earth, but he *was* waging war.

Seth's eyes drifted to Rachel. Despite everything, they had come out stronger. She had inspired him to live for Christ. She continued to inspire him. And he felt a surpassingly great strength come from knowing that in Christ they would change their world together.

Epilogue

Joppa's voice finished strong, his eyes wet with tears. "It is beautiful."

"Joppa?" she asked, a childlike tone possessing her, as the fear and realization came to her that her uncle was soon to breath his last. Reesthma threw herself beside him and put her hands in his.

"What will you do, Reesthma?"

"What do you mean?"

"Follow in your mother's steps or mine?"

"I pray there is no need for a warrior now," she answered. "But if there is, I will do what I must."

He patted her face. "King Evan relies on you."

It had been over a year since the adventure, and Reesthma had grown from a young teen to a young woman. As she had gradually assumed Joppa's duties, the king had installed her in his council. She had taken a great place of honor in the new kingdom, one that she doubted she deserved but was determined to use well. She recalled her own folly in Nadine's cave. That was her inspiration never to make a decision that did not come from prayer and the guidance of the Scripture.

Her uncle was staring out the window.

"Joppa?" she called to him. "What is it?"

"I saw history completed," his voice waned as he spoke. "You will go on to tell the tale."

"What tale?" Reesthma questioned him.

"Look!"

Hesitant and knowing his time to be short, Reesthma's curiosity won her over. She rose and stared out the window. Moving through the gates was a girl both innocent and learned; young and old; dead and alive. Her brown locks fell down her shoulders; three rings glittered on her fingers; a smile of anticipation caused the lines of her face to rise. "Nadine…"

Xsardis

Can't get enough of The Xsardis Chronicles?

The adventure continues on the fan page of www.jessiemaehodsdon.com with an alternate ending!

Fans will get a first glimpse of the future projects, tour dates, and more of Jessie Mae Hodsdon.

Visit www.issym.com

Email jess@issym.com to have her come to your school or church.

Xsardis

Rebirth Publishing, Inc is committed to using adventurous literature and high quality writing to shine Christ in a dark world.

Xsardis

About the author:

Jessie Mae Hodsdon is an author, a junior in college,
the founder of Rebirth Publishing,
and an inspirational speaker.
She lives in Bangor, ME, and travels the country
as a speaker.

Learn more at www.jessiemaehodsdon.com

Xsardis